DEVOLUTION

CHRIS PAPST

A POST HILL PRESS BOOK
ISBN: 978-1-61868-805-7
ISBN (eBook): 978-1-61868-804-0

Cover Design by Christian Bentulan

Post Hill Press
275 Madison Avenue, 14th Floor
New York, NY 10016
posthillpress.com

PREFACE

"Humanity will never forget this moment," he stated, sitting down at his carved English Oak desk. Centered on its front, a soaring eagle evoked the prestige that once embodied the office. Towering behind his chair, a pair of wilted flags separated three large rectangular windows.

The weary man looked up with defeated eyes. "Are we sure we want to do this?"

The forlorn dignitaries standing around him couldn't even bring themselves to match his stare, let alone answer his question. With an unbearable reality, his head hung loaded with regret.

Did it have to come to this?

A calm autumn breeze drifted through a cracked window, yet did little to dilute the oppressive air.

Seated deep within his chair, the man reluctantly reached for a single piece of paper on the opposite side of the desk. He slid the document toward him.

The dozen witnesses, all dressed in black suits, stood motionless, but not emotionless. This unprecedented moment would not allow for apathy. The man drew a pen from his breast pocket. An overwhelming sense of duty and honor stopped him from using it. The idle seconds that followed only intensified the agony. Eventually, a bleak sense of sanity filled the void.

"We have no more options," his secretary whispered. Her trembling voice matched her stricken eyes, which remained fixated on her folded hands.

Crippled with remorse, he reluctantly nodded.

His signature gradually manifested itself at the bottom of the page: President Madison C. Harris. His eyes eased shut when the pen broke contact with the page. Though the fault was not his own, he could not help but feel the immense weight of history pressing on his shoulders.

The circular room, draped in old Victorian styling, emptied for the final time.

As word spread, millions revolted. But millions more rejoiced.

The United States of America had just been signed out of existence.

CHAPTER ONE
YEARS LATER

"**M**r. Nolan," scolded Professor Sorenson, peering over his bifocals.

Startled, John Nolan looked up, covertly sliding his hand over the fresh markings on his desk. "Sorry, Professor." His baritone voice softened from embarrassment.

"As I was saying," continued the professor, "in *The End of Christendom*, Malcolm Muggeridge made this powerful observation about society:

"*I conclude that civilizations, like every other human creation, wax and wane. By the nature of the case, there can never be a lasting civilization any more than there can be a lasting spring or lasting happiness in an individual life or a lasting stability in a society. It's in the nature of man and of all that he constructs, to perish, and it must ever be so. The world is full of the debris of past civilizations and others are known to have existed which have not left any debris behind them but have just disappeared.*"

The aging professor forced a deep breath, knowing his upcoming analysis would fall hollow on the young man he had admonished.

While the professor droned on, John peered through the window at the tumbling October leaves. He thought back to a few months prior, when he got the news that changed his life.

John sat at an ornate wooden desk. Dusty books and golden replicas of the globe furnished the musty room. The haughty-looking man opposite him was clad in plaid and corduroy. The door read, *Dean Darrin Pricart, Department of History*. It reeked of elitism.

"What do you mean I didn't get in!?"

"My deepest regrets, Mr. Nolan." Despite his words, the dean was not at all sympathetic. "We simply have no more room in the program."

"I don't understand," John said frantically. "I met all the requirements. I did all the suggested activities and—"

"Yes," the dean interrupted. "You did the minimum. However, if you want in this grad program at the University of Cambridge you must exceed the minimum."

"What do I need to do?" John pleaded. "Tell me. I'll do it."

"I'm sorry, Mr. Nolan. It's too late."

John felt sick. He had planned his life around this graduate school.

"You can try again next year." The dean leaned back in his polished leather chair. "If you wish, I can see if other departments have openings. Sociology may have availability."

John nodded. He had never felt so empty.

John awoke as the professor was summing up his lecture.

"Muggeridge concluded by saying, '...*but the realization is impossible for the simple reason that a fallen creature like man, though capable of conceiving perfection and aspiring after it, is in himself and in his works, forever imperfect. Thus, he is fated to exist in the no man's land between the perfection he can conceive and the imperfection that characterizes his own nature and everything he does.*'

"Thank you for coming today." The elderly academic gently closed the book from which he read. "Remember, your thesis topic is due by the end of semester. I am here if you need me."

"Have a topic?" Christian Blaire asked John as they gathered their belongings. His British accent was thick, but unlike other natives of the island, it was highly unrefined.

John and Christian were close friends, yet appeared very dissimilar. John was about six feet tall with rusty brown hair, similarly colored eyes, and a slim physique. He was not particularly handsome, nor was he terribly unfortunate looking. Christian, conversely, had a mass of distinguishing features. His stumpy 65-inch frame was half as wide as tall. Two cavernous dimples quartered his round cheeks earning his nickname – the chubby chipmunk. His dirty blond hair was dirty due to actual dirt. The 22-year-old's most characterizing attribute sparkled in his clear blue eyes.

"Nope. Not yet." John's accent was more in line with what the United Kingdom had become; a random mix of British and American dialects. "I'll figure it out."

"It be nice if *that* were your topic," Christian said, studying the humbly elegant April Lynn as she tossed her backpack over her shoulder. His lip curled under his stubby yellow teeth.

John rolled his eyes and chuckled.

*

"Hey, can you get me another box of the 1190?" yelled Milt Sirrah as he carefully backed out of the shower.

John's boss was only 45 years old, but his choice of profession wore heavily on his body. Straggly dark hair and an unkempt beard complemented his Mediterranean skin tone.

John walked across the unfinished hall with the marble. The bony young man was dripping with sweat from grouting the secondary bath.

Milt reached for the box. "Must I check your work, again?" he asked, only halfway joking. The other half was serious.

John smiled.

"Make sure you cover that floor before you leave," Milt said, ripping the cardboard box. "This dude has kids. You know, it's a bitch to get dirt out of grout."

"I know," John said. "Hey, Milt, do you mind if I leave early? I have schoolwork."

"Fine." Milt crawled back into the shower. "Hey," he said, his voice echoing off the reflective walls. "When are you done anyway?"

"All I have is my thesis."

Milt finished the final row and rose to his feet. "So I guess I'll need a new laborer?" His joints cracked as he stretched his back and sighed in relief. "Things are slow. I might go solo for a while."

John unsnapped his knee pads and brushed himself off. "Well, I don't even have a topic, so I'll be around for a while."

Milt chuckled and reached for his water. That was not surprising.

Seconds later, John was running towards his old red hatchback. Home was minutes away.

*

With a burdened mind, the robust man sat on a frigid metal chair, his elbows resting on his knees, eyes fixated on the concrete below. His cement enclosure harbored a damp aroma. In a room that reflected noise nothing could be heard, not even a faint breath amongst the chill of the moment.

The man wore a black armored suit with thick soled boots, laced halfway to his knees. Dense gloves protected his hands. A lone pistol, ammunition, and a long knife encircled his waist. The black mask, folded above his eyes, revealed his only exposed skin. The dim room cast a powerful shadow, concealing his identity. His soul appeared as dead as his demeanor.

A similarly dressed man appeared at the door, his arrival marked by silence. He stood feet soldier-width apart, chin high, hands locked at the small of his back. "Everyone is here, Captain."

The man in the chair continued to stare at the foundation beneath, elbows perched with a sagging brow.

"The literature is here as well, sir." The man's voice reflected no emotion. "It is time." His words were as lifeless as his spirit.

"Are we doing the right thing?" Within the captain's equivocal tone, a hint of certainty arose.

No answer was forthcoming. There was none to give. The debate was over.

The captain rose until his back arched in perfect posture. His thick chest and broad shoulders formed an impressive silhouette. With both hands, he rolled the ski mask over his shadowed face.

*

John's bedroom was filled with pictures from history's most famous and infamous moments: the 1945 photo taken by Joe Rosenthal of five U.S. Marines and a sailor raising the American flag over Iwo Jima; a snapshot from the battle of Gravelines, which contributed to the defeat of the Spanish Armada; the destruction of Napoleon's La Grande Armée following the invasion of Russia; and the Ides of March as depicted by Vincenzo Camuccini.

John's fascination with history ran deep. He'd planned to turn that passion into a career, however, the Cambridge history department's rejection letter, which lay on his dresser, had shattered that dream.

The young man sat at his desk deeply engrossed in a book when his father, Theodore Nolan, approached the doorway.

"Are you coming to eat?" he asked.

John remained huddled over his book.

"Son!" his father raised his voice and stepped into the room.

Startled, John shook the thoughts from his mind. "What? I'll be down in a second. I'm ..." he stopped and exhaled.

He rotated his chair to face his father, whose cavernous wrinkles had unfairly aged him, as did his thinning gray hair.

"This...this thesis has me lost."

Theo felt his son's frustration.

John said, sulking in his own doubt. "If you didn't know the College Officer I probably wouldn't have got into Cambridge at all."

"Well, as an aspiring—"

"It has to deal with Great Britain," John interrupted. "I need to find an aspect of society and predict how behavior will evolve."

"You're limited."

John haplessly concurred.

"Well," his father said, making his way to the door, "dinner's limited, too. And if you don't get there before your sisters, you'll be frustrated *and* hungry." He stopped at the doorway. "If this isn't what you wanted, why did you stay in school?"

"I don't know," John said. "Maybe I wasn't ready for the *real world*." He wrapped his fingers in quotes.

Their eyes locked, exchanging the type of silent smiles reserved for family.

"Come on." Theodore draped his arm around his son's scrawny shoulders and they walked down the hall.

*

That night John awoke to the faint sound of screaming. As the cries steadily grew louder, he forced open his eyes. Although blurry, the flash of red and blue lights was unmistakable.

He jumped out of bed and bolted to his window, where the intense rays proved overwhelming. He backed away from the frosty glass, his head buried in his arm. His groggy eyes were slow to adjust.

He ran to his door and swung it open. His father was already standing in the hall.

Although panicked, John remained in control. "What is that?"

"It looks like the police have stormed the Santos' house." The cutting light flashed throughout the hallway. "Come on!"

The Santos' were a popular couple. The family had been in the neighborhood for decades. They were social and took an active role in the community. The husband was pushing 70 and his wife wasn't far behind.

6

Within minutes, the dazed neighbors had gathered in the street, watching in curious disbelief as handcuffed people were escorted out of the house—people no one recognized, barely clothed and greatly dispirited. They held few belongings. Authorities packed windowless vans with sealed cardboard boxes.

It wasn't long before the husband and wife emerged from the darkness of the front door. Their appearance triggered gasps and loud whispers. With high chins, they walked to the squad car and slid inside without acknowledging their gawking neighbors. The police eventually blocked off the street and forced back the crowd. But it didn't matter any longer. After the couple was taken away, there was nothing left to see. The street returned to the night.

*

The following day's news made no mention of that morning's incident. The lack of information forced concerned neighbors to talk amongst themselves, and the conspiracies thrived.

"I knew them for years. They seemed to have nothing to hide."

"Maybe they were spies."

"Do you think they killed anyone?"

"You know, I always thought they were a little suspicious."

"They had to be corrupt. They got what they deserved."

The head of the Neighborhood Watch called police, who had no comment. Local politicians remained quiet.

"What's happenin', man?" Christian's high voice was easy to hear in the crowded pub. "I want to be trustin', but the government's not makin' it easy."

John snickered as he finished the day's first beer—it was noon.

John and Christian had been friends since primary school. John was immediately drawn to his glowing smile and infectious laugh, neither of which seemed to wane regardless of the situation. Christian was the only son of a military parts supplier, and his family was well-off. Unlike many children of new money, the spirit of giving was not lost upon him. But the refined nature of high society was.

"Elections are comin'," Christian proclaimed. "Maybe we can kick some asses out."

"What will that do?" John smirked at his friend's blind faith. "If you want to change the circumstance, you have to change the system."

"No," Christian argued, "it doesn't need to be drastic. We just need some honesty."

"New players in the same game is not the answer," John replied. "Voting out the dishonest does little if a new set of dishonest people take their place. If there's something about the current system that produces counterproductive politicians, that is what needs to be changed."

"We spent years rebuildin' our overseas colonies," Christian stated. "We can't chance losing all that."

"Sure, but sometimes a new system is *needed*—like in America or Rome."

"Rome?" Christian signaled the waitress for another round. "I thought Rome was conquered."

"It was. But what caused that to happen?"

"A weak military?" Christian guessed.

"Yes, but it's much deeper than that. The Roman *Republic* was a mix of democracy and oligopoly. Many of Rome's magistrates were elected. But the senate, which was their most powerful body, was not elected. They were appointed by the ruling class. Over time, an aristocracy arose that became so powerful the elected governance lost control. The leadership could only be overthrown by revolution."

"A change in the system," Christian added.

"Exactly." John was glad to see his friend was listening. "The republic had a strictly hierarchical society with slaves at the bottom, freedmen in the middle, and freeborn citizens at the top. Women could not participate in politics, the poor vote was many times not counted, and many senators were corrupt. Soldiers had more loyalty to their generals than to Rome. The need for slaves grew as the country's men fought in wars. And, of course, slaves were not loyal to the nation. The groundwork for revolution was laid. They only needed a catalyst."

Christian again signaled to the waitress. "What's she doin' over there?"

"There was a civil war and Julius Caesar was made dictator for life. The republic was gone forever. The *system* had to change... and it did."

Christian finally got the pub-maid's attention. He pointed to his empty glass.

"The empire that followed the civil war did well. It thrived for hundreds of years until weak emperors came to power. The country split in the 4th century and the most powerful nation the world had ever seen was eventually conquered by Germanic tribes."

"But, that doesn't make sense," Christian said. "How can that happen?"

"Well, there are a bunch of theories," John replied. "As the emperor gained power, the people felt less involved. With less devotion came less willingness to fight for Rome. Others say the empire became too large to secure its own borders, and the taxes they levied on conquered lands were too high, angering the people. Skirmishes disrupted trade and slowed the economy.

"It really was the perfect storm. You had economic decline, Germanic expansion, depopulation due to a plague that killed millions. Rome no longer could sustain a tax base or military. Similar epidemics hit in the third century as well. Their dense population could have made them a victim of their own success.

"One interesting theory is that Rome depended too much on its ability to conquer land and not on sustaining the land it had. The empire didn't have a strong monetary system to regulate spending or the value of its currency. It depended heavily on gold. As their ability to conquer diminished, so did the supply of gold. They were forced to coin currency with less gold, causing inflation. Citizens began bartering for what they needed, limiting tax revenue."

"So with less money they couldn't pay a strong military," Christian said, quite interested now that the beers arrived.

"As the economy got worse, food became scarce and people left the cities to farm. That created a heavy reliance on slaves, which made a strong middle class impossible. Eventually they fell behind the world in technology. The horseshoe, for example, out of Germania and gave their cavalry a huge advantage."

"How do you know this?"

"My undergrad was history."

"Ohhhh," Christian said, "yeeaahh, I forgot."

"When a country grows, it depletes its resources. In the case of Rome, they needed more raw materials like grain, metals, and slaves, so they 'solved' the problem by conquering more land. That's not sustainable. As the empire grew, the cost to maintain it also grew. They got so big and weak that any disaster, like a famine, plague, invasion, or rapid inflation would break its back. And there's your catalyst for revolution."

Christian set his beer bottle on the table. "There's got to be a lesson in all that."

John raised an eyebrow. "Of course, but if we haven't learned it by now, we never will."

*

"'Give me 26 lead soldiers and I will conquer the world.' Those words were uttered by a man who did his fair share of altering the map." Professor Sorenson paced in front of the class, his head down and hands folded behind his back.

"More people have been persuaded by those 26 lead soldiers than by any military. Those little figures are in many ways invincible. But can they conquer the world?"

The old academic removed his spectacles to clean them on his faded flannel shirt. After securing them back on his nose, he cleared his throat.

"Sociology is the study of human behavior. If our goal is to predict behavior, then how do we analyze these 26 lead soldiers? What does their power say about us?"

He stopped again to study the vapid stares of his students, challenging someone to muster the courage to opine.

John thought back to the words of Dean Pricart. *You did the minimum.* He reluctantly raised his hand.

"Yes. Mr. Nolan?"

"I believe that speaks to our need for hope. Rhetoric, regardless of truth or reality, gives us reason to think the future will improve on the present."

"How so?"

"We want to believe more is possible," John said, choosing his words carefully. "No one wants change when things are good. During bad times, we look for someone to guide us, and there is never a shortage of power hungry people looking to exploit a crisis. These leaders convince us to follow them to a better future and we are happy to be part of the movement, even if we don't know where it's taking us. All the great revolutions throughout history occurred during tough times, when people needed something to believe in. It gives us a sense of personal meaning."

John paused to collect his thoughts. "Most times what leaders propose has already been tried and oftentimes failed. But when we're vulnerable, we're easily manipulated. We're told we can do better. "

"Keep going with that," Professor Sorenson encouraged.

"Well, take America, for example. What that country built in a matter of a few centuries was astonishing. However, when they faced a substantial problem, they abandoned the principles that created their prosperity. Real problems take time to fix. It takes effort and hard work—not accounting tricks. America didn't want to wait, so they voted for politicians that fed off that energy. It was the abandonment of the very system that built that country that tore it apart. No military in the world could have conquered them. Instead, they fought a battle of ideas. The rival armies fought with speeches and pamphlets. A war of words. A war of lead soldiers."

"So was Karl Marx right?" the professor challenged his student. "Can you really conquer the world with only the 26 letters on a keyboard?"

John nodded. "If they can dismantle the most powerful country the world had ever seen, why not?"

*

"Hey, what are you reading?" John's dad asked as he entered his son's room. John was sprawled out on his bed, a book resting against his chest.

He showed his father the cover. "It's about the fall of Greece. The author claims the pursuit of wealth tore families apart, which led to moral decay."

"Yeah?" Theodore took a seat at the foot of the bed. "I always thought internal wars did them in."

John leaned over the far side of the sheets and grabbed a thick book. "This one talks about that."

Theodore's smile was more one of pity than pride. *If only he had gotten into that school.*

"This author does a great job explaining how influential Greece was. He talks about how they invented democracy, philosophy, astronomy, and advanced mathematics like geometry. They had the world's first professional military, too."

Theodore's smile never faded. It was rare his son got excited about anything.

"It talks about how the wealth and power of Athens attracted the most talented people." John paged through the book double-checking his facts. "A strong middle class led to advancements in arts, leisure, and education. Boys *and* girls learned how to read, write, and do math. No one else was doing that. As a result, architecture, philosophy, literature, and mathematics thrived. Some of the most influential people of the ancient world—Socrates, Aristotle, Plato, Herodotus—emerged out of 5th century B.C. Greece."

"Why Greece?" Theo asked.

"That's the really interesting part. In Greece, at that time, the laws changed. Up until then only free, land-owning, native-born men could be citizens entitled to full protection of the law. When that law expanded to include more people, Greece thrived. It was the first experiment in individualism and it worked brilliantly. For the first time in human history, potential was unleashed. Prior to that, people were held back by authoritative rulers who refused to limit their own power by allowing their subjects to acquire their own. And you're right, eventually, constant fighting between city-states caused the birthrate to plummet since men at war could not reproduce. Their aging population made them vulnerable and Rome conquered them.

"There is another theory that makes sense. A lot of people argue that life became too good. Greece became too wealthy and the people were unwilling to sacrifice their quality of life by fighting to maintain it. Once families didn't need to stay together to survive, society decayed."

"Is there a way to use this stuff in your thesis?"

"That would be nice," John replied wistfully.

*

That evening the Nolan family gathered in the dining room for dinner. Theodore always sat at the table's head, near his grandfather's rustic oak clock. John's mother, Charlotte, settled across from her husband, half-blocking a wall full of family pictures. Theodore smiled as his twin daughters entered through the hallway. To his right, John squeezed his slender frame by a window that overlooked the community.

The Nolans, like many of their neighbors, were implants from America. Instability had convinced the family to relocate to Great Britain from Pennsylvania when John was an infant. Their house, a modest gray-white cape-cod with groomed landscaping, was a near duplicate of the home they'd left behind. It had once stuck out in the quiet Cambridge suburb. Now, it simply blended in among the classical wood/stone European architecture and new American-influences.

John's father, an unremarkable, yet caring man, was a school teacher of 31 years. His profession had spared the family from the tough economic times that had befallen the country. Charlotte had worked until John was born. Now, with three kids in university, money was tight.

John was the oldest of the three Nolan children. His sisters, Elizabeth (Lizzy) and Rose, were two years younger, and not at all similar to John. He struggled to maintain decent grades, while they would graduate with distinction. John usually kept to himself, while the girls struggled to choose which parties deserved their attention. At school and in life, John blended in and his future was uncertain. The twins were on a field hockey scholarship to Saint Mary's College of London. The freshmen marketing majors were destined for careers in the corporate world.

Rose placed her silverware on her plate and wiped her mouth before she spoke. "Do you know what you are doing for your thesis yet, John?"

"No." He piled a forkful of mashed potatoes on some bread. In mid-chew he mumbled, "Dad had an interesting idea of combining history with sociology."

"What are the requirements?"

"I need to pick an aspect of society and predict how behavioral patterns will evolve."

"Are you leaning towards anything?" Charlotte asked, raising her glass of red wine—her only vice.

"Not yet."

"So, you need a topic by the end of this semester," Lizzy said, "and you have nothing?"

John cut a piece of his pork with the side of his fork. Her questions required no answer.

"When's it due?" Lizzy prodded.

"End of next semester."

Charlotte stood and walked into the kitchen to pour another glass of wine. "Why don't you do something on technology?" she suggested.

Theodore eyed his wife as if to say, *That's your last, right?* But he couldn't be too critical. There weren't many 50-year-old women who looked like Charlotte. Toned and tanned, despite the English weather, with glossy dark hair and straight, white teeth, it was obvious where her daughters acquired their vanity. At times, Charlotte was even mistaken for the third daughter—a notion that never sat well with the twins.

"I had thought of that," John said, careful not to hurt his mother's feelings.

"What about drinking laws?" Rose offered. She loved giving advice.

Lizzy shot her a nod of approval. "Yeah, that's good."

"That seems hard," John said. "Plus, I don't know anything about law."

"Well, what about government?" his father said, reaching for the pepper.

BEEEEEP! BEEEEEEP!

A piercing tone shot through the kitchen and into the dining room. The British News Network alert siren was used sparingly. Hopefully, this was merely a test.

"We have breaking news," the impassioned voice of the newscaster announced. *"At this hour, terrorists have stormed the House of Commons and have taken four unidentified members of Parliament hostage. It is not known how they entered the building, but sources say they are heavily armed. Initial reports put the number of terrorists around twelve. We have a crew heading to the scene and will have*

more information as it becomes available. Stay with the British News Network as this situation unfolds. "

The family sat in a somber silence, John's issues a distant memory. The focus instead turned to Charlotte, whose brother was a sitting member of the House of Parliament. Wide eyed and unable to vocalize their concerns, the family's appetite vanished. Naturally, they feared the worst.

Theodore took the lead and stood up, pushing in his chair. His family followed him into the family room. Without a word, they sat down on the couch and turned on the television.

"...not yet know who the hostages are." The reporter stood in front of Westminster, the seat of government in the UK. In the background, dozens of law enforcement officers were perched behind armored vehicles, their rifles fixed upon the building. Flashing lights and police tape distracted the attention, but the reporter's words cut through the chaos. *"Police are telling us the group responsible is a terrorist organization known as the LAF, Loyalist Ali Front."* The faint sound of sirens emerged from the background as reinforcements approached. *"The building is surrounded."*

*

"How did this happen!?" yelled Colonel Levanetz. The broad, daunting soldier dressed in fatigues seethed with anger. "We had them tapped. We should have known this." He slammed his fist against the heavily armored truck he stood behind.

"A-A code of some sort," the specialist sputtered. "They never mentioned this in our surveillance."

"This does not happen without planning!" the colonel raged. This failure fell upon *his* head.

A young private came sprinting from behind another armored vehicle holding a phone. "Sir, the prime minister!"

The colonel reluctantly placed the receiver to his ear. "Colonel Levanetz here."

"Colonel," the prime minister said, hiding his irritation well, "how did he get authorization into that building?"

"We will get this resolved, Mr. Prime Minister."

"But now the media is involved," the PM replied. "What will you tell them?"

"We will soon release it's the LAF. There is no reason for them to think otherwise. We will handle the situation then hold a press conference."

"You know the press, Colonel," the prime minister said irritably. "They're not going to wait long. What happens if they find out?"

"They won't," Levanetz assured him.

After hearing a click, the colonel paused to gather his composure. He then lowered the phone from his ear and gazed up towards the window where the situation was unfolding.

*

"What do you want?" The distraught member of Parliament sat bound on the floor. His back leaned against a fallen board room table. The other three MPs sat by his side, all tied together, facing the tinted windows that spanned the opposite wall. It happened so quickly they couldn't even loosen their red ties or take off their navy blue coats. The four men looked like mirror images: pale skin with brown hair and terrified eyes.

"We only want what is ours," one of the masked terrorists, dressed all in black emphatically stated.

The MP shook his head. "This is not the way to get it."

The man's eyes gleamed a reddish hue. He reached up and ripped off his mask, exposing a marred and disfigured face. The left side bubbled from severe burns. The right side bore deep scars courtesy of a sharp blade. The man eased down toward the MP. The hostage tried to be strong, but his eyes conveyed a rare type of fear. With his mangled face mere inches from the MPs, the man uttered, "Yes, it is." The heat from his pungent breath lingered on the MPs nervous skin.

"Captain!" One of his comrades rushed into the room. "The prime minister wants to talk to you."

The captain eyed the hostage as he extended his arm for the phone. The MPs were perplexed. *The prime minister?*

"You have no idea what's happening," the captain said in a near whisper as the phone settled in his waiting hand. "If you knew, you'd be with us." He clutched the phone in his leather glove and marched out of the room.

"Mr. Prime Minister, what took so long?" He strode down the hall to an empty office.

"Captain Brooks, I advise you to reconsider. We *will* defend ourselves."

The captain would not be deterred. "The country will soon know, Mr. Prime Minister. Whether I'm dead or alive, they will all know."

"Captain, think about what you're doing..."

"I have."

The conversation was over.

Meanwhile, a large, loud, and curious crowd had gathered behind the police tape that surrounded the building. Riot control officers, in full protective gear—masks, shields, body suits and batons—stood firm. "They are here!" The captain stood next to the window with his arms folded across his chest. "The people. The media. The police." He turned to his second-in-command who had entered the nearly vacant office. "A little bit longer, my friend."

"What have *we* done?" cried out one of the hostages when the captain stomped back into the room. "Why us?"

"Don't flatter yourself." Stopping in mid-stride the mighty soldier turned. "It's not you we want, it's your position."

"How'd you even get in here?"

He smirked. "We have some friends who share our interests. Be calm, you won't be hurt, we just needed the audience." He gestured towards the window where thousands of people and hundreds of media waited. "And you gave us a global one."

"Who are you?"

The captain grabbed a black backpack from next to the windows. He unzipped the top and pulled out what appeared to be a rectangular pamphlet. The backpack contained thousands. He counted out four.

"My name is Captain Erik Brooks." He crouched down next to his hostages and cut their hands loose. "I served in MI6 for decades. Many of us have," he nodded towards his colleagues. "But you know nothing."

The hostages listened intently; void of the fear that once paralyzed them.

These pamphlets highlight some of the worst I saw, and did. Torture, extortion, embezzlement, mass murder." He handed them the pamphlets, one-by-one. "Everything you need to know is in there. You will see pictures of our most beloved politicians making crooked deals with terrorists and dictators. You will see the bodies, the drugs, the weapons, the money. Our work over the past few decades spelled out before the world. The people must know the truth."

"Why all this?" asked one of the hostages.

"We needed a big impression," the captain sneered. "We had to separate ourselves from all the nonsense. This is no conspiracy, my friends. This is real."

"Oh, my God," uttered one of the MPs as he scanned the material. He looked up at the captain in shock.

"The government's been on to us for a while." The captain walked towards the windows with his hands folded behind his back, chest out. "They wiretap our phones. Read our messages. But it's hard to catch the people who perfected those strategies."

"If this is true, it will ruin us," warned one of the MPs as he read. "You're a damned traitor."

The captain smiled. "History may judge me however it wishes, gentlemen. I am a patriot of the highest order."

He looked at his watch, then peered outside. "First Lieutenant, it's time. Head to the roof and enlighten the world."

The MP on the end whispered, "He's going to throw those pamphlets off the roof while the world watches." He looked down at his copy. "And we're his legitimacy."

The lieutenant snatched up four backpacks and threw them over his shoulder. After one step towards the door, he stopped in his path. His eyes widened and his mouth dropped.

With great intensity, the British military burst into the room and opened fire. Though the sound was deafening and unmistakable, all the masses saw from the street below was shattering glass and the flash of high velocity rounds.

*

"You're going to have to go out there eventually," said Colonel Levanetz to a somber Commissioner of the London Police Department. The men stood looking out a small window at a swarm of reporters.

"I know," he acknowledged. He turned to the colonel with sympathetic eyes. "I deal with some of the worst scum you can imagine, and those people scare me most."

The colonel patted the commissioner on the upper back, then made his way down the hall. The four MPs sat alone in a guarded office. They were visibly tired, stressed, and traumatized.

"I gather you remember your mission?" The colonel's question sounded more like a command. "Your country is counting on you."

Although the situation was over, the four men still felt like hostages. Yet, being in no position to ponder the consequences, they followed the colonel's lead.

When the ornate doors of Westminster opened, the hostages, military guards, and Police Commissioner, emerged into a media frenzy.

The flash of cameras and screams from the massive crowd defined the moment. The press shouted their questions, trying to overreach security with their microphones.

"Back away!" commanded the guards.

The media did not heed the warning. "Move!" With his massive forearm a guard drove a reporter into the ground.

In emotion unbecoming of the circumstance, the faces of the former hostages appeared vacuous. The energy surrounding the moment appeared to have no effect.

Following an arduous trek, they eventually reached the podium. It seemed cold and, notwithstanding all the people, very lonely. The front of the podium displayed the seal, "Metropolitan Police." In reality, the local authorities couldn't have been less in control.

Wasting no time, the commissioner approached the podium. He was greeted by a seemingly endless sea of microphones, cameras, reporters, and inspired citizens.

"At approximately 5:45 this afternoon, members of an extreme Islamic militant group known as the Loyalist Ali Front, or LAF, infiltrated the Palace of Westminster and took four members of the House of Commons hostage." His eyes remained glued to his notes. "There were ten men involved in this terrorist act. Not knowing their weapon capabilities or if they intended to harm the hostages, we had little time to act. To ensure the lives of our MPs, we saw no other option but to take swift action. With the help of the military..." the commissioner took a second to acknowledge the soldiers that stood behind him, "...we carried out a successful raid and killed the terrorists. As with most terrorists, we can only assume their primary goal was to disrupt our quality of life. At this point we have no reason to believe more attacks are imminent. I would now like to bring forward MP Richard Sykes. This is obviously an emotional time for the MPs and all their families. We ask the media to be respectful. He only wishes to say a few words."

The commissioner stepped aside and proudly shook the MP's hand as he reluctantly stepped to the podium.

From his breast pocket, Sykes pulled out a postcard sized piece of paper and unfolded it carefully. His eyes purposely avoided contact with anyone in the crowd or beside him on stage. The onlookers and media remained amazingly quiet, eagerly awaiting his testimony. He delivered his speech in much the same way as the commissioner—with stunning apathy.

"When confronted with a tragic situation, you never know how you'll react. Such was the case for me and my three fellow countrymen. At first, it was simply some yelling from down the hall. Before we knew what happened, four masked men burst into our room. They put guns to our heads and began shouting out commands in what sounded like Arabic. We could not understand their orders, so they beat us with their weapons."

Sykes took a step back to calm his emotions. In a touching display of solidarity, one of his fellow MPs placed a caring hand on his shoulder. The surge of camera shutters embraced the moment which would come to symbolize the ordeal. With the help of his colleague, Sykes managed to gather his composure. He returned to the podium with a quivering voice.

"They tied us all together and put us in a closet. All I could think about was my family at home and wondered if I would ever see them again. We sat tied, blindfolded, and gagged while they spoke amongst themselves."

Despite his best efforts to remain strong a tear formed in his eye. The pride he regarded as his greatest virtue disallowed him from wiping it away. As a result, the tear broke free and gracefully rolled down his cheek.

"When our brave military stormed the room and started shooting, we all thought we were going to die. It lasted barely a few seconds, but as you can imagine, it felt like an eternity. I know many of you want more information. We ask that you please respect our wishes and let us heal." He took a deep breath. The next words would be the most difficult. "God save the Kingdom."

A few more tears quietly broke free as he retreated from the microphones. His written speech remained behind on the podium stand.

Despite his request, the media bombarded the MPs with questions. "Did the terrorists talk to you? Did they tell you anything about their objective? Commissioner, tell us more about this LAF? We need more information!"

The thousands of onlookers erupted in cheers. The four men had instantly become national heroes. With the crowd noise growing to insurmountable levels, the media screamed their questions. Some even tried to leap onto the stage. What audiences saw, from around the world, was nothing less than a controlled riot. All the while, the four MPs remained huddled together, wishing it would all go away.

Colonel Levanetz stood near the doors, concealed in the back. The line filed past him as the stage emptied. His phone began to vibrate.

"Yes, sir?"

"Is everything taken care of?" the unyielding voice demanded.

"I'm assuming you watched."

"What about the backpacks?"

"We have them, Mr. Prime Minister."

"I am glad, Colonel. Have another talk with our MPs. Make them understand what the Crown expects."

"Yes, sir." A shrewd sense of accomplishment flashed across his face as he lowered the phone.

By this time, the four MPs were nearing the brilliant doors of Westminster. The colonel nodded at them in approval but was ignored.

The crowd and media dispersed. The struggling nation was blessed with a newfound sense of pride in what its fellow countrymen had survived. But what nobody saw, the pamphlets in the back pockets of each of the former hostages, had the power to transform that pride into disdain.

Only four people knew those pamphlets existed. Soon, the whole world would know. And the person responsible would have unknowingly sparked a revolution.

CHAPTER TWO
THE GENESIS

A solemn Nolan family sat in their living room enraptured by the media coverage. Charlotte frantically paced behind the couch, dialing her phone hysterically. Minutes prior, her brother, Tony Manning, had stood before the world as a hero who had just survived a terrorist attack. Every number she tried went to voice mail, and her anxiety mounted.

"Honey, your brother is fine," Theodore said. "Please. Relax." He held her in his arms. "Tony is safe."

Her anxiety morphed into a somber release of tears.

The hostages were unknown before they took the stage to address the world. When Charlotte's brother emerged from Westminster, the response was not relief, but desperation when she realized how close he'd been to death.

"I-I-I don't know what-what to do," she sobbed.

Theodore held his wife tightly. After a moment, he gently pulled himself away and took her hands. "You saw him," he said soothingly, his thumbs rubbing her fingers. "He's okay!"

Charlotte would not be consoled. "I have to talk to somebody. I have to talk to *him*."

"What do you want to do?" Theodore asked, continuing to caress her hands as she sobbed.

"I need to see him."

"You want to go to London?"

Charlotte nodded.

Theodore turned to his children. "I think you should stay here." He swung open the closet door and rooted through the clutter. "I am assuming we won't get back until late, maybe tomorrow morning." He ripped two coats off the hangers, and handed one to his wife.

Charlotte grabbed a few things off the foyer desk and shoved them into her purse. The couple raced out the door. "We'll call tonight," Theodore called back, opening the car door for his wife.

The uncertainty surrounding the terror attack loomed in the minds of the Nolan children.

"Please be careful," Rose said, grabbing her twin's arm.

Charlotte managed to compose herself as the car backed out of the driveway. Her children stood at the doorway and waved a heartfelt goodbye. Forcing a smile, she returned the gesture.

Theodore put the car in drive and powered down the road. As soon as her children were out of sight, Charlotte's emotions broke free. For the entire hour drive to London she fought back the tears, occasionally giving in.

*

"Excuse me," Colonel Levanetz apologized as he interrupted the Manning family reunion. It had been fifteen minutes since the media blitz and the family had embraced for the first time. "Can we have a moment more of your time?"

The colonel didn't appear to be bothered by his unwanted interruption. He towered over the family, displaying a semi-polite authority.

Manning was not understanding. "I would like to be with my family right now, Colonel." "This will only take a few minutes," the colonel insisted, gripping Manning's arm. "I assure you," he said to Manning's wife, "this will be the last time."

Manning had no choice. "Wait here." The MP's support group included his parents, brothers, nephews, wife, and baby boy. They had all been through a mental hell.

"I won't be long," he assured them. Seconds later he disappeared behind a metal door.

The MP was led through a long tile enclosed corridor. The lights flickered as they silently advanced into the darkness. Their short journey ended at an unobtrusive looking door. The colonel pushed it open, and a sweeping light fell upon the three other MPs. They sat in wooden chairs in the middle of a dark, empty room.

"Please take a seat, Mr. Manning," offered the colonel. He motioned to the only remaining chair. "We'll be with you shortly."

The colonel stepped out, allowing the door to slam shut. The blow resonated in the void chamber. Despite the absence of barred windows and ratty bunk beds, the ambiance was prisonlike. It smelled of mold and floral air fresheners.

"What is this?" Sykes asked, highly irritated.

"Bullshit! That's what it is," Manning said, more cynical. "It's all a damn lie."

For the next few minutes, the four MPs stared at the door. There was nothing left to say. They wanted this behind them. They wanted their lives back.

The faint sound of a turning knob and the creak of an opening door soon replaced the silence. The room gradually illuminated with the shrill release of a rusty hinge.

The men who entered the room appeared as dark silhouettes against a bright background, intense beams of yellow outlining their imposing figures. When all six had cleared the threshold, the door again slammed shut.

A few struggling lights gradually rose to a dull dim.

A short, leather faced man in the middle spoke first. "Good evening, gentlemen. Please remain seated." His voice was raspy and unimpassioned. "This will not take long."

Despite their dark suits and dress shoes, something about their presentation appeared soldier-like. They emitted that certain swagger unique to the military.

"Please forgive me if I do not introduce myself. Given the situation, you surely understand."

"Let us go," Sykes said, refusing to be intimidated. "We did our part."

"You did." The man's lack of emotion and monotone delivery was unsettling. "And we appreciate your cooperation. But your loyalty to the crown is not yet over. In fact, must never be."

The man reached into his breast pocket and pulled out an unwrapped cigar. Holding the dark leaf at a 45-degree angle, he torched the end and placed the fresh cut to his lips. With a swift breath, he blew out the flame, then drew a sweet cloud into his mouth.

The smoke rose from deep within his throat. "Gentlemen, you're some of the brightest in Britain. Therefore, you can appreciate our duty to this nation." He drew heavily from his Dominican. "Our job is to keep the people safe, happy, and free—by any means." He flicked his ashes onto the cracked vinyl floor. "Whether you four like it or not, you are now part of our fraternity." He swirled his cigar, weaving a trail of smoke around the men who accompanied him. "We know Captain Brooks spoke with you. What he said will remain between you four." He paused to ensure his words were understood. "Captain Brooks was a traitor. We let him into our world, and he betrayed us. He served his country with valor and distinction, until he didn't. He failed to understand the mission and its greater good."

The man puffed, creating a halo that rose towards the ceiling. He continued in an apathetic voice. "Gentlemen, ordinary people cannot handle what you now know." He lowered the sweet Pacifica from his mouth. "I am going to make this clear..."

He gestured with his cigar towards the MPs, the smoke rising from the tip. His eyes were distant. His soul dead. "Never mention what happened here today, outside the statement we provided you. National security trumps the individual good. It's how we survive." He paused as the smoke once again encircled his head. "Please do not think we are the enemy, gentlemen. In fact, it's just the opposite."

With a crack of the rusty hinge, the men were gone. But this time the door gently closed behind them. The MPs watched the cigar smoke dissipate as it spread along the ceiling.

MP Sykes reached into his back pocket and pulled out the pamphlet Captain Brooks had given each of them. "I want nothing to do with this damn thing." His act of tearing it into little pieces must have been contagious, and two other MPs repeated the action.

Manning, however, took the pamphlet out of his back pocket, but could not bring himself to destroy it. In all the confusion, the other three didn't even notice he sat with his elbows resting on his knees, staring at it.

When his pamphlet had been turned into a pile of confetti Sykes approached the window, removed the dark covering, and threw the tiny pieces out into the rain that had begun to fall. Satisfied, or maybe relieved by his action, he left the room quietly. The other two MPs followed suit.

Manning was now alone, still staring at the pamphlet. His mind raced uncontrollably with grand thoughts of pride and country. The room cooled rapidly as the outside air rushed in through the window. His breath became more visible with each exhale. His uncertainty mounting, he drew in a large breath. His aching chest and knotted stomach expanded. A warm cloud of moist air blew onto the pamphlet when he heaved a heavy sigh. Before the vapor could fade, he tore it into two, then four, eight, 16, 32 pieces. Soon dozens of tiny bits of paper littered the floor.

"Tony!" screamed Charlotte when he walked back to where his family was waiting. His sister ran up and threw her arms around his neck.

"Thank God!" she gasped.

Soon, his entire family had surrounded him, all of them thankful for the blessings in their lives. Despite their energy, Tony remained without joy.

"The drive felt like an eternity," Charlotte cried, holding her brother tightly, her head pressed against his chest. "Thank God, everything is okay! This nightmare is finally over."

*

"Class, we are about to begin," announced Professor Dayton Sorenson. A popular nickname among the students for him was 'Old Sores', a fitting name considering his ancient age and grumpy demeanor. "Before today's lesson, let's discuss thesis ideas."

He pulled a folder from a hemp satchel, resting it on his desk, rifling through the sections. He looked up from under his glasses. "Jody." He pointed to the Asian girl in the front row. "Do you have a topic?"

"I think so." Her lack of confidence suggested otherwise.

The professor nodded for her to go on.

"Well, I have been studying death and bereavement. I'd like to look at how we've changed concerning mortality."

"Okay." Old Sores displayed a little authentic excitement—but only a little. "That may be a bit overbroad. With technology, the Earth is becoming one big culture. Given our timeframe, try to make it more specific. Maybe just burial practices."

Jody hurried to jot down his recommendations.

Professor Sorenson glanced around the room. "Anyone else?"

A few brave souls raised their hands. Old Sores pointed to an older Indian woman next to John.

"Juvenile dependency." Her proposition sounded more like a command than a suggestion. "It seems kids can't be kids. When I was young, I played with friends. Today's kids have to work."

"I like it. But focus on a certain type of job."

The professor shifted his focus to the entire class. "Pick a topic that is specific. This is not a dissertation."

A few more students raised their hands.

"I want to look at the sociology of aging." The Kenyan in the back row blurted out. "My generation can expect to live well into our 90s, but we don't want to look older than 50, while being active like we're 40."

The professor tilted his head in thought. He was not sold. "I feel that has been overdone. Stop by my office after class. I think we can make it more interesting. Not only for you, but for me. I have to read it." The class chuckled at his brutal honesty.

Old Sores returned to his desk to page through his lecture. "I have office hours after class. I will stay as long as needed. Now," he marked the day's lesson with a pen, "the sociology of quasi-sport..."

Christian leaned partially across the aisle, towards John. "Whatcha doin' after class?"

"I need to stop by his office."

"Really? I'm goin' to the pub. Meet me when you're finished?"

"Sure."

Their focus shifted back to the front of the room. Even though the old man couldn't hear, his eyes were keen.

When class finished, John made his way to Old Sores' office. He sat in a chair outside the door.

The professor allotted fifteen minutes per appointment and John was second. He unzipped his backpack and as he pulled out his notes, the sweet smell of floral perfume caressed his nose. He looked up to find April Lynn sitting next to him. They exchanged pleasant smiles.

Despite her reserved appearance, John considered April to be stunning. At a thin five-foot-seven, she more resembled a Norwegian skier than a student at one of the world's foremost universities. John didn't date much. The thought of rejection terrified him. But for April, he was willing to make the effort.

While John searched his brain to initiate a conversation, fate offered him an opportunity.

"I heard one of the hostages in the House of Commons was your uncle," April said. In her words, John detected a strong southern American accent.

"My mom was born in America. Tennessee."

John nodded.

She smiled. "Everyone asks."

April and John had taken a few classes together. Yet, their conversations never went beyond classroom discussion.

"Yeah." John lowered his head, figuring the sympathy card was a good one to play. "It's been tough."

"I'll bet." The compassion in her voice matched that of her empathetic gaze. John didn't know her well enough to be sure it was genuine. In reality, he didn't care.

"My mom freaked," he said, acting strong, yet sensitive. "What were the chances my uncle was one of the four?" He paused for dramatic effect. "We were close to losing him." John peered into her clear blue eyes.

"You poor thing." She placed a caring hand on his knee and gently squeezed. "I can only imagine."

The moment was perfect. As John inhaled the breath intended to ask April to discuss this further, he heard the door creak open. *Damn it!* His eyes closed in disappointment. He was next.

"Mr. Nolan, how can I help you?"

The professor's room more closely resembled a closet than an office. John thought surely a scholar of his tenure should have better accommodations. The short expanse of the floor allowed for only two small, rickety chairs. Rows of rotting books spanned the height of the walls. John wasn't entirely sure the room was safe. Gravity's tenuous hold could give way at any moment. If John had been claustrophobic, he would have been in trouble.

The nervous young man rooted through the notes he had not prepared while talking to April. "I have some ideas."

"Alright."

"Well, I love history. I'd like to do something on the evolution of government. Maybe pick a specific type." John bit his lip, waiting for a reply.

"Okay." The few seconds leading up to that lonely statement were agonizing. John had no other ideas. This was all or nothing. "The sociology of government?"

"It's specific, especially if I pick a certain aspect of governance, and it doesn't seem stale."

The old man leaned across the desk to study John's notes. "Can this be done by May?"

"I'll start now. "I've already done a lot of this work as an undergrad." He scooted to the edge of his chair. "I will look at the great nations of the world: Rome, Greece, the Mayans, Persia, Ottoman, Byzantine, USSR, United States. Based on their successes and failures, I can predict how we will govern ourselves to create a more perfect union. Our civilization is the result of centuries of trial and error. How will we implement that knowledge going forward?" His stomach twisting, John sank back in his chair, but could hardly relax.

The old man's bushy eyebrows arched up when he peeked above his thick bifocals. "It might work."

The knot in John's stomach loosened slightly.

"But..." the professor extended his finger, "I do fear this is a lot to handle in our timeframe. I'm also skeptical of the work's significance. It must be relevant."

"Sir," John stated, "I will not let you down."

Old Sores could never reject such zeal. "I want to see progress. At the end of January, let's get together. If progress is lacking, we'll change topics." He allowed John time to consider his caveat. "Deal?" Old Sores extended his shaky gray hand across the desk.

John enthusiastically extended his own. "Deal!"

*

"Well?" Christian was already a few deep by the time his friend arrived.

"I'll take the usual."

Christian reached out to the passing waitress. "Ma'am, a pint of your house pilsner please."

She smiled.

"So," Christian turned back, "get yourself a topic?"

"I did," John said proudly. "I am going to write a Constitution."

His friend cocked his head. "You're aware this is a sociology class, right?" Sarcasm was one of Christian's finer traits.

The beer placed in front of John was so cold a thin surface of ice floated on top. A frigid rush chilled his throat as he gulped it down. "Well, Old Sores doesn't actually know it yet."

"Why should he?"

"Ahh, no worries. Look, I don't really like sociology. If I am going to spend a few months working on this, I have to be interested. So I gave him some line about the sociology of government. *I* thought it sounded terrible."

"It does." Christian gurgled in his glass. "He bought it?"

John nodded.

"What kind of constitution will you be writin'?"

"A flawless one. I am going to study past civilizations, determine what made them strong, and what then led to their downfall. From that, I'll write a Constitution that emphasizes what works and corrects for what doesn't. We have enough human history to draw upon. There's no reason any nation should fail—or even struggle for that matter. They can *all* be successful. I will find that perfect formula and write a Constitution that ensures lasting prosperity."

"Damn." Christian was authentically shocked. "That's intense. How'd you...." He stopped in mid-sentence. His friend had zoned out. Christian knew the look. It was usually followed by a...

"Look at the Mayan empire of Central America."

...tangent.

"They were the most powerful of all the ancient 'American' civilizations. They built temples and pyramids and vast cities that were untouchable during the first millennium. Their cities had a population of 2,000 per square mile, more than many of our cities today. Then it all vanished. Why?"

Christian shrugged. He knew the answer was pending.

"Some believe they simply ruined their environment. Scientists found lake sediment around 900 AD had no tree pollen. It was all weeds. The Mayans deforested their land. Without trees you have erosion of topsoil. One scientist said the change in ground cover could have increased the regional temperature by six degrees. That could have dried out the land, affected rain, lowered the groundwater table and reservoirs. The bones found from ancient Mayan people show severe malnutrition. It may not have been purely environmental, rather a combination of war, migration, and disease. These could be related. The worst drought in the past 7,000 years happened about when the Mayan empire collapsed. Cities were abandoned, causing economic collapse."

"Ahh."

"They couldn't have been invaded because armies conquered for resources. The cities were abandoned. But if there were a drought, a war over water seems likely. It couldn't have only been disease. Disease doesn't wipe out 100 percent of a population."

"Nope."

"The northern cities like Chichen Itza and Coba lasted a little longer, but their water tables were closer to the ground than the southern cities." John took a slight break to finish his beer. "If that was the reason the Mayan civilization fell, I would also look at what made them so powerful."

Even as much as he liked to look bored, Christian actually found John's knowledge interesting. A small part of him even envied his insight.

"The Mayans made great structures that instilled pride. They tracked a solar year, including eclipses. They mapped stars and were expert farmers." He ticked off the items on his fingers. "They developed their own mathematics and system of writing. They studied architecture; established strong trade routes. Unlike many nations that conquered their way to power, the Mayans relied on intellectual achievement. They spent a large portion of resources educating their children. That may have been why they lasted so long. They prospered through education, not warfare. So what do you think about my thesis?"

"You know what, man?" Christian said honestly. "Lesser ideas have changed the world."

*

January of the following year

"Pugh, Cunnington, and Sykes to Step Down"

The headlines were stark. Three of the four men taken hostage that fall day in London wouldn't return to the House of Commons after May elections. Speculation in both Houses, media, and the public mounted. What were they afraid of? Why would they quit? The only member running for reelection was Tony Manning. The country decried the loss of its most revered leaders.

"You've got to be kidding me!" A disgusted Manning clutched the kitchen table after reading the headline.

"What's wrong, honey?" Manning's wife, Emma, entered the kitchen holding their baby. Soon, she'd set out on her morning run.

Emma Manning was the appropriate wife for a young politician. She was tall and thin, pale skinned, with flowing red hair. Emma was an admired wife in the Commons. Her socials were an honor to attend. A practicing Catholic—one of a few left in the Kingdom—she carried on the religious traditions of her Irish ancestors. But her looks and faith were deceiving. Underneath her disciplined exterior lay an erratic temper.

"They all told me they considered stepping down, but I didn't think they would actually do it." Manning's irritation was growing with every breath.

"They didn't handle the situation as well as you," Emma said, preparing the baby's formula in the sink. "It was obvious."

Tony approached the kitchen window. The overnight snow was finally beginning to taper off.

"They are giving up!" He slammed his open hand against the granite counter and the baby began to cry.

Emma flashed her husband an unforgiving glare as she calmed the child. "What do you mean?"

"The terrorists."

Emma put the baby on her shoulder and faced Tony.

"I have to talk to them." He fiddled in his pocket for his phone.

Emma looked perplexed. Her husband's anger seemed misplaced.

Tony first called Pugh, then Sykes, and finally, Cunnington. They all agreed to meet at noon for lunch at a cafe in downtown London.

Tony was the first to arrive. He informed the waitress of their meeting and requested privacy.

In House-of-Commons-style, the other three arrived on time. They sat down in an awkward manner.

"Tony, we can't do this anymore. I don't *want* to do this anymore," Sykes said softly as not to be overheard. "I can't sleep at night knowing that I lied to my country. My constituents trusted me. I think I might even leave the island for some time."

"Me, too," Pugh said. He appeared unusually skittish. "I feel like *they're* listening. I don't feel safe in my car, at work, on the phone, in my house. If I leave politics, maybe I can get my life back. Right now, I don't feel like I have one."

"This is not right," pleaded Manning. "How can you walk away? The people deserve more." He placed his elbows on the table and folded his hands. "I don't want to start a war, I just want to be honest. We came into the House on a platform of transparency. Let's *honor* that commitment."

"It's not worth my family," Cunnington said unapologetically.

"If we do this together, the four of us, they can't retaliate," Manning insisted. The nation is behind us."

The waitress placed water glasses on the table for each of them. As instructed, she left immediately.

"How do we know they are not listening, right now?" Cunnington asked, watching the waitress approach another table. "It freaks me out." He lifted his glass to inspect his water. "Does the waitress work for them? I can't handle this. I have to rid myself of this torment."

The other two agreed.

"Tony, how long have we known each other?" Sykes asked. "Decades, right? You're one of my best friends and I have always been there for you. And you, me. But on this, I am out. We're all out."

Manning, however, could not let it go.

"Think of the people who are being wronged. All the tax dollars wasted. How many innocent people have died? We took an oath." His voice quivered. "We have a responsibility!"

"Tony, I'm sorry." Sykes stood up and pushed in his chair. "I appreciate your passion, but I can't help you." He turned and walked away.

"Tony, I am not interested in taking on the government," Pugh said, standing. "We have a responsibility to our families first. Good luck my friend. I'd hate to see something happen to you." He followed after Sykes.

It was now only Manning and Cunnington.

"Tony, what are you going to do? The pamphlets are gone. Who will believe us? We may be in Parliament, but we have no power. We are moving on. I suggest you do the same."

"Will, please," Tony said, offering one final plea.

"Tony, that guy in the room was right. They *are* the good guys. They *are* on our side. If I have to live in ignorance to keep my life, then so be it." Will leaned towards Tony and spoke caringly. "We were in the wrong place at the wrong time." He looked his friend in the eye. "Please, Tony, let it go. This is a battle you won't win. In fact, it's one you may not want to win."

"I don't want a battle," Tony declared, shaking his head.

"It doesn't matter what *you* want. And that is what scares the hell out of me."

With that, Cunnington stood and pushed his chair under the table. "I will serve my country until May. Then I am done."

Manning soon found himself alone, watching his final ally shrink with each step down the snow blown street. Without help, he knew he could not continue. He would need a conduit to deliver his message. But anonymity was key.

He removed his phone from his pocket, jiggling it in his hand. With a stern look of determination, he stood up. He knew what he had to do. And he was going home to do it.

*

When night fell on that pleasant January day, it brought with it a cold front laced in a deep freeze and unforgiving wind. The snow that fell the night before had melted in the mid-morning sun. Only scattered patches remained throughout the yards in the Nolans' neighborhood.

John was holed up in his room, where he had spent much of the prior two months. His desk was stacked high with history books and encyclopedias, littered with notes and markers. As he read, text scrolled across his monitor; "minimum is never enough."

Although he was hurried, his room remained orderly. The bright, hot lights of his desk kept him awake. The silence kept him focused.

After finishing his latest book, John sucked in some stuffy air and settled in to type out the history of the Ottoman Empire, the rise and fall of this once great civilization. It didn't matter if it took all night. Soon, he would present his work to the professor. There was no time for sleep.

When he was done, the paper read:

The Ottoman Empire was the most powerful Islamic-controlled nation, ever, a multi-ethnic and multi-religious state that reached its peak in the 15th and 16th centuries. Its rule spanned three continents and was once greatly feared and respected. In the end, it was reduced to a pejorative sobriquet, "The sick man of Europe."

The Turks thrived during the Middle Ages when Christian Europe was stuck in stagnation. The Ottomans utilized this time to set up business centers where schools of theology and advanced studies flourished. The government subsidized many of these institutions, which did not discriminate on the basis of class or religion. The system worked to develop powerful working and ruling classes. These institutions, called Akhis, grew very powerful, which would become a problem centuries later.

The key to the longevity of the empire was its tolerance and acceptance of different faiths, which attracted many of the world's greatest minds and most ambitious entrepreneurs.

In 1453, it conquered the Serbs, extending the empire into Europe. Constantinople became its new capital. Trade routes blossomed, the economy prospered, and its military grew in power and influence.

However, it stretched itself too far. The strain of consistent conflicts, up to and including the 16th century, stripped the empire of its resources. Supply lines crumbled when they could no longer communicate across long distances. The military need for defense eventually made greater expansion impossible. Its enemies formed alliances in the Mediterranean. Although the Turks weren't hated in the region, they were the most powerful nation, and therefore targeted.

The colonization of the new world corresponded with the height of Ottoman power, and also provided the catalyst for its collapse. New trade routes limited its power as a trade center in the Mediterranean, which was no longer the center of trade in the world. The giant influx of Spanish silver from the new world weakened its currency.

While the Industrial Revolution had swept through Western Europe, the Ottoman Empire was still relying mainly on medieval technologies. It had no railroads or telegraphs. Poor communications made it difficult for Constantinople to control its provinces and facilitate advancements. Thus, many provinces became autonomous. A corrupt tax system depleted revenues. Lack of industry meant their raw materials were not being harvested. Chaos sparked revolution. It lost large portions of its Jewish population (the Hebrews originally immigrated there to flee religious persecution), further crippling the economy.

On Friday, May 9, 1873, the Vienna Stock Market crashed and took with it the entire economy of Europe. The Ottoman Empire was unable to deal with the situation. Regional wars led to WWI and soon after, the Empire was dissolved.

In many ways, the circumstances surrounding the fall of the Ottoman Empire paralleled those of the Roman Empire, particularly in terms of the government's inability to deal with tensions between ethnic groups in tough economic times which were mainly caused by inflation.

Its trading philosophy depended too much on the Greeks and not enough on themselves. When the Greeks demanded independence in the early 19th century, the Turks were unprepared to trade on their own. This made the Empire more of a producer rather than a manufacturer of raw materials.

Unstable leadership was a problem. The second most powerful man in the Empire was the Grand Vizier, the adviser-in-chief to the Sultan. To prevent a coup, the Sultan would often replace him. This prevented a stable government, the thing most required in turbulent times. Also, to preserve their rule, Sultans would take male relatives and sequester them. If the Sultan died, the heir would not be prepared to lead. Any efforts to modernize or reform the empire—especially when

DEVOLUTION

it came to technology—were always opposed by the powerful (the Akhis). The introduction of such advances would have limited their power as others gained it. As the world became more democratic, the empire remained autocratic. Revolts broke out. Unlike other nations in Europe where a weak leader could be balanced by another governmental body, the Turks could not atone for a weak Sultan.

The empire's problems were, in fact, the result of an inability to deal with weak leaders, rising nationalism between ethnic groups, powerful internal factions unwilling to reform and the inability to change with the global economy.

It is a common theme throughout human history that once power is obtained, those who obtain it will do what is necessary to preserve it. In the case of the Ottomans, the ruling party resisted technology and scientific advancement, leaving the Ottomans at a great global disadvantage. But the strategy worked brilliantly; up until the empire's demise, as power was never lost upon the ruling class.

A system must be put in place where the people determine their ultimate destiny, and are free to evolve, and not devolve. A nation mustn't march into the future under the pompous command of a few, but rather the acute vision of the many.

Pleased with his research, John powered down his computer and stumbled to bed. A few hours later he would wake and continue.

*

As John was laying down to sleep, his uncle quietly arose to peruse his own ambitions. With his wife and child asleep, Tony Manning embarked on what would be hours of planning. His office was similar to John's in that, despite his frantic determination, it remained tidy. Illuminated by only the light of the monitor, and entertained solely by the dull drone of the cooling fan, he worked tirelessly throughout the morning hours.

Tony had returned home from his disheartening lunch meeting that afternoon. Despite the snowfall, Emma was out on her daily run, and his son was sleeping in the back room. With a heavy mind, he sat on the couch to gather his thoughts. He learned not long ago that major mistakes are made when one lets their emotions control their actions.

Like most freshmen MPs, Manning felt invincible when he first entered the House of Commons. And after garnering 61 percent of the vote, the most of any member of the incoming class, why shouldn't he? He was 32, newly married, and full of ambition. It fostered a mindset that was asking to be challenged.

Days after his arrival, he took to the House for his first session.

"This guy will go on forever," MP Henry Bodwell whispered, leaning towards Tony. The red haired Irishman motioned to the MP who had the floor.

"Yeah?" Tony kept his gaze forward. He had no desire to converse. The novelty of his surroundings had far from faded.

"You know, I don't understand this initiative," Bodwell went on, ignoring Tony's disinterest. He leaned in closer. "I mean, who cares about Congo Free Trade, anyway? This is a waste of time."

"Give it a chance." Tony flashed a courteous smile.

Tony's naiveté served as fuel. "Henry Bodwell." The husky man extended a hand in faux friendship.

Tony responded in kind. "Tony Manning, Kensington and Chelsea district," he said with enormous pride.

"Yeah, I saw your victory," Bodwell recalled. "This must be exciting for you. I remember my first week in the Commons."

Tony nodded halfheartedly, then turned back to the proceedings.

Bodwell didn't get the hint. "You had an impressive election," he continued. "Congratulations. Don't let it go to your head. People are fickle."

Tony kept his focus on the floor. "I'll keep that in mind. Thank you."

Later that day, the Congo Free Trade bill came up for debate on the House floor. Unlike the House of Lords, which was more ornate in its styling, the Commons' chamber was small and modestly decorated in a green art deco amongst Gothic-related architecture. Located in the Palace of Westminster, it featured rows of benches on opposite sides of the floor. On the far end of the aisle, in towering wooden booths, sat the speaker and high ranking officials. Despite the relative simplicity of the all-wooden structure, its rich history and storied past created an inspiring aura that transcended its appearance.

Members of the Speaker's majority party sat to his right side, while opposition party members presided to his left. Tony constituted the latter. In front of each bench was drawn a red line, which members were forbidden to cross during debates. The space between equaled two sword lengths. The more powerful and tenured members sat in the front with the lesser in the back. Again, Tony was the latter. The members outnumbered the available seating, forcing late arrivals to stand near. Tony arrived early to ensure his seat.

"We are here today to discuss the Congo Free Trade agreement," announced the Speaker of the Commons, Dan Chin, bringing the House to session. The room echoed with the sounds of shuffling feet and adjusting bodies, which quickly dissipated.

"This bill, which will necessitate a vote upon conclusion of debate, will decide whether the United Kingdom will engage in tariff and tax-free trade with the Democratic Republic of the Congo, a nation endowed with ample resources and vast potential for wealth. However, it has the potential for instability."

The Speaker removed his glasses. His chiseled chin and beady eyes scanned the assemblage. "We shall begin the debate with the bill's sponsor, the Honorable Member for Hackney."

"Thank you, Mr. Speaker." Rick Bryne took the floor. "In this time of economic hardship, we must secure the value of goods and services from overseas." His thunderous voice reverberated throughout the wooden chamber. "Unemployment, inflation and interest rates are rising to levels we haven't seen in quite some time. This agreement would help calm the markets. The Democratic Republic of the Congo has a tenuous past. But if we are to expand our global influence, we must feed our markets with fresh resources. The region has stabilized. The government has control."

The impassioned MP paused for a moment to sift through his notes before continuing.

"This is a market the industrialized world has yet to corner. By eliminating the tariff and opening up free markets, we can work with them to not only grow our economy, but grow our relationship with an African nation whose neighbors are also rich in resources.

"This free trade would spur competition in the raw materials marketplace, prices will drop, and quality of life will increase. For our future, we need free trade. Mr. Speaker," Bryne turned to the bench, "you have the floor, sir."

"Thank you, Honorable Member for Hackney. Rebukes?" He surveyed the hall. "Yes, the Honorable Member for Hammarsmith and Fulham."

Bodwell rose. "Mr. Speaker," he nodded in much the same fashion as Bryne. "This free trade agreement is too risky. Yes, our economy is stagnating, but we cannot allow our companies to invest in such an unsteady nation. The Congo has been a battlefield for decades. I ask you, where is our common sense? If we allow free trade, existing British companies will suffer. Wages in that nation are low. They can undercut our workers and our companies will suffer. We must protect ourselves. Mr. Speaker, I now turn the floor over to you."

The Speaker eyed the MP from Hackney.

"Mr. Speaker, history has shown," refuted Bryne, "that isolationism helps no one. In the 1930s, America was in the Great Depression longer than any other country in the world. And it was their isolationism that prolonged their own misery. The Smoot-Hawley Tariff was the driving force for the reduction in U.S./European trade. The lack of competition and the artificially high prices it created suffocated the nation. Trade is wealth! And competition fuels innovation and lower prices. Mr. Speaker, free markets are the path to a recession-proof Great Britain. We *must lift the tariff.*"

After ninety minutes of the debate, Tony, the ambitious young representative, decided to make an impression. He motioned towards the Speaker.

"The Honorable Member from Kensington and Chelsea has the floor."

Manning began with a gracious nod. "Mr. Speaker. While we each have our own constituencies, we ultimately serve the United Kingdom. We have a responsibility to look out for the entire nation, not a select few. Our country, as a whole, will benefit from this free trade bill. And that, as Members of Parliament, must constitute our grandest of intentions. Thank you, Mr. Speaker." A sense of accomplishment rushed through his being.

The Speaker panned to his right. "If there are no more comments then, we can move to a vote."

The hall was still. Then, Bodwell arose from his chair. "Mr. Speaker. The Honorable Member from Kensington and Chelsea fails to understand reality."

Manning immediately perked up. "We *are* looking out for the nation. To assume otherwise is reckless. Looking out for jobs *is* looking out for the country."

Bodwell was right. Tony's choice of words was poor. Embarrassment set in and heads turned in his direction.

"Just because we believe prosperity can be achieved through a different channel does not mean we wish to cause suffering to the nation. Mr. Speaker, I would like the previous testimony stricken from the record."

Tony's grave embarrassment morphed into anger and his pride took over. "That is absurd."

"Sir, you will not speak in this chamber unless called upon!" the Speaker snapped at the MP.

"Mr. Speaker, that was completely—"

"MP Manning!" the Speaker said indignantly. His commanding voice consumed the room. "Your actions are unacceptable. I order you suspended, effective immediately, from this House of Commons!" The Speaker pointed towards the door. "You may leave."

Manning stood up and shuffled his way through the row. Despite the humiliation, he marched with confidence. The freshman MP refused to play the victim.

Bodwell brandished a condescending smirk. The click of the door signaled Manning's departure.

"We will now vote on the Congo Free Trade Bill. All those in favor?"

"Aye."

"Those opposed?"

"Nay."

The bill was defeated.

Weeks would go by, and numerous letters of apology written, before the Speaker would lift the suspension.

Manning had learned his lesson well. He learned to control his emotions and use them to his advantage.

*

Despite his uncertain course of action, Manning was sure of his ultimate goal, and knew where to start. He marched across the house to his office, powered on the computer, and disconnected the Internet. He realized this particular computer could never be connected again. From the bottom desk drawer he removed a connecting cord; a wireless transfer would be too risky. By the time everything was connected, the computer had booted.

With mouse in hand, he guided the cursor. A program opened and began downloading the pictures from his phone. He worked to finish before his wife returned from her run or the baby awoke.

As the download neared completion, he took the available images and arranged them onto a horizontal page, careful to ensure the pictures and text lined up. He leaned forward, his nose inches from the radiant glow of the monitor. His rapidly adjusting eyes reflected the intensity of his work.

What was meant to take minutes took hours. Tony wasn't even aware his wife was home when she knocked on the door. Dressed in a blue robe tied tightly around her waist, her hair was still damp from an evening shower.

"Honey," she remarked drowsily, "I am going to bed. Are you coming?"

"Soon." He swiveled around, careful to block the screen. "I can finish in the morning."

"What have you been doing up here all night?" She approached him, and he placed his back against the monitor.

"It's just something for the House."

Emma was skeptical, but she was also tired. "Please, come to bed soon."

He rose to kiss her forehead. "I'll be in soon."

The second she left, Tony was back to work. Pleased, he placed his hands on his head, leaned back, and inhaled deeply through his nose. A steady release of the breath calmed his nerves. He placed his hand on the mouse and positioned the pointer. Leaning over, he turned on the printer. The green light soon flashed a bright red. He pushed the "print" icon.

The printer slid a page from the bin and processed the command. Seconds later, a replica of the pamphlet Tony had ripped up a few months earlier sat on the tray.

He saved his work, shut down the computer, and went to bed, knowing there would be little sleep. In a few short hours he would rise again to plan his attack.

CHAPTER THREE

"BECAUSE SOMEHOW, THEY KNOW WHO WE ARE."

It was a mild January day in Cambridge, a welcomed break from the frigid weather that had besieged the city. John Nolan's red hatchback puttered around the crowded parking garage, eventually squeaking to a stop near the top level. John gathered his things from the passenger seat.

Founded in 1209, the University of Cambridge was the second oldest university in the English-speaking world (behind Oxford). Academically, it was ranked among the world's best, and was historically the choice of the royal family. Graced with gothic, colonial, and post-modern design, much of the institution lined the River Cam. The manicured grounds and freshly scented air attracted visitors year around.

John strode purposefully across campus.

"Hey stranger." In his intense focus, he didn't even notice her. "Aren't you a sight?"

That Tennessee accent was unmistakable, and John's heart raced. "April!" She walked towards him, and he nervously lifted his backpack onto his shoulder. "I'm sorry, I didn't even see you. I have a meeting..." He paused to steady his voice.

April found his jitters endearing. "I just got finished with Old Sores myself."

"And?"

"It went well. Really well."

At that moment, John noticed a vulnerability—another opportunity. A warm feeling of accomplishment resonated in her eyes.

"I have my meeting with him now." John nervously rubbed his hands together. "It shouldn't take long. Want to get together afterward?" *Awkward pause.* "Have a drink or something?" His forehead dripped in a cold sweat.

The corners of her mouth curled up. "Well, I am going to the library now. Here's my number." She ripped some paper from her bag and jotted it down. "When you're finished with Sorenson, I might be ready for a break."

They shared a pleasant smile as she handed over her number. The caress of her hand on John's tingled his body.

*

Professor Sorenson looked up from his cluttered desk when John entered. "Mr. Nolan, take a seat."

The chair creaked in pain as John sat down. Before removing his notes, he glanced up at the room's overburdened shelves. "I think you are going to like what I have so far."

Old Sores motioned with an upwards palm. *Let's see it.*

"Well," John began with confidence, his notes now in his hand. "Before, we talked about the sociology of government." He scooted forward and sat up straight. "I have researched numerous civilizations and found their downfalls were largely preventable and self-induced."

John looked at Old Sores in an effort to soften him up before revealing his ultimate plan.

"Professor, I want to write my own Constitution. In fact, I have already started." The tense young man presented his rough draft. "What better way to predict the future of governance?"

The professor studied his student's work, and John was unable to decipher the expression on his wrinkled face.

"I have divided the Constitution into six articles," John went on. "The first three outline the branches of government, or departments as I call them. The fourth describes how the government will operate. The fifth article details with the rights of the people. And the sixth sets forth laws."

"The Department of Military and State?" the professor questioned.

"Yes," John replied. "The other two are Treasury and Commerce, and Justice and Law. That's all that's needed. I explain why in there."

The poker-faced professor skimmed though John's work. His ancient chair moaned in a series of high pitched squeaks and pops as he leaned back to read. The minutes slowly ticked past.

Eventually, Old Sores removed his glasses, leaning forward to toss them onto his desk. The springs of his chair cried even louder.

"This isn't what we discussed," he said.

"No, not exactly, sir," John nervously replied. "But I—"

"It is a stretch to consider this sociology. It's more political science."

The empty feeling John associated with academia, reappeared.

"However, you have come so far."

The void began to fill.

"I have always thought that my primary job as an educator was not to teach sociology, but to help students achieve their fullest potential. If you don't plan to seek a doctorate in this field, what harm would it do to continue?" The professor shrugged, his stone expression slightly relenting. "Being candid though, I still question the paper's significance. Your work must be applicable to pass this course."

"I believe it is, Professor," John said, doing his best to mask his jubilation. He could sense the old man's approval. "I will prove it to you."

"Fine." Old Sores handed the papers back to his student. "However, your final paper must sell itself. I'm still not convinced. If you need help, don't hesitate to ask. I expect the finished copy on my desk by April 30."

"Yes, sir." John stood up and flung his bag over his shoulder. With a smile that encompassed his whole face, he proudly walked out of the office.

*

"Sir, you have a phone call on your personal line," Shalid Ali Hannan whispered in his boss' ear as he finished his prayers. Alam Jabbar required assistance to rise from his southeastern kneel.

"Did they give a name?" Jabbar asked with a thick African accent.

"No, sir. He just asked to speak with you."

An injury to Jabbar's leg left had him partially disabled. He limped down the hall to his plush office.

"This is Alam Jabbar," he said into the telephone receiver, making no attempt to hide his Kikongo dialect. The Arabic emblem of his organization hung proudly on the wall behind him, a bright crescent moon against a black backdrop, surrounded by brighter stars.

"Mr. Jabbar, it is a pleasure. I have something that may be of interest to you," said a male voice Jabbar did not recognize.

"Really?" Jabbar replied. "To whom am I speaking?"

"I would like to meet with you."

"I meet with no one I don't know."

"Do you know who Captain Brooks is, sir?"

Jabbar was one of few who knew the name well. "What is the point of this? I do not have time for nonsense."

"Meet me tomorrow night at nine at the corner of St. Andrews and Downing."

"Why should I?"

CLICK.

Jabbar lowered the phone and laid it onto his desk.

"Who was that, sir?" Hannan asked, re-entering the room with a tea set.

"I do not know," Jabbar said, slightly agitated. His curiosity, as always, would trump his judgement. "I guess we will find out tomorrow."

*

"Ready for a break, yet?" John asked April Lynn as he exited the Sociology building.

April sat behind a dozen sprawled out books, her eyes tinted a mellow red. "Sure."

"How about All Bar One? Edible food. Cheap beer."

She marked a page with yellow tape. "Give me a few minutes."

John rushed through campus to arrive first and the pub, which was jammed with students and faculty decompressing after a long semester. John managed to secure a table directly in sight of the door.

All Bar One was your typical English college pub. Its central location on campus made it a Cambridge favorite. The inside was crafted of various shades of stained oak. Pictures of the Royal Family adorned the walls, and it reeked of stale beer.

When April entered, she spotted John and went over to sit with him.

"How'd it go with Sorenson?" she nearly shouted, placing her bag on a chair. The pub was known for being loud.

"Good. Very good!"

John noticed April's lips were shining a fresh bright red, the buttons on her shirt were no longer closed at the top of her chest, and her silken blonde hair had been released from its tie.

She chuckled. "Thank God, right?" She drew out the 'i' as if she had spent her entire life in Tennessee.

"I'll get your drink orders in a second." The waitress placed two glasses of water and darted off.

What do you drink?" April asked, her eyes scanning the menu.

John was hesitant to risk a common interest by recommending the wrong cocktail. Plus, he found himself fixated on the loose buttons of her blouse.

"What kind of whiskey do they have?" she said.

Whiskey? His jaw dropped even more.

"What can I get you guys?" The waitress seamed to appear out of nowhere, and John was not prepared.

"I'll have a whiskey and soda," April said. "Light on the soda."

"And for you, sir?"

"Uhh..." John's usual light pilsner was suddenly not an option. "Stout. A local stout. The biggest mug you have."

"Got it." The husky waitress disappeared amongst the patrons.

John planned to use that day's crowd to his advantage. It forced them to lean in a little closer as they conversed, which allowed him better access to her provocative perfume—another addition to her character he had never noticed.

"So what's your topic?" John asked, wanting their conversation to go smoothly, no awkward pauses.

"How families with special needs children socialize."

"Okay." John enthusiastically nodded, fighting the urge to peek down her blouse. *Keep your eyes high.*

"I'm going to be a social worker," she went on. "Help families with special needs. My brother has Down Syndrome. It can be hard. My family really needed help growing up, and I want to help others."

April leaned back to give the waitress room as she lowered their drinks. She pressed out her chest as she arched against the back of the chair. John barely noticed their order had arrived.

"Good for you," John said when the waitress had walked away.

"It's a tough industry. We depend on government grants. Politicians are hard to lobby. There aren't too many votes in our community. You know what I mean?"

April emptied her drink down her throat in one shot. "We'll see what happens. So, what are you doing?" she asked.

"Uhh..." *Are you kidding me?* "Well, I am writing my own..." *Was there whiskey in that?*

April tilted her head in confusion, her hair gently falling off her shoulder. "Your own...?" she prompted.

"Uhh..." He had never seen a woman who looked like her—drink like that. "My own Constitution."

She now looked even more confused.

"The idea is to create the perfect form of government. One that will last."

"Wow!" she exclaimed. "Good luck with *that*."

John smiled, while taking another quick peek.

*

Dressed in her blue nightgown with her red hair pulled back, Emma Manning leaned against the doorframe of her newborn's room, watching her son sleep in his crib.

"He's beautiful, isn't he?" she said when her husband walked up behind her, affectionately putting his arms around her waist.

He gently placed his chin on her shoulder. "Can I talk to you for a second?"

Emma turned to look at him, wondering. She silently followed Tony down the hall, where he closed his office door behind them.

Emma stood reserved with her arms wrapped in her nightgown.

Tony opened the top desk drawer. "Remember that day I was held hostage?"

The question required no answer.

"I said I wouldn't tell anyone." He removed a pamphlet from a manila folder. "But I have to."

His wife stood perplexed.

"We were not taken hostage by Muslim terrorists," he explained, walking towards Emma. Her eyes followed him across the room. "We weren't even taken hostage. We were used as publicity tools so *this* information could get global attention."

He handed her the pamphlet.

"They worked for MI-6," he gestured towards the document which had already captured his wife's attention. "That is what our government *really* does."

Emma began to tear up as the unknown mounted in her mind. *What does this mean?* The shock forced her mute. Much of what the pamphlet highlighted were well-known events, which now took on new meaning.

"When the military came in and opened fire they didn't care who they hit." Tony pulled up a chair for Emma to sit. "If we would have been sitting anywhere but where we were, we would have been killed instantly. I think the only thing that saved us was Cunnington. He got free and called his wife. They couldn't kill us with her on the other line, but I feel they wanted to."

Emma continued to study the pamphlet while listening to her husband's confession, covering her mouth with her free hand.

"When the shooting stopped, some of the captain's men were still alive. They were taken away. All the dead were put into bags. It happened in a matter of seconds."

"I never asked you... I figured you would talk when you were ready," Emma declared, regretting what she now knew.

Tony went on as though he didn't hear her. "The four of us sat there terrified. We feared our military more than our capturers. Not long after the shooting a man came in and told us to follow him. We walked to a room where they gave us information and told us to memorize it. We stayed in that room until the press conference."

"Do they know you have this?" Emma asked, the pamphlet shaking in her nervous hands.

"No," he assured her. "The originals were destroyed. That is a replica."

"What are you going to do with it?" Emma looked up in fear of the answer.

"I believe this country has a right to know. The government told us to stay quiet. This is why the other guys are stepping down. They can't trust themselves."

Emma raised her hand as if to say, 'stop!' She handed Tony the pamphlet. What she was about to tell her husband would go against her better judgment and contradict all she believed in—specifically love of country. But ultimately, she saw the significance. Fighting back intense urges to say something completely different, she managed to utter, "God help us."

*

The full winter moon lit up the University of Cambridge campus in a pale blue, with heavy cumulus clouds floated across the sky. The air was calm and crisp. A thin layer of snow covering the ground reflected much of the moon's light. A long black car eased to a stop one block down from the intersection of St. Andrews and Downing.

"Do you want us to go with you, sir?" the man in the front seat asked Alam Jabbar while pulling his coat aside to slide a pistol into a holster.

"Get out and be within sight, but I will go alone," Jabbar replied. "I did not get the impression I was in danger."

The men opened the doors to exit, spreading out between the buildings. Cane in hand, Jabbar limped his way to the meeting point. He positioned himself under the glow of a fading yellow light post. With the exception of a few stragglers, the street was empty. The only sound was that of the sharp breeze whispering its way past the university walls to fill the street. The cold air it delivered stung the inside of his nose.

Jabbar peered down at his watch: 8:59.

When the minute hand struck twelve a hollow thud echoed off the buildings. Simultaneously, all the doors that lined the sidewalks swung open. Hordes of students emptied out of their late night classes. Jabbar was soon surrounded by hundreds of grads and undergrads who had been stuck in small wooden desks for hours. The narrow streets turned into a scene of madness as everyone jockeyed for position to board one of the many buses that instantly appeared, their conversations buzzing.

"Where are you going?"

"Let's go to the pub."

"What did you think about the professor?"

"Tom! Tom! Hey, Tom!"

All the energy suppressed during their classes discharged, creating a chaotic display.

Jabbar tried to maintain his position under the light pole, but the flow of the crowd forced him down the street. With the masses unwilling to slow their advance, his balanced wobbled and he collapsed to the concrete.

His men lost sight of him and rushed against the surge but progress was difficult.

Jabbar's phone began to ring.

"Sir!" his bodyguard yelled in distress.

WHACK!

Before Jabbar could respond, a hard knee to the back knocked the phone from his hand. He held on all fours to catch his breath. Then, as quickly as the rush began, it was over. All the buses had left while the remaining students filtered between the buildings. All of a sudden, it was quiet, peaceful, and for the exception of a few stragglers, desolate.

Jabbar scanned the sidewalk for his phone and spotted it several feet away. Heavily relying on his cane, he hobbled towards it.

"Sir!"

Jabbar sighted one of his guards running from across the street. He brushed the dirt from his knees and straightened his suit. "I'm fine."

"Sir, your back." Another guard approached from up the street and pulled a white envelope off Jabbar's coat.

Bewildered, he studied it for a few seconds and then peered up at his guards. His meeting was apparently over.

*

"Harry!" Chris Nash hollered to his young reporter after assigning him the closing of an assembly plant. "This company has hundreds of workers. You better be able to interview one."

"These people are corporate," Henry countered. "They will not talk!"

Chris glared at his reporter. "Why are you still here?"

Harry stood his ground, but decided not to waste more time. He hastily marched out the door.

At the same time, Ashleigh Blair entered with the day's mail. "Mr. Nash, how are you this afternoon?"

He sighed. "Alright, Ashleigh, how are you?" Nash was now two weeks into his 50s—evident by the drooping party balloons in the corner. Time had not been good to the newsman. With slumping shoulders, a tired voice, and white hair, he more closely resembled a man fifteen years his senior. His wrinkled shirt and loose tie completed the stereotype.

"I am well, sir." The old widow flashed a pleasant smile.

Chris's office was straight out of the media handbook. It appeared to be a wasteland of piles of paper, but to the trained eye, it was a highly organized mess.

Most days, Nash received a large bundle of letters, magazines, and memos wrapped tightly in a rubber band. This day was no different. As news director of the BNN—a radio, television, print, and Internet conglomerate—he was a popular man.

"Thank you," Nash said dismissively.

Ashleigh turned to exit his room. She could tell Nash was not in the mood to talk. If she were lucky however, someone along her route would be.

Every day the mail contained the same nonsense—companies looking for free press, lame stories, free magazines, political letters, resumes, etc. Yet, a nervous anticipation always developed in his belly when he snapped off the rubber band. Every day was one closer to when he would get the story of a lifetime.

As he dug his way towards the bottom of the stack, he noticed a letter addressed in an odd font. The envelope had no return address, but had been mailed in Cambridge. He ripped open the top. Inside, he found a typed note:

```
Dear Mr. Nash:

    I have recently come across some information
in which you might be interested. A few months
ago, terrorists gained access to Westminster,
taking four MPs hostage. The military
subsequently stormed the building, killing the
terrorists and sparing the representatives.
Unfortunately, this is not the true story. I
have proof that what the government called a
'necessary action' was actually a deliberate
cover-up. I wish to earn your trust and
cooperation in exposing this fraud. However,
due to the sensitive nature of the material, I
hope you respect my wish to remain anonymous.
I will write in the coming days with more
information. In the meantime, re-watch the
press conference from that day, and listen
```

closely to the words of MP Richard Sykes in
particular. You will begin to understand.
   Good day, Sir.

Dubious, yet quite interested, Nash put down the letter and made his way to the archives. He paged through the dates to find that day's copy and skipped to where Sykes began to speak:

"When confronted with a tragic situation, you never know how you'll react. Such was the case for me and my three fellow countrymen. At first, it was simply some yelling from down the hall. Before we knew what happened, four masked men burst into our room. They put guns to our heads and began shouting out commands in what sounded like Arabic. We could not understand their orders, so they beat us with their weapons. They tied us all together and put us in a closet. All I could think about was my family at home, and wondered if I would ever see them again."

Nash stopped the video immediately and hit rewind.

"All I could think about was my family at home, and wondered if I would ever see them again."

His eyes glazed in disbelief and his mouth dropped open. In the gravity of the situation, it must have been overlooked. It was well-known Sykes *had* no family. They had all perished in a car crash three years earlier.

*

The rotation of the cooling fan had become a comforting sound for John Nolan. The research that would lay the foundation for his Constitution was nearly finished. He sat at his desk on this mid-February evening putting the finishing touches on the rise and fall of one of the greatest and most-feared superpowers in history, the USSR. It read as follows:

To become a superpower, a nation must have a strong economy, a dominant military, and immense international influence. The Union of Soviet Socialist Republic (USSR) was established in 1922 and grew into one of the world's most powerful and influential states. Prior to WWII, the USSR was strong. Following the war, it became a superpower as it filled the power vacuum in its hemisphere brought about by a war-weakened Europe.

By partitioning Germany after the war, the USSR and USA effectively limited competition. To ensure its power, the USSR annexed its border countries instead of fostering communist revolution within them.

The acquisition of land, resources, money, and people expanded the Soviet economy. However, as past nations learned, there is only so much wealth to be confiscated. Eventually it would have to be produced. A dramatic decrease in demand for oil (a main export), competition for material/raw goods, and increased military spending emptied the Soviet's coffers and led to bankruptcy. It collapsed in 1991.

Prior to its dissolution, the USSR had the second largest economy in the history of the world—more a result of its sheer geographic size than its economic efficiency. This deceivingly large economy proved the reason for its collapse. The nation's problems stemmed from a weak financial system in which the State Planning Commission controlled the production and price of all goods and services. Price fixing rendered the market useless. Stores oftentimes had surpluses of undesirable items and a scarcity of products people wanted, creating tax-free black markets. Due to the ineffectiveness of the Ministry for Construction Materials and Equipment Supply, companies were forced to produce products they were not designed to make. Businesses kept large surpluses of material in inventory since the state-run shipping companies were unreliable. Profits were not kept by companies, they were given to the State. Initiative was suppressed and the quality of work suffered. Information flowed slowly through the central planners, causing the Soviet economy to respond slowly to change or adapt cost-saving technologies.

Companies under the communist system had no competitive incentive to conserve and treat resources as scarce or valuable. Soviet industry used more energy and raw material than its western counterparts to produce the same products. The Soviet ministries in command of distribution did not directly work in the fields they supplied, hindering their ability to accurately estimate costs and needs. This wasted resources, the most of which may have been the workers themselves. Five to fifteen percent of all workers, in fact, did not work. They were employed by companies to be there, "just in case." The Soviets had arguably more resources than any other country on Earth and an educated population, however, they lacked an economic system in which to utilize their strengths.

There were two main problems with the Soviet economy. The first was there were no property rights. Therefore, the incentive to grow, expand productivity, and increase efficiency was lost. And the nation that was founded on anti-capitalism forbade foreign investment, which crippled its ability to raise revenue and develop its markets.

The USSR proved an economy, and thus a nation, cannot survive when too much control is held by the government.

*

"I heard you received a letter of interest," Aasir Abdulah Kabul said to Alam Jabbar when he entered his chief deputy's office.

Jabbar pulled out a chair for his boss. "Please sir, sit."

Kabul was a large, imposing figure. His salt and pepper hair followed the contours of his face, culminating in a perfectly groomed beard. His exquisite suits were usually light in color, with a white shirt and bright tie. While he managed to keep his public image clean, he'd developed a dubious reputation with authorities. Legally, he developed real estate; Jabbar supervised his projects.

Jabbar's desk was crafted from a dark hardwood. Cast iron lights, original artwork, and Indian rugs encircled the sleek centerpiece.

"So where is it?" Kabul's powerful voice nearly shook the room.

Jabbar pulled the envelope from his breast pocket and slid it across the desk. "I received a call on my private line and—"

"Was it tapped?" Kabul fitted his managers with monitoring technology. If a conversation was being intercepted, the line would emit a faint pulse.

"No." Like all of Kabul's men, Jabbar feared the consequences of an incorrect answer. "The man refused to identify himself."

Kabul lifted the document free of the envelope. "So then who gave it to you?" He glanced up at Alam and then back to the pamphlet.

"I do not know." Jabbar swallowed hard. "He planned it perfectly."

Kabul studied the document in pure fascination. At certain points, he nodded. At others, his eyes closed in reflection. Jabbar remained silent and a few uneasy minutes passed.

"Can we trust this?" Kabul folded the paper back to its original size.

Jabbar sat up straight. "Could be a setup, he suggested. "The government knows our past."

"Possibly," Kabul hesitantly agreed, though Jabbar knew his boss' instincts told him otherwise.

Kabul leaned forward and placed the pamphlet on Jabbar's desk. "They would never give us this."

"So you believe it?" Jabbar asked, now more interested than timid.

Kabul blankly looked at his subordinate, then stood up and made his way over to the window with his hands folded behind his back. In the evening light, his wide shoulders cast a large shadow across the room. From Jabbar's position, he looked a ghostly black as his body blocked the retreating sun. Kabul gazed out the sixth-floor window at the darkening city below. As if it helped him think, he rocked from his toes back to his heels.

"Whoever compiled this, knows."

Jabbar patiently waited.

"And they want it out." Kabul turned towards his subordinate. "Which is why we have it."

"Why us?"

"Because," Kabul raised his eyebrows in incredulity, "they know who we are."

*

"Your mail, sir," announced Ashleigh Blair, presenting Chris Nash with an exceptionally tall delivery that required two rubber bands.

It had been nearly a week since Nash received that anonymous letter. He had hardly slept since.

"Thank you," he enthusiastically replied, hoisting the stack off her wavering arms and dropping it onto his desk. Before the 'thud' had finished reverberating through the room, Nash was tearing through the pile.

Ashleigh hoped her boss' good disposition would translate into a conversation, however, she was wrong and quietly left unnoticed.

Midway through the stack, Nash came upon a promising envelope. It had no return address, was mailed in Cambridge, and was typed in a recognizable font. He reached for his letter opener. Inside was a short note.

"Sir!" his assistant news director hollered, dashing into the room.

"Not now, Ryan," Nash replied.

"Sir," Ryan pressed. He took a few steps into the office. "I think you should hear this."

"Can't it wait?"

"The prime minister is about to make an announcement about elections."

"I'll be out shortly." Nash finally looked up. "Please shut the door."

Ryan found his boss' apathy misplaced.

After hearing the latch lock, Nash removed the letter and unfolded it and read it.

Dear Mr. Nash:

I hope you got a chance to view the speech by MP Sykes. Now that I have your attention, I want to make sure we handle this carefully. Meet me on April 10 at 12:15 under the Vauxhall Bridge. I will be alone; I expect you to be the same.

Good day, Sir.

Nash folded the letter and placed it back in the envelope. Every reporter wanted notoriety for exposing the powerful and corrupt. Nash had paid his dues, and now he was ready to join the ranks of legendary. He opened his bottom drawer and placed the envelope on top of the first. He then made his way to the door.

The newsroom staff was huddled around monitors waiting for their leader to fill the screen. As Nash walked up to the group, the prime minister emerged from behind a curtain. He strode steadfastly to the podium.

"My fellow countrymen," he began, "at 9:00 this morning, as tradition requires, I received a formal request from the Queen to dissolve Parliament on April 11, thereby confirming—based on recently passed law—April 28 to be the date for the next general election. The final day of Parliament will be April 10. On the date, April 28, the British people will decide their leaders."

As the prime minister continued his speech, Nash looked on with intrigue. This can't be a coincidence. April 10 could not come fast enough.

CHAPTER FOUR

IN BLOOM

"Dunant, Dunbar, Dunkirk, Dunno—come on!"

John Nolan's frustrations grew as he searched through the archives of the Cambridge University Library, his outburst provoking the ire of his peers studying at adjacent tables.

America was the final civilization John would research before writing his Constitution. He already knew about its downfall, but he was motivated by Dean Pricart to learn more.

It was easy for John to see why Americans had lost confidence in Washington. The nation founded on the rejection of government interference was ripped apart by it centuries later. America, during its demise, was similar to what the United Kingdom had become: a tenuous, lone superpower amongst faux-friendly nations. In order for his Constitution to be viable, John knew he must directly address the issues that had forced America's disintegration.

"The damn book *has to* be here!" John said aloud, again drawing the ire of those nearby.

He abruptly stood up, grabbed his book bag, and shoved in his chair, refusing to acknowledge their pretentious reaction.

The library was congested with fidgety students scrambling to complete their work. In a few weeks, the semester would be over.

The line at the elevator was long. The line at the stairs was longer, but at least the steps afforded some exercise therapy to calm his irritation. Eventually reaching the fourth floor, John traversed towards the back.

What am I going to do if it's not here?

He made his way along the aisles, glancing over the indexes.

There it is.

DU—EA.

Cambridge had an impressive library, one of the best in the world. However, as the school acquired books, it did not acquire the space to store them. Instead, sliding metal columns were installed, where a large wheel accessed the archives. These columns consumed the entire rear section of the floor.

John grabbed the partially rusted, one-inch thick, circular metal bar with both hands. With his body weight behind him, he rotated the wheel clockwise, grinding the gears, the metal rows squeaking as they moved. The columns separated until enough space formed for him to squeeze in. He stuffed his body into the narrow aisle. "Dunant, Dunbar, Dunkirk." He ran his fingers ran along the rows of books above his head. "Dunn!" He yanked it from the row.

The Fall of The World's Greatest Empire by David Dunn. This would tell him all he needed to know.

As he strode back to the stairs, his cell phone rang.

He ducked behind a column and answered it. Phones were prohibited in the library, and he didn't need any more frowns shot his way.

"Hello?"

"Hey, honey. What are you doing?"

He instantly forgot about his big discovery. "Uhh. Nothing. You?"

April giggled. "You can come out from behind that column."

With his phone pressed tightly to his ear, John emerged from his hiding spot. His eyes darted around the floor. Off to the right a hand rose in the air. He lowered his phone and made his way over.

"Hi," he said, his voice quivering with nervous excitement.

She gestured for him to sit. "I am sorry I haven't returned your calls. This paper's been brutal."

"No worries." John forgave her, even though he'd promised himself he wouldn't.

"No, I feel bad. It was rude." She tilted her head, causing a band of golden sun to fall along her face. "You thirsty?"

John leaned forward ever so slightly. *Did I hear that right?* "S-sure," he stuttered. "Of course."

"All Bar One?" she asked with a smile. "Meet me in thirty. I need to run home for a minute."

With all the stress of the thesis and his uncle's kidnapping, John could barely remember being more filled with joy.

*

"So how's the paper going?" John asked after they sat down at the same table as before. While at home, April had traded her jeans for a black skirt, her book bag for a handbag, and sneakers for pumps. Her tight blue tank top and golden hair looked too perfect. With each subtle move, a not-too-subtle band of provocation wafted John's way.

Once again, he found himself struggling to suppress an unfamiliar urge.

"The paper's not bad." April leaned forward to grab a menu, and John again found himself fighting the urge to peek. "I'm fixing to get it done a little early and run it by Old Sores. You?"

John summoned the waitress as an excuse to look away. "I just got my last reference book. I'm ready for the final paper."

"The Constitution, right?" Her southern U.S. dialect rang prolonged the 'i' in 'right'—an accent John found overly alluring.

"That's right. You want a whiskey and soda?"

"Sure."

The same husky waitress as before appeared, took their order, and vanished.

All Bar One was not nearly as crowded as the first time John and April met. Most students were too busy completing their course work to engage socially. The relative quiet afforded them a more civil environment. For the next two hours, the couple sat talking about their lives, their families, their wants, their needs, their failures, their successes. Their connection was real and conversation came easy. April was grounded, funny, laid back, yet motivated. To April, John seemed like a honest guy trying to make his way, yet she detected a hidden passion she found intriguing. But mostly, he afforded her access to a valuable resource.

John looked at the bill and threw some cash on the table. "Are you about ready to get out of here?"

April looked somewhat disappointed. "I guess." She grabbed her coat off the neighboring chair.

As they strolled through campus, they continued their carefree conversation. April wrapped her arm around John's elbow. He felt awkward, but special.

"You know, I never asked you..." April stopped to face John. "How's your uncle?"

John's demeanor instantly turned less joyful. "I guess he's good. I don't see him much. My mom is close to him."

"I'd like to meet him sometime," she squeezed John's arm against her chest. "I really admire him."

John quivered when his elbow pressed against April's breasts. *Should I pull away? Should I not?*

He searched for a poignant statement. "I admire him too, I guess." But instead, he espoused his true feelings. "He's a politician."

April released John's arm. "Yeah, I understand."

"You do?" John looked down, catching a strong drag of her scent.

"I've had some family members in public life." She looked very uncomfortable. "We don't talk about it. My political ancestors... well, my family is not real proud of their legacy."

"Like what?" John pressed.

April looked at John and flashed an innocent smile. "I have to go." She lifted herself onto her toes and placed her soft lips on his cheek. He inhaled her essence. His arms began to wrap around her waist as she gradually pulled away.

74

"I had a really nice time," she whispered near his ear.

John could feel the warm moisture of her kiss begin to evaporate off his face. The cool sensation emanated throughout his body. "Me too."

She gently took his hands in her. "Call me soon," she flashed her eyes as she turned away. "And I promise I'll call you back this time."

John wanted to her to stay, but the effects of her kiss had nearly paralyzed him.

※

That night John took public transit home. He sat alone, next to a window towards the back. He hunched down, bracing his knees on the seat in front of him. He felt the chill of the evening filter through the glass. It smelled of cold metal and exhaust. His new book lay secure between his legs. An array of shadows danced across the pages as the aging machine powered down the deserted streets of London. When John got home, he scurried past his family and rushed to his room. With the information fresh in his mind, he booted up his computer. Unlike the other civilizations he documented, there was no need to greatly detail the rise of the United States of America—it would consist of the exact opposite of what had led to its demise:

In President George Washington's farewell address, he predicted the conditions necessary to collapse the republic and urged future generations to act accordingly. He warned of partisan politics, stressed the importance of maintaining a strong currency and paying debts in a timely fashion. He encouraged America to make friends with every nation and avoid foreign entanglements. How did he know?

America's Founding Fathers created a limited government designed to ensure a society based on individualism, rights, and property. The much-fabled pursuit of the American dream— to live the life you desire with limited government intrusion—attracted the best and most motivated talent in the world. Its relative isolation shielded it from global threats. Its abundance of natural resources and raw material guaranteed independence.

It was understood that America would never be conquered by soldiers marching across its borders. Rather, it would fall by financial mismanagement and the implementation of ruinous policies. Though years of American intrusion into world politics had soured relationships, the decline started with American politicians pursuing more power than the Constitution afforded.

The seeds of America's downfall began during the Great Depression. In an effort to help the country, the government expanded its influence. Alone, the initial government programs were not the culprit. However, the desire for politicians to grow government did not end when the economy recovered. In the decades that followed, more programs were created and existing ones expanded. Following a series of Supreme Court decisions, the once limited government became limitless.

Eventually, the size of the government created instability. National and budgetary debt grew to dangerous levels. Central banks around the world began to question the stability of the dollar and many dumped it as a reserve currency.

Over time, the country's government expanded beyond the tax base's desire or ability to support it. The apathetic nation, unwilling to compromise the life it felt it deserved, and the life it was promised by its leaders, refused to address its unsustainable path. Washington was forced to default on the promises of previous generations. The people revolted. In the chaos, America no longer attracted the best the world had to offer. In fact, many of its citizens left for more stable nations that offered better opportunities.

The states wanted to be disconnected from the Federal Government's fiscal disaster. Most had balanced budget Constitutional amendments, but Washington refused to adopt the same. For decades the states watched their rights being gradually usurped by the central authority. This was their opportunity to once again control their own destinies.

The states separated from Washington D.C. and combined to form sovereign nations. A few years after these secession movements began, the president signed a bill dissolving the Federal Government. America broke up into seven nation-states.

America bankrupted itself as it abandoned the very principles it was founded upon. As with any strong nation, there is a fabric.

And when that fabric is frayed, the people are no longer united under a single cause.

A nation's direction is guided by its officeholders. America lacked congressional term limits, which spawned corruption and encouraged distrust among the populace. In order to acquire more control, career politicians established political allegiances and forced the public to follow suit. Politicians embraced loyal constituent groups, and pitted them against others. As the political issues grew in importance, so did the degree in which the people separated. Many representatives simply did not concern themselves with the nation's future, only their next election.

John took a deep breath and exhaled. He saved the document and closed it, revealing a solid blue screen. His aching eyes eased shut and he leaned his head back. The research stage of his thesis was now complete. His shoulders sank forward. It felt good to relax.

With a new document opened, John placed his hands on the keyboard and typed: C-O-N-S-T-I-T-U-T-I-O-N.

Theodore and his wife sat together on the living room couch, him watching television while she read a book.

"Is he still working on his paper?" he asked.

His wife looked up from the page. "I think so."

"Wow," Theo said, impressed. "I've never seen him work this hard."

*

BANG!!!

The bang of the Speaker of the Commons' mallet resonated throughout the chamber. Dan Chin commanded the hall's attention. The leader of Great Britain's lower house wore the traditional black robe, as did his presiding officers.

"Honorable members of the House of Commons," he said, his delivery uncharacteristically lighthearted, "I welcome you to the final full day of this Parliamentary session on this April tenth. This Parliament has achieved much on behalf of the people."

In reality, that was debatable. The UK was in a steep economic downturn. But the cameras were always on—as were the politics.

Chin looked up from his notes with a far less jubilant expression, his protruding chin pointing skyward.

"A few months ago, we saw a tragedy play out when four of our own were taken hostage in this very building. A despicable act of terrorism we will not forget and must not allow to repeat."

Sykes, Cunnington, Pugh, and Manning looked on from their respective positions scattered around the congested floor. The attendees offered a round of tempered applause.

Speaker Chin raised his right hand after the mild ovation trailed off. "Three of those fine men and patriots..." he acknowledged each via open-handed gestures, "will move on from this Parliament. We, of course, wish them the best in their future endeavors. As for the rest of you vying for reelection," the gravitas dropped from his demeanor, "may only my members be victorious."

A loud roar consumed the House.

Shouting over the merriment, the Speaker proclaimed, "We will have our final meeting of committee members after lunch."

Following another smack of the mallet, this brief session of the Commons came to a close.

Tony Manning casually made his way down the rickety wooden steps. From across the floor, he spotted Richard Sykes. The MP's morose disposition separated him from the jovial mood of those around him. Manning was in no hurry as he walked over. Sykes spotted his approach and excused himself from the group.

Manning extended his hand as they neared. "How have you been, my friend?" They hadn't spoken since that afternoon at the cafe.

"I'm getting by." Sykes' defeated eyes, however, told a different story. "It's still tough."

Tony understood, and he did not envy him. Without a family, Sykes had no one to comfort him, no one to console him. No one to love him.

Manning placed a compassionate hand on his old friend's shoulder. "It's not too late."

The expression on Sykes' face remained unchanged: stern, yet weak.

Off to their right, Tony noticed a figure emerge.

"Gentlemen," William Cunnington said with a heavy soul.

To Tony's left, MP Pugh entered the conversation. "So, this is it." Pugh's spirit was on par with the others: joyless and somber. "I was sort of hoping this day would never come."

The remaining members of the House suspended their own conversations to witness the embrace. The four heroes stood together, possibly for the last time. The hall silenced.

"I'll be honest," Cunnington confessed, fighting his emotions, "I thought about running again. But I need more time."

Manning and Sykes tried to console him; they felt his pain.

The rest of the House looked on sympathetically. No one dared to even move. The hall had never been so full, yet so quiet.

Pugh removed his hand from Cunnington's shoulder and placed it in the middle of their small circle. Sykes followed by placing his on top. Manning and Cunnington joined in solidarity.

"To us..." The four men tightened their grips. Pugh spoke softly, his words intended for their ears only. "...the men performing the greatest patriotic service that no one knows."

Touched by the reality they shared, the other three replied, "To us."

The tight embrace of their hands fell away, and their inner circle broke apart. If they had only known one of them would not live to see the afternoon session, they may have prolonged the moment.

*

It was a chilly, overcast April afternoon in London The Members of Parliament broke out of Westminster for one last lunch break before elections. A strong westerly wind signaled the approach of a cold front and possibly rain. Under the Vauxhall Bridge stood a man dressed in a full-length tan coat and matching hat. The pillars of the bridge acted as a funnel guiding the gales over the River Thames. Newsman Chris Nash battled to keep his balance. Hunched forward with his fists clenched in his pockets, he shivered in the rushing current, wondering why he was asked to meet here. Under the bridge lay a few vagabonds, huddled together under layers of worn-out cardboard and raggedy blankets. In the distance, up river, Nash spotted an approaching figure. His heart began to pound and gelid beads of nervous sweat formed on his forehead.

The figure was wrapped in an ankle-length khaki trench coat, with a hood pulled securely over its head. Sporadic gusts lifted the bottom half of the coat, revealing dress shoes and pinstriped pants. With taut arms jammed into the pockets, the figure battled the headwind. Nash noticed the face was hidden behind dark sunglasses and a tightly wound scarf.

The man was soon upon him, his head held low. "Mr. Nash?" the figure called over the loudly blowing air.

"Yes!" Nash yelled.

The man removed a piece of paper from his pocket and presented it to the newsman. Nash leaned in.

The man's voice rose to a barely audible level. "Few in Parliament know of this. The prime minister is your contact."

Nash battled the wind trying to view the pamphlet. "Where did you get this?"

"Do the right thing, Mr. Nash. Your country needs you."

The man turned and walked back along the river. The wind seemed to carry him away, leaving Nash to stand in amazement, gazing at what could be the story of the century.

*

RING!!! RING!!!

The sound of the incoming call echoed through his posh office. Alam Jabbar casually put down his book, rose from his leather sofa, and limped to the phone.

"Hello?" He rubbed his tired eyes.

"Mr. Jabbar," said a deep, cavernous voice.

He recognized it immediately, but played it off as unimportant. His fatigue faded. "How can I help you?" A faint pulse mildly thumped in his ear.

"Have you made a decision?"

"Why do you keep calling us?"

"All you need is what I provided you."

"I am through playing these games with you," Jabbar blurted out.

"No, you're not," the man said calmly.

He had called Jabbar's bluff, and they both knew it.

"What do you want from us?"

"You're a smart man, Mr. Jabbar. What do you think I want?"

Click!

The line suddenly went silent.

Jabbar groaned, placing the phone on its base. His stomach churned while he impatiently awaited a call back. His fingers danced nervously across his desk. Five minutes passed before he reluctantly reached for his other phone.

"Yes, Jabbar," answered Aasir Abdulah Kabul, as if the call were anticipated.

"Sir, we just got a call. It was tapped and then disconnected. We spoke of nothing important." Jabbar was about to apologize for failing his boss—he wanted a name. Then Kabul uttered, "Standard protocol. I know it well."

"Sir?" Jabbar was puzzled. "British intelligence," Kabul explained. "They hung up for you."

*

William Cunnington was sitting at a table with many of his fellow Parliamentarians. The men often spent the noon hour at the Soba Noodle Bar, not far from Westminster. The sleek interior blended variations of stained hardwoods with yellow radiance. There was no better place to enjoy their final lunch as representatives.

Richard Sykes was the last to arrive, and excused his tardiness. "I had to get something out of my office." He shook off his coat and hung it on the back of the chair.

Pugh and Manning also sat at the eight-person table, and Sykes settled across from them.

"So this is it," Cunnington commented. "The last time we'll sit here."

"How about we talk about something else?" Manning pleaded.

"Think you guys will run again, someday?" asked a fellow MP who filled one of the remaining seats.

Pugh reached across Manning towards the sugar bowl. "I might," he said absently.

"My wife won't let me leave," Manning joked. "I have to make some money."

"Don't give me that," Sykes mocked. "That wife of yours makes enough cash."

"That was my mistake," chimed another PM. "I went for looks."

"Really?" Cunnington questioned. "Slim pickings where you're from, huh, Paul?" The table broke out in laughter.

The light prodding helped to lift the suffocating cloud that hung above the table. For the remainder of lunch, the men avoided discussion of the hostage crisis and its aftermath.

The check was paid, and soon afterward, they all had their coats heading towards the door.

"After you." Manning reached for the handle ahead of Sykes.

When the door swung open, it ushered in a gust of cool, moist April air. The patrons turned towards the door when the refreshing breeze fell upon them. The men embraced the harshest of the draft, their coats and scarves swinging freely in the opposite direction.

In what appeared to be slow motion, the expressions of the patrons turned to horror as three bullets punctured Sykes' chest. The blasts from the shots violently ricocheted off the restaurant walls. The force of the blow knocked Sykes into Manning's arms. Plates and glass chattered as tables were thrown onto their sides for protection. Women screamed and men yelled to get down.

"Call the paramedics!" Manning cried, clinging onto his dear friend. The blood gushed from his body.

The other MPs rushed to assist Manning in lowering Sykes' to the floor. The door quietly closed as they pulled his limp body from the entrance.

Manning opened his friend's shirt, revealing three flowing holes. "Oh, my God!" His fellow MPs stood in horror. "Is there a doctor here!?" Manning screamed, clutching Sykes' lifeless body. "Please, is there a doctor here!?"

"Hang in there," Manning begged, the tears rushing down his face. He knelt on the floor, his friend resting in his arms.

Despite Manning's pleas, Sykes lay motionless, his olive complexion turning to a pale blue.

"The paramedics are coming!" Cunnington hollered.

Manning pressed his fingers to Sykes' neck. Feeling nothing, he placed his friend on the floor and began pumping his chest. With each thrust, hope faded from the eyes of the onlookers. Their concern morphed into a solemn stare of inevitability.

Cunnington stepped forward, placing a hand on Manning's shoulder. He gave a sturdy squeeze. Bathed in blood, Manning stopped pumping and lowered his head to Sykes' chest. He wept as patrons began to emerge from behind the fallen tables. Off in the distance, the faint wails of an ambulance grew louder.

*

April 15

The final toll of the bell faded as the pastor began the service. His voice calmly echoed off the stone walls of the cathedral.

"Ladies and gentlemen, we are gathered here today to celebrate the life of a friend, a father, a husband, and a son."

Mourners continued to enter under the large expanse of Gothic arches, yet the pews were barely a quarter full. MP Richard Sykes lay in state at the front. His friends and loved ones, dressed in a dull black, struggled to compose themselves. The church's stained glass windows cast a spiritual light.

Manning, Pugh, and Cunnington sat in the front pew. They appeared lost and abandoned, despite the support of their families. Sykes was now a central player in the two most dramatic experiences of their lives. The pastor continued with his sermon, but the men discerned only ambient noise. The pain of the moment was too consuming, and no one could understand their pain.

While the manifestations of their internal struggles appeared identical, the fuel of their thoughts was very different. Pugh and

Cunnington focused on Sykes and what he had meant in their lives. They remembered the times they shared. In Tony Manning, however, a rage was building. In that church, at that moment, he vowed to avenge his friend's death. And he knew his target.

Across town, within earshot of the tolling bells, the London Chief of Police opened a very contentious news conference.

"I know, I know," he stated to a badgering media, his arms held high. "If you give me a second, I can answer your questions." He tried to show as little frustration as possible. "We have a suspect in custody. He is a member of the Loyalist Ali Front. Right now we can't link it to the hostage crisis, but we are looking into it. We do not know why MP Sykes was targeted. But the man has confessed."

Chris Nash squeezed his way to the front of the media mob. Normally, news directors didn't leave their offices, but the newsman had an inkling this was somehow connected to *his* investigation. "Do you believe the other three hostages are in danger?" Nash hollered.

The rest of the media followed with their own queries, flustering the chief and giving him no time to answer.

Aasir Abdulah Kabul and many of his comrades, including Alam Jabbar, were watching the press conference from his office.

Kabul's office was even more magnificent than Jabbar's. Animal heads from his hunting expeditions hid the Versailles paneled walls. Visitors stood upon bamboo flooring and Tabriz Haji Jalili rugs.

"Turn that off," he barked. "This does not seem right." Kabul's keen instincts told him something was amiss.

"What does not seem right?" Jabbar asked, admiring his boss' intuition.

Kabul motioned towards the blank screen. "This guy—something does not seem right about his death. Why would that terror group who took him hostage kill him and not the others?"

One of his subordinates spoke up, "They could kill them one by one."

"All the MPs were in that restaurant. If they wanted them dead, that was the moment," Kabul said.

"Maybe it was not the LAF," suggested Jabbar. He rose from Kabul's red sofa and reached for his cane. "Remember the letter we received?"

Kabul rubbed his chin. "You never received a call back from that person, did you?"

"And it was tapped." Jabbar was pretty sure he knew where his boss was going with this.

Kabul was now in deep thought. *Could it be coincidence?*

"Do you think whoever killed him will come after us?" Jabbar asked with concern.

"When you last spoke with this person," Kabul said, ignoring his question, "did either of you mention anything about the pamphlet?"

"No," Jabbar recalled, though he was uncertain. It had happened so quickly. "We didn't get that far into the conversation."

"But you got far enough for someone to recognize his voice." Kabul grinned with nefarious excitement. "Mr. Jabbar, I think your mystery man was Richard Sykes."

A blast of intrigue rushed through the room.

"My comrades," Kabul proclaimed, "we now have the upper hand."

The leader's grin grew more prominent as he rose to his feet and proudly advanced towards the window. The realization was nearly overwhelming. Their opportunity to exact revenge was possibly at hand. He relished in this revelation as he overlooked downtown London.

Kabul's gaze fell upon a long black sedan creeping down Victoria Street below. For no particular reason, he watched the vehicle vanish among the brick edifices of the aging city.

In the rear seat sat Colonel Levanetz.

"Yes sir, it's taken care of," Levanetz said through the car's wireless system.

"I watched the press conference," the vapid voice on the other end replied confidently. "Any problems with media or city officials?"

"No sir. And our guy's condition is progressing quickly. He should be dead in a year. He'll remain quiet."

"Make sure his remaining days in prison are gentle."

"His family has already been moved out of the red zone," Levanetz assured him. "They are on their way to London with full payment. Their house is ready and we have alerted a Mosque of their arrival."

"Perfect, Colonel. Has his real name been erased?"

"Yes, Mr. Prime Minister."

"Good day to you, sir. Great Britain and her people appreciate your patriotism."

The line went dead.

Colonel Levanetz basked in the sensation of accomplishment. Another disaster averted. When the black sedan braked for a red light, his body slightly shifted forward with the momentum. They were now driving through the University of Cambridge on their way to a retreat in Norwich.

As the "WALK" light began to blink, John Nolan came sprinting through the intersection, darting past the sedan when the light turned green.

Upon reaching the sidewalk, he slowed his pace. Waiting on the steps of the library sat April Lynn. When she spotted John, she sprang to her feet and rushed towards him.

"Ready?" John asked.

April leaped onto him, flinging her arms around his neck. There was no alluring scent or unbuttoned blouse. April had secured her initial desire. She was now onto her next goal.

She squeezed him tightly. "I couldn't be more ready."

Hand-in-hand, the two strode down the sidewalk.

"Do you feel good about that job?" John asked. The semester was nearly over. Campus was nearly empty.

"Yeah, it should happen. They're still getting some funding. But who knows for how long."

Unemployment in the UK had recently hit eight percent; a few years prior it was half that. The boom years leading up to the fall of America, and then following it, were over. The proverbial bubble had burst. As a result, ominous political winds were swirling throughout the United Kingdom. Calls for a change in government grew louder with each updated economic figure. It was not for lack of action. As the economy spluttered, the government tried to mitigate the pain. Some politicians called for tax incentives and free trade, while others favored tax hikes to redistribute wealth. To placate the masses Parliament passed some laws. Yet, the people were impatient and demanded more.

The abrupt spike in job losses gave rise to opposition movements that looked to capitalize off the misery. Never let a crisis go unrealized. Few employers were willing to expand with such an uncertain future, which contributed to the economic slide, further empowering the minority party's claims against the current power structure.

"What about you?" April gently squeezed John's hand as they passed the Unitarian Church of Cambridge. Like many holy places in the country, it was turned into something more desirous of the population—this one an art gallery. "Hear anything back yet?"

"No. But we got a new tile job. It will last a few weeks."

April sighed. "If I get this job, I don't aim to make much." They turned a corner and crossed a footbridge that spanned the River Cam.

"I'll get a professorship," John said and smiled. "I promise."

The couple approached a set of white marble stairs and climbed.

April looked up at John in critical approval. "There has to be a small college that would love to hire a Cambridge grad."

John opened the door and after a short walk, the pair stood before a set of metal doors. "Doesn't that sound good, though? I can work my way up. Eventually get to a larger university."

DING!

The elevator doors struggled open. They stepped in and turned around.

"I can do my job most anywhere," April said. "In case you get a job far away."

John looked down at her and smiled once again.

DING!

The doors shuddered open and their conversation came to an end. For the remaining voyage down the hallway, the only noise came from their shoes striking the dull laminate. Silence in their relationship was no longer awkward.

Hand-in-hand they walked, eventually turning to face the door with the nameplate, "Professor Dayton Sorenson."

Following a slight sigh of anxious relief, April broke the silence. "Here we are." Those simple words encapsulated this remarkable moment in their lives.

They swung their book bags forward and unzipped the tops, pulling out their prepared reports. In their hands, they now held the culmination of months of work. The old professor preferred paper to digital.

April knelt down, placing her binder on the floor, as did John.

"You know," John remarked, "I have spent so much time on this, I don't want to let it go."

April understood what this paper meant to him. This was his chance to prove his worth after being rejected from the history department. This paper was more than simply a thesis to graduate. It was a statement.

"This paper is a part of me." John took a deep breath. "You ready?" he asked.

In unison, they both slid their theses under the door and into the darkness of Old Sores' office.

They stayed knelt down, enjoying the giant weight that had been lifted.

For April, it was a tribute to her family.

For John, it was vindication, and the hope that his work would be recognized.

*

While John and April were waiting for the elevator to return, a door creaked opened behind them. They turned to find Professor Sorenson holding what they had slid under his door.

"Hello, Professor," April said. "We figured you were out."

"I should be." He smiled politely. "Mr. Nolan, can we have a word?"

Moments later, John was sitting in Old Sores' office.

"I've glanced through your paper," the professor said, leaning back in his chair. "This seems a bit presumptuous, don't you think?"

"Presumptuous?" John's back arched in discomfort.

"Here at Cambridge," the professor said, attempting to mitigate his words with a non-insulting pitch, "we attempt *realistic* scholarship."

"It took me years to write this, Professor. I have the research to back it up."

"John, I told you I was concerned. You're not a lawyer, you're not a political scientist, you're not an historian or a politician's son. I fear you don't have the pedigree to write something of this nature." The professor flipped through the pages of John's report. "What do you expect to do with this?"

John had no real answer.

"Who will take this seriously?"

"My work is sound," the young man stated. "It's rooted in the human experience. No, I don't have a *name*, but I have ideas and an honest approach. And if anyone is willing to give them a chance..." the young man paused. "Well, maybe I can *get* a name."

"*The people within this jurisdiction, under their own free consent,*" the professor read from the preamble, "*establish, preserve and ensure the blessings of human rights, personal liberties, common defense, just competition, individual property, a stable currency and the moral justice required to form a more perfect union, do ordain and authorize this Constitution."*

He turned to a random page. *"Congress shall make no law abridging the freedom of the press—unless such press or their ancillary corporate partnerships profit off government contracts."*

"Doesn't that make sense?" John argued.

Old Sores placed John's paper on his desk and leaned forward. He appeared less skeptical. "You will receive the grade you deserve—like any other student. But just so we are clear, you *do* understand my concerns?"

"Someday, Professor," John replied confidently, "our society will seek a new direction. Maybe even a new government. And when that day comes, your *concerns* will be meaningless."

CHAPTER FIVE
THE CONSTITUTION

The People within this jurisdiction, under their own free consent, establish, preserve, and ensure the blessings of human rights, personal liberties, common defense, just competition, individual property, a stable currency, and the moral justice required to form a more perfect union, do ordain and authorize this Constitution.

Article One
Department of War and State

Section 1 – Mandate

All defense and foreign relations powers herein granted shall be vested in a Department of War and State which shall consist of a single representative body.

Section 2 – Powers of the Department

To declare war, grant letters of marquee and reprisal, declare a national emergency, make rules concerning detentions on land, air, space and water;

To raise and support a functioning military, and all aspects thereof, but no appropriation of money shall be for a longer term than two years;

To make rules for and regulate land, air, space, water and all other forces;

To set policy and provide for calling forth Municipality militias to execute the laws of the Union, suppress insurrections, secure borders and repel invasions;

To provide diplomacy between foreign states and military operations domestic and foreign;

To dispose of and make all needful rules and regulations respecting the territory not under the jurisdiction of this Constitution;

To negotiate and approve treaties with foreign nations with appropriate ratification from Article 4, Section 4, of this Constitution;

To provide consulate and dignitaries to foreign nations;

To define and punish terrorism, piracy, or aggression, and all felonies committed on the high seas, and offenses against the law of nations;

To, with understanding the purpose of war is victory, allow Secretarial authority to act as necessary during declared wars. Periodically, the Secretary shall appear before his/her Department to outline strategy, in secrecy if required, upon which the Department can vote to remove the Secretary with a three-fourths vote.

Article Two
Department of Treasury and Commerce

Section 1 - Mandate

All financial powers herein granted shall be vested in a Department of Treasury and Commerce which shall consist of a single representative body.

Section 2 - Powers of the Department

To levy and collect taxes, duties, imposts, and excises, to pay down debt and perform necessary operational functions. All duties, imposts, and excises shall be uniform throughout; with the understanding that direct taxes, those which are levied on existing property or wages, shall be apportioned equally among the People or the businesses for which they are employed;

To borrow money on the credit of the Union;

To regulate commerce with foreign nations, and among Counties, Townships, and Cities/ Towns;

To coin money, regulate the value thereof, and of foreign coin, and fix the standard of weights and measures;

To provide for the punishment of counterfeiting the securities and current coin of the Union;

To establish lines and access of communication for Government and private sector enterprises;

To promote the progress of science and useful arts, by securing for limited times to authors and inventors the exclusive right to respective writings and discoveries;

To ensure that private contracts among individuals and corporations which do business within the jurisdiction thereof shall be upheld;

To establish uniform laws on the subject of Bankruptcies;

To exercise exclusive financial legislation in all cases whatsoever over such districts as may be under the seat of the Government of this Union;

To dispose of and make all needful rules and regulations respecting the territory or other property belonging to this Union; and nothing in this Constitution shall be so construed as to prejudice any claims of the Union, or of any particular County, Township or City/Town;

To create an annual budget adhering to the laws and regulations of this Constitution;

To ensure the free flow of goods and services, with respect to the environment, People and Government.

Article Three
Department of Justice and Law

Section 1- Mandate

All judicial and legal powers herein granted shall be vested in a Department of Justice and Law which shall consist of a single representative body.

Section 2 - Powers of the Department

To oversee and regulate the creation of common law-based Courts within the various Counties, Townships, and Cities/Towns, as many as deemed necessary by the Department and overseen by that District's representative, who shall choose justices for the Courts for a term determined by the Department;

To oversee and regulate the creation of a Federal Supreme Court, with an uneven number of justices, no less than seven, understanding a majority vote in all trials is required, and whose members must be elected Department representatives who may choose to separate themselves from normal Department activities;

To oversee and regulate the creation of regional Courts, as many as deemed necessary, and to appoint Federal judges under the recommendation of the Secretary and majority approval by the Department body;

To review all bills, measures, laws, taxes and budgets from the various Departments for constitutionality;

To have original jurisdiction, to be heard by a predetermined body, to adjudicate all cases that gain certiorari, within the jurisdiction of this Union or any matter pertaining to this Union for which the constitutionality, or interpretation of law, is in question. This includes treaties, international disputes, declarations of war and national emergency.

To ensure the passage of laws to ensure public safety, productivity, and freedom of action and/or expression without infringing on any statute in Article 6 of this Constitution.

To pass laws on treason against the Union that shall include, but are not limited to, levying war against the Union, or in adhering to its enemies, giving aid and comfort to its enemies. No person shall be convicted of treason unless on the testimony of two witnesses to the same overt act, or recorded, or on confession in open Court, and determine the punishment of treason, but no attainder of treason shall work corruption of blood, or forfeiture except during the life of the person attained.

To regulate the availability and legality of intoxicating substances.

To settle disputed boundaries for Counties, Townships and Cities/Towns and issue necessary warrants.

To create law governing Citizen and Registered Resident registration.

To determine the age limits of voters.

To determine the location of a trial if the alleged crime is not held within the jurisdiction of this Union but still falls under the auspices of the Court.

To interpret this Constitution when reviewing laws, bills, measures, taxes and budgets, and any case not covered by this Constitution shall be left to the discretion of the People via referendum.

Article Four
Government Operations

Section 1 - Elections

The national electorate shall be divided into districts of no more than 500,000 Citizens, and no more than four regions divided equally by population, to be chosen and amended every ten years by a committee of nine representatives, three from each Department. Each representative shall be a member of the Department he/she represents, nominated by the Secretary, and affirmed by a majority vote within their respective Department.

All national elections shall be determined by popular vote. Members of the Departments shall be elected once every six years by their respective districts in which they shall reside outside the Capital, and shall serve no more than two full terms or one full term and more than 80% of another. Upon ratification of this Constitution, a nationwide vote shall ensure for all Departments, which then stagger every two years beginning with Treasury and Commerce, followed by Justice and Law, then Military and State.

Initial Elections which determine district representatives shall be held on the first day of the seventh month of the year, excluding weekends. The victors who desire the position of Department Secretary shall run in the Regional Elections, which are to be held on the first day of the ninth month of the year, excluding weekends. The four regional winners then shall run for Secretary in the National Election, held on the first weekday of the last month of the year, excluding weekends. The new Department shall be sworn in, with Secretary, on the third weekday of the New Year.

In the event of a tie on any electoral level, which is defined as any election where the total vote count for the top candidates is within one percent, the candidate who spent the least amount of money shall be the victor. Campaign spending shall be reported to Department officials on a weekly basis during the campaign. Failure to comply, or fraudulence, shall immediately result in expulsion from the campaign and a return of money to requesting donors.

DEVOLUTION

No candidate shall be a member of a political party and shall not be endorsed by any political parties.

No candidate shall hold a public office different from that which he is a candidate.

Candidates, who receive a certain number of signatures determined by their respective Department, shall appear on the Initial Election ballot.

Voting requirements of Article 5, Section 1 of this Constitution shall apply except for the first two elections following ratification, in which case all legal Citizens within the jurisdiction of the adopting Union shall vote, and the following election two years later.

Section 2 Members and Secretary

Department representatives may serve one of their two-term limits, or 80 percent of one remaining term, as Secretary. The Secretary on the first day of session shall choose a Lieutenant Secretary from the respective Department. If the Secretary cannot perform his or her duties, the Lieutenant Secretary shall assume plenary powers, including the authority to call the Department to session.

If a Department member cannot perform his/her duties, a new member, who shall reside in that district, shall be chosen by the Secretary and confirmed by the Department with a majority vote.

Members of the Departments shall regulate their own Rules of Order, ethics and meetings, and shall meet no less than once a month.

Any action against a fellow representative, including the Secretary, shall require a two-thirds vote for the exception of expulsion, which shall require a three-fourths vote. Expelled representatives shall appear before the Supreme Court, if granted certiorari, to face appropriate charges.

Department members shall be sworn in reciting the following: "I do solemnly swear that I will faithfully execute the Office for which I have been elected, and will to the best of my ability preserve, protect, and defend the People of this land and the Constitution of this Union. Failure in this endeavor shall result in my rescinding of office."

Section 3 – Campaign Finance and Compensation

Department candidates shall not use personal wealth to fund their own campaigns more than 100 percent of monies they have raised.

Foreign money, including that which changes hands, is prohibited in campaigns within this jurisdiction.

Department members' salaries shall be determined by the Department Secretaries. Changes in specific Department wages shall be approved by a majority vote with that specific Department and shall not take effect until the following session begins.

Violation of the measures listed above shall result in immediate and indefinite expulsion from current and all future political races.

Individuals hired by the Federal Government to count votes shall be charged with Felony Tampering of the Democratic System, and punished to the fullest extent of previously determined law, if guilt is proven in a Court of law.

Section 4 - Mandates, Procedures, and Prohibitions

The State shall not endorse or establish any religion, nor shall it restrict any person who desires to practice.

Bills, declarations, and measures that originate in either the Department of War and State or Treasury and Commerce, and pass with a majority vote with approval from the Secretary, shall be passed with a similar vote and approval from the other Departments.

If the bill or measure fails, the disapproving Department shall make changes and return the document to the Department where it originated.

Upon passage of any bill, measure, treaty, declaration of war, or budget, the Department of Law and Justice shall grant judicial review.

This Constitution, and the laws of the Union, which shall be made in pursuance thereof; and all treaties made, or which shall be made, under the authority of the Union, shall be the supreme law of the land; and Judges in all jurisdictions shall be bound thereby to this Constitution or laws of any Municipality to the contrary notwithstanding. Such treaties shall not override any existing law in this Constitution.

The Secretary, Departments, and all Government officials shall be held accountable and shall not have sovereign immunity. All legitimate grievances against Federal Government officials shall be reviewed by Federal Courts, which shall hear all cases necessary.

Department Secretaries shall have line-item veto and full veto power of bills originating in their respective Departments. Vetoes shall be overridden by a two-thirds vote by the Department body.

Department Secretaries shall have the authority of appointment when necessary with advice and consent from the remainder of the Department from which the appointment is pending.

During crises involving national security where an immediate response is necessary, shall a Secretary be allowed to restrict this Constitution, or violate the human rights of individuals in pursuance of vital information, upon which that Secretary shall go before his/her Department and face a vote of expulsion where a one-third vote is required.

All that applies to the Citizens of the nation shall also apply to Federal Government.

At no time shall all members of the Federal Government be gathered.

That which is not specifically enumerated in this Constitution shall be left to the discretion of, in order of authority, the individual Counties, Townships, and Cities/Towns.

Should the Federal Government assume powers not enumerated in this Constitution, the validity of such laws shall be determined by the individual Counties, Townships, and Cities/Towns until proven otherwise in a court of law.

This Constitution shall guarantee to every Municipality under this Union a Republican Form of Government, and shall protect each against invasion and upon request from the Municipal governing body, against domestic violence.

The Federal Government shall be prohibited from withholding funding from Municipalities based on mandates for which the individual Departments are not constitutionally permitted to legislate. The Federal Government shall withhold funding for non-compliance of laws passed within the framework of this Constitution. The Federal Government shall be prohibited from passing any law impairing the obligation of contracts.

No Preference shall be given by regulation of commerce or revenue to the ports of one Municipality over those of another, nor shall vessels bound to, or from, one Municipality, be obliged to enter, clear, or pay duties in another.

The privilege of Writ of Habeas Corpus shall not be suspended, unless when in cases of a declared national emergency, rebellion or invasion, to which the public safety may be required.

No person holding office of profit or trust under this Federal Government shall, without the consent of the Department of Law and Justice, accept any present, emolument, office, or title, of any kind whatsoever, from any King, Queen, Prince, or foreign Head of State.

The Government shall have no obligation to provide prosperity to individuals, but may provide assistance on a limited basis when necessary. The Federal Government shall never own or operate or control a stake in more than 15 percent of the national economy, or any sector thereof, and at no time shall the national debt rise above 50 percent of annual Gross Domestic Product, nor shall necessary payment of annual debt service exceed eight percent of the Federal budget, except in times of declared war or national emergency.

Section 5 - Budgets, Taxes and Duties

To ensure an informed Citizenry, all wages shall first go to the People who shall deliver the appropriate taxes to the Government.

The Secretary of Commerce and Treasury shall present a budget to the Department during the first month of the calendar year. If a budget is not established and approved by the other Departments by the end of the second month, the previous year's budget shall remain active until new is passed.

A regular statement and account of the receipts and expenditures of all public monies and actions shall be published periodically or upon request, unless the Union can prove the release of such material jeopardizes national security.

Section 6 - Acquisition of Land and Ratification

The acquisition of Union land shall be approved by all Departments with two-thirds majority vote and approval by the Secretaries.

A majority from the citizenry of the acquired land shall approve annexation.

All debts contracted and monetary engagements entered, before the adoption of this Constitution, shall be valid against the new Union under this Constitution.

Section 7 - Powers Granted to Counties, Townships, and Cities/Towns

Rules of governance under which they shall operate shall be created by the Municipalities. These include: organize and levy taxes, establish and train a militia, appoint officers, and all duties not specifically enumerated in this Constitution.

Full faith and credit shall be given in each Municipality to the public acts, records, and judicial proceedings of every Municipality. And the Department of Justice and Law shall, by general laws, prescribe the manner in which such acts, records, and proceedings shall be proved, and the effect thereof.

A Person charged within the Union with treason, felony, or other crime, who shall flee from justice, and be found in another jurisdiction of the Union outside where the crime occurred, shall on demand of the executive authority of the prosecuting jurisdiction from which he fled, be delivered.

Counties include the combination of various Townships, set by the Department of Law and Justice, that agree upon the merger by popular vote. Townships include the combination of various Cities/Towns, set by the Department of Law and Justice, that agree upon the merger by popular vote.

A new County, Township, or City/Town may be chartered by the Federal representative from that district. But none of the above shall be formed or erected within the Jurisdiction of any other without approval from the encumbered party. Nor shall any of the above be formed by the junction of two or more without majority consent from all parties.

The rights, privileges, and freedoms not enumerated in this Constitution shall be delegated to the local Municipalities, and the People.

Section 8 - Powers Prohibited by Local Governments

No County, Township, or City/Town shall enter into any treaty, alliance, or confederation; grant letters of marquee and reprisal and make rules concerning captures on land, air and water; coin money; emit Bills of Credit; make any but precious metal currency a tender in payment of debts; pass any bill of attainder, ex-post-facto law, or law impairing the obligation of contracts; or grant any title of nobility; or lay any imposts or duties on imports or exports, or tonnage, except what may be necessary for executing inspection laws, in which case remaining revenue shall be delivered to the Department of Treasury and Commerce.

No County, Township, or City/Town shall, without the consent of the Department of War and State, enter into any agreement or compact with a foreign power, or engage in war, unless invaded, or in such imminent danger as will not permit a delay.

Section 9 - Amendments

The Department of Law and Justice, whenever two-thirds of the other Departments shall deem it necessary, with Secretarial approval, shall propose Amendments to this Constitution. Upon a two-thirds popular vote by three-fourths of districts, the amendment shall be enumerated in this Constitution. For this execution, no timeline exists.

Article Five
The People

Section 1 - Citizen

A Citizen of this Union shall have all the rights listed in Article 6, Section 1, of this Constitution. Citizens may hold Federal office and vote in Federal elections, and work on all levels of the Federal Government.

The requirements to become a Citizen shall be set forth by the Department of Justice and Law. They shall include, but are not limited to, a Registered Resident who completes two years of public service to the nation, whether military or otherwise, beginning on or after the Resident reaches 18 years of age and has resided permanently within the Union for 15 years.

Section 2 - Registered Resident

A Registered Resident of the Union shall have all the rights listed in Article 6, Section 1, of this Constitution.

Registered Residents, of appropriate age who have resided permanently within the Union for ten years, may hold Municipal office and vote in Municipal elections; they shall not hold Federal office or vote in Federal elections.

Registered Residents may work for the Federal Government in limited roles in accordance with ordinances set forth by the Department of Justice and Law, and shall register with the district in which they live at time of birth or settlement.

Registration, including foreign visas, shall be free unless otherwise stated.

Section 3 - Non-Registered Resident

Non-Registered Residents of this Union shall have all the rights listed in Article 6, Section 1, of this Constitution.

Non-Registered Residents shall not be entitled to the privileges, licenses or grants provided by, or regulated by, the Federal Government and Municipalities.

Non-Registered Residents shall not hold any Municipal or Federal office or vote in Municipal or Federal elections.

Non-Registered Residents, upon notice to authorities, shall pay a fine determined by the Department of Justice and Law, and register with the Union. Failure to do so, whether voluntary or by lack of funds, shall result in deportation at their expense. If the individual cannot pay for deportation, he/she shall work for the Union until the hours have been accrued to cover the appropriate costs.

Article Six
Laws of the Land

Section 1 – Human Rights

Every individual under the jurisdiction of this Union shall have the right to life, speech, property, and equal opportunity under the law which shall not be infringed.

No right, or legality to vote, or desire of freedom, shall be denied or abridged by the Union or any jurisdiction thereof, on account of sex, religion, race, disability, or heritage, or any other personal characteristic for which the individual is deemed beholden.

The right of Federal information shall exist in its entirety unless the Union or local Municipalities can fully demonstrate a valid state-interest in its secrecy.

The right of workers to participate in solidarity with a private vote shall not be infringed. Such organizations that service government, in more than 25 percent of their operations or membership, are prohibited.

Congress shall make no law abridging the freedom of the press—unless such press or their ancillary corporate partnerships profit off government contracts—or that of the People to peaceably assemble, or petition the Government for a redress of grievances.

DEVOLUTION

Understanding that it is essential for individuals within a free and just society to protect themselves and their families, the right of the People to keep and bear Arms, and protect their property, shall not be infringed.

The right of the People to be secure in their persons, houses, papers, and effects, against unreasonable searches and seizures, shall not be violated, and no Warrants shall be issued, but upon probable cause, supported by oath or affirmation, and particularly describing the place to be searched, and the persons or things to be seized.

No person shall be held to answer for a capital, or otherwise infamous crime, unless on a presentment or indictment of a Grand Jury, except in cases arising in the military forces, or in the militia, when in actual service in time of war or public danger; nor shall any person be subject for the same offense to be twice put in jeopardy of life or limb; nor shall be compelled in any criminal case to be a witness against himself, nor be deprived of life, liberty, or property, without due process of law; nor shall private property be taken for public use, or by the Union or local Municipalities in general, without just compensation.

In all criminal prosecutions, the accused is entitled the right to a speedy and public trial by an impartial jury in the district wherein the crime shall have been allegedly committed, which district shall have been previously ascertained by law, and to be informed of the nature and cause of the accusation; to be confronted with the witnesses against him/her; to have compulsory process for obtaining witnesses in his/her favor, and to have the assistance of Counsel for his/her defense.

In suits of civil law, where the value in controversy shall exceed an amount set periodically by the Department of Justice and Law, the right of trial by jury shall be preserved, and no fact tried by a jury, shall be otherwise re-examined in any Court of this Union.

Excessive bail shall not be required, nor excessive fines imposed, nor cruel and unusual punishments inflicted.

The rights of parents to raise their children under their supervision, but within the context of the law, shall not be infringed.

The powers not delegated to the Union by the Constitution, nor prohibited by it to the Counties, Townships and Cities/Towns, shall be reserved for the People to determine by popular vote.

Section 2 – Privileges, Immunities, and Licenses

Citizens and Registered Residents shall be entitled to all privileges, immunities, and licenses earned, in the several Districts, Municipalities, and Federal Government, unless it has been determined by a jury of their peers that they shall not hold such privileges, immunities and licenses.

For the exception of declared national emergency, or by voluntary action, the People shall not pay Federal taxes totaling more than 25 percent of wages and income.

That which is not defined in Article 6, Section 1 on this Constitution shall be left to the discretion of the local Municipalities as privileges for which they may establish immunities and licenses, necessary and proper to operate, within the confines of this Constitution.

These privileges, immunities and licenses shall be established and abolished with the consent of the People with the undeniable understanding that the rights and overarching mission, detailed in the preamble of this document, shall never change.

CHAPTER SIX

A LOOSE DEMOCRACY AT WORK

April 28—Election Day:

"**P**eople, please stay in line. Be calm," commanded the disgruntled poll worker. His pleas for cooperation only caused the crowd to grow more restless. The long, slow-moving line stretched down the hallway of the old school, out the door, and onto the sidewalk. "You will all get to vote. Please!" He walked along the line, cordially escorting people back to single file. The bright sun and warm spring air fueled an energy pent up through a long winter.

The Nolan family had just parked their car and stepped in line. The family preferred to vote together. When the twins were ready, they'd continue the tradition.

"Damn government!" yelled a man not far ahead of the Nolans, his impassioned voice deeply tinged with resentment. "Do *something* right!"

This election was vital. Contempt with the government was approaching critical mass. The future of the nation was at stake more than any election in recent memory. The minority party, which ran on a platform of responsible reform and cautious reorganization of the markets, cut heavily into the majority's numbers in the Commons. They were in position to lose the majority as they advocated patience in letting the market correct itself.

"We grew so fast for so long. A correction was bound to happen," they explained.

This election, however, threatened to swing the pendulum in the way of a third party, who favored major market reform. Though the UK had many smaller parties, one was able to break through, and they were perched to make history by riding the electoral disdain to Westminster.

"I have never seen things this bad," observed Theodore, his family huddled close together. "I don't like to see our country going down this path."

His family held silent in agreement, watching uneasily as the crowd grew even more frustrated and antagonistic. The current government was quickly becoming the enemy.

It was safe to assume many waiting in line had lost their jobs. Unemployment was now at more than ten percent—the highest in years. Lagging government revenues from a reduced working class had forced Parliament to deficit spend and consider tax increases. Interest rates skyrocketed as government money became less attractive. Expanded social programs advocated by the minority party helped the jobless, at the expense of the working. The nation was pitted against itself.

These were not the steps the majority party wished to implement, and it fought the change. The growing power of the minority parties, however, commanded influence. This uncertainty in government created uncertainty among the people—a disastrous combination right before an election. The media fed off the fear; the people were scared, and needed something new to believe in.

In the years prior, people believed in Great Britain. Leading up to dissolution of the United States of America, Great Britain saw an opportunity to reclaim its superpower status. As the USA became unstable, the UK lured its most talented with economic opportunity via tax breaks and reduced regulations. The huge influx of wealth, both material and mental, jolted the UK economy. In a few short years, it reclaimed its spot as the world's largest and most influential economy. Colonies in Africa, Southeast Asia, and South America soon followed.

Unemployment dropped to near statistical zero. Billionaires and millionaires were being made by the day as the stock market soared. But as in any boom, the bubble would burst, and it threatened to take the entire country with it.

The poll worker stepped outside the schoolhouse door. "Ladies and gentlemen," he said, his voice quivering. "We are experiencing problems with the ballot machines. We will have them back online very soon."

The crowd released a monolithic groan.

In between the ceaseless moans and embittered complaining, the sounds of a distant chant steadily grew louder. The crowd noise tapered as the cadence became more dominant and intrigue set in. The words were not yet decipherable, but the enthusiasm and energy was unequivocal. Familiar melodies erratically bounced off the brick walls, making it hard to pinpoint its origins.

"There!" A man up front pointed to just over the near horizon. Though at first only the occasional glimmer of homemade posters broke the crest of the suburban road, the muffled tune of an impassioned protest spurred a sense of wonderment.

What started as periodical visions developed into a plethora of symbolic art. Soon after, the protesters broke free over the hill releasing the full force of their voices. The voters stood by, their internal reactions mixed.

The protesters marched down the hill directly towards the voting line. Dozens of third party supporters proudly barked the obligatory and trite protest tunes that never seemed to die.

"Hey, hey, ho, ho our government has got to go." Their signs depicted the majority and minority leadership with circles around their heads and slashes through the middle. Children sported handcrafted shirts that read "Take Back Our Country,", "End the Exploitation," and "Don't Ruin it For Me/ Give Me a Chance."

"What does that mean? 'Take Back Our Country,'" Charlotte all but whispered in her husband's ear.

CHRIS PAPST

"Whatever you want it to mean," was all Theodore had to say.

The protesters closed in on the soon-to-be voters.

"What do we want?" cried a tall, thin man in front. He wore ripped jeans and a bright yellow shirt picturing Nick Clekk—a former party leader. He beat a wooden stick on the pavement, keeping rhythm like a human metronome. His long, straggly dark hair was pulled into a ponytail.

"Justice!" roared the protesters, including the young children.

He delivered his follow-up question with affliction.

"When do we want it?"

"Now!" the followers cried.

"You know what?" John overheard a young woman in front of him mention to her

husband. "Their party has never been in power. Maybe it's time they get a chance." Though her husband remained silent, it was obvious he agreed.

When the activists arrived at the school they spread out. The lead protester approached an older couple behind the Nolans.

"Do you like where the country is going right now?" they asked, receiving no answer.

"Look at what this government has done to us. Look at all the people who have no job. All those people left behind while a certain few get rich. Please consider us. We will get everyone back to work. And those who can't find jobs will be taken care of."

He handed them some literature explaining their positions. "With the wealth of our country no one should be hungry. No one should be out on the street. No one should be without medical care. They've had years to get this right. Please, give us a chance."

John surreptitiously turned his head to study the man as he approached the next set of voters. Beyond his obvious message and ambush-style tactics, something just didn't seem right. His emphatic voice and body language appeared friendly, but his green slivered eyes held a hidden story.

"Are you happy with where our country is going?" he asked another couple.

John turned away.

"Don't people understand this is how growing economies work?" Charlotte asked. "The market goes up and down. It's healthy."

"He is using fear to get votes," John said matter-of-factly. "People don't want to wait. And we like to have purpose in our lives. We want to be part of something bigger than ourselves, even if we are ignorant of where it's really taking us. That's how some of the worst tyrants in history came to power."

"T.S. Eliot said, *'Half the harm that is done in this world is due to people who want to feel important and think well of themselves,'*" Theodore chimed in.

John leaned a little closer to his mom and his father angled in as well. "Waiting does not give people *hope* that things will improve. Change does."

"They are using ill-will to their advantage," Theodore said, finishing his son's thought.

John lowered his voice when one of the protesters approached the group in front of them. "While bad times lead to change, it's often the worst time for it. Uncertainty does not help a struggling economy."

"Hi, how are you guys? Can I interest you in some information?" The group seemed willing to hear more.

"Should we believe they have a magic formula that's never been tried before?" Theodore said.

The protesters soon progressed down the street, chanting the entire way. Their message would reach thousands of voters before the day was through.

That night, the Nolans sat in their living room watching the election returns. The orange light of the evening sun faded along with any aspirations they had for a lasting financial recovery. Their fears had mutated into a grim reality. Their churning stomachs made it nearly impossible to speak. The nation had given that third party, the Centre Party, a huge victory in both Houses. The new Parliament would officially be opened by Her Majesty, the Queen, on June 1.

*

"Hon!" a crabby Emma Manning hollered down the hallway to her resting husband. "Come here, please?"

Tony awoke from his deep trance. He shambled down the hall, the scope of his recent ventures heavy on his mind.

"Please get me a clean diaper?" Emma asked when he entered the room.

He grabbed a new pack, opened it, and handed her one. Emma remained hunched over their child.

"Thank you." She grabbed the white cloth and slightly elevated the baby's feet. Tony stood by, watching his beautiful wife assist their even more beautiful son. Emma was dressed in black workout shorts and a faded light blue t-shirt. Her fire-red hair remained uncombed, and she had yet to apply any makeup. To Tony, it didn't matter. For the first time in a few weeks, an authentic smile grew upon his face. She was his jewel in an otherwise morbid time.

Emma finished changing the diaper. "Follow me," she said to her husband, shuffling by him with the baby cradled in her arms. Tony locked eyes with his son. He scrunched his face and stuck out his tongue. The baby grinned.

Despite Tony being one of the most powerful men in Great Britain, as a Member of the Commons, he was not the most powerful person in his household. They sat together on the couch.

"Tell me what's wrong," Emma said, her tone filled with compassion. "For the past few months, I figured you were in this funk because of Richard's passing and the other guys not coming back to the Commons, but this is going on too long." She peered at her husband, knowing he could not resist her. "Please."

"I can't stop thinking about Richard." Tony dropped his head, unable to meet his wife's gaze. She waited patiently for him to continue.

Tony's heart raced and he nervously massaged his face. "The LAF didn't kill Richard Sykes."

Emma leaned in towards her husband. This was not the answer she'd expected.

Tony's hands dropped from his face. The words came hard. "The Crown did it." He looked up at Emma with uneasy eyes. "And I don't think the bullet was meant for him." He sighed. "It was meant for me."

Emma gasped, placing her hand over her chest. "Why would you think that?" She felt a tear streak down her cheek.

Tony took a second to not only gather himself, but allow his wife to come to grips with what he told her. He reached for her hand, intertwining their fingers. He then confessed everything. "The final day of the session, I hid my identity and walked to the Vauxhall Bridge. I met a member of the media to give him the pamphlet I showed you. I thought I did everything right. I thought I was smart about it. I never called him. Everything was through regular mail. I don't know how they figured it out." His voice trembled. "When I walked up, I saw some guys that looked like homeless people lying under the bridge. We talked briefly. But it was so windy. How could they have heard? I gave him the pamphlet and went to lunch."

Up to this point, Tony could not bear to look at his wife. He struggled to find the strength to continue. "Emma, they know what I gave the media. They thought I opened that door. Those bullets were meant for me."

"Why would you assume that? You don't know—"

"I killed one of my best friends!" Tony wailed. "Me!" He jammed stiffened fingers into his chest. "It's my fault!"

The man she loved reduced himself to a confused, vulnerable shell. Emma scooted towards her husband, placing her free arm around him; their baby still secured in the other. She couldn't help but feel partially to blame. After all, she had given him permission to pursue his path. They grieved together.

"So what are you going to do now?" she quivered.

He sulked under the weight on her comforting arm, both hands cradling his leaden head.

"At this point, if they are going to kill me, they are going to kill me." He had come to grips with that reality. "So I have no choice," he paused to assure his words were not mistaken. "I *have* to strike first."

*

"PM Has Time to Reflect"

The headlines the following day served as a stark reminder.

I don't have much time.

Chris Nash sat ensconced at his desk, suffocating under piles of paperwork. Payroll and scheduling, in addition to the everyday grind of a metropolitan area news director, proved overwhelming.

I need to get out of here.

He shoved some papers into a filing cabinet and slammed the door shut. Swirling around in his swivel chair, he flung open his desk drawer in reckless search of his contacts.

There it is.

Paging through, he blindly reached for the phone.

"Office of the Prime Minister," answered the secretary.

"Delores, how are you? It's Chris Nash."

She gasped. "Chris! My Lord. How long has it been?" Delores was a sweet old woman whom Chris always admired. She'd worked in the prime minister's office for more than forty years. Retirement never appealed to her. "You become big time and you can't call an old friend anymore?" She chuckled. "How have you been?"

"I'm good, Delores. It's nice to hear your voice. I was wondering if the prime minister has any time today to talk with a little guy like me."

She snickered. "I'm sure he'd love to. Let me see..." Chris heard her shuffle some things, and then she said, "He's in his office now, and might be available. Should I try?"

"Please."

"Okay, hold on."

Being placed on hold reminded him of the old days—the classical hold music, *Love on the Dole Suite* by Richard Addinsell, was the same as a decade earlier.

"Chris Nash! What a surprise!"

"Sir, it is a pleasure." Nash was honored to have received such a jovial greeting from the nation's highest ranking elected official.

Chris Nash and the prime minister had known each other for years. They'd developed a strong professional relationship when Nash worked the political beat. They fought and scrapped their way up their respective vocational ladders together, and the hundreds of encounters they had in the early part of their careers made them lifelong acquaintances, with a mutual respect for one another. At the same time, however, their guards were always up.

"What can I do for you, my friend?" asked the PM.

"I need to talk to you. I have nowhere else to go."

The PM was already intrigued.

"A few months ago, I received this anonymous letter that caught my attention," Nash told him. "I followed it and got an interesting piece of literature. It describes government dealings over the last couple of decades. I am not sure what to make of it."

"What do you mean, government dealings?"

Nash held the pamphlet in front of him, trying to decide which section to use as an example. "Remember a few years back, large reserves of oil were discovered in Angola? And the FLEC, which everyone thought disbanded, led a failed rebellion against the Republic? A massive civil war erupted over the oil rights."

"Of course."

"Well this, um," he paused, looking for the right word, "*document* says the FLEC was revived by the Crown. It claims we funded them in exchange for oil rights once the FLEC took power. But when the Republic got the upper hand, we bailed out of the agreement. It details the murders of hundreds of thousands."

The other end was silent.

"Sir?"

"S-sorry about that, Chris," the PM stammered. "My secretary needed something."

Nash knew better.

The skilled politician quickly regained his composure. "I'll be glad to take a look. Do you have time this afternoon?"

The PM's response, and willingness to meet on such short notice said it all. What Nash held in his hand was legitimate.

"When is good for you?" the prime minister prompted.

"You're a busier man than I, sir."

"I love that about you. You're always so accommodating." The forced chuckle between them was terribly uncomfortable. "How about two o'clock?"

Nash looked down at his calendar, tracing his finger along a continuous string of meetings and corporate conference calls. "I think that should work."

"I'll see you then. Hey, Chris!" Nash raised the phone back to his ear. "When you were given the document, did the person say anything to you?"

Nash paused briefly, solely for dramatic affect. "No. He didn't say a word." The newsman always played by the mantra: less is more. The phone went dead.

Daunted by this revelation, the PM sat back in his chair, loosely spinning the phone in his right hand. He dialed a familiar number.

"Mr. Prime Minister," answered a raspy, passionless voice. "You know I don't like receiving calls from you."

"Major General," the PM said unapologetically. "Are you sitting down?"

*

"Society and power."

Professor John Nolan felt more uncomfortable than he thought he would as he took command of his first college class. He forced a hearty breath and fought through his fear of unfamiliar groups.

"Every aspect of our lives contains a tiered hierarchy. Whether in sports, literature, fashion," he gestured towards his surroundings, "higher education." His dynamic, yet smooth, baritone voice fell gracefully over the students.

"The people who sit atop the pyramid, in many aspects, dictate how those below behave. If you step outside this world of unwritten rules, you risk banishment from that society or glorification of your maverick ways—a distinction for which you have little control."

The small class appeared captivated with John's inaugural lecture. He'd spent the whole night crafting it. Similar to their professor, this was for many their first college class and the novelty of advance thought and critical thinking was stark. The question was: Could John manage to command the same level of attention by semester's end? "In this class we will look at the hierarchy of power in our government. Her Royal Majesty, the House of Commons, the House of Lords, the prime minister, our military and so on. We will examine how they control our lives—in ways we may not want them to." He lowered his voice as if the following words were secret. "Or ways we don't even realize." He briskly inhaled and continued as normal. "We'll briefly look at the history of our government and how it came to be. And we'll examine where we think our society is heading in terms of government influence. Questions?"

The classes' hearty acceptance of John's opening monologue sent a rush of confidence and pride through his being. His new career, which he planned to take to the grave, had begun in that cramped, undecorated, and otherwise unmemorable classroom. And only twelve students were there to witness it.

The crooked smile on his face served as a sponge, soaking up the spirit of the moment. He knew it would never feel like this again.

That night the Nolans met at the dinner table to celebrate John's professional leap from student to teacher.

"To John!" toasted Theodore, raising his beer high into the air. "Congratulations, John," Theodore could not have been more proud. The family kitchen was filled with the harmonic ring of chiming glass.

"John, I'm so proud of you," his mother beamed. "We are all really proud of you."

His sisters expressed their regards with authentic smiles. *Yeah, John, congratulations.*

The table was made complete by April Lynn. She sat to John's immediate right. She and John had now been dating for a few months. Whatever awkwardness existed around his family was minimal.

"I wonder what kind of nickname my students are going to have for me," John wondered aloud, half-joking. The other half was true concern: *Old Sores.*

"So how many classes are you teaching?" Rose inquired.

"For this first summer session, only one." John reached for April's hand underneath the table. "By the fall, I should have a full schedule."

The couple shared a celebratory gaze.

"What if you're not any good?"

"Lizzy!" scolded her mother.

"What? It's a valid question."

"That's why he only has one class," Theodore bellowed.

Effective comedy must contain an element of truth. And John's father was right.

Charlotte even found herself chuckling. However, her motherly instincts caught herself. "The City University of London is lucky to have you."

"Thanks, Mom."

"So do you have a curriculum planned out?" Rose asked, refilling her Chardonnay glass.

"I have the course materials from my predecessor. I'll follow that, then introduce my own work."

April beamed up at him, locking eyes. "That's the plan."

"The plan?" Lizzy asked, puzzled.

It took John a second to break April's alluring stare. "My old professor from Cambridge encouraged me to get my paper published."

"Wow!" his sisters blurted out.

"What does that mean?" Charlotte asked.

"Well, in order for me to use literature in my class, it has to be published. So Professor Sorenson set me up with a small publishing company. They might publish my thesis as a book."

"It will contain all the research he did on the civilizations. The Constitution, too." John mildly blushed under April's excitement.

"Oh! Haven't y'all read it?" She looked around at the family. The answer was obvious, they hadn't. "It's quite good."

"I had to do some work to get it book-ready. But that's pretty much it." John could have regaled his family for hours about the process, but he figured he'd spare them the minutiae.

His father was stunned. Charlotte quietly radiated with pride. "I always knew you had it in you, John," she said.

His sisters looked at each other as if to say, *we didn't.*

John had been waiting for the right moment to tell his family. This was as good as any. "Since I am teaching about society and power, the government plays a large role. My plan is to teach my book in class."

"That's awesome, John," Rose said. "And who knows, maybe it'll catch on and your ideas will spark some sort of change. That'd be wild."

The family chuckled at the statement's absurd degree of optimism. But for John, he simply laughed out of courtesy. How sweet a revenge that would be.

*

The reticent storefronts and lack of commerce on Bridge Street typified the dreary weather that had befallen London. Chris Nash sat nervously in his silver vehicle parked below the magnificent Gothic vaults and pointed arches of Westminster. His watch ticked ever closer to 2:00. The anticipation of his meeting sent his emotions on a wild ride of uncertainty. He didn't want things to get contentious, but he understood the sensitivity of the material could lend itself to such an encounter. Nash believed everything in the pamphlet was true. He knew the prime minister would deny its authenticity.

Tick. Tick. Tick.

With each pulse of the second hand, the knot in his stomach tightened.

Two o'clock.

Nash inflated his slender chest with a deep drag of balmy spring air. Under a controlled exhale, he grabbed his briefcase off the passenger seat and reached for the door handle. It was time.

"Hello, Mr. Nash." Delores' warm welcome scarcely served to calm his nerves.

She walked out from behind the desk, greeting her guest with an embrace. "It is

nice to see you after all these years."

For the moment, the scope of Nash's upcoming parley escaped him, replaced

with friendly reminders of a past life. The customary sights and familiar sounds of the office assuaged his near crippling anxiety. And perhaps none brought back such powerful feelings as the pungent aromas. Much like the classical hold music still in use, Delores' sweet perfume had also remained unchanged.

For many years, Chris Nash was the Capital reporter for the British News Network—the largest media conglomerate in the United Kingdom. He always revered the Gothic Revival characteristics and old Victorian feel of the office. With its tall, ornate cathedral ceilings and busy, yet simple, stained glass windows, it perfectly exemplified the power and prestige of the elected official it housed.

"The prime minister will be out momentarily." Delores gestured towards the short procession of chairs that lined the wall. "Please take a seat. There is coffee in the break room down the hall, if you would like." She smiled warmly. "We also have a cappuccino and a hot chocolate-maker now."

"No kidding!"

Delores was the only person he knew who had a delightful snicker. "I love how you use my own money to make me feel at home."

"Isn't it wonderful?" She strolled back behind her desk, grabbing her purse. "I'm off to lunch. Try to keep in touch, stranger." The door closed behind her as she exited the room. Nash was now alone.

The newsman took a seat in one of the newly upholstered, dark mahogany chairs. *I could go for some French vanilla.* He immediately stood back up.

Nash received his promotion to news director a few years after the fall of the United States. The influx of people caused a boom for every industry, especially the media, which up to that point had seen years of cuts and layoffs. The press once again had become viable and influential. They had proved that professional reporters were a vital part of a healthy and stable democracy, mostly by holding government accountable. Chris felt he had anonymously led this media revolution. And somehow, the pamphlet in his back pocket was his reward.

To Chris Nash, this room meant power. During his time inside these walls, the UK saw the spawning of its greatest years. However, this time around, he didn't feel that same awe or sense of patriotism. The energy had changed.

With his nerves reappearing, Nash made his way down the hall for a tall French vanilla, ultra high-fat, cappuccino. *Hell, if I'm paying for the fat, why not?*

Twenty minutes, and one-and-a-half cappuccinos, later there was still no sign of the prime minister. Nash's anxiety had morphed into an unpleasant mixture of irritation and guilt. The second cappuccino tasted fatter than the first.

The long wait was not a pleasant one. *Is he playing with me?* Nash watched the time creep by, as it always did when one was obsessed with its progression. The gravity of the situation only weighed heavier on his mind as three o'clock approached. His years of reporting on-air, sometimes in front of large tempestuous crowds, had taught him how to eliminate nervous energy and internal discomfort. But that strategy only suppressed the symptoms, and nothing he had ever done prior quite compared to this.

Eventually a loud clamor jolted Nash in his chair. The large wooden door across the room creaked open, revealing the prime minister. The PM may have been the same person Nash first met decades ago, but their rich past could not make up for lost time. Both men had reached the pinnacle of their respective careers, and the scars they bore in the process seemed to separate them like strangers. Under different circumstances this overdue reunion may have been more of a celebration of the other's success. However, it was not meant to be. On the phone their discourse was smooth and cordial, but in person it became awkward, coupled with a tenuous peace.

"Chris Nash." The PM forced a coarse smile. "Old friend, how are you?" He reached out his hand as Nash rose to his feet. The newsman towered over the much shorter politician. Physicality aside, their intellects were similar in many ways, a quality they mutually respected.

"I am good, Mr. Prime Minister." Nash was equally as inauthentic. Their cold palms met in an assertive embrace. "Thank you for meeting with me."

The PM placed a stiff hand on Nash's rigid shoulder. "We have a short walk, my friend." With his free hand, he pointed. "This way."

As they approached the door from which the prime minister first appeared, he asked, "What do you think? We've spent a lot of time refurbishing the place."

Nash looked around. *Really? It looks the exact same.*

He reached for the handle. "This was getting pretty run-down." Nash walked past him and across the threshold. "They did a good job." The door fastened behind them.

The hallway they entered no longer held that old Victorian feel. The need for certain aesthetics ended where the public's vision stopped. This section had more of an aristocratic, contemporary feel, complete with detailed crown and chair molding, gold-accented wallpaper, and burgundy-carpeted floors that they seemed to float upon. The soft brilliance provided by stained glass windows was gone. Bright track lights now illuminated the route.

The PM pointed up the hallway. "Straight ahead."

The Prime Minister of the UK was about as physically average a man as they came. Hovering around five-foot-seven with an unimpressive build, he intimidated no one. His meager 140-pound weight, squeaky voice, and high hair parted to the left supplied his critics with an assortment of punch lines. However, what he lacked in physical stature, he made up for in intelligence and the ability to communicate. At 55 years old, he was still relatively young and had a bright future.

This PM was a strong leader who the people had respected. Yet, with the massive landslide victory of the Centre Party in the April elections, his time was running out. In less than a week he would step down. A scary proposition for not only him, but for a number of Brits who feared what the Centre Party would do to the country. Since they'd never held political power, their governing style was an unknown.

The men entered the PM's office which, despite the time of day, was depressingly drab with layered shadows eerily strewn in every direction. "Please, sit."

Nash was quick to oblige.

"I love this office," the PM stated as he plopped down in his chair. "I don't want to leave, Nash." Though his dispirited acceptance of the circumstances was no surprise, his willingness to discuss it was.

Chris had no idea how to respond. *Why is he making small talk?*

"I hope they appreciate and understand the responsibility this office brings." He spoke of the incoming party. "Just sitting in this chair reminds me of all those great men and women who preceded me. I think about all the people we've helped. All the freedom we've spread. All the prosperity."

Nash was dumbfounded. This was not how he'd expected the meeting to begin. The awkwardness had vanished, replaced by a sense of weakness and vulnerability on the part of his perceived adversary. Maybe Nash's first impression of awkwardness was misinterpreted. Maybe to the PM, time had not distanced them. But Nash was too jaded by the system to be fooled by a skillful politician. The prime minister never said a word without its impact being carefully weighed.

"I understand," Nash replied. "But it is not all—"

"I have so much unfinished work," he interrupted. "These are hard times and the people turned on us. What we did worked!" He tapped his chest with an open hand. "This market correction had to happen. We even predicted it! *Now* is the time when the ones with the experience are most needed!"

Chris remained silent. *What the hell?*

After a few seconds, the PM became much calmer. "I have no idea what the Centre Party is going to do. I fear for our country." He lowered his head in defeat, releasing a sigh of humility. "They will force major change that this fragile economy cannot handle."

134

As if jolted by an instantaneous burst of energy, the PM raised his head, white-faced and wide-eyed, somehow transformed into a new person. "So, Chris, what do you want to show me?"

Nash's desire to grill the PM for answers had all but dissolved. Stalling for time he reached into his breast pocket for the pamphlet. "This is what I told you about." He handed the document desktop the PM.

The PM closely examined it, his face unwavering. "Do you mind if I have this?"

Nash nodded. "That's a copy."

He continued to study its contents, occasionally gesticulating as if what he had read was so absurd it was humorous.

"Well," the PM said with quite the poker face, "I don't know what to tell you."

Nash intently looked for any signals that could give away the PM's true thoughts, but there were none.

"I don't know what this is." The Prime Minster placed the pamphlet on his desk. "Who gave it to you?"

"I don't know."

"You don't know?" He seemed incredulous.

"I didn't see his face or get his name. I met him under the Vauxhall Bridge."

The location instantly caught the PM's attention and Nash noticed his intrigue.

"The Vauxhall Bridge? When did you meet this person?"

"Second week in April. The tenth, I believe, around lunchtime."

"Really?" The prime minister's poker face briefly slipped before he corrected himself.

Nash caught the slight infraction; he was getting close to something, though he had no idea what. "All the man said was I should talk to you."

The PM casually leaned back in his chair and lightly cast himself away from the desk. "Well, I don't know anything about this. For all I know, it's a fraud. I will have my people look at it."

He was lying and they both knew it.

"I would appreciate any information," Nash said. Despite his ill feelings he remained respectful. Their political game was far from over.

The PM again examined the document.

"Well, Nash, it's not every day someone like yourself calls my office with something like this. It's interesting. But I have to be honest, with the new majority party coming in, it'll be a while before we get back to this."

Nash now understood the Prime Minister's initial misdirection. He feared the pamphlet's release during his administration.

Pretend like we're still old buddies, right?

Realizing additional efforts at acquiring information would be futile, Nash stood up and extended his hand. "Sir, thank you for your time. I will keep in touch."

And prove this information without your help.

The PM rose to escort his guest out of the office.

"No need, sir," Nash announced kindly. "I can show myself out."

After Nash left his office, the PM carelessly tossed the pamphlet on top of a stack of papers and spun in his chair to face his monitor. "That was interesting." His hands rose to the keyboard.

"Do you think he believed you?" a hoarse voice said from the far back corner of the room. The lack of light perfectly hid his position behind a bookshelf.

"Not a chance," the PM replied. "But I didn't give him enough to go on." He rotated his chair again, this time to face the blackened windows that overlooked a decreasingly vibrant city. "Thoughts?"

The man emerged from the shadows and into the scattered light, a freshly-lit cloud of cigar smoke encircled his head. Despite the gravitas of the situation, his monotone voice displayed no gravitas itself. It sounded as though his words were dead. "We need to know who met him under that bridge."

CHAPTER SEVEN
THE FALL

Early September

"Ladies and gentlemen, welcome to Society and Power S151."

By his time, Professor John Nolan felt like a seasoned classroom veteran. After teaching two summer sessions he felt in command. Yet his shy and quiet nature still had a tight grip.

"I gather all of you are in the correct class." His cheesy line received a slight chuckle, mostly out of respect.

"It's an interesting time in our nation's history to be taking this course," John began. "Our economy is weak. Some people think it's collapsing and we are heading towards a depression. Others are less pessimistic. To understand our power structure, you must understand economics and government. By the end of this semester, you will."

The class staring back at the professor was far from full. The struggling economy forced many students to work to help feed their families or save money for what may lie ahead.

"How well do you follow our economy?" John pointed to a young man sitting in the front row. "What is the unemployment rate?"

The young red-haired, freckled-faced boy, who appeared to be right out of high school, shrugged.

"Does anyone know?" John asked, careful not to damage the student's self-esteem.

A young, heavyset brunette girl with braces raised her hand. Before the professor had time to call on her, she blurted out, "15 percent."

"Right." John nodded in approval. "What about inflation?"

The same girl exclaimed, "11."

John eyed the nameless young woman. "Would you also like to tell me about interest rates?"

Stumped, she sat befuddled a moment before shaking her head.

A young Indian boy sitting in called out, "19 percent?"

"Yes. Unemployment, inflation, and interest rates all in the double digits—stagflation. It has drastically changed the power structure in our country."

John approached the board, grabbed a marker, and wrote in large block lettering, "S-T-A-G-F-L-A-T-I-O-N."

"Our new Parliament has tried to stabilize the economy over the past few months. Has it worked?" He paused to let his question sink in. "The government has bailed out a few companies. Did it save them? Or did it make them dependent and encourage others to act recklessly? Did they learn from their mistakes? Do they even have to? Is the government now their boss? The government didn't *save* other companies that failed. Is that right?"

John snapped the cap back on the marker and dropped it on the aluminum slide at the base of the board. "Global investors are less likely to look at our markets. Who controls the money? Is that who ultimately has the power?"

He paused again. This was a lot for the young minds to process. "If you would have taken this class in the fall before the election, this would have been different. A lot has changed in the past few months."

John took a seat behind his desk facing the class.

"When the Centre Party took office they had to make immediate changes to appease the nation. That is what they campaigned on. But major changes create uncertainty because no one knows what the affects will be. This is especially true in a fragile economy where companies are hesitant to hire or invest, and rather wait to see what happens. When the first set of changes didn't work, they said it was because they didn't change enough. So, they changed more. Now we have this mess of an economy."

"Who knows who John Maynard Keynes is?" Most all the students raised their hands. "Was he right? Can deficit spending save an economy? Will it save ours?" John asked. "What can slow a recession or stimulate an economy? Hard work or accounting tricks? What message are we sold?" John expected some argument from his students. But that was for a different day.

"So, the government had to increase interest rates to tighten the credit market and decreased the money flow to halt inflation. As a result, businesses cannot borrow. Now, unemployment is rising and our money is devaluing. That's stagflation."

His students could not have been more confused. Maybe that was a little much for the first day. "What caused this drastic change in our nation's thinking? What if we had done nothing? Why did we vote for a party that had never led before? These are types of questions we'll answer during this semester. You will leave this class with a different understanding of who holds power in our nation. Are there any—" His phone started to vibrate in his pocket. He pulled it out and glanced at the incoming number. "Please excuse me," he said, and stepped out the door.

The empty tile and concrete-laden hallway providing a slight echo to his voice. "Professor Sorenson. How are you, sir?"

"I am wonderful, John." Old Sores was far more jovial and mild-mannered outside the classroom. "I gather your first day of classes is going well?"

"Yes, sir." John regretted to have to cut off the conversation. "I am actually in the middle of lecture right now."

"Well, this won't take long. John, the publishing company has agreed to print your book."

John's jaw dropped. His body went numb with a paralyzing excitement.

"Congratulations, John!" Although Professor Sorenson was not there, he could picture John's reaction. It made the old man smile. "Call me when your class is finished and we'll go over the details."

"Yes, sir! Thank you, thank you, sir!"

John stood motionless in the hallway with the phone pressed tightly to his ear. With his head drifting backwards, his eyelids softly fell, shielding this moment from the rest of the world. *YES!* A tingling sensation rushed through his body followed by a cool, mellow charge of pure joy. For that brief period in time, he felt weightless, invincible. He had just learned of the greatest achievement of his life. Nothing could duplicate this overwhelming sensation of pure bliss.

John lowered the phone from his ear and dialed the numbers. He heard three rings and then, "Hello?"

"Hi."

Surprised, April said, "I thought you were in class?"

"I got the book deal!"

Her piercing shriek echoed through the hollow halls more than John's own words. "Oh, my God, honey! Are you serious? That's awesome!"

"I know." He could barely believe his own words. "It's finally coming together."

I am becoming worthy.

*

CRACK!!!

A shattering glass bottle on the sidewalk outside Westminster only added to the intolerant cries of the already antagonized British people. The enraged crowd of thousands grew even more indignant, shouting down their elected officials and public servants. Police in full riot gear stood at the gates of Britain's governance, limiting the people's advance. The occasional protester would break through the line of officers in a futile attempt to scale the fence, only to be dragged down from behind and taken into custody. These individuals never got far, but they served to fuel the crowd's belief that the catalyst for revolution was at hand. The massive citizen army was as angry a crowd as the dilapidated streets in downtown London had ever seen. The harrowing screams and hollers for justice were unmistakable. And they didn't fall on deaf ears.

"Equal rights! Equal rights!" bellowed some who had felt the government favoritism was unfair.

"Let us live! Let us live!" averred others who felt the government had already done too much.

"Action now! Action now!" bawled still more who thought the government hadn't done enough.

Thousands, all with a different solution. How could they please them all?

Homemade signs, many distributed by grass roots organizations, peppered the swelling ranks. Some contained encircled pictures of Parliamentary leaders with lines through their faces. Others expressed thoughts, like 'Revolution Now!' and 'Break the cycle!'

Kids too young to walk wore shirts of protest while strapped to their parents' backs. Older children, tethered to their guardians, contributed with shirts of their own that evinced their personal interests: "I'm Already Drowning in Debt," "Don't Kill My Dreams."

This massive protest had been planned for weeks, and the biting pain on the faces of the beleaguered was contagious. Food had grown scarce in some parts of the nation. And for some, food became too expensive. Winter was only a few months away and many feared they would be unable to pay their heating bills. The government was out of money, and foreign nations were unwilling to invest, either out of concern for their decreased credit rating or eagerness for the superpower's possible demise.

Some feared without police protection, the building would have been ransacked, and the leaders of the country would be at the mercy of the masses. But fears of a riot were few. Nevertheless, the Centre Party majority was ill-prepared and ill-equipped to deal with the circumstances.

The still relatively new prime minister watched the protest amongst a few of his closest advisers. His mood manifested as a heavy-hearted mellowness. His team stood in the chief executive's office looking out the window at the indignant and enlarging crowd.

"How did we get ourselves into this mess?"

No one dared to answer his question.

The PM lumbered away from the window and sulked in the false comfort of his chair. The faint cries of the crowd could be heard off in the distance. His staff, although slower to exit from the window, followed him to his desk. The wearisome sound of silence filled the room.

In the House of Commons and House of Lords, all negotiations had stalled. Under the fear of further failure, the Centre Party was hesitant to use its majorities to act. It was those very majorities soon after inauguration that pressed through sweeping reforms that knocked the economy off its axis. Although those immediate measures succeeded in placating the frustrated masses—for a while. As a result, the government had become as unstable and polarized as the country itself. The leaders had effectively lost control. And no one in that room had any answers. They sat staring at each other.

"What now?" questioned the spiritless PM as he fiddled with a pen on his desk.

One of his subordinates mustered the courage to speak. "We take our time and make sure this gets done right."

That passive, weak strategy, which unfortunately was the only viable one available, would prove fatal.

*

"The pain is palpable," explained the casually-dressed reporter holding the microphone firmly in her right hand. Standing a few feet in front of her, the photographer fought off the crowds to keep the camera from wobbling. Despite the scene she managed to keep her composure.

"The people who gathered here today wanted nothing less than a solution." The people around her realized she was live, and tried to use it to their advantage. The signs behind her all turned to face the camera. These signs were accompanied by the yelling of slogans that represented each person's particular hardships.

"Freedom is not free!"

"Unionize the banks!"

"Vote for gold!"

There was no laughter in these people's hearts; no joy on their faces. They were scared.

The crowd was reaching the point where its size trumped the ability of the police to contain it. For now, the people knew where that imaginary line was that kept the police at bay, however, that didn't stop them from inching ever closer to it.

The reporter concluded, "There is no telling when this crowd will disperse. Their energy is growing and so is the power of their message, even though there's no consensus on what that message is. Live outside Westminster, Lindsay Bothwell, BNN News."

"This is it," declared a defiant Aasir Abdulah Kabul. He and his most loyal followers stood in an office witnessing the events at Westminster. His deep, powerful voice rumbled in the room. "This is the time we've been waiting for. Weak leadership, a struggling economy, people out of work, hungry, angry." Nodding his head, a sinister grin blended with an already intense stare. "It is time. We now prepare."

Kabul nostalgically peered at his subordinates who had all been to Hell and back, together. Their chance to avenge The Cause was finally at hand. That realization was a testament to their storied past and infamous future. The journey they were about to embark upon would undoubtedly be their last. With a means to an end within reach, the reason they had survived when few others did not had become clear—they were the chosen ones.

Kabul was a man his people trusted unconditionally. They believed in him and put their faith in his resolve. He'd singlehandedly resurrected the Front for the Liberation of the Enclave of Cabina and nurtured it into a viable and powerful entity. When oil was discovered on their land in Western Angola, he led his people out of the slums. The seemingly endless cycle of poverty and destitution finally began to reverse itself. Access to quality education was suddenly possible. Vaccines for simple illnesses flowed abundantly. Small communities dotted with respectable houses replaced infested ghettos. Kabul was able to broker a peace with the Angolan government setting suitable tax rates and mandates that equally benefited both parties. The Cabina region's spirits and hopes for a better future were higher than they had ever been. Those spirits translated into productivity and a better life, but it also created a wide wealth gap with the nation's other citizens.

It didn't take long for the tenuous peace between the FLEC and the Angolan government to waver. The hundreds of millions of dollars the FLEC acquired from the oil reserves were put to good use developing infrastructure and brokering global trade contracts. Meanwhile, the Angolan's government profits were squandered via corruption—the same *policies* that had kept many African nations perpetually poor. Skirmishes between the rich Angolans and the rest of nation's poor arose. Calls for greater Cabina autonomy rang loudly.

At that time in world history, calls for regional nationalization, within existing states, reverberated globally. The fall of America inspired other successful regions to declare independence.

Every government dealt with these changes differently, but they all had the same goal: maintain power over the prosperous.

The FLEC struggled for more autonomy, but with only a fraction of the nation's population, they were outnumbered.

The irregular skirmishes between the classes soon became daily occurrences as the state's poorer residents sought refuge in Cabina. The exchange of words quickly escalated into an exchange of fists; then bottles; then bullets. The country was on the brink of civil war when the FLEC defiantly defended the way of life it had worked so hard to create.

Despite the situation, Kabul believed an all-out war could be avoided. Then the British government secretly stepped in and convinced Kabul that with their help, a decisive military victory was attainable. Kabul brokered a deal: in exchange for clandestine assistance in the civil war, they would guarantee future oil exploration rights to the Crown.

"We want to be free," Kabul would tell the British ambassadors. "And I do fear this is the only way."

The nation fell into a terrible civil war.

Eighteen months into the fighting and it was obvious they had underestimated the preparedness of the Angolan government. In fact, it was apparent the FLEC would eventually lose. The state simply had too many willing bodies to sacrifice. The countryside was littered with millions of Angola's sons and daughters that lay in various stages of decomposition. The air reeked of rotting flesh. The nation's greatest rivers ran red with the blood of its people.

Kabul attempted to broker a deal with the Angolan government, but in the middle of negotiations, the British government pulled their support. Kabul could no longer supply his armies. His ability to arbitrate a peace crumbled with his capacity to maintain a resistance. As a result, hundreds of thousands of men, women, and children were massacred in their own homes, schools, and businesses. The international community stood by as the Angolan government extracted revenge on the defenseless FLEC. Once the government captured the oil fields, the war was over.

In a scene resembling the fall of Saigon, the FLEC frantically tried to escape their capital as the government closed in from all directions. If they could get out before the military arrived, they could escape into the hills and blend in with the commoners. If not, they would be killed. As leader of the resistance movement, Kabul was a wanted man. The Angolan government purposely refused to declare victory in the war until he was captured, dead or alive. This delay also allowed them to further crush the resistance and keep the international peacekeepers at bay. For days helicopter loads of refugees, mostly high ranking officials in the FLEC, fled the nation and sought exile. The final helicopter out of the capital carried Kabul and a few of his closest and most loyal followers. Their families had lifted off minutes prior. His final act as head of the FLEC was to broker one last deal with the British government. In exchange for his silence concerning the Crown's involvement, he would be allowed to live as a protected man in the UK. That decision, to leave his homeland, was his most painful. He vowed to his people he would defend the motherland until his own blood nourished its fields. He broke his promise. He would never forgive himself.

As his helicopter took off, he watched below his people valiantly fighting to the end. Though he had to abandon them in favor of protecting his own family, it was obvious by their unwillingness to surrender that his followers had not abandoned him. The guilt was all-consuming.

When there was no one left to carry on the resistance, the Angolan government declared victory. The international community converged on the country to offer support. It was assumed Kabul had perished somewhere in the killing fields.

Their war was now over. But a new battle emerged—one with a different objective and target. This time around, he would learn from his mistake. He would be more patient. He would be more opportunistic. He would follow his better judgment. He would wait for the right time to strike his new enemy. The enemy he blamed for the guilt that kept him awake every night; the enemy he blamed for the heinous scene involving his family seconds after takeoff that remained etched into his psyche; the enemy that promised their support only to strip it away when it mattered most; the enemy that was now vulnerable.

*

"Get down there, NOW!" Chris Nash yelled to one of his reporters. He rose abruptly from his desk, pointing towards the door. "GO!"

The young reporter strode out the door, halfheartedly calling for his photographer.

"He better not miss this story." Nash, cheeks flushed red, turned to his assistant. "The biggest protest in years and he is worried about— UGH!" With his arms hanging freely at his side and shoulders lurched forward he flung his head back, staring at the tiled ceiling.

"Sir?" One of his producers poked her head into his office. "You have a call."

"Who is it?"

"I don't know. He said it's important."

Nash flopped back into his ratty leather chair. "Send it in."

The phone rang.

"Chris Nash here."

"Mr. Nash." The newsman sat up. A chill ran through his erect spine. The man didn't even wait for Nash to reply. "Do you still have the literature I provided you back in April?"

Nash was careful with his words. "I do." He waved for his assistant to close the door on his way out.

"Why haven't I seen it reported?"

"This is not the type of information you just publish," Nash said honestly.

"The outgoing Prime Minster didn't help you, and the current one has no idea, does he?"

Nash was stunned by his accuracy. *Who is this guy?*

"What if I help you prove it?" The man knew if a respected journalist, such as Nash, published this material, the public would lend it viability. "Will you run it?"

"Why do you want this material to get out so badly?"

"Our people have the right to know what their government has done, the man snapped back. "If you do not want to break this story, I will find someone who will."

Nash was in no position to call his bluff. Plus, he would not miss this opportunity, even if it meant damaging the country he loved. Most journalists believed their right to inform trumped any greater good.

"What do you say, Mr. Nash?"

Nash tried to slow his racing heart. "Where do we start?"

*

With great social unrest comes the need for greater education, John Nolan thought as he approached the door to his Society and Power class on the afternoon of the protest. He crossed the threshold of the room, hiding behind a colossal cardboard box bursting its contents. His legs wobbling and spine arched backwards, he desperately tried to balance the weight of the box with his rapidly failing sternum. The students leaned out of the way, praying the box wouldn't burst as he waddled past. He eventually reached the front of the room. With a grunt, he hoisted the mammoth square on the metal desk. He emerged from behind the hulking box to find that, to his surprise, the class was full.

He was shocked at the day's attendance. "It is nice to see you guys chose to come here rather than participate in the protest. I figured I was killing myself getting this here for nothing." He patted the box. Its sides were stretched to their final threads.

"It is not safe down there," one of the girls in the front row said earnestly. "It is actually getting pretty bad."

The others wholeheartedly agreed. John could sense they were greatly troubled by what the nation had become.

"I went for a while," admitted one of his male students. "But I got the feeling something bad was going to happen." He appeared a bit frightened.

John looked at his students and proudly nodded. "Then you made the right choice."

Content, Professor Nolan dropped his focus to his desk to arrange the day's materials. "Okay."

He turned his attention to the very colossus that caused every muscle in his narrow body to ache. Brandishing a small cutting device from his pocket, he intently studied the box in search of its most vulnerable point. The flaps on the top and bottom had been secured with a thick layer of clear packing tape.

The following showdown of man vs. box served to provide the class with some much needed levity. The box won the first few rounds, but man eventually got the better of it.

"Class," a winded Professor Nolan proclaimed as if he had just slain the dragon and saved the village, "this is a proud day for me." He finished tearing at the top until all four flaps hung wide open.

From the box he brandished a hardcover book that was obviously new but looked almost ancient. The coloring appeared a faded-manuscript yellow, as though it had been aged for centuries in some dark cellar. Fractures that looked to have developed in the same fashion wove their way around its facade like a spidering crack in a windshield. Old English cursive writing in varying fonts and sizes spread out horizontally on both sides.

A copy of the Magna Carta? thought the students at first.

A closer inspection of the cover art spelled it out. Bold letters that appeared impressed into the manuscript itself read: *Constitutional Correctness*. Inscribed in the same crude fashion as the title, the bottom right corner revealed the author, John Nolan.

"Class." The professor held the book above his head as if it were the head of the dragon. "I am pleased to present you with the initial copies of my first published book."

"This is a big deal for me," John announced. "How about some applause?"

Seeking refuge from the day's turmoil in his jocularity, John's students began to applaud enthusiastically. As if their energy were a rejuvenating fuel, their teacher's weary body sprang to life. He plunged into the box, grabbing an armful of books to pass out.

"This is a book I wrote when I was a graduate student at Cambridge." He handed them out as he walked down the aisles. "I was obsessed with this paper." The students eagerly accepted his offering.

"Throughout the next few weeks, we will read this book, analyze it, and augment it with class discussions. I want you guys to understand past power structures and their current relevance. All of the research in this book culminates with me drafting a Constitution, which we will read and analyze."

He stopped for a second to assure the class. "I will *never*," he greatly emphasized the word, "judge you on how you judge my work." He now stood in front of the class. "It is the greatest achievement of my life, but that does not mean it's perfect. I welcome any suggestions or constructive criticism. And there is one more thing. This is not ideological. This book is a direct result of research. Some of these measures I don't even necessarily agree with. But, it's not about what we feel, it's about what has proven to work. And what has proven to fail." He looked down at his notes and arranged them in the proper order. "Now let's continue with today's lesson."

For the rest of the class period, Professor Nolan and his students discussed and analyzed the prior night's readings, forgetting largely about the deteriorating situation not far away.

For 90 minutes they weren't Brits. They weren't the sons and daughters of the unemployed or the hungry. They weren't young people who soon would be forced to make critical decisions about the future of a nation they barely knew. They were just freshman and sophomore students who wished to enlighten themselves on a path towards something better.

After class, Professor Nolan sat at his desk next to the cardboard box, writing down notes for the following day.

"Professor?" a young woman said, approaching him.

John looked up and gave her a welcoming smile.

She held out his book. "Can you sign it for me?"

John was slightly taken aback, but very proud. "I would be honored." Little did she know how much her simple request meant.

He wrote:

"TO KELLY, MY FIRST EVER SIGNING. THANK YOU FOR APPRECIATING MY WORK - JOHN NOLAN."

*

It would be one week before the Westminster protests dwindled down. The angry masses had made their voices heard, but they wouldn't give their elected officials much time to act.

To the credit of those who demonstrated, the week was generally non-violent.

The streets around Westminster calmed as winter approached. The roads and back alleys that split the city were quiet as the recession hit urban areas the hardest. The proof was left in the boarded-up windows.

Vacancy.

For Rent.

Closed.

What little commerce remained struggled to hang on. Despite the protests ending, a lonely few refused to abandon the cause. They sat quietly on the sidewalk outside of Westminster, unshaven and unshowered, in torn, raggedy clothing. Their signs from the prior week were propped up on the fence behind them. Occasionally a pedestrian would stroll by, most barely acknowledging their "sacrifice." Every half day, a fresh batch of like-minded persons would relieve the old. They hoped *their* action would encourage more official action. In reality, however, they achieved little more than filling a void in their own lives, a desire to matter.

While the incessant protesters favored the passive approach, others were more proactive in fulfilling their ambitions for the country.

"Does everybody have their assignment?" roared Aasir Abdulah Kabul. He stood tall in a pressed, dark blue, pinstriped suit, perched on a chair casting a broad shadow over his followers. They had gathered in his waiting room decorated with original abstract artwork, stained oak furniture, and imported Indian rugs—a peculiar location in which to rally the troops for a revolution.

"This is your last chance to back out," he warned. "Neither I, nor anyone else in this room will look down upon you if you choose not to participate."

He stood before his people feeding off their energy. Kabul had an uncanny ability to read emotion and the text of his men's demeanor was clear.

"Men," he began in a mellow, yet potent tone. "Understand, this government will hunt us down." The mellowness in his voice faded as a deep-rooted contempt emerged. "You must be prepared to give your life. I am willing to avenge our fallen countrymen. Are you?"

His men erupted in thunderous agreement.

Kabul looked down at the stack of papers he clutched in his right hand. Dozens more stacks lay waiting on a table in the back. When the roar tapered off, he continued, his inflection turning dulcet. "My friends, there has never been a better time. This country is on edge. And this," he held the stack of papers high in the air as if it were a trophy, "will send them over it."

His men's guttural response lasted one-second and sounded more like a deep-throated grunt. The echo was quickly swallowed by the room.

"Men!" Both his arms were now elevated high above his head in preeminent victory. "The protests are over. The headlines will be ours."

Their joy, this time, was more prolonged and exuberant.

"Once the world knows what this nation has done in secrecy, our mission will be complete."

Following his last word of motivation, Kabul and his men solemnly made their way towards an adjacent suite via the back of the office. Their holy room was painted in a brilliant white. The opaque, single-stained windows shielded the lavish prayer rugs that graved the hardwood floors from outsiders.

Kabul and his men removed their shoes, neatly placing them next to the threshold before entering single file. The first man walked to the upper right-hand corner of the room and stood erect with his head down, arms loosely hanging by his side and feet evenly spaced at shoulder width. He stood motionless as the rest of the men lined up next to and behind him. Soon all twelve men had entered and assumed a similar position.

Without warning or command, as if summoned by a higher power, they simultaneously placed their hands to the sides of their heads, palms forward, thumbs behind the ears.

"God is great," they harmonized in a low, melodic tonality.

With eyes shut and chins ever so slightly elevated, they placed their right hands over their left, below the navel and chanted, "Glory to you, O' Allah, yours in the praise. I seek refuge in, Allah from Satan. God is great. Holy is my lord the magnificent." They followed this with a prolonged bow of silence.

They placed their hands on their knees and lowered their bodies to kneeling positions. A forward bend, ending with their palms supporting the delicate union of their foreheads and the sacred matting, symbolized their devotion.

They rose to sitting positions with their eyes now fixed on their laps. Turning up the heels of their right feet with bent toes, they recited the following prayer in perfect unison, possibly for the final time: "O' Allah! Our Sovereign Lord, grant us good in this world and the world hereafter and protect us from the torment of Hell. O' Allah! We implore You for help and beg forgiveness of You and believe in You and rely on You and extol You and we are thankful to You and are not ungrateful to You and we alienate and forsake him who disobeys You. O' Allah! You alone do we worship and for You do we pray and prostrate and we betake to please You and present ourselves for the service in Your cause and we hope for Your mercy and fear Your chastisement. Undoubtedly, Your torment is going to overtake infidels."

Moments later, the door shut behind them as they embarked on their mission. The room they left behind was unchanged but for the exception of the thousands of papers stacked high on the tables, had vanished. The literature and illustrations would circulate around London, and then the globe.

It has always been said that one must be proactive to achieve the unachievable. The problem is that when the unachievable is achieved, so are the unintended consequences, which may never have been considered, or even worse, blindly ignored.

*

Kabul's plan worked perfectly. Word spread among the discontent citizenry with a bent fury.

Kabul and his men entered stores, movie theaters, bus stations, food markets, sporting events, shopping malls, schools and universities, handing out the pamphlets. A few of the men walked around London distributing the incendiary literature, complete with corroborating illustrations, to anyone willing to accept it. A few more spread the message digitally. Minutes after being dispersed, one of the documents found its way to the cluttered desk of Chris Nash.

A young reporter charged into the newsroom with an imminence rarely seen even in the media.

"Excuse me!" He dashed through the cubical laden office, the air in his wake lifting papers off desks. "I am so sorry. Excuse me." He swiftly snaked through a group of producers conferencing around an empty space. Onlookers wondered what could be so important.

"Sir!" He urgently rushed into Nash's office unannounced and out of breath. "You have to see this."

Winded, yet energized, he darted to his boss's desk, handing him the document.

Nash's eyes swelled a bright white. "Where did you get this?"

"These guys are handing them out on the streets. It's all over the internet."

Nash hastily swung his chair around and ripped up the blinds that shielded the office from the bright morning sun. His eyes took a second to adjust to the vivid light.

As his vision cleared, the image of people suspending their daily routines to process the claims came into focus. Although he was elevated a few stories above them, the litany of reactions were unmistakable: surprise, wonderment, intrigue, anger, and fear.

Under the intense spell surrounding his own emotions, his abashed heart decelerated. Nash sulked back into his chair appearing physically drained. He gradually lowered the blinds, again shielding himself from the outside world.

I can't believe this is happening.

He could literally feel his aspirations for media immortality vanish.

In the few seconds that passed, everyone realized what had possessed the reporter to sprint through the newsroom. By the time the mentally defeated Nash rotated his chair around to his desk, his office was filled with eager journalists, editors, photographers and producers.

What are our orders?

Oddly, Nash, who lived for breaking news, was somber and subdued and his staff wondered what was wrong. They waited for their commands, dumbfounded by his apathy. Their confusion rang loudly in their blank or befuddled expressions. You could feel the excitement drain from the room.

Nash appeared a broken man. The look of defeat encapsulated his being. After a short while he mustered the strength to speak, albeit lethargically.

"Get some reporters outside to get reaction as people read it. Somebody get a hold of the prime minister's office. We need reaction."

His staff wasn't quite sure how to respond. They knew this situation was urgent, and they needed information fast. But the mental state of their leader somehow seemed more important.

Nash continued, following a doleful sigh. "And find the people who are this passing out. We need sound from them."

Springing to action, his assistant Ryan Loben took command. "Go! Go! This is the biggest story of the year! We need sound! We need information! I want the prime minister himself!"

With the room now empty, Ryan turned to Nash, who remained in a pitiful state.

"Sir?" he said carefully.

"Put this on the Internet immediately. I need some time, Ryan," Nash said dolefully. "Please."

The assistant took a few steps towards his desk. "Sir, don't we want to verify this first?

Nash opened his top desk drawer and pulled out an innocuous-looking brown folder. "I got this a few months ago," he explained. "I've been working with the man who gave it to me. And yes, it's true. I wanted to wait until we proved it all before releasing it—we were so close."

Nash opened the folder to reveal what looked like a pamphlet, which he unfolded and handed to his assistant. Instinctively, Ryan compared the document to the one he already possessed. It was a perfect match.

"I waited and waited, trying to be as thorough as possible. I thought a lot about the implications. Apparently someone else already made that decision. All that work. I've lost it all." He paused. "Run it now. At least we can be the first to confirm its authenticity."

His assistant fully understood his boss's mood. Chris Nash had blown his chance.

"This will do great harm to our country," Ryan said, hesitant to follow the order. He lowered his voice to a near whisper, "But our job is to report the news. Our emotions cannot get in the way."

"You're right." Nash's apathy morphed into a sudden burst of cynicism. "It's no coincidence this information was released now, at a time when the nation is at its weakest. This was calculated. We need to find out why."

*

"What the hell is this?" demanded an enraged prime minister, throwing the pamphlet on his desk. Those who filled the room remained silent. In his short time in office, the PM proved to lack the leadership skills of his predecessor. But what he lacked in confidence and ability, he made up for with a powerful physical presence and masterful oratory skills, both of which he skillfully utilized to usher himself and his party into power.

"Mr. Prime Minister," the icy female voice emanated from the speaker phone on his desk. "You have a guest, sir."

The PM leaned in to press "talk." "Not right now, Deloris. This is *not* a good time."

"He said it's urgent."

"About what?"

"The information released today."

The prime minister leaned towards the speaker, his imagination running wild with speculation. "Send him in."

"Why not? *This* isn't getting us anywhere," he uttered under his breath, yet loud enough for his administration to hear.

Moments later, the door to the PM's office eased open. In walked a leather-faced, middle-aged, dark-haired man dressed in a black pinstripe suit. His white shirt and solid blue tie perfectly complemented his pressed outfit. His hair, parted off to the right, and brilliantly patent leather shoes made him a distinct presence that demanded respect. He carried himself with great authority, pride and confidence. Yet his eyes told the story of a different man.

"Can I help you?" asked the prime minister.

"I need to talk to you, alone."

In all the excitement, the PM hadn't even thought to ask his secretary how he had gotten into the building. However, the seriousness of the man's demeanor convinced him. He waved for his cabinet to exit.

"Please take a seat."

While the prime minister reclined back, crossing his legs at the knees, his counterpart sat with a rigid back and feet flat on the floor.

"Well," the PM inquired somewhat haughtily. "Do you have a name?"

"I prefer to be addressed by my title...Major General. I work for the Bushtell Counter Intelligence Division of MI-6."

The PM tried to ignore the man's cold and abrupt delivery. "I've never heard of that department."

"I know."

The PM was quite skeptical, yet intrigued. This was obviously not someone who just walked in off the street. "How did you get into this building?"

"I am here to help you."

"Are you?" The PM's pronounced arrogance was typical of his weak character. As the nation's highest ranking public official, and subsequently most powerful person, he believed there wasn't much he didn't already know.

The man looked down at the pamphlet that the PM had carelessly thrown on his desk. "That information, I know where it came from."

The PM sat relatively unstirred with a smug look.

"It comes from a former officer of mine," the man said, his tone remaining void of emotion—though that fact must have troubled him. "At the end of his career, he defected and created this pamphlet using the information he had acquired throughout his years at the agency. It somehow got into the wrong hands and now we have a problem."

The prime minister was now leaning intently forward with his elbows perched on his desk and his stately frame resting on the last few inches of the chair.

"My men and I specialize in the preservation of the Crown. Our involvement goes undetected. But I assure you, our impact is immense. Without us, Mr. Prime Minister, Great Britain and the world is a very different place, and not for the better, I assure you."

"Why have I not heard of you until now?"

"There was no reason for you to know of us."

"I'm the prime minister..."

"Which means nothing," the man said unapologetically. "There have been many men in your position whose paths we've never crossed. We only invite people into our world when it is necessary."

The PM's cavalier perception of his own power and influence had suddenly fallen into question.

"So this is accurate?" the PM asked, looking at the pamphlet.

"The truth is irrelevant. All that matters is what the public believes."

"Did my predecessor know of this?"

"We had great trust in him."

"And me?" the PM inquired.

"Right now," said the major general, "I don't have a choice."

*

The greatest fears of many and dreams of others had come to fruition. The pamphlet and its contents spread around the globe in a matter of hours. By nightfall it went from the streets of London to nearly everyone in the world. It was accompanied by little media skepticism, thanks to Chris Nash's signature of authenticity.

The nations of the world took to the news unkindly. After all, the true agenda of many of their allies had been exposed. What the former members of the FLEC failed to realize in their selfish pursuit of revenge was in order to out the British government, the actions of other nations must also be unmasked. This would inevitably turn allies against one another and strengthen the animosity between existing enemies.

With modern technology, the PM and the major general had little time to prepare before the barrage of phone calls. Their attempts to divert attention with oblique rhetoric would fail. The evidence against them was overwhelming. The history, too deep. Still, they had to try.

The prime minister spent the entire night on the phone attempting to heal the wounds with heads of state from every continent:

"Please reconsider."

"Allow us to explain."

"We have been allies for decades. Don't walk away."

"This had nothing to do with my administration."

"If you feel it is best."

"Give it some time. I am sure we can work through it."

"We don't know who released that information."

"Anyone could have put that together."

"Who knows what is true, someone with a grudge did this."

"Do you really want to end our relationship this way?"

"We've been friends for so long."

"Your constituents are upset? Ours are as well."

"So, this is how it ends?"

"It pains me it got to this point."

"Good day to you, sir."

"Hopefully, we can settle our differences."

"Our alliance will one day be strong."

"I promise we will again earn your trust."

"You have my word, we will find out who did this."

"Please calm down."

"Those responsible will renounce these blatant lies."

"Yes, it disgusted me as well."

"There is no need to raise your voice."

"Great Britain looks forward to continuing the relationship between our two great countries."

"Europe must unite and look past this nonsense."

"How can allies exist without trust? I assure you it is all lies."

The useless platitudes went on for hours.

For the PM, the task was exhausting. And tomorrow, the start of a new week wouldn't get any better.

When the stock markets opened Monday, the dire financial situation in the United Kingdom developed into a worldwide crisis. One could all but hear the sucking sound as victimized nations (which at one point was most all of them) pulled their money out of oppressor countries (which at one point was also most all of them) sending the global market into an uncontrolled tailspin. Mutual funds, money market accounts, retirements collapsed under the strain of the sell-off.

Jingoism kicked in as nations protected their own assets by selling off foreign-held securities and investing at home. No one knew how to react or how any action would affect global or national economies. They just knew they had to protect their own companies that had lost massive amounts of capital when foreign shareholders bailed. If they didn't, they risked a national uprising, or at best, a crippling depression.

When the initial panic subsided, the market freefall began to stabilize. Now, the attention of the world could focus on the one country that would be blamed for it all. That nation and its people would have a whole new list of challenges, and the concerns of its former allies and newfound adversaries would be a distant thought.

CHAPTER EIGHT
ASCENSION

Professor Nolan's students shuffled into class as they always did—silent and still drowsy from the early rise. As first-year students, the once-convenient notion of early classes was a mistake none would make again.

Professor Nolan, on the other hand, was wide awake and in great spirits. He strode to the front of the room, placing his briefcase on the empty metal desk. "Good morning!" Gazing out over the sea of dark circles and coffee cups, he jubilantly asked, "Comments?"

The young red-haired, freckle-faced lady in the front row appeared less tired than her peers. "It's complicated," she said.

"We'll work through it," John said, knowing the material was not simple to digest.

Another girl chimed in, "I like how no *one* person has much power."

The first male student opined, "It spreads out the risk."

"There's a fundamental flaw in humans," Professor Nolan said frankly. "We crave power. Those who crave it most must be kept in check. Civilization is most efficient when authority is shared, and public officials can focus on an area of expertise. Hence, three departments with their own elections. Local and federal governments must be strong, yet limited in their strength. In my government," he gestured toward a copy of *Constitutional Correctness* on a nearby desk, "no one person, no one group of people will have significant influence in the nation's direction. It will move as one."

"It's also important to spread out election turnover. Voters tend to follow momentum and make hasty decisions. With only a third of the government up for election every two years, change will be gradual, and less susceptible to fads."

John jolted himself up from the desk onto his feet. "Come on. What do you think? As citizens, you need to think on this level. These are the issues that control your lives."

"Voting," a blond, rugged-looking boy with a protruding jaw blurted out. "Why can't everyone vote?"

"Everyone *can* vote," the professor emphasized. "It just requires more than an age and a pulse. Voters must hold the well-being of the nation above themselves. *My* voters will have invested in the nation, since they spend two years in service to it. People who have nothing will often vote for those who promise them something. That system will fail."

"Redistribution," the boy blurted out.

John could see the student's energy levels rise. "It gets politicians elected," John said. "However, once it starts, it never ends. At first in America, only those who owned land could vote. The nation's founders knew that people who did not own property would vote for the candidate who would give them someone else's. And their Constitution did not limit the largesse of politicians." He paused allowing the accuracy of his words to sink in.

The silence was soon broken.

"Why no political parties?" the brown-haired girl asked, looking somewhat disgusted.

"Political parties are allowed," John responded politely, sensing her disagreement. "Politicians just can't be affiliated with one. This eliminates voting blocks and forces people to educate themselves about the candidates. Most importantly, politics are limited when there are no parties to politic for."

"Everyone in federal office has term limits?" The question came from the far back corner.

"Everyone." For John this was a vital provision. "Many politicians will do what is necessary to get re-elected, regardless of future consequences beyond their years. Term limits force them to focus on the *present*. Plus, the longer someone is in office the more they consolidate authority, and voting blocks. That is never good."

As the conversation dove deeper into John's ideas, the students searched for grievances.

"What's this about parental rights?" asked a student reading from the passage marked by his finger.

"Parenthood is the basis of human rights," John stated ardently. "Parents must be able to raise their children in their image, within the law. That law will be determined by the courts' interpretation of statute. Parents also have the right to information about their children."

"I like that human rights are consistent no matter your status in society," said a young Asian student who likely had contradictory experiences.

"Thank you," nodded John.

"This isn't actually in the Constitution, but...you talk about cooperative federalism. Can you explain that?" asked one of the older students on the window-side of the room.

"Let's take the old United States of America for example again," John said. "It's the most recent example of what can go wrong. The U.S. started as a dual federalist system where the federal and state governments remained separate, focusing on their own duties in the Constitution. With the civil war and Great Depression, the discrepancies that system created among the states became a problem, and a cooperative federal system developed where the federal government set standards and helped the states achieve them. That system worked well. It brought the states on a level playing field. But the federal government wanted more. The system evolved into new federalism, where Washington acquired as much authority as possible. If the states didn't cooperate, they were punished with fewer federal dollars, creating major problems."

John massaged his chin. "There must be a consistent balance between all levels of government and the people. That is why my

Constitution has strict mandates. Civilizations with a weak central government fall apart because the people lose their identity. Civilizations with too much central government fail because they become oppressed."

The professor could see the students' thoughts turning.

"Things will always go wrong. It is how a nation responds that determines the outcome. If the result is government-based, politicians prefer short-term fixes to keep them popular. If the result is people-based, the fix may be slower, but it will be longer lasting because that is *their* concern. Of course, the latter isn't good for the politicians, who can't benefit. However, it's best for the health of the state."

"What about *now*?" the freckled girl asked, referring to the current plight of Great Britain.

"Great question," John said, pleased it had come up. "Last year, when the economy slowed, it felt comforting to hear someone with new ideas say they would save us. But we didn't need to be saved. We just needed to work our way out of it. Sure, if laws need to change to prevent it from happening again, that should be debated in the legislature. But the government cannot cure a recession any more than it can create prosperity. That can only be done by the people working hard."

"I feel so helpless," one girl said.

"*That* is what politicians count on. Listen, no matter what happens in the near future, the people always create their own destiny. So why not start with a government that fosters that outcome, rather than one that reaches it through less favorable means?"

"How will this end, Professor? What will happen?"

"It will end the way we want it to," John said confidently. "The one thing I know is a nation must have a strong economy first. When the economy struggles so does everything else: military, infrastructure, education, social programs. Then the country becomes vulnerable. The only way to maintain a strong economy is if people work. People must have incentive to work. But the state needs tax dollars to operate. I think I found that balance in this Constitution. Entitlements are the same, though there needs to be a balance. We have an obligation to take care of the less fortunate. However, dependency helps no one. Entitlements should only be for people *truly* in need. That's why I place a 15 percent limit on government involvement in GDP. It will limit what can be distributed after essential services are funded." He paused. "Shrewd politicians will use your money to control you."

"The right to bear arms?" The wheelchair-bound freshman's question was more of an affirmation.

"The government cannot protect you at all times," explained Professor Nolan. "Citizens must have the ability to protect their families. Security is vital to a lasting society. But those securities can be limited based on public safety, common sense, and responsibility. Society will determine the limits. Did you guys ever hear the phrase, *'With guns, we are citizens. Without, we are subjects'?*"

A few of his students nodded. Others looked confused.

"That doesn't necessarily mean that gun control *subjects* us to the brutality of tyrants—like Hitler, Stalin, Mussolini and Pol Pot, which all favored gun control." John knew this type of history was not taught in public schools. "It means we become more subjected to terrorists and criminals. Another piece of history that is often forgotten is that the Japanese didn't invade America after the bombing of Pearl Harbor because General Yamamoto, their Naval Marshal, went to Harvard University. He knew many Americans had guns. How do you conquer a nation when every citizen is essentially part of the army?"

"Judicial review?" asked an Indian girl in the front row.

"The more checks on power the better."

"No progressive taxes?" The portly, red-cheeked sophomore didn't even seem to know what that meant.

John handled this topic gently. It was always a touchy subject with the capability to ignite a discussion on class welfare. "All citizens must be treated the same, regardless of sex, race, gender, religion, or income."

"But why do people have to pay the government for every tax? That seems time-consuming."

"Only with direct taxes, but a great question." John was pleased with their concern for what most people their age found meaningless. "First off, a direct tax is one that is levied directly to the person such as income tax or property tax. There are also indirect taxes that are levied on commodities, like sales tax." The professor stopped to think. "Everyone must know how much they are paying in taxes. It will keep the system honest. When money is taken out of someone's wages automatically, the impact is not the same."

"Back to taxes," another student added. "The government cannot take more than 25 percent of a worker's income?"

"That is the balance I talked about earlier. Twenty-five percent makes sense. Of course, local municipalities will have their own taxes, but this provision gives the people some protections."

"What's a line-item veto?" asked a student in the front.

"That allows the Department Secretaries to nullify specific provisions of a bill without having to veto the entire bill. It makes for stronger legislation. But any veto can still be overruled by the representatives in the departments."

John was shocked. *Questions about a line-item veto?* While vitally important to a nation's health, such issues were oftentimes disregarded, especially by youth.

"The federal government does not have that many responsibilities," he clarified as his students hurriedly paged through *Constitutional Correctness* looking for more topics. "Chiefly, it is only there to protect the citizens from foreign and domestic threats, maintain order, uphold individual rights, and make and pass laws to protect the people."

"I like the right-to-life clause." The African exchange student came from a nation where the slightest infraction could cost you your life.

"You're talking capital punishment, right?"

The student nodded.

"I don't think the government should ever take a life."

"What about abortion?"

"Is it in the Constitution?" the professor asked.

"I didn't see it."

"Then the individual municipalities should decide via referendum, unless an amendment is passed."

"The difference between rights and privileges is interesting." The statement came from a freshman, who only wore jeans and a short, gray pullover.

"There's a big difference. They had to be defined."

One of the most important questions came much later than John anticipated. "What do you think the role of the media is?" asked another student. "You gave them special rights."

"The media is a crucial part of any democracy. It serves as a watchdog. Not an attack dog and not a lapdog, but a watchdog. You may have read that any media outlet cannot do business with the government. That is essential."

"You limit public sector unions?" the same student pressed.

"With government unions there is no one to effectively bargain on behalf of the taxpayer," John espoused. "Especially when the union funds the campaign of those writing the contracts."

"*Nor shall private property be taken for public use, or by the State in general, without just compensation,*" the student read directly from the book.

"Eminent Domain. Private property is the foundation of freedom."

"Why are you so concerned with debt?" asked another student. "You say debt can't climb above 50 percent of gross domestic product."

"Debt plays a large role in an economy; the value of currency and the ability to borrow, trade, and invest. The purpose of this document is to place specific limits on government to protect the people. This one is very important."

Professor Nolan returned to the chair behind his desk. "Just remember one thing as you review this document. There are two quotes I remembered as I wrote this book." He held up his own copy. "The first is by Thomas Jefferson. You guys know who that is, right?"

Most everyone nodded.

"Jefferson said, *'A government big enough to give you everything you want, is strong enough to take everything you have.'*" He paused, letting that sink in. "The other goes like this, *'Those who attempt to level, never equalize. They simply concentrate power in their own hands.'* Class, the lack of those two realizations triggered the downfall of a staggering number of civilizations."

*

"The first mass gathering was more of a protest," the reporter explained, standing nervously in front of the rowdy crowd. The pain in the eyes of those behind him manifested in wild screams and violent gestures. The cool, moist air was accented by the pungent odor of burnt wood and melted asphalt. As the morning fog lifted, it was soon replaced by a dark cloud of expanding smoke. "This one appears to have the signs of a riot."

It had been more than a month since the citizens of Great Britain took to the streets in protest. Since, Parliament had remained gridlocked. The majority feared further financial collapse and looked to compromise and therefore spread the blame. The minority parties refused to negotiate, however, hoping the discontent would force new elections sweeping them to power.

The reporter continued. "This demonstration is not only larger than September's, the tone is different." The cameraman swung off the reporter to scan the angry crowd. "As you can see, there are no signs, no chants." He paused. "There are also no children."

Reality was not important to the elected officials. The millions who lost their jobs, hundreds of thousands who lost their homes, and tens of thousands who were hungry only served as potential voters. Culpability was vital.

"There's a lot of negative energy." The camera panned back to the wide-eyed journalist who began to edge his way through the crowd. "And for some people, this protest never ended as the economy continued its slide." The reporter bounced around between the protesters. The crowd was much more forgiving for the cameraman.

"Zander," asked the anchor from the desk, seeing the reporter struggle to negotiate a path. He pressed in his ear piece, shielding the noise. "What are people saying?"

"Well, Leah, it seems these people want Westminster and the world to know who's in control." He pressed deeper into the crowd.

"Are there police?"

"Yes. But they were late to arrive."

"What about—"

"As I mentioned, for some, the protest never ended." He emerged into a small circular opening. A group of five unkempt vagabonds sat blank-faced on the edge of the sidewalk in front of the entrance gates.

"These people have been here since the beginning."

It looked like they hadn't showered, shaved, or changed their raggedy clothes since.

The reporter lowered a knee to the curb to a single man. "Why have you remained for so long?" he asked loudly.

The shaggy, bearded man dressed in old gray and black clothes looked up. His eyes appeared soulless. "For our country," he said, his voice uninspired.

The reporter held the microphone firmly, waiting for him to elaborate.

"We realized," he continued, "this nation was being misguided. We can't simply be content to voice our opinions. We must demand more." His intense rhetoric failed to match his vapid delivery.

The camera panned to his right to the others in his party. At the end of that line sat a thin man dressed in ripped jeans. His long, curly brown hair was pulled back in a ponytail. He no longer wore a bright yellow shirt. It had been replaced with another that simply read, "Join the Resistance."

The reporter stood up to hold the microphone at his center. "And Leah," the reporter motioned towards the crowd, "many here also told me it was that mysterious pamphlet that convinced them to come here. Reporting live, outside Westminster, Zander Woods, BNN News."

"Zander," asked the anchor from the studio, "before you go, how many people are there?"

"It's hard to tell. It's a good number."

"Thank you, Zander." The anchor turned to another camera. "Now we're going to speak with a riot-control expert as we continue to show you these amazing pictures from Westminster."

"My God," stated a disbelieving Theodore. He and his family watched the coverage from their quiet home. "How did this happen?"

His question required no response.

"Hey!" John lunged forward on the couch pointing at the television. "Did you see that?"

"See what?" His sister looked at him strangely. All she saw was a sea of people accompanied by the dull drone of a helicopter.

"I saw... something."

The image soon reappeared.

"There!" John yelled. "Look!"

Off to the right stood a man unfamiliar to the Nolans. He was taller than most in the crowd and a little heavyset. He was jumping up and down. His blond hair was cut short, and his thick glasses bounced in sync with his movements. Despite the chilly temperatures, he wore only jeans and an orange t-shirt, which displayed unremarkable lettering. The crowd was too large to hear his words. Yet, it wasn't his appearance or actions that caught John's eye. It was the object in his left hand, raised high above his head.

It appeared small on the shaky screen. The Nolans couldn't make out the illustrations or lettering. But, they didn't have to. The color gave it away.

*

"We are not going out that easily! I've worked too damn hard!" asserted an enraged prime minister. He pounded his heavy fists upon the desk. The large window behind him vividly depicted the focus of his discontent. Somber and dispirited members of his own cabinet and party moped into the room. "We have only been in power for six months! What do they want?"

He slammed down onto his desk again, this time with open palms. He exploded to his feet. The violent thrust upwards sent his chair heaving backwards. The PM leaned forward towards a diminishing number of advisers. Purple veins in his neck pulsated rapidly, fueling the blood that colored his face a bright red. "These people voted for us." He turned sideways, pointing out the window. "They voted for us!" he cried.

"Sir," said one of his advisers, "we have to call for elections."

Exhausted by his repeated outbursts, the PM's temper subsided. However, his imposing body remained perched on his arms. He spoke slowly, emphasizing every word. "*We* will not."

The men and women who filled the room had no faith in his leadership. Their depressed body language spoke louder than their silent stares of hopelessness.

The PM jabbed at his own chest with stiffened fingers. "If we call for elections and admit our defeat, our party is finished. I cannot allow that."

"But sir," said the same adviser, "the country is failing."

All the eyes in the room focused on the PM.

"There will be no vote," he stated.

*

On the other side of the fence outside the PM's window, police deployed in a hasty march. Adorned in full riot gear and armed with rifles, they filed along the streets forming an intimidating wall of black and blue uniforms. To the demonstrators, the dispatch of law enforcement was seen as an oppressive measure, perpetrated by an incompetent government. As the parade of "peacekeepers" darkly outlined the crowded blocks surrounding Westminster, opportunism arose.

It began with verbal cries lobbied towards the officers.

"You can't stop us all!" A stark reality revealed in five words.

The desperate cries roared louder as the sun edged its way across the October sky. The demonstrators wore their anguish for the world to see: the white collar father who lost his job and couldn't pay his mortgage; the new mom who'd wisely left her baby boy at home, but held his uncertain future close to her heart; the lifelong mason who had no work and no real options; the secretary who, like her boss, had lost everything when the market collapsed. Each person had a unique story, but their grievances were similar. At this point, no one knew what to do. All they had was frustration and nervous anxiety.

The breadth of the crowd continued to swell as it approached noon. Off in the distance, helicopter blades signaled the next round of government action—military personnel to assist the outnumbered police. The sight of the heavily armed soldiers jumping out of low lying choppers was not well-received. Feelings of intimidation threatened the peace.

Some of the soldiers rushed to assist the riot police at the base of Westminster's pointed steel, reinforced brick wall. Others stayed on the outskirts in a vain attempt at containment. They sprinted into position as if time were precious, proceeding with a cautious reserve.

The clone-like soldiers seemed intent to not acknowledge the growing discomfort of the mob. With rifles drawn, the indignant nature of the demonstration turned to paranoia. The mob continued to swell in numbers, but it was kept from swelling in size. Some tried to expand farther down the streets, only to be forced back at the end of a gun barrel.

Hysteria turned to fear, and then to anger. Like the waves of a curtain flowing in a soft breeze, uncontrolled mass movements of bodies collided in brilliant displays of aerial grace. Blocks of irritable and resentful Brits violently slammed into one another. Everyone was at the mercy of the invisible hand that controlled the mob.

The multitudes were forced to rely on the strength of those around them as the wave arrived. Not an inch existed between people. One could smell the hot, panicked breath of their neighbors. The intense feeling of claustrophobia struck those who never knew they suffered from the illness. The weaker citizens fell to the cold pavement, never to rise under the weight of the legions. Witnesses were rendered helpless under concern for their own safety. Hundreds would perish before a single shot was ever fired.

"Get our people out of there, now!" proclaimed an unnerved Chris Nash, watching the frightful event unfold from his office. With his arms stiffly crossed and feet firmly planted on the floor he quietly murmured, "God save us."

One of his producers ran into his room, holding a phone tightly to her ear. "We can't get a hold of them, sir. It's too chaotic."

"Keep trying." A regrettable nervousness set in. "See if the helicopter can pick them up. They need to leave, now!" He wiped the sweat off his forehead with an open palm. "Figure it out!"

Tony Manning sat perched on his couch restlessly watching society deteriorate on live television.

"Thank God I got out of there."

His wife, who was far more relaxed, sat next to him holding their son. The boy squealed with delight as he bounced on his mother's knee.

What kind of country will he inherit? Tony thought to himself. He broke his stare of the television to lovingly observe what little bliss he had left—his family.

"What happens if this erupts?" Emma asked.

"I think you mean *when*."

Emma remained silent, while her question remained unanswered.

On the other side of the city, the major general closely observed the day's events by himself in a dark, windowless office. A single desk lamp partially illuminated his body and the meager contents of his desk. The rest of the room appeared and disappeared with the flicker of the screen. He sat reclined with the remote resting upon his left leg. His elbows lay comfortably on the arm supports and his head tilted ever so slightly to the left. His gray pinstriped suit-coat hung on the back of the chair, his tie high and tight. He appeared apathetic, hardly reacting to the turbid scene.

KNOCK! KNOCK!

The harsh echo of bare knuckles upon his door frame served as a reminder of what reality had become. He rotated in his chair to find one of his subordinates standing at the doorway.

"Sir," he said solemnly, "our investigation is nearly complete."

The major general nodded for the man to enter. He sat up, muting the television.

The soldier handed his boss the documents. "This won't surprise you."

The major general offhandedly studied the information even though it really didn't matter how the pamphlet was leaked. The damage had been done. And, as a result, the nation, socially and financially, was collapsing.

"Thank you, Tad. Go home to your family." He tossed the papers onto his desk and grabbed the remote.

"Thank you, sir." Following a straight-legged solute, the man marched out of the office.

Upon his assistant's departure, the major general glanced down at the report. A tight grin appeared on his face and a single chuckle emanated through his body. "Son-of-a-bitch." He was not surprised and maybe even a little humbled.

You got me.

Leaning back in his chair, his attention shifted back to the television and the streets surrounding Westminster. He increased the volume just enough to could hear faint fragments of natural sound. For the rest of the day he would remain in that reclined position, drifting in and out of consciousness.

"Gentlemen," barked Aasir Abdulah Kabul, leaping onto a chair. The congested room rejoiced at his arrival. Yelling over their cheers, he announced the obvious. "You should be very proud of yourselves."

"YEAH!" his men shouted in unison, pumping their fists into the air.

Kabul stood tall at the head of the room absorbing their energy. The screens behind him displayed the decaying scene outside Westminster.

"What did I promise you?" he continued after the roar died down. A smug, arrogant leer developed on his face. "We got our revenge." His words sparked yet another round of jubilation.

Kabul hopped off the chair and powered through the crowd to his private office. Shielding the view with his left hand, he typed the code. When the red light flashed green, he turned to observe his men memorializing their victory. They had no idea what was coming. The massive oak door closed behind him and a click from the brass latch sealed him inside. The ebullience of his men softened into a faint, far off cry for attention.

Considering the decor and brilliant architecture through the complex, Kabul's private office was not the magnificent spectacle one would assume. It was dark, shaded by thick canvas blinds. The only illumination came from the natural light that fought its way through the curtains. The walls were relatively bland, absent of the Muslim adornments of his subordinates. The wood furniture was nice, but not elegant. The simple rugs appeared to only lessen the echoes of hard-soled shoes as they knocked against the worn out wooden floors.

Kabul's desk was as banal as the rest of the office. It was also void of personal remembrances. No pictures, no art projects from his children, nothing. The desk was in keeping with the rest of the interior design: impersonal.

Kabul leaned back in his chair, listening to the faded merriment of his devoted followers. Their abundant joy brought him great sadness. Lowering his right hand, he typed another code into a security pad on the bottom drawer. The sharp high-pitched tone generated by the broke the relative silence of an otherwise vacuous room.

BEEP! BEEP!

A green light again signaled the code had been broken.

He pulled on the handle, displaying the contents.

The insides looked plain at first glance—stacks of documents and illustrations, some protected by plastic folders of varying thickness, while others existed alone. Kabul removed a wooden picture frame that sat atop everything else. The perimeter was crafted of one inch wide, darkly stained pine. The soft wood was aged, however, the glass that protected its contents shined like polished crystal.

Kabul ran his index and middle fingers along the circumference of the exposed edge as if he were rubbing the face of a dear lover. He gently placed the frame on his desk.

The picture inside portrayed a happy and loving family of four. Mom sat perfectly postured in the middle, her two early teenage sons proudly perched on either side. Their smiles portrayed a bond reserved only to a mother and her sons. The professional-looking portrait had been folded. Deep creases that ran down the middle, vertically and horizontally, cut the mother in four, yet did little to distort her beauty. As the focal point, the matriarch held the attention. Her powerful pose embodied the dominance she wielded over the family, and possibly beyond. The two boys were handsome in their three-piece suits. Astutely pressed, they resembled their mother in physical appearance and their father in stature. The portrait was set against the backdrop of a sun-burst, gray canvas creating a peaceful atmosphere. Standing proudly off the right shoulder of the sacred feminine, with his left-hand placed on her shoulders was Kabul. The patriarch wore the same suit as his sons. They were only differentiated by the reddish hues of their neckties. Unlike the picture itself, the love they appeared to share could not be fabricated.

Kabul gazed at the picture, replacing the distress he felt just minutes prior with a rush of adoration. It was this photo and all it symbolized that motivated him. It led him to convince his men, who were otherwise content with their lives, to damage the nation that was their greatest ally.

Kabul teared up, tenderly caressing the sides of the frame as if it were his wife's flowing dark hair.

"How are you guys?" he said through the glass and into their souls. "I hope ya are doing well...what?" He leaned towards the picture turning an ear. After a brief chuckle he jestingly scolded, "Listen to your mother! Can I speak with her?" He waited with an anxious patience. "My love!" She was his reward. "Our plan is working perfectly." The response came quickly. "Yes, I will see you soon. I am almost finished here. Tell the boys I love them." His heart nearly leaped out of his chest. "I love you too."

Two beeps later and his most valuable possession was again secure. Recharged with a new sense of being, he vigorously rose from his chair to join his men in their triumph.

*

"It can't be!" John's sister Rose exclaimed, hoping her own eyes were deceiving her.

The family sat perched on the last few inches of the couch watching the aerial coverage of the mass demonstration that most certainly would become a riot.

April was less skeptical and more confused. "I saw it, too," she said, her southern American accent more prominent with her nerves. She and John sat close, arms intertwined.

John was neither doubtful nor bewildered. He knew what he was looking at. "There's no way."

All the journalists and photographers had fled the scene. The only reports came from a half-dozen helicopters that hovered above the crowd. Plumes of alternating light and dark smoke stretched high in the clear sky. New fires seemed to appear by the minute. The choppers dodged the towering lines of soot interspersed between the once magnificent buildings. Down below, the hapless military and police forces tried to hold back the surging populace. With each passing minute, it appeared less likely they would succeed.

While the cameras were focused on the congested streets surrounding Westminster, a few blocks away the real rebellion was taking place.

A man wrapped his hands around his mouth to amplify his voice and shouted, "Keep them coming!" He rose to his toes, projecting his commands over the crowd. "Go! Go! Go!"

The tall, hairy man stood by a series of large cardboard boxes. A parade of scurrying workers deposited the heavy containers, while others arrived immediately to snatch them away. Dispersed throughout the block lay the boxes' flattened remnants. The peculiar commotion garnered the curious attention of the media, hovered above.

"Any more?" asked a woman, rushing up to the bearded ringleader.

"We are almost out," he replied. "More are coming."

"Do you think this will work, Warren?" she asked with a twinkle of wonderment in her eyes.

"It has to," he stated resolutely.

BAM!

A box slammed down at their feet. It barely had time to settle before it was off to its new destination, where its cargo would be distributed.

Within seconds, the cardboard coffer landed one hundred yards away. The workers attacked it, frantically tearing at the top to expose its freight, hundreds of books entitled *Constitutional Correctness*. As quickly as the box was opened the books were gone and in the hands of the embittered masses.

A thin, squirrelly-looking man that delivered the box barreled up to the bearded commander. "We have one box left," he huffed. "There!" he blurted out, flinging his arm sideways.

The approaching freight arrived.

"Pass it out and then we will get started," the bearded man instructed. The box was swept away as soon as it arrived.

Among the urgency of the situation, the bearded man was approached by an innocent looking, short, portly fellow with red hair. "Sir, your weapons." He gleefully held them at the end of his extended arms. The artisan's utensils exchanged hands—a four-foot wooden stepladder, and a red and white bullhorn. "You must hurry, sir. The peace will not last."

The bearded man nodded and took a deep breath to calm his racing heart. "Here we go!" His nervous energy instantly morphed into a steadfast desire. He and his group had planned this moment for months. He mustn't allow its surreal nature to affect his performance. This was the place. This was the time.

The tension in the air was palpable. No one felt safe, and that crippling fear was the only stitch holding the mob at bay. But that threat was straining. The crowd had now grown to staggering numbers taking up more city blocks than anyone wished to count. The police and military further attempted to force the crowd into designated sections.

"Ready?" screamed the bearded man. With affirmation from his supporters, he spread the ladder's legs, slammed them onto the ground, and scaled the steps.

"My fellow countrymen!" he hollered loudly enough that his words were only slightly distorted. He wildly swung his torso, echoing his cries in various directions. Those within earshot turned to see who had called their attention. His right hand gripped the bullhorn while his left held firmly to the off-yellow colored book. "Our rebellion is justified!"

The crowd erupted. He raised the megaphone. He knew he could play the crowd, but he must be careful to not get lost in the moment. The ability to control a large group was a power often abused.

Like dominoes falling in every direction, bodies turned to see who had generated such a commotion. Within seconds he attracted the eyes and ears of thousands. Though he didn't know it, his audience was about to get much larger. The hollow thumping of helicopter blades would soon expand his reach into the millions, then billions.

He kept the crowd's attention while awaiting the media.

"People of Great Britain, will we allow this government to ruin our lives?"

"No!" the crowd chorused.

"Will we let this government destroy what we have built?" He pounded his chest with the book.

The response was deafening. "No!"

The dominoes continued to fall as the roar of the crowd demanded more attention.

Knowing dissension was the fuel of disorder, the bearded man continued, "Should we trust those who created this mess to fix it?"

"No!" The response to each successive question grew in veracity.

"Will we stop until we win?"

"No!"

The media was now in position.

"Then I ask you to follow us," he wailed as loudly as he could. "Join our movement for a *freer* Great Britain! One controlled by its people. Please find a copy of our book." He held *Constitutional Correctness* high above his head. "Read it. Study it. Pass it on. Learn of the failures of government. Learn how only *we* can save ourselves. You will find us on street corners, at stop lights, and outside stores." His eyes reddened with passion as spit flew from his mouth. "Join us for a *freer* Great Britain!" He shouted freer as if it were painful. "A United Kingdom once again controlled by its PEOPLE!" He rode out that final word as long as his fatigued lungs would allow.

The masses erupted in overwhelming support.

Knowing his window was closing, the bearded man again placed the megaphone to his mouth. "Go back to your towns, cities, and neighborhoods and tell them about us. Tell them about our book and our ideas. We are called," he paused to allow enough oxygen to enter his lungs. "F-r-e-e- GB."

It may have been a coincidence, but the catalyst for the riot appeared to coincide with the conclusion of his brief speech. As the bearded man jumped from the ladder and onto the street, the mob leaped to action. In a violent display of raw power, stores were raided, looted, then set ablaze. Street poles fell, cars, trucks, and buses were overturned and lit on fire. Fearing for their own safety, police and military fired their weapons into the advancing mob. But the numbers were overpowering. The historic and once majestic city of London was about to burn, and it would all be caught on camera for the world to see.

At the Nolan household, not a word was uttered. The family simply watched the situation unfold while understanding what just happened: John had unwittingly been thrust into the national rebellion.

By the following morning, untold hundreds would lay dead on the streets and in the alleys; some stomped to death, others shot by terrified riot police. The area a dozen blocks in every direction of Westminster would be nearly unrecognizable. Small and large business owners arrived at daybreak to find their livelihoods destroyed. Few solid window panes could be found, nor a car not beaten into ill-repair or charred while resting on its roof. The streets were littered with the looted commerce that twenty-four hours earlier had struggled to keep the city's economy alive. Smoldering fires sent off signals of desperation into the cool blue morning sky. That pungent combination of burned rubber and melted steel spread over the land, carried by a brisk October breeze. Homemade pipe bombs and other explosives chipped away at the delicate facades of historic buildings. The pride of downtown London, the architecture, was now laced with jagged edges and blackened brick. The emerging sun that once glistened off the royal framework, now only served to cast light on a horrifying reality. What hope London, Great Britain, Parliament and the Crown had of a swift recovery or lasting resolution to the nation's problems, had instantly dissipated.

CHAPTER NINE

IT'S US AGAINST THEM. PICK A SIDE.

KNOCK, KNOCK, KNOCK!

Charlotte Nolan's blue slippers shuffled quietly along the hardwood floors. She tied a sash around her robe as she scurried to the front door. The rich aroma of bacon and buttermilk followed behind her. Like a silent alarm, the smell crept through the house waking her husband first, then her son. Her daughters would be last to rise, then the groggy scuffle downstairs would begin. It was safe to assume few of them had slept the previous night. The events of the previous day were racing through her mind, similar to every other Brit. The Nolans, however, shared a unique bond no one could understand. As a result, Charlotte didn't open the door the way she would have one day earlier. Instead, she cautiously pulled back the window curtain to peek out.

Her spirits instantly rose.

"Tony!" she cried, swinging open the door. "It's so great to see you." She lunged towards her brother with open arms. "I was worried about you last night."

Their tight embrace yielded as she pulled back to see his face.

"I'm fine," he assured her.

"We'll, I'm making breakfast," she said. "Join us."

Tony smiled and stepped inside.

In the time it took Charlotte to answer the door, the entire family had surrounded the kitchen table.

"Where's Emma?" Theodore asked. He was hunched over his plate awaiting his meal.

"She's at home with the baby." Tony pulled up a chair at the far corner. "She regrettably couldn't make it." With Charlotte's back turned, Tony snuck a piece of bacon off the stove. Charlotte Nolan liked her bacon crispy, making it impossible to steal quietly.

"Hey!" Charlotte whipped around armed with a spatula. With half a piece of bacon left in his hand, Tony was caught.

He changed the topic. "Hey, is this your girlfriend?" Tony walked over to April and extended his hand. She stood up and quickly adjusted her appearance.

"Yes," John said proudly. "Uncle Tony, this is April Lynn. Sorry I haven't had a chance to introduce you earlier."

"Nice to meet you," Tony said, shaking her hand.

April had wanted to meet the representative for quite some time, and said warmly, "It's nice to finally meet you."

Tony's brow bent in thought. "Social work, right? I remember seeing your name cross my desk."

She smiled. "Yes, sir. I have some thoughts I'd like to share with you. Maybe we can talk sometime soon?"

"Absolutely." Though their hands stopped shaking, they remained connected. "It's a worthy cause.

"So what happened last night?" Lizzy blurted out and every eye in the room snapped towards her. "What? How long were we *not* going to talk about it?"

She was right. It was the main topic at every other breakfast table in the United Kingdom that morning, if not the world.

"I have no idea," Tony felt obliged to respond, "that is why I am here, though." He pulled out his chair and sat down. "This country is about to split. Even in the Parliament, people are taking sides." He leaned forward, placing his elbows on the table. "This is bad."

"What does John have to do with any of this?" Charlotte asked, close to tears.

"I saw that too," Tony said.

"This is not something I asked for." John meant no disrespect, but his tone was harsh. "I don't want to be caught up in this."

Tony nodded. "Unfortunately, you don't have a choice. You're now on the list."

"List?" Charlotte spun around from the stove, nearly dropping her utensils. Theodore abruptly stood up to comfort his wife. "What are you saying, Tony?"

"I am sorry," Tony said sincerely, "but you need to know. The government is taking this burgeoning rebellion seriously. It will begin monitoring you, if it hasn't started already. It has to."

"You're in Parliament!" Theodore exclaimed. "Can't you do something?"

Tony shook his head in regret. "The Crown will protect itself."

The family was lost. Even the normally reserved April appeared visibly shaken. She asked the obvious question.

"Why John's book?"

"This book was a godsend for these people," Tony said matter-of-factly. "John put into words what they feel and think. As a college professor, he has credibility."

"What do you mean?" Theodore asked, his firm grip on his wife preventing gravity from yanking her to the floor.

"John's book discusses the failures of government and puts forth an alternative. And right now, that alternative is very appealing."

"This doesn't make sense," Rose said desperately, attempting to rationalize the irrational. "What do they want from John?"

"I'm not sure." The sizzling sound of bacon cooking filled the silence.

"What I do know is these people have waited years for this moment. The people don't trust their government, the economy is terrible. Everyone is tired, hungry, and scared."

"Maybe I should publicly denounce this," John said, looking around the kitchen for encouragement.

"It won't matter." Tony's eyes felt for the young man.

"What should he do?" Charlotte nervously inquired.

"I'm not sure," Tony said. "I'm sorry. I know that doesn't help."

Charlotte freed her hand from her husband's to cover her mouth. Her eyes watered. This was not the outcome she'd hoped for. She turned to Theodore and buried her face in his chest, wracked with sobs.

The Nolan patriarch appeared defiantly strong. On the inside, however, he may have been the most distressed. Many had already died in the chaos.

Lizzy and Rose were too stunned to react. It was unclear if they were even able to fully understand the situation.

April appeared mournful.

John Nolan, like his father, was not an excitable man. He was always able to control his emotions. But the sight of his mother crying instilled in him a powerful sentient response. He fought back his own tears.

"I have to do something," John asserted, looking down at the table and away from his mother. He could no longer bear to watch her sob.

The bacon had now stopped sizzling, and the stove began to cool. The room took on a funereal tone.

"I should get back to Emma." Tony reluctantly stood and placed his napkin on his empty plate. He felt awkward leaving, but this family needed time to process the information.

Charlotte eased from her husband's consoling arms to escort her brother to the door.

Tony stopped her with a mild-mannered raise of his hand. "Charlotte, it's okay," Tony said. "I can show myself out." He gave her a kiss on the forehead, then turned to April. "It was nice meeting you. We'll talk soon."

April stood to shake his hand, forcing a pleasant smile. "It was an honor to meet you, sir."

Before stepping over the kitchen threshold to enter the family room, Tony turned to the confused family. "I'll do all I can," he promised.

The family remained silent while Tony approached the front door and gently closed it behind him. They looked blankly at one another as the breakfast Charlotte had lovingly prepared gradually cooled to room temperature.

While walking to his car, Tony Manning placed a phone to his ear. It rang once before it was picked up.

"How did it go?" the voice on the other end asked with a curious excitement.

Tony sat in his car and closed the door, sealing his voice inside. He answered the question as if nothing dramatic had just happened.

"He will come around. I just need some time."

*

BANG!!

Aasir Abdulah Kabul's head bounced off the metal table. The impact echoed sharply off the bare gray walls of the near-empty concrete enclosure. Blood dripped from the tip of his nose and his right eye had already swollen shut. The hand that tightly gripped the back of his head was that of the major general.

"I can do this all day, Aasir." Even in torture, the major general's emotions remained dead.

Kabul sat defiantly in his torn white dress shirt and stained khaki pants. A laceration on his forehead produced a horizontal line of blood that accumulated in a few wrinkles. His arms were chained to the back of the chair. Though the interrogation had been going on for a while, the blood-soaked grin of revenge on his face had not faded.

Kabul intentionally created the illusion of deliberate defiance. In reality, he had nothing to hide.

Disgusted with his lack of progress, the major general walked around to the side of the table opposite his captive. He leaned forward, placing his hands on the red-splattered table. "You *will* tell me."

Kabul inhaled deeply. "I told you." His swollen mouth made it difficult to speak. "I don't know. We never saw his face or heard his name." The aggressive beating had begun to take its toll on Kabul's weary body. His head bobbed as he fell in and out of consciousness.

In a back room, a group of men huddled around a monitor monitoring Kabul's rapidly fluctuating body temperature.

"He contacted us," Kabul said, enjoying the fresh flow of blood on his lips. Revenge had never tasted so good. "He said he had something we would want. He was right."

The men in the back room watched intently. "He's telling the truth," one of them said into the major general's earpiece. "He's never been a good liar."

The soulless interrogator grabbed a chair from the corner and placed it at the table, a few feet away from his former comrade. "You know what this means, Aasir."

Kabul sat motionless with his shoulders hunched forward and head hanging low. Nothing he could have said would matter. He had known the Major General long enough. The African Muslim's body slumped as the adrenaline subsided. The slightest of movements triggered his wounds to sting.

The major general tried a different approach. "Why did you do it, Aasir?"

Kabul peered up with pride. His reason was obvious.

"Aasir, there was nothing we could have done. We gave you enough money, equipment, support." He paused, the words came hard. "We lost."

"A peace agreement was within reach," Kabul muttered.

"They would have killed everyone. They wanted you to sign some phony document and hand over your records so they *knew* who to kill. Our withdrawal saved many lives, including yours."

The resistant prisoner finally began to disintegrate. Sporadic and uncontrollable fluctuations in Kabul's diaphragm caused him to gyrate in his chair. He tried to fight the intense release of energy, but the urge was overwhelming. With his arms still tied behind his back, he struggled to catch his breath. The tears broke loose from his eyes, mixing with the dried blood on his face.

Kabul was unaware his men sat in a neighboring cell, watching. They had never seen their leader so vulnerable.

Kabul could no longer live a lie. His true intentions would be revealed in a pathetic display of self-pity. "I cannot get it out of my head. It replays over and over again every day." His words were interrupted by brief fits of hysterical distress. "I had to justify their lives."

"So you convinced your men to join your plan for revenge, when it had nothing to do with them? It was all about you."

Kabul mustered the strength to lift his head. His watery eyes cried for forgiveness.

Kabul's men sat in the adjacent room realizing at that moment that the very man to whom they had entrusted their lives had betrayed them. And it was too late. Their fates had been sealed.

It had been many years since the major general thought back to that day. The capital and final stronghold of the FLEC lay in ruins following months of aerial and ground assaults from the Angolan government. Since the beginning of the conflict, an agreement had prohibited aerial combat, but missiles were exempt. No building inside the compromised walls remained untouched. People evacuated by the thousands, seeking shelter in the countryside. They filtered into underground tunnels, impervious to spy planes and satellites. But the unforgiving Angolan government would provide no amnesty. Those left inside when they entered would be slaughtered. Those who fled would be hunted down.

The sounds of the weeks leading up to this moment were few, but distinct. Explosions were so common that unless the heat could be felt, it was not even acknowledged. The echoes of gunshots were less prevalent everyday as the rebels saved what little ammunition they had. Hundreds of rebels were stationed on top of the city walls to ward off government forces as long as possible. Resources were limited due to the sound that garnered the most attention: helicopter rotors carrying people to safety. The relief effort ran unimpeded, day and night, carrying survivors and those less-injured to neighboring countries that granted asylum. However, the return flights brought few supplies. The nations that granted asylum wouldn't interfere enough to upset the imminent victor.

The capital for the FLEC was situated in the province of Cuando Cubango at the old city of Menongue, on the river that shared its name, far away from the Angolan capital of Luanda. A ten-foot thick wall of steel-reinforced concrete was constructed before the war ever began to guard the FLEC's possessions. This barricade was later used to protect the aristocracy of the rebellion. The Inner City shielded one square mile, allowing the rebels to regulate their inner circle, thus maintaining authority and most importantly, authenticity.

When the government would break through, its soldiers would encounter just a few recalcitrant souls, who refused to give up. They would easily be toppled, and the most devastating war in Angolan history would be over.

"Are you sure there is no one else?" yelled a young and vibrant major general, who, at the time, was not yet of that rank. The powerful roar of the rotors and discharges in the distance nearly drowned him out. He sat in full infantry gear in the front of the helicopter. The pilot next to him had a long, narrow scar on the right side of his face. It appeared to have been courtesy of a sharp blade.

"We have to get out of here, now!" the pilot screamed. The city walls were being breeched and government soldiers were rushing in. "They are closing in!"

The major general tore off his safety straps and whipped around, facing the rear of the helicopter. "Where the hell is Kabul!?" he barked to a teenage Alam Jabbar.

"A few more seconds!"

The major general's eyes glanced down at a makeshift bandage wrapped tightly around a shrapnel wound that engulfed the young man's leg. Everything below the knotted cloth was saturated in blood, a pool of thick red liquid covering the floor.

Jabbar ignored the pain. "I will be fine."

"There's another!" The major general's head snapped toward port side. Another part of the wall bore a hole.

The major general's admonition was clear. "We are leaving in twenty seconds whether he is here or not."

Jabbar didn't argue.

The initial surge by government soldiers through the opening was tempered by the remaining resistance forces. The valiant last ditch effort would soon dwindle. In a matter of seconds after the holes opening, all the rebels in that vicinity converged in an attempt to plug it. As soldiers poured in, they were mowed down in a hail of bullets. However, those bullets would run out long before the government's availability of soldiers. As the breeches multiplied, the number of forces available to plug them thinned.

"Go!" yelled Kabul, leaping into the helicopter.

"Finally," the major general said, his voice quivering with anxiety.

Kabul hastily prepared himself for liftoff. "My family just took off."

"Are they good?"

The addition of gunfire a few hundred yards away made conversation nearly impossible.

The soon-to-be-exiled leader of the FLEC nodded as he strapped on his helmet. Kabul's family was on their way to Liberia, and then Great Britain. Kabul and his men had some final business with the Crown before heading for their new home. Great Britain had agreed to escort his wife and children to London weeks prior. Kabul had refused to leave them, until now.

"Hold on!" announced the pilot, signaling for takeoff.

The helicopter rose from the ground, and Kabul and his men watched as the last of the resistance was decimated. The wall surrounding Inner

City now looked more like a series of columns. It was shortly before midday; the war would be over before nightfall.

Kabul nudged Jabbar and leaned forward to tap the major general's shoulder. He pointed to a helicopter not far off in the distance that carried his family.

The unfortunate angle of the two choppers offered the military men an unobstructed view of a land-to-air-missile racing across the clear blue sky toward that lead helicopter. As if in slow motion, the ballistic missile collided with the aircraft and detonated. The brilliant ball of fire it produced spread in all directions. The explosion raged with such intensity the helicopter appeared to incinerate in mid-air.

"Nooooo!" Kabul cried out in horror, his arms outstretched toward the orange burst.

The major general closed his eyes and lowered his head to utter a short prayer. He felt for his friend. Throughout the years, he had grieved for countless souls. Over time, the recurring pain would harden his reserve. If he were to rise to the top of his field, he must not be weakened by grief. It was just a matter of time before this philosophy would rid him of all emotion in the quest for power.

Kabul and Jabbar looked on in horror as the fireball extinguished into a plume of black smoke that lazily ascended toward the heavens. That crippling feeling in Kabul's stomach would never subside. In a matter of minutes he had lost his country, the respect of his people, and his family. He reached into the breast pocket of his fatigues and pulled out a folded picture. It showed a happy and loving family of four. His wife sat perfectly positioned in the middle, their two early teenage sons proudly perched on either side. The preeminent patriarch, Kabul, stood tall behind them. This picture was all he had left.

In the room where Kabul's men watched, it was silent. Their fearless leader had degenerated into a sobbing coward. The power of symbolism had never been so caustic. And this time, they could not blame their troubles on the British government.

"I have no choice," stated the major general.

Kabul didn't acknowledge his captor. The man who sat huddled in the chair was but a broken-down skeleton of his former self. The relentless memories and painful realities of what could have been proved an enormous weight around his neck, one that became far too heavy. He lacked the mental ability or desire to ever release himself.

The major general eased himself out of his chair. He walked over to his old friend and placed his left hand on his right shoulder. "I am sorry," he whispered in a voice so low only Kabul could hear. As he removed Kabul's chains, he took a few seconds to admire the man he once revered as a great and powerful leader.

When the major general exited, the sound of his shoes knocking against the hollow concrete floors echoed eerily throughout the room. The latch of the chamber unlocking signaled the end of their relationship. The loud crash of the door slamming against the metal frame finalized the deal. Kabul was now left to himself, with an eternity to ponder his life.

A few minutes later, Kabul stood up and shuffled over to a bed at the far corner of the room. He lay down on his back to stare at the ceiling. Reaching down, he grabbed the sheets and violently attempted to rip them apart. The maddening release of energy served to ease his mind. Pleased with the quality of the fabric, he smiled letting his head fall backward to rest against the bare wall. The blanket barely covered half his ravaged body. The dried blood on his face resembled war paint. He heard the locks on his cell door jiggle once again. Eternity would not be much longer.

A few cells down, a door swung open, revealing the major general to Kabul's men. They sat in the room dispirited from what they had just witnessed. Most didn't even bother to acknowledge his entrance.

The military man stepped into the room and without any emotion, simply asked, "Who's first?"

*

Professor Nolan walked into the already-filled classroom. "Good morning, class."

John was last to arrive. He performed his normal rituals of first placing his bag on the desk, then hanging his coat on the back of the chair. The previous instructor always left the chair halfway pushed in under the metal lectern. John would have to finish the task. The room was quiet as he went about his routine. No talking, no shuffling of papers, desks or chairs.

He opened his briefcase in search of the day's lesson. When he reached to grab his notes, an awkward feeling of discomfort flowed through him.

He peeked up from the tops of his eyes. The students had not moved. In fact, he wasn't sure if many had even blinked. He scanned the room from left to right.

Off to the right, outside the door, John saw an increasing number of students walking past his classroom and peeking inside. Many of them pointing and whispering. Some held copies of *Constitutional Correctness*. Confused, John turned his attention back to his class. Their blank stares did not help.

"What?" he said, and the students unleashed their barrage of questions.

"How did they get your book?"

"Did you give it to them?"

"Will you join the resistance?"

"Are you making money in book sales?"

"I heard it's sold out everywhere."

"Did you write the book hoping this would happen?"

"You have to be making a ton of money. Everyone wants a copy."

As John's exam continued, the hall swelled with onlookers and the subsequent noise they generated.

"Myra!" John blurted out, startling the young girl. The class quieted immediately. "Please shut the door," John said.

When she had done so, the background noise vanished. "Alright," Professor Nolan started in a calm voice with his arms outstretched, palms facing the floor. "I am just as stunned as you." He pulled out the chair he just pushed in and took a seat. "I did not volunteer for this. I don't know how it happened. I don't have any answers to your questions. I wish I did."

"Sir?" said a young man in the front row.

"Yes, Peter."

"If you need help, we'll be there," the boy said with compassion well beyond his years. When the rest of his students expressed similar support, John couldn't help but smile.

KNOCK! KNOCK!

Unfortunately, his moment of comfort did not last.

Without any formal invitation to enter, the door creaked open again, filling the room with the clamorous chatter from the hallway. The piercing squeaks of the rusted metal hinges gave way to an old, humpbacked, gray-haired man. Thick, goggle-like glasses hung at the tip of his nose, and his attire was a worn out, earth-toned suit.

John rose from his desk. "Chancellor Landon!" He briskly made his way to the old man with his hand extended.

The chancellor shook John's hand. "Professor Nolan, it's a pleasure to make your acquaintance." His voice was tired but exultant.

For John, this was an honor. He had never met the chancellor. In fact, he was rarely seen outside of speeches and commencement addresses. At his age, public appearances were tough.

"How can I help you?" John asked, somewhat stunned by the unannounced arrival. He signaled for Myra to again close the door.

"Well, John," the chancellor said with a downward smile, "may I have a moment?"

"Absolutely, sir." John reached for his briefcase. "Alright, class, I want you guys to read chapters ten through fifteen. Next class, we'll go a little longer to make up for today. Schedule appropriately."

The students gathered their belongings.

"Thank you for your understanding," John said as they filed into the boisterous hallway. "Please shut the door."

Within seconds, the room was again quiet. The old chancellor sat down in a chair in the front row. John leaned against his desk.

"Wow," The chancellor remarked, looking around the classroom. "I haven't been in one of these chairs in a while. It's quite uncomfortable."

John grinned slightly. The old man's levity was easing the awkwardness of the moment.

"John." He seemed to finally settle in. "You know why I am here. I read your book. It's brilliant. Congratulations."

"Thank you, sir."

"I've been around for a long time, son." With shaky hands, he removed his glasses and placed them upside down on the desk. "I've never seen things this bad. This country has some very tough decisions ahead. You know, when I was a younger man, I was in a similar situation as you find yourself now." He drew in a long, slow breath. "Not long after the turn of the century, I did some international relief work. You know, to pad my resume." The chancellor leaned back and stretched upright in the chair. "The doctor told me I need to work on my posture. I get yelled at."

John was surprised by Chancellor Landon's disposition. He had not expected that from a man of his stature.

"Anyway, I ended up getting a job working for the Solomon Islands' government. Soon after, a man by the name of Snyder Rini was elected prime minister. In April of 2006, he was sworn in. Riots broke out in the capital of Honiara over rumors that Rini used bribes from Chinese businessmen to buy votes in Parliament. Those riots were severe. God, it was scary," he vividly recalled. "Resentment against local Chinese business was intense. Many Chinese-owned businesses were destroyed. Talks of money being exported to China made it worse. China evacuated many of its people to safety. I watched it all."

He again repositioned in the chair, wincing in discomfort. "In the end, the riots worked. Rini stepped down. He faced a no-confidence motion. Even if he survived it, the fact that a no-confidence motion happens can ruin a politician."

John found himself immersed in the story, yet wondering why it was relevant.

"The sad reality was Rini was misunderstood. This man's political career, what he fought for his entire life, was taken away from him." His voice dropped to a sorrowful tone. "And I allowed it to happen."

"You, sir?"

The Chancellor appeared lost in his own reflection. "I didn't want to get further involved in another country's politics," he admitted. "I think about it a lot. Over time, I've convinced myself to not regret it." The old man shifted again, turning towards John with a look of great seriousness. "Professor, you have a rare opportunity. Your family, your friends, polls, they will tell you many things." He pointed at John with a quivering finger. "*You* must live with your decisions. If you do what is *right*," he emphasized that last word, "you will have no regret, no matter the result."

"What is right?" John inquired. "How will I know it?"

The professor replied with a crooked smile. "You will know. Sometimes, we just choose not to realize it."

John's mind raced as he pondered the chancellor's words.

"Joseph Schumpeter was an economist from Austria-Hungary." The chancellor placed his bony hand on John's shoulder and looked at the young man as if to view his soul. "He said, *'The first thing a man will do for his ideals is lie. And that first lie is usually to himself.'*" The old man kindly patted John on the arm.

John's attention shifted back to the Chancellor's anecdote. "You said you didn't do anything because you didn't want to get *further* involved in another country's politics?"

The chancellor's mischievous smile revealed more than he had intended. "Help an old man up," he instructed.

"You said the prime minister was misunderstood," John pressed. "How did you know?"

The chancellor remained silent, and the not-so-subtle hint was understood.

John gripped the chancellor's frail arm and helped him to his feet. As he rose and got a look out the window, they discovered a small crowd had gathered on the university lawn in support of Professor Nolan. The two men walked over to the high windows that had previously shielded them from view. When John stepped into the beams of warm sunlight that radiated through the glass, the students erupted in cheers. They had chosen their allegiance.

*

"My fellow countrymen," began the prime minister as he addressed the nation. He sat tall at his desk with the nation's flag draped on the wall behind him. His office and appearance had been as carefully prepared as his speech. "We find ourselves in unprecedented times."

While the prime minister spoke, the printing presses spun tirelessly, producing copies of John Nolan's *Constitutional Correctness*. The books barely had time to cool before they were boxed and shipped.

"Our country is being torn apart by forces of change. I fear these forces will transform us into something we no longer recognize. This system that has provided us and our ancestors with the greatest and most consistent quality of life in the world is now in jeopardy."

The streets of London were mostly empty, except for the litter that piled up as social services faded. A few children with less protective parents played and laughed without a care. They all huddled around the few remaining street lights that still shined. Understanding the uncertainty that had gripped the Kingdom, most Brits held their children as they listened to their leader.

"It is the highest priority of this government to resolve this situation soon. If all sides can come to an agreement, if we can come together, we can begin the work to fix this great nation. But we will certainly fail under the current divided state of our union."

Somewhere within the city limits of London, the man who not long ago preached from a podium and proclaimed the beginning of the revolution, watched the prime minister deliver his speech. He stood with one foot on a crate, leaning forward with his elbows resting on a raised knee. Behind him, his loyal legion of revolutionaries feverishly worked on banners, posters, and newsletters in an effort to gain converts. Some people mass-produced basic handwritten signs, while others utilized computers to draft more professional documents. As the Prime Minister spoke, an insidious smile grew on this man's face. He knew he was winning.

"Tonight, as we begin the long road to recovery, I ask for your patriotism. But before you can commit, first ask yourself if your kids are safe in school. Is your job secure? If you have lost your job, ask yourself what the chances are of getting another, soon—one with a living wage. Are you optimistic that your electricity will be there in the middle of the night when you need it? If you get sick, will your doctor be there to give you medication? Will that medication be available? When will your trash be picked up? Will the grocery store be stocked? And if it is, will it be too expensive to afford?"

Chris Nash sat at his computer in a dark, lonely room, listening only to the audio of the prime minister's speech. He, like every other media boss, did not get a pre-speech copy of the address and listened for a theme that would serve as a headline. With each sentence, Nash would amend his work, typing a few words then deleting them. The headline which would eventually lead all the outlets of his media empire was simple, yet powerful. It was sure to make people stop and think. And most importantly, watch or buy. His seven words would resonate throughout the land:

"Prime Minister Uses Fear to Quell Fear"

"We are a country centered in unity, a country that has survived the darkest days this world has seen. That unity has been at the core of our greatness. We can't give that up. Our choices in the following days, weeks, and months will determine the Great Britain we will become. The Great Britain our children will inherit."

Somewhere within the city limits of London, another secret factory making revolution paraphernalia was seconds away from an unwanted surprise. In mass movements, government officials scrambled to surround the building. One by one they swiftly exited armored, unmarked military trucks in night camouflage, complete with assault rifles and body armor. Using only basic sign language, they positioned themselves at doors, windows, and any escape route. The commander peered at his watch with his back pressed against a brick wall. The second-hand approached the twelve. The night was dark, chilled, and calm.

"What path will we follow? Will we choose the Great Britain our ancestors chose, the Great Britain they fought and died for? One of laws; one of civility; one of peace? Or will we choose the chance of an uncertain future, one that lacks peace of mind, and where great doubt exists?"

"NOW!" screamed the commander. At once, all the doors surrounding the compound were kicked in. The government soldiers swarmed the building, weapons raised.

"GET DOWN!"

The screams of the workers could be heard blocks away. The swift, carefully planned attack allowed no time for their horrified targets to react. Most didn't even try to resist. A few attempted to run, only to find every exit sealed. The tireless copying and printing machines were shut down at the behest of assault rifles. The workers were led out of the hot, brightly lit room and placed in dark passenger vans, their destination unknown.

"I assure you. Your government, my administration, has not given up. And we will continue to fight for the people of this nation. Right now about 25 percent of you are out of work. The government has less tax revenue with which to help. Many of you are running out of money.

If we don't act now to save ourselves, people will go hungry. More will lose their houses. Winter is coming."

That night, John and April watched the prime minister's address from the relative safety of her dimly lit apartment. The air smelled of hours-old macaroni, the remnants of which were strewn around the kitchen. They sat on the couch, her legs draped over his, arms interlocked. A light blanket kept them shielded from the chilly breeze that wisped in through a cracked window. April positioned herself on her side to tightly hold John.

With her head pressed firmly against his chest she whispered, "I'm scared."

John looked down at her, smiled, and kissed the top of her head without a word. She didn't need to know he was scared as well.

"In order for us to unite, we must first address some misinformation circulating in our homes, on the street, and on the internet. And let me be clear, that information is untrue. Members of a small, extreme Islamic militant group known as the Loyalist Ali Front or the LAF printed those lies and spread it during this time of economic uncertainty to cause further harm to our country. Their goal is to disrupt our quality of life. Sadly, it has worked."

Tony and Emma Manning watched the address as they ate dinner. Tony's eyes never broke from the television as he stabbed raviolis with his fork. Emma was more focused on not only feeding herself, but also their baby boy, who sat between them. Tony's blood burned as he watched the leader of the country blatantly lie to the people. For him, reconciliation was not an option. He vowed revenge.

"Your government, my administration, has not and would not jeopardize your trust or violate the sacred bond we share. I speak of a bond that only a democratic people and their democratically elected officials can possess. We are an accountable government. Accountable to you."

"AHHH!" April screamed, covering her head as the door to her apartment burst open. Armed men dressed in dull black flooded the room in much the same fashion as the men who had raided the factory earlier that night. John and April jumped up from the couch, turning to face the door in horror.

"Hands up, now!" a man yelled. Facing a half-dozen rifles, they complied. April cracked under the intensity. "Come with us," the man said, grabbing John's arm and dragging him through the door. April was not far behind.

"My fellow citizens, we currently stand on the precipice of history. What we do here will be judged for generations to come."

While John and April were being shoved into the back of a car, similarly-dressed men ransacked the Nolans' house. His parents and sisters were forced out. When the marauders reached John's bedroom, they began seizing its contents. His room would soon be just bare walls and vacant drawers.

"Our system of governance allows us to achieve our fullest potential. And that will continue if we allow it."

The vehicles that contained the Nolans sped away as quickly as they arrived. The thundering sound of engines tearing down the road faded, returning the dark streets to the peaceful night.

"My fellow countrymen, we are simply borrowing this land and passing through its legacy. It is not our duty to change its foundations and remake it in our own image; but to preserve it for the next generation so they can inherit the blessings it contains. I greatly fear what will happen if we choose another path. Good night. And God save the Queen."

*

John sat alone in the corner of the cell, ignoring the two aluminum chairs centered along the minimal expanse of the room. Off-white laminate floors and beige walls spawned a musty atmosphere. The overhead lighting cast dark shadows under his bloodshot eyes. With bent legs and elbows perched upon his knees, John's fear slowly subsided. The longer he waited, the more annoyed he became.

Before long, he heard the door unlock and pivot inward.

"John Nolan?" The short, leather-faced man marched into the room as if this meeting had been mutually arranged. "My name is Major General Bernard Harris."

John was not impressed. "Where is April?"

"She's fine." Harris admired the young man's moxie, however specious. "She is waiting in another room, as is the rest of your family."

"You took my family!?"

"We had no choice."

His frigid and enigmatic temperament wore at John's frustrations. "We could not chance someone calling authorities," Major General Harris continued in a monotone. He sat down in the chair closest to the door and gestured for John to join him. His flawless posture and pressed suit was beyond peculiar.

John rose from the floor, cautiously made his way towards the chair, and sat. "Why am I here?"

"Great Britain requests your services." At John's confused expression, Harris explained, "You are an emerging figure in this nation's struggle." He removed a black folder from the brown leather briefcase that lay upon his lap and pulled back the top fold, revealing a series of pictures.

"This is Warren Wickham." He presented the photo to John. Wickham appeared to be mid-30s with brown hair and hazel eyes. With his soft jawline, he more resembled an office worker than the leader of a burgeoning revolution.

"You may not recognize him. He grew a long beard to conceal his identity. However, we hear he has now shaved. He is the person who dragged you into this mess."

After the initial shock subsided, John grew less irritated and more ambivalent. The uncertainty that lay ahead was indeed disconcerting. But in it, he saw opportunity.

"This is a bad guy." Harris gestured towards the picture that still held John's attention. "There has never been a riot, protest, or any type of civil unrest he didn't like. Unfortunately, he seems to have found a message that has stuck."

Harris selected the next photo. Unlike the first one, this image instantly caught John's eye. The man had a darker complexion than Wickham. Darker hair, darker skin, and demented green eyes that John had never forgot since he first saw them last spring while waiting in line to vote.

"I've seen this guy," John admitted. He explained to the major general how he had watched this man try to stir up votes for the Centre Party.

"He has been around for years desperately trying to find a way to matter," the major general replied. "These guys are smart and very devoted. They could actually help this country if they weren't always trying to subvert it. His name is Paul Harris. We think he's the brains, but he's too radical to be the front man."

John looked up from under his brow. *Paul Harris? Major General Bernard Harris?*

"No relation," the major general snapped, looking mildly disgusted at John's insinuation. "His nickname is Paulie."

Harris' focus abruptly dropped to the folder on his lap. "These guys aren't quite as high profile as the first two. The one on the right is Colin Tudor and the other is Clive Rodriguez."

John did not recognize either.

"As I said, all these guys want is to *matter*." Harris sealed his briefcase. "They have been involved in these types of dealings for a long time. For some reason, it makes them feel worthy; gives their lives meaning. They have no regard for consequences."

"If these guys are bad, how do they get a following?" John's asked.

"It's not about who they are. It's about timing." *The one thing I can't control.* "They finally got lucky."

Those words and their significance bounced around in John's head. "What do you need from me?" He was now more intrigued than anything. A new feeling also began to creep into his being, one that greatly bolstered his confidence and his sense of worth.

"Your service to your country," Harris spoke simply. "These guys will come after you, try to recruit you. Your book is their Bible. They need you. John Nolan will be a household name in Great Britain. Whether that name is synonymous with patriotism or traitor is up to you." John wasn't sure how to respond.

"Keep us informed. They will contact you, maybe they already have. We need information. This movement must be defeated, Mr. Nolan. If we fail, so will the country."

John nodded. He had always considered himself a patriot.

*

After John's meeting, he reunited with April and his family. The urgency of the situation had been explained to them, along with the Crown's expectations concerning their loyalty. The same jet black cars that abruptly swept them away earlier that night calmly returned them to their once-quiet suburban lives. The confounded family exchanged few words as they wandered up the winding path that partitioned the browning grass of the front yard. Before reaching the door step, Theodore pulled a bronze key from his pants pocket, unlocked the door, and they filed into the brick and stone Cape Cod.

They entered the foyer, finding it exactly how they had left it, orderly and clean.

"I know they went through everything," Charlotte said. "I saw them."

John was the first to venture farther into the home. He proceeded delicately. "Looks alright." He ran his hand along the top of their brown, nubuck leather couch as he walked past. The family carefully searched the home.

Theodore stood in the entryway to the kitchen, looking back at his family. "Are we being too paranoid?"

"Dad's right," John stated, popping his head up from behind the television. "We have to live our lives." He made his way out of the corner and towards his father, briefly stopping to peek under a lamp shade. "Sorry."

"Y'all think it's...?" April's eyes dashed around the room from one potential target to the next.

No one was prepared, or willing, to answer that question.

Charlotte released a deep sigh of exhaustion and buried her head in her husband's chest. "I can't live like this."

Theodore put his arms around her, gently squeezing with his chin resting upon her head. Rose and Lizzy silently consoled each other.

John nudged April and signaled for her to follow. They discreetly made their way up the stairs to John's room, where April remained at the threshold, leaning up against the wood molding.

"What's the matter?" she asked.

John was already squatted, sifting through his papers and examining the order and contents of the drawers. "I know how I left everything." He pulled a six-inch thick binder out of the bottom drawer of his desk. He rapidly paged through the color-coded sections of the giant notebook. "This is nearly perfect." Impressed with their keen attention to detail, he snapped around to look at April. "These guys are good."

DING DONG.

A flash of terror ripped across their faces.

"Come on." John grabbed April's hand and rushed down the hall toward the stairs. They hit the bottom step as his mother opened the front door.

Charlotte was surprised to see her brother, maybe even a bit shocked. "Tony?"

"May I come in?" he asked politely.

"Oh!" Charlotte exclaimed. "Absolutely." She stepped aside. "I'm sorry, Tony. It's been a long day."

April quickly tossed her hair and straightened her outfit.

"I just wanted to stop by and check on you guys," Tony explained, drifting through the foyer into the family room. His focus nervously shifted around the room. "You've been through a lot."

Theodore smirked at his understatement and vanished into the kitchen. "Beer?" he yelled.

"Sure," Tony replied. He watched Theodore disappear behind the refrigerator door. He then turned towards John, who was sitting on the stairs. "How are you two?"

John nodded. "Fine."

April released John's hand as she addressed Tony. "It's nice to see you again, Mr. Manning." Her tone was awkward, but not uncomfortable.

"Please, call me Tony."

April smiled.

"I stopped by earlier this evening, but you guys weren't around." A beer suddenly appeared over Tony's shoulder.

As he took a swig, Charlotte flashed a look of trepidation. So did the twins.

Tony's suspicions were correct. He changed the topic.

"John," Tony began, "I am tiling my master bathroom and I wanted your opinion. I have the porcelain in my car. Can you take a look? They're heavy." Tony chuckled. "It'd be hard to bring them in."

John and April shared a fleeting glance of incredulity. "Sure, Uncle Tony."

"Emma wanted to go with marble," Tony explained as they approached his car. "But I am trying to do this myself and I don't know if I feel comfortable cutting that."

He popped the trunk. "This is what I ended up getting." Tony leaned into the trunk and ripped apart the cardboard box that held the light blue porcelain. He handed a piece to John.

"Well," John said as he examined the specimen, "porcelain can be sharp. But if you're careful, this is fine."

"I wanted to run it diagonal."

"I wouldn't." John handed it back. "Diagonal is risky—less room for error. If something goes wrong, you may not be able to match the pattern. Then you have big problems."

"Emma likes it." Tony placed the tile back in the box with the others. "I'll tell her what you said."

Tony shut the trunk, and the two casually meandered back to the house. With his hands in his pockets Tony kept his focus on the walkway. "They took you away, didn't they?" he asked under his breath.

John peered down, blank-faced, at his shorter uncle, confirming his presumption. Their carefree stroll slowed to a standstill halfway up the walk.

John assumed his uncle's Parliamentarian connections had tipped him off.

"Look, this revolution is building real momentum, John. The Crown is scared. They've lost much of this country." He paused for a second. "They can't lose you. The government has made you a pawn in its game to control the people."

Despite the nation's dire situation and John's obscure involvement, he embraced the attention. That feeling of prestige and virtue he felt with the major general had returned. He thought of those bastards at the Cambridge history department. He thought of April and of his family.

"I'd like you to meet someone." Tony turned to the house and continued his walk. John followed. "I think you'll like him."

CHAPTER TEN
WHAT IS PATRIOTISM?

Winter had set in. The abbreviated days and elongated nights only served to augment the depression, a word that only spoke half the story, in the national and psychological sense.

More than a quarter of Brits were in need of work. Foreclosure and For Sale signs became the quintessential suburban lawn decorations. Homeless shelters were brimming with previously employed men and women who had turned to drugs and alcohol. Even those who remained strong and defiant of their circumstances did what they never thought they would—accept a handout. Pride was no longer an issue. Everyone was just trying to survive.

Downtown city districts throughout the UK had lost their brilliance. Some were ghost towns, abandoned. No one shopped along the once bustling storefronts that had been replaced with broken glass, crumbling facades, and scores of vagabonds.

For many, outside the necessities, commerce had largely stopped. Desperation had led to an increase in crime, further crippling the recovery. Some of the only workers remaining were city employees who struggled to maintain essential infrastructure and utility repairs. After all, Westminster was still open for business. But for every pothole fixed, three more would open up in the rotting streets. Hope was lost. However, not *all* activity had ceased.

The autumn riots and protests which became more or less daily occurrences were forced off the streets by the frigid temperatures. Climate-controlled venues were less visual in terms of PR, but proved more effective in terms of solidarity. Winter weather and emotional fatigue limited attendance, making the rebellion appear less formidable. If that were only the case.

"Who's got the north side of town above Winchmore Hill?"

Warren Wickham stood at the head of a long wooden table lined with his henchman. A giant map of London, pegged with names and artificial boundary lines, hung on the wall behind him. The boardroom in which they sat was drab and cluttered.

"Brooks." The response came from his immediate right. Like others at the table his dress was casual and unrefined.

"Does he need backup or do we have the support of that area?" Wickham turned, arms folded, to study the map.

"He is making progress," the heavyset man replied, his chins jiggling. "That town has fared slightly better than others. Those people are a little harder to recruit."

Wickham stood pondering the board. His chin rested upon a stern thumb, fingers curled along his mouth. "I know there are a few gas stations left in business."

The husky man nodded as he examined the papers spread out before him. "Yes, sir."

"Have Brooks take them out. That should convince them to join us. Then we'll reassign Brooks and send our people to gain the area's support."

The rotund henchman dutifully wrote the orders. "The police force just had more layoffs." He looked up from his notes. "This should be easy."

"Perfect." Wickham flipped the map up, revealing a similarly detailed ground plan of Leeds, Britain's third largest city. "Now, we still have work to do *here*. These people are being stubborn." He closely studied the map, dissatisfied. "Ideas? We have to control this city before moving forward."

"Sir?" The young, nervous man slipped into the room interrupting the meeting. "You have a call."

"Can it wait?"

"It's Mr. Manning. He says he needs to speak with you right away."

Wickham reached for the phone. "Yes?"

Tony could barely contain his excitement. "It will happen soon."

A toothy grin formed on Wickham's cleanly shaved face.

Wickham lowered the phone to address the room. "Well," he stated with a newly found enthusiasm. "We need to prepare for a special guest."

*

While the rebels held a meeting to plan their strategy for victory, their enemy sat down at a similarly long rectangular table, not far away, with near identical goals.

"Where are they focusing?" asked Major General Bernard Harris, studying the massive amount of paperwork that lay in front of him. The entire table was littered with documentation, surveillance imagery, and half-empty coffee cups.

"Our sources tell us they will soon aggressively campaign in Leeds," answered the thin, rugged-looking man sitting opposite the table from Harris. He, like others in the room, was either dressed in military fatigues or a suit. "They aren't polling well there."

"Do we have resources to send? We must keep their support." Harris removed his dark oval-cut glasses and looked up from his papers. "Food, clothing, shelter? Even a little bit of street work would be fine. We need a presence."

"We don't have much." The pale woman who sat off to the right of Harris wildly poked at her calculator. "But we have *some* funds."

"Mr. Prime Minister." The PM's head jarred up from his own stack. "Can you go there and gain support from those people?" Harris' words were hollow. He believed the PM to be incompetent, a sentiment most of the country shared.

The prime minister even questioned his own ability to lead. He had failed within his own party to rally support in the House of Commons or House of Lords. Not one significant bill had been passed since the early days of his administration. Attempts to assuage the withdrawal of foreign monies from the British economy fell short. The effort to garner new investments proved a further embarrassment. The man, who'd confidently promised a "new and more powerful Great Britain" eight months prior, couldn't even be an effective figurehead. He had lost the support of the nation, his party, and the government. The inevitable vote of no confidence would come at the choosing of the opposition parties.

The prime minister appeared remote and disinterested at Harris' request. "I'll try." He truly felt he could have been a great leader if not for the awful hand he was dealt.

I should be running this meeting, and the nation.

He could no longer use his imposing size and dominant voice to cover his shortfalls. His ineptitude and deep rooted lack of confidence had been exposed.

"Good." Harris eyeballed the prime minister before returning his attention back to his notes. "Have we confirmed Wickham is behind much of the crime?"

"We have captured some who are setting fires and looting stores" the bitter man averred in disgust. "They aren't giving us anything."

"That's because they don't have anything to give," a bald man to Harris' left said with a slight degree of admiration. "Wickham needs chaos to further his movement, but he can't be connected to it, so he organized these outside groups. The actual saboteur doesn't know their orders are from the resistance. This is well-organized."

"We could bring in the military to guard the neighborhoods." The suggestion came from the back.

"Perhaps." The major general thought hard. "Will that scare the people into thinking we have further lost control, or will it reinforce our commitment to them?"

"We don't have much of a choice," the rugged man from across the table said. "These people must be stopped."

"We are wasting our damn time!" the prime minister roared in a thunderous voice, attempting to take control. Every head in the room whipped in his direction. "We should focus on the economy, not this!" He stretched his arms out, indicating the papers that covered the table. "With an improving economy, this 'revolution,'" he used his fingers as quotes, "would crumble. That is how it started and that is how we end it."

"Mr. Prime Minister." The Major General removed his glasses. "The reason we can't grow the economy is *because* of this 'revolution' and the crisis it's creating." He mockingly used his own air quotes. "The more they succeed, the more control we lose. *This* is our priority for now." He tapped the papers on his desk with an index finger. His delivery, as always, lacked any semblance of emotion.

"Let's inform the media about what this Wickham guy is doing." The more the prime minister spoke, the less respect he garnered, if that was possible. Through the bereaved expressions on their faces, he could see those in the room feel sorry for him. Their head of state appeared a hapless peon.

A young woman who the prime minister had never seen before answered his question. "Wickham is paying people to cause chaos. But they don't work for him, and we haven't located the money trail. The media is not an option right now. Plus, they are not our friends."

"Then let's use the military." The PM's previously potent voice quivered with frustration. "We can crush them. Let's go after them."

Harris kept his voice at a patronizing pitch. "They have grown too powerful. Any aggressive action on our part will only strengthen them. Plus, it didn't work the first time. Why would it now?"

"Wait!" the sullen PM interrupted with a more passive voice. He now realized his main weapon, the tool he mostly used to garner high office, was useless. "What do you mean 'the first time?' Why wasn't I informed of this?"

Harris continued as if the Prime Minister hadn't even asked a question. "The people have lost faith in us." Harris eyed the PM.

Thanks largely to you. "FreeGB wants to be a political force. That is how we beat them."

"Wickham has to infiltrate from within," the bald man continued in his preferred mellow voice. "They used that pamphlet and the economy to demonize us. Then they ridiculed us by saying a Constitution some college kid wrote should replace us. And now, they are overwhelming the system with violence. They could gain majority support. We can't let them."

The silence that followed spoke volumes to his analysis. He was right. And it was terrifying.

The prime minister wasn't even listening. He was too humiliated to even care.

What has happened to me?

BEEP BEEP.

The incoming text was a welcomed interruption.

"Well, my friends," stated the major general, reading the message. "Our boy is going in. Hopefully we'll get some answers."

*

"All right, class."

Professor Nolan's students feverishly began cramming their books and binders into their bags. It was Friday, and they never wasted time getting off campus. Plus, finals week would begin the following Monday. They didn't have much time to blow off steam.

"Remember, the final is next Wednesday at 10:00." John now had to speak above the dull roar of whisking zippers, sliding chairs, and rustling papers. "It's not what you know, but how you apply it."

He got in his final words as the students swarmed out the door.

John patiently stood at the front of the room waiting for all his students to exit. He would then begin to pack his things. The vacuum left by their departure afforded the young educator time to ponder his first full semester as a college professor. Was he any good? Had the kids learned? Was it a good idea for him to prohibit discussion about the revolution and his involvement? Evaluations would come after grades were submitted; evaluations he would never get the chance to read.

This class had been John's sanctuary; his escape from life. He flung his strap over his shoulder and took that first step towards the door, then his shoes squeaked to a stop. Once he walked through that door, weeks would pass before he'd enter it again. Thoughts of winter break, and what may lie on the other side, swirled through his head. There was no doubt things would change in the coming days and weeks. The doubt came from not knowing *how* it would change.

"Congratulations, Professor Nolan."

John was startled out of his daze by April Lynn's seductive voice. She stood in the arched doorway with her hands folded at her waist. The dark, 19th century lighting cast alluring shadows across her face. Struck by her beauty, John's thoughts eluded him.

April walked into the room and took a seat at one of the desks near the door. John stood his ground at the front. An amorous smile hung high under his glowing eyes.

"So," she said, her eyes surveying the room. "This is what your students see?"

A slow nod accompanied his deep adoration.

"How did your first full semester go?" April had a slight, leftward head tilt, where her flowing blonde hair partially covered her face. It was a seductive look she used when she wanted something.

"I think it went pretty well." John made his way down the aisle adjacent to hers. "I'll find out in a couple of weeks." He removed his strap and sat down in the seat next to April's. "You know, I've never really sat in these chairs." He shuffled trying to find a point of comfort. "How do they sit in these for three hours?"

April chuckled at the irony. "I'm sure *they* think, 'how can he talk for three hours?'"

"Yeah," John's chuckle echoed off the stone walls of the hollow room. "That's for sure."

"John..." April looked down at her folded hands that lay on the desk. Her mood quickly changed. There was no more joy or levity in her voice. "What is going to happen?"

John knew what she was referring to, but asked anyway. "With what?"

She remained fixated on her intertwined fingers. "John, we were kidnapped by our own government."

He sighed. Words of inspiration eluded him. Not wanting to upset her, he opted for silence.

Much like Emma Manning, despite April's petite build and delicate good looks, inside lay a very powerful woman. John was always very careful not to trigger her release.

"This whole *revolution*," she said the word as if it was a euphemism or somehow inaccurate, "has me terrified. And somehow *we* are in the middle of it!" The fervor John wished to suppress began to emerge. "I don't want this! People have died, John! And you show no emotion at all. It's like you find this a game. Do you understand what is happening?"

John knew she was right. He didn't afford the situation the seriousness it deserved. He was too caught up in his own involvement. His new and potent feelings of self-worth and importance trumped that of responsibility and fear. April's questions highlighted concerns John would have rather ignored. He didn't want to ponder the alternatives. He didn't want to recognize the consequences or impact of his decisions. He wanted to blindly enjoy the ride. "I in no way intended this to happen. You know that," John said, sounding somewhat defensive, as if he had been unjustly ambushed. "I was just as shocked as you when my book appeared in that riot. I don't know, April! I don't know what you want me to say."

April wanted to speak, but she chose not to interrupt. It was rare that John spoke from the heart.

"I ask myself, 'what is the patriotic thing to do?' I love my country and I want to defend it. But what the government has done is wrong.

They failed us. I can't support that. Yet, if I join the resistance, history could view me as a traitor, even if the best option is a new government." April's austerity softened. "I mean, what is patriotism? Is it working to fix a flawed system? Or fighting to replace it with another one? I will do what *I* think is best for Great Britain. But the level of patriotism I have, it's not for me to decide. Historians, not yet born will determine that. After I am gone no one will know what's in my heart. They will only know my actions. That is terrifying to think about." John loaded his empty lungs and released the breath slowly to settle his voice. "And the winner does not always write the history books. Look at *our* Civil War."

Out of the corner of his eye, John saw how April reacted oddly to his last statement. She lost her quasi-domineering tone in favor of a more timid one. John's bewildered eyes silently requested an explanation. But he could tell she was reluctant to speak.

"Remember how I once told you that my family was not too proud of our ancestors?" she said abashedly.

John erupted with excitement. This had bothered him for months. He did his best to conceal his euphoria. He nodded.

She tightly shut her eyes and grumbled. "I'm a descendant of Oliver Cromwell." Her chin fell as the words leaked out.

"That's awesome!" John blurted. "Why are you so ashamed? Many people see Oliver Cromwell as a hero."

April peeked up at John from her shameful posture. "He was a dictator accused of genocide." She didn't find this as enchanting as John, although it did serve to lighten the mood. "People still hate him. Did you know when the Royalists returned to power after his death, his corpse was dug up, hung in chains, and beheaded?"

"Sure, that makes it seem bad. But..."

Her glare was unmistakable. *Don't even try.*

"Please don't tell anyone," April pled. "We don't want people knowing."

"All right," John said, "but I'd tell people if *my* family had a legacy."

RING!!!

April welcomed the interruption of John's ringing phone.

"Hello?" He paused, listening. "Okay. I'll be right out."

John threw the phone back in his briefcase. "I have to go."

"I'd like a little more time with you."

John disregarded her polite request. "I told these guys I would meet with them."

He stood up and walked to the front of the room, grabbing his coat. April remained seated, her eyes followed him.

"Is this about the resistance?" she asked, fearing the answer.

His back remained towards her and he did not respond.

"God, John. I don't think you should go."

"Please, April," John said, "don't do this. I know what I am doing."

"No!" she fired back. "No, you don't. You have *no* idea what you are doing!"

John knew she was right. Yet, his ego would prevail over her better judgment.

"Please be careful," she pleaded as he approached the door. "You are a good person, John, a kind person." She could see his mind was made up. There was no stopping him. But her final words came close. "The people you're dealing with are not."

*

John entered the rear passenger-side door of the long, black car head first. His initial scan found only one person in his company, his uncle, Tony Manning. The plush leather seats were nearly as black as the limousine's tinted glass. Stained cherry-oak rails, bottles of Banyuls red wine, and ornate crystal goblets graced the elegant interior. Neon lights lined the ceiling and lush carpet separated the back seats. If the point was to prove the movement had financial backing, they pulled it off well.

"Today will be eye-opening, John," Tony said with high optimism.

The professor grew less enthusiastic and more skeptical following his conversation with April. "Uncle Tony," John asked, "why are you doing this?" The smile fell from his uncle's face. John felt comfortable, asking the question. But the answer would determine if his poise would endure.

Tony acted calmly, as though he had anticipated the question. "I have not turned my back on the nation, if that's what you're insinuating. I am serving the people in their best interest. The current government is not." Tony was a politician, so it was hard for John to determine if his heart matched his rhetoric. "The Crown and Parliament have failed us. Unemployment, inflation, crime, poverty - nothing is getting done. That is why I joined FreeGB. And you, John," Tony pointed at his nephew, "are the reason we will not fail. Your book, your Constitution, has opened our eyes to how government should be. We want your Constitution as the new governing document of Great Britain. That is our purpose. *My* purpose. That is how I am serving my constituents, by giving them a better government. Just like you envisioned in your book. We will earn their trust and win at the election box."

April was more right than John could have ever imagined. He hadn't even come close to understanding the scope of the situation. He was not just an ancillary part of the revolution, he *was* the revolution.

Tony leaned forward in his seat to look deep into his nephew's eyes. "I. Am. A. Patriot." He placed heavy emphasis on each word. "I know you'll be, as well."

*

"My friends," began Warren Wickham, speaking to the giant hall full of exuberant followers. "This movement is truly historic." His words resonated off the splintering wood of the old barn as the faithful cheered wildly in agreement. "Historic, not in our actions but in our purpose. Our desire is not to control this nation, its resources, or its people. Our desire is to control those who want to."

The ebullient crowd erupted. Wickham fed off the deafening ovation by gripping the microphone and proclaiming over their roar, "We are fighting to choose our own destiny as a people and avoid the inevitable failure of corrupt and greedy politicians!"

The fusion of his energized voice battling the crazed crowd made for a contagious atmosphere. If it wasn't already, this movement would soon be formidable.

He raised his arms, signaling for quiet. The microphone rested atop a stand as his voice normalized. "Now, we have some important business."

The hall in which he spoke was an old cattle barn. About 150 feet long and at least half that wide, it uncomfortably held a few thousand people. The thickening cloud of dust kicked up by the dirt floor steadily rose to the sharply-angled ceiling. In the rear, the incessant hum of powerful fans circulated and expelled much of the air, making conditions tolerable. Years of agricultural use had produced that unmistakable odor of stale urine and rotting hay. The fraying wooden planks that formed the building shell had been sloppily painted off-white. If not for the high density of the crowd, the temperature would surely be as frigid as the weather outside.

Hanging sporadically from the ceiling, and waving in the force of the fans, were red, white, and blue banners depicting their cause: "Freedom for All," "For Love of Country." A finely-groomed Wickham stood on a raised wooden podium dressed simply in blue-jeans and a brown cardigan. Behind him a giant national flag was draped proudly across the entire rear wall.

"In violation of our rights, the government is trying to break us," he continued. "They have raided our factories, they have arrested our patriots, charging them with treason and other unfounded crimes. And as they continue their war against freedom, we continue to gain more support."

The crowd erupted once more.

"In the coming days, weeks, and months expect to fall victim to the injustices of this Crown. Your rights may be stripped. You may be imprisoned. But as you sit in a jail cell, I challenge you to think." His followers looked on with cult-like stares. "Think about what is happening to you and to our country. Think about our youth and the nation they will inherit. Most of all, never lose sight of the goal. In that cell you *are* the movement! You symbolize all we fight for. And as more people in this great country come to our side, pressure will be put on the government to free you, in so many ways. And never be mistaken about this..." He paused to let the cheers taper off. "We will not forget you. We will honor you and your heroic sacrifice."

The assembly's spirited acclaim morphed into a unified chant of "FreeGB!" The congregation's raised arms pumped in unison as they loudly proclaimed their mantra.

Among the collective celebration, John and Tony entered the hall.

"They cannot imprison us all!" Wickham yelled, pumping his own fist into the air. "We are too many!" He and the masses fed off each other. "I want to leave you tonight with a quote."

Off stage left, Wickham noticed the arrival of their guests and an insidious grin flashed across his face.

"The economist Adam Smith said, *'Examine history, and you will find that misfortune arises from not knowing when we are well.'* My friends, many times we cause our own misfortune by taking action when action need not be taken. That is why our country is in disarray. We got what we voted for. But the time has come when we are no longer well. WE-MUST-NOT-BE-CONTENT!"

He signaled for the rowdy crowd to quiet. "Ladies and gentlemen, before you leave, I have a very important announcement. Actually, why don't I just let *them* make the announcement." From atop the stage he waved for John and Tony to join him.

"I have some people I would like you to meet." Wickham pulled the microphone off the stand and made his way towards the stairs. The mob had quieted in anticipation. While Tony made his way up the creaky wooden steps, John bashfully backed away.

"How are you, Tony?" Wickham gleefully extended his hand as his friend emerged onto the stage. "Tell them your name."

With the microphone by his side, Wickham motioned for John to join them on stage; he didn't budge.

Wickham turned to face the audience. "My friends, today is a big day for our cause." He rotated his shoulders and proudly looked at the MP. "Tony, please introduce yourself." Wickham extended the microphone.

"I am Tony Manning."

"Tell everyone what you do," instructed Wickham.

"I'm a Member of Parliament from the House of Commons. I represent the Kensington and Chelsea districts."

The crowd wasn't sure how to react. Despite his national celebrity with the *terrorists*, wasn't it the government they had gathered against?

"That's right, my friends," Wickham announced, grabbing the microphone from Tony. "The government is now abandoning itself!"

With the meaning now clear, the mob cheered appropriately. A toothy smile expanded across Wickham's face. He turned to silently thank his friend with a nod.

John stood a safe distance away by the stairs, engrossed in the spectacle. The energy was real, the passion was infectious.

"What did I walk into?" he murmured.

"We have one more special guest today." Wickham walked towards the side of the stage were John stood. The freshman professor's heart sank into his stomach, realizing all the attention was about to center on him. Unlike his uncle, he did not do well among unfamiliar crowds. "It's not every day you come face to face with greatness. Today is one of those days." He walked down the steps to escort the hesitant young man onto the stage.

"Would you please tell everyone your *first* name, sir?" Wickham's right arm was anchored around John's shoulders as they made their way up the steps.

"My name is John." The large lump in John's throat hardened and the knot in his stomach swelled. He had never been in front of so many people. The sea of faces—some friendly, some not so friendly—seemed to expand indefinitely.

The two reached the middle of the stage. "My friends, this is an exceptional man who has done exceptional things in his short life." The crowd's interest was now piqued.

The beads of sweat on John's brow doubled every second, along with his heartrate and breathing. The now quiet crowd only intensified his desire to get off that stage. He could faint at any second.

This is not why I came here.

"Please," Wickham continued, "tell everyone your full name." He extended the microphone towards his guest's mouth, and John apprehensively scanned the crowd. They awaited his identity with widened eyes, desirous of hope and longing for meaning.

"My name," he swallowed hard, "is John Nolan."

The monolithic mob was stunned. Some managed to cheer while others simply gasped. A few appeared spellbound as if the greatness of the person who stood before them caused temporary paralysis. Despite whatever initial reaction, everyone was taken aback. In front of them stood the man whose ideas the entire movement was based upon.

"That's right, ladies and gentleman!" Wickham yelled into the microphone so loudly his words distorted. "The author of *Constitutional Correctness*, Professor John Nolan." In grandiose nature he swung his right arm in John's direction, as if to reveal his assistant following a magic act. This time the crowd knew exactly how to behave.

Wickham stepped up to John and leaned towards his ear. "They are cheering for you, John," he all but screamed to overpower the energy that engulfed the building. "This is all for you and your ideas."

John didn't know how to respond. But standing on that stage all of a sudden felt real. His nerves vanished, giving way to a new type of overwhelming sensibility, one that he'd only felt briefly a few times before. For the first time in his life, as he gazed over the adoring crowd, it seemed as though he'd been called to a higher purpose. These people appreciated his work. They believed in him, and for that moment he felt worthy.

"John No-lan, John No-lan" the congregation chanted. Their universal love propelled a tingling sensation that rapidly spread throughout John's being. A more dynamic sense of pride he could not recall.

There was just one lingering problem that dampened this otherwise euphoric moment. How would he explain this to April, his parents, or the government?

*

An exhilarated Warren Wickham floated into his office with John and Tony following closely behind.

"Wow!" he exclaimed. "That gives me so much hope." He extended an arm, offering his guests a seat. "Can I get you guys something to drink?"

He grabbed a water bottle out of a small refrigerator next to his desk.

"No, thanks," John said, too wired to consume anything.

Wickham's office looked more like a makeshift meeting room than the central command center for an intricate revolution. Rudimentary street maps and satellite images of nearby cities hung on the peeling red walls. Uneven ceiling tiles shifted with each creak of the old wood building. It smelled of a strange combination of old dirt and men's cologne.

"How about the energy in that room?" Wickham opened his water. "I know, it's not the most beautiful office," he said when he noticed

John's wondering stare. "We never know when the government is going to raid us." He chuckled. "So it doesn't make sense to decorate."

Wickham and Tony laughed as John forced a smile. His nerves had returned via his conscience.

"John, I'm very happy that you came here today," Wickham stated. "It truly is an honor to make your acquaintance."

"Thank you."

"You know," Wickham continued after swigging from his water bottle, "I don't know what you've heard about me. I'm a simple man, John. I didn't want this to happen." His smile appeared real, matching his sincerity. "But it had to. I hope you don't mind we used your work. Your ideas are brilliant. People are hurting. The nation is hurting. Now is the perfect time for your ideas to take hold. We can't control everything, but we can still control our future."

Wickham smiled. "And hey, our membership buys thousands of your books *every week*. Tens of thousands, even. Perhaps more."

John nodded.

"This movement is about the country, not any one person or group of people. We certainly can't keep living like this." He gestured towards a copy of the leaked Bushtell Counter Intelligence pamphlet that rested upon his desk. "Because of you, John, and your ideas, we will be a force like this nation has never seen."

They were already well on their way.

"Come on!" Wickham stood up, throwing his water bottle into the trash can. "Let me show you around."

The three men walked out of the office and back into the now-empty barn. The cold air hit John as he entered the old structure. It didn't take long for the heat to escape after the people dispersed, though it still held a magical aura that lingered in their absence.

"As you just saw, we hold our rallies here," Wickham explained as they continued on the dirt floor. "Soon, this place will be too small. The first few rallies we had a couple months ago attracted, like, 200 people. The one you just saw had about 2,500 and it was the second one today."

He stood tall and with deep pride, gazing around at what he had built, a gaze in which he seemed to get lost.

"Do you charge for these rallies?" John asked, breaking Wickham from his trance.

"No. People contribute. We don't force anyone to pay." He continued towards the far door. "This is all voluntary."

When the three exited the barn, they entered into a long, narrow concrete hallway that seemed 200 years newer. It had hard vinyl and bright lights. The vibrant sound of hundreds of energetic voices rang clear. The continuous operation of machines distorted the recognition of any individual word.

"These are our offices." Wickham held his arms out to the side as he walked past the rooms. "We make recruitment calls, ask for donations. We have people printing newsletters and updating websites. Creative comes up with slogans and sayings. We lobby people for their support. And I am very happy to say the federal government is making our jobs pretty easy." His smile seemed a bit disingenuous as they meandered down the hall.

John didn't expect the movement to be like a business. "How many people are here?" he asked.

"It's hard to say," Wickham replied as they passed the accounting offices. John, who walked slightly behind Wickham and in front of his uncle, peeked into one of the rooms where large stacks of money were being placed into briefcases. "Many people want to help. As we expand, we can put them to work. This was our first property. Now we have dozens across the Kingdom."

"So that rally you—"

"Yup," Wickham interrupted his guest. "That was just one of dozens from all around this great nation of ours."

They traversed through the labyrinth of hallways and offices, rounding a corner, and something peculiar caught John's eye. He stopped as the others continued. Inside a room workers were writing from that afternoon's rally. On the cover was a picture of John waving to a maniacal crowd with the headline, "The Moment."

He rushed to catch up to his host.

"You see, John," Wickham was saying, "we believe in our cause. We all do. We are motivated." He stopped and placed his hand on a silver door handle. "Right now, it's not a glamorous life. But someday it will be."

He turned the handle and pushed open the door, filling the stuffy hallway with an influx of chilled air.

"This is our last stop," Wickham announced, stepping out into the winter sun.

He led his visitors up a small hill that evolved into another. After cresting a third, Wickham proclaimed. "Look."

John turned, setting his eyes on a vast maze of metal shoots and rectangular extensions. The section they walked through was merely a scintilla of the network.

"The old barn is the least impressive aspect," Wickham joked.

John was in awe of the sheer size of the complex. Wickham pointed out where new recruits were trained, where they housed the needy, where they produced their own electricity. He explained where the maintenance, custodial, and culinary offices were located. It was a self-sufficient community.

"This is why we bought this old dairy farm," he explained. "It gave us space. It might have a little smell, but we deal with it."

"Does the government know this is here?" John asked, though he knew the answer.

"Of course. But we're *pretty* safe," he explained. "The Crown controls the media, but they have to be careful. They don't want to give us more attention by reacting to us."

John was now beginning to understand the scope of his involvement. And it terrified him.

"This movement is real," Wickham said directly to John with a semblance of mysticism. "Join us, John. Your Constitution could be the Constitution of *this* nation. I want it. Everyone here wants it." He paused to allow John to think.

"Your name could be spoken in the same breath as Washington, Bonaparte, and Caesar. But *you* have to want it."

*

Before John knew it, he was trudging up the stairs towards April's apartment. With her at work, he was destined to spend the evening pondering his life—something he could not do at his parents'. As he approached the door, he reached into his pocket for the keys. From behind, a low, raspy voice spoke.

"You had quite the day, Mr. Nolan."

John whirled around, wide-eyed, to see the major general emerging from a cloud of smoke. The young man released the breath he had trapped in his lungs.

"We have plenty to discuss," Harris said, taking the keys from John's petrified hands.

He rotated the knob and pushed the door open.

"After you."

CHAPTER ELEVEN

THE NEW MACHINE

The next morning, John awoke to find April sleeping peacefully by his side. A rare blanket of snow thinly coated the battered city in a neutral serenity. Like in slow motion, the flakes tumbled aimlessly from the heavens. The tranquil aurora made it possible for one to follow a single white dot until it landed. John remained in bed, gazing through the window at the temporary peace that had befallen London. He would enjoy it while it lasted.

It wasn't often that John stayed with April at her apartment. She insisted their relationship progress slowly, in keeping with her family's religious heritage. Although recently, John's sleeping over had become more frequent. The city had deteriorated to where April felt safer in his company.

"Are you awake?" April asked from the depths of her pillow.

John broke his stare with the dawn. "I am."

April rolled over, partially throwing her body on top of his. A warm gust of air from underneath the covers caressed his face. "How'd yesterday go?"

John took a deep breath of his own. As he exhaled he mumbled, "I don't know. I don't know what to do."

April groggily opened her blue eyes to see the falling snow. John turned his head towards the window to share in the moment.

"I can't make a decision," he reluctantly admitted. "I can't do it. I just can't. Maybe I shouldn't... for now. See what happens."

"Is that what you want?" April asked, knowing it wasn't.

"At least I can't lose," John answered honestly.

"It seems cowardly to me," April said abruptly, catching John off guard.

He glanced down at the top of her head which was partially resting on the left side of his chest. Even though he didn't necessarily like it, John saw her point.

"Great leaders make decisions." April slightly lifted herself up, locking eyes with the young man. "John," she said with great sincerity, "at first, I didn't think you understood the situation. Now you do. And you must decide. Whatever you choose, I will support you. But you must also support yourself."

April gently laid her head back on John's chest. He hated when she made sense.

*

"Gentlemen," Warren Wickham said urgency as he stood at the head of a long table containing his highest deputies, "Mr. Nolan is not yet ready to join us. We must convince him. Ideas?"

Confused eyes stared back, hungering for some sort of answer.

"We gave him our pitch," Wickham continued. "He knows what we stand for. He knows our mission. We have to go beyond that."

"Could we bribe him?" asked someone from the back of the room.

Wickham shook his head. "We need his heart."

A dirty looking woman in the front spoke up loudly. "Offer him a paid position."

Wickham smirked at her suggestion out of conformity. "This is a 20-something professor who has spent his life in academia. We can't give him authority. We just need his name."

"I have an idea," proclaimed a confident voice from the back corner. The focus of the room shifted to a confident man leaning against the wall. "Trust me," stated Tony Manning. "This can't fail."

*

"Do you have to go?" John pleaded from the comfortable confines of the bed. April stood in front of the mirror applying her makeup.

"I won't be long," she promised. "You can come if you want."

"It's cold. It's snowy. It's the perfect day to stay home."

"I told these people I would meet them." She put on her jacket and grabbed her purse out of the closet. "I aim to keep my promise."

Apparently his allure was not quite as enchanting as her job.

"I only have this one appointment." She pulled her hair and pulled a black wool beanie over her head. "This kid is so cute, though." She briefly vanished into the back where she kept her work papers. "I'll be home before noon."

"The life of a social worker," John stated halfway annoyed.

April hustled out of the room, sneering at John's tone. "Families with disabled children don't get a day off."

April walked over to his side of the bed, placing an affectionate kiss on John's forehead. "Any plans?"

John crossed his arms, determined to resist her little game. He did not want to make lunch, which he knew she was going to ask. She held her smile, flashing her eyes until he wore down.

"What do you want?" he said in defeat.

April took a seat on the bed. "I have been fixing for some sloppy Joes. Homemade sloppy Joes, with French fries." She collapsed forward onto John's chest. The gentle pressure of her body pressed against his, combined with the euphoric aroma of her perfume, rendered John defenseless.

"Fine!"

They both knew he'd give in.

April sat up and gave him another kiss on the forehead. "Bye," she said, hopping off the bed and skipping towards the door. "Don't add too much mustard. I don't like bitter Joes."

"Hurry back," John commanded, though he couldn't help but smile. "Be safe!"

After hearing the door shut, John again turned his attention to the window and the weather it kept at bay. This time, his enchantment did not come from the snowfall. It centered on how April made him feel when she was with him, and how much he anticipated her return when she was gone.

*

"Hopefully, this won't take long," said Major General Bernard Harris as he marched into a crowded board room in Westminster containing many of Great Britain's most powerful officials, including the prime minister. Despite the dozens of people packed into the small space, very little noise was made.

"Thank you all for coming on such short notice." Harris stood at the head of the long table hastily arranging his things. Stress had worn greatly on his mind and body.

"We are losing," he asserted. "The resistance is gaining converts faster than we can count them. We estimate they have the loyalty of 35 to 40 percent of the British people. Ladies and gentlemen," his brow furrowed and his voice coarsened, "this is serious. It is projected our economy will not even *begin* to climb out of this depression for another six months to a year. We do not have that much time."

Harris' words fell on blank, worn out faces.

"Pass these around." The documents Harris handed out revealed detailed pictures of resistance facilities and data, rallies, fund raising efforts, and the intricacies of FreeGB's propaganda machine. "Here's what we're up against. They have hard money, manpower, and offices all around the country."

The sophisticated scope of the enemy had been realized. And it was terrifying.

A mellow voice emerged from the back of the room. "How did they set all this up?" The Prime Minister had not been privy to the intelligence.

"Mr. Prime Minister," Harris chided, "at this point, it doesn't matter."

The room exploded in fierce whispered conversations. If there was one person to blame this on, it was him. He had yet to be in office for a year and control was lost. He was determined to get it back—somehow.

"You are wrong, Major General," the PM countered, controlling his voice. "It does matter. I am the prime minster as voted by the people. I deserve to be briefed."

As much as Harris wanted to, he couldn't argue. "Agreed. Deputy Freeman will fill you in when we conclude."

The two leaders shared an unpleasant stare.

"Despite how bad this looks, we still have John Nolan," Harris explained. "We *must not* lose him. So we will protect him. I have placed guards around his girlfriend's apartment and parents' house. I have informed him of this protection." He spoke slowly, stressing every word as if it were of great notability. "We cannot lose the man upon whom the resistance has built its entire movement. And Warren Wickham will do anything to get him."

*

"Thank you for coming." April Lynn unlocked the door for her departing client. She knelt down to give little Michelle a big hug. "Now you be good for your mom." A wink and smile accompanied April's soothing tone.

Michelle smiled warmly. Down Syndrome children have a unique way of capturing our hearts.

"Thanks for coming in this morning to meet with us," Michelle's mother said, truly grateful. "I know you were supposed to have today off."

"You don't have to thank me. I'd never miss a chance to be with this one." She patted the nine-year-old on her tight brown curls.

"Be safe," the mom stated in what had become the contemporary way of saying goodbye in Great Britain, especially London.

April appreciated her concern. "This door will lock as soon as you are out."

With her hand still grasping her mom's leg, Michelle lunged forward with every step her mother took out the door. Yet, she still managed to turn and wave goodbye with her free hand.

Though April's job didn't pay well, it was moments like this that made her feel rich.

"How are you guys doing, you know, with the economy and all?" Michelle's mother asked with real concern as she helped her child in the car. "Will you be able to stay open?"

"We should get the funding we need." April smiled with certainty. "I've been working a great contact in Westminster. He wants to help us. In fact, I'm going there now before I go home. He just wrote me. He needs me for something."

The mom nodded in relief and drove away. April locked the door, grabbed her coat, scarf, and gloves off the rack, and made her way to the back door and her car.

Her drive home vividly detailed the expansive scope of London's desperate situation. Homeless, some covered by a thin layer of snow, lay huddled around smoldering piles of wood and debris. Many were either dead or on the verge of death. It served no purpose to even beg for money. There was little to beg for. They lay curled against a backdrop of abandoned and boarded-up buildings.

The once familiar sound of gunfire and gang violence had faded just as quickly as the retail and entrepreneurial spirit before it. In harsh reality, there was nothing left to steal. Most anyone who owned anything had left. The people who remained were desperate and not to be trusted.

If you looked hard enough, you could still find some commerce that managed to survive. April's company was one of the lucky few. Despite Britain's troubles, its desire to help the disabled had endured.

"I'll be home in a little while. I have to make just one quick stop. I'll only be about 20 to 30 minutes."

"Where are you going?" John inquired. He found it odd she shouldn't come straight home.

"It's no big deal. Don't worry about it." With one hand on the steering wheel, April blindly searched her pursue for lipstick and perfume.

John didn't want to press her. But something didn't feel rights.

"I'll be very careful." April promised. "I know, I know. I won't get out and yes, the doors are locked. I'll see you in a bit." When John hung up the phone, the call disconnected. From the sound of nothing in her car, a relaxing jazz instrumental emerged.

The snow had ceased to fall in the time that April had counseled her family, and the warmer temperatures brought a heavy blanket of fog. Like an expanding wave, the dense air engulfed the city in a ghostly white. Visibility was mere feet. The few inches of melting snow made for slick roads.

BEEEEEP.

The piercing, high-pitched tone wailed out from behind her small two-door car. April's heart thumped. Her eyes darted back and forth from the rear-view to the side-views mirrors. All she could see was a solid cloud of nothing. Gripping the steering wheel with white knuckles, her panicked breath matched the intensity of her heartrate. She vaulted forward in her seat, grasping the wheel even tighter. Then it came again.

BEEEEEP.

She recoiled into her seat, releasing a panicked shriek. Her body trembled. In her rear-view, a flash of blue lights emerged from the milky shadows.

"I didn't do anything wrong," April quivered. "Why is he pulling me over?" She rolled her car to a stop and tightly clasped her eyes shut, reciting an impromptu prayer. The melting snow sloshed beneath her tires. She removed her seatbelt and reached for her purse in the back seat.

As the police car approached, the flashing lights reflected off the condensed haze. Despite the close proximity of the parked car behind her, April could only make out the grille. The rest of the vehicle vanished into the pearl.

The slamming of the car door jolted April off her seat. Out of the corner of her eye she saw a dark figure emerging from the fog. Her palms moistened, and she attempted to calm her breathing.

The officer rapped his baton on the glass

With great caution and even greater reluctance, April lowered the window just enough to allow for conversation.

"Hello, Ms. Lynn." The officer was far friendlier than April had anticipated. He was a younger, nice looking man, with dark skin and a smooth complexion. "I noticed you were driving very slowly. Is everything alright? This is not your normal way home."

His mellow, amicable demeanor was trumped however, by his knowledge of her identity. John failed to mention that morning the government was now their protector.

April began to unravel. "How do you know my name? Why was I pulled over? I was just driving to—"

"Ma'am, will it be okay if I follow you home?"

April's shakes gradually subsided as the officer explained the situation. She smiled nervously. No one could know where she was going. "I appreciate it. But, no thanks. I can make it on my own."

The two shared a brief smile as he turned to make his way back to his squad car. While their eyes were still locked, two powerful gunshots echoed throughout the city's shattered facade. April cried out as she watched two holes open in the officer's chest. Stumbling for his gun, he fell sideways, shattering April's window and partially falling into her car. As he struggled to stand, his hand became wrapped in her seatbelt. She screamed frantically as his blood splattered her interior. Struggling to move him, she unbuckled her seatbelt to free his hand.

With the last of his life, the officer pushed himself out of the car. The front of his body was now saturated a crimson red. Wobbling, he fell to his knees, his eyes rolling deep within his head. With his final breath, he murmured in a liquid voice, "Go!"

Behind her, off to the right and left, April spotted numerous black, silhouetted figures charging towards her car. She threw it in drive and slammed on the gas, tossing gobs of slush under her chassis. The surface of the road delayed her acceleration, giving the dark figures time to converge.

The ravagers pounded on the outside of her car with bats and batons, trying to break the windows. They reached for the door handles as they ran alongside the vehicle, which had finally begun to gain traction. April's screams were nearly drowned out by the shattering of glass and cracks from by bats beating her door. April's stressed engine finally pulled away from her attackers. In her haste to escape she didn't even notice her rear window had been shattered and the front windshield was badly cracked, and had begun to spider.

Her short, fast breaths placed her on the verge of hyperventilating. She desperately wanted to grab her phone and call John, but her hands wouldn't let go of the wheel. The sweat raced down her panicked face despite the chilled air rushing through the broken windows. The car roared down the streets of London at an ever increasing speed. April could no longer see or hear the men who savaged her vehicle, but the air was so dense she couldn't be sure she escaped the threat.

As her eyes shifted from the rear-view mirror to focus on the road ahead, a large vehicle emerged from the mist. Her momentum was too great. There was no time to stop. She jerked the wheel to the right, launching the small coupe onto the curb. Ripping the wheel back to the left she tore down the sidewalk. Scared of what, or who, lay ahead, she again spun the wheel. This time, the road conditions took control. She stomped on the brakes as the car spun, slamming into a metal telephone pole.

Instantly, the vehicle went from 40 to zero, catapulting April through the windshield and into the afternoon air.

April came to rest 100 feet from the car, face down and unconscious. A 20-yard-long skid mark outlined her path. All the noise, confusion, and panic of the moment had faded into an eerie silence. The only sound to be heard was that of her smashed car settling against the base of the steel beam it was wrapped around. The street was desolate as the melting snow around her body ran red.

*

The rooftops surrounding April's limp body dripped with the remnants of the melting snow. As the droplets plunged to the sidewalk, they created eloquent harmonics laced with various hollow pitches. The slush around the young woman's body had diffused, allowing her blood direct access to the street. The otherwise menacing silence of the foggy afternoon was broken by the tone of a ringing cell phone. The endless rings rang out from inside the demolished car. The chimes were only separated by the time it took for the caller to hang up and press redial.

Back at the apartment, John paced with his phone pressed tightly to his ear. April should have been home by now. His mind conjured up terrible images magnified by the guilt he felt for not accompanying her to work—or pressing her on where she went afterwards.

"Have you heard from April?" he asked her parents. They had not.

"Mom, did you happen to hear from April this morning?" Pausing to hear his mother's reply, he said, "Yeah, I am sure she's fine."

Frustrated with his lack of progress, John flung open the closet door and snatched his coat off a hanger. Seconds later he raced down the stairs as the apartment door eased shut behind him. His stomach churned as he ran through the complex to the underground garage. His red hatchback roared to life and he sped through the twisting tunnels towards the exit. The government guards assigned to protect him watched from a distance, and as John peeled away, they followed.

John followed the route April would have taken home from work through the soupy fog. He tried to remain calm. The ability to control his imagination helped control his anxiety. However, there was no controlling his reaction when among the near white-out conditions he came upon a yellow two-door coupe partially wrapped around a telephone pole. Though the dense vapor made the totality of the picture difficult, there was no mistaking what he had found.

John's brakes squealed to a stop and he leaped out. Dashing through the heavy mist, the terrifying image became clearer. With blood pounding through his veins and breath ripping through his lungs, he frantically searched the vehicle. April's purse, cell phone, and keys were all there. But she wasn't.

"April!"

"April!?" he called in every direction.

He studied her vehicle for clues. Why were all the windows smashed? What were those dents? The peculiar scene only contributed to the tension.

After receiving no response, he took off in search of her in a panic. He ran around the car calling her name, "April! April!" Visibility was getting worse; down to just a few feet now.

John sloshed through the melting snow, drenching his feet in freezing water. He soon came upon a short expanse of pavement absent of snow—a trail? Fearing the worst, he reluctantly followed it.

The fuzzy image that revealed itself halted John's progression. Initially, all he could make out was a person face down near the intersection of the sidewalk and the street. His hands shot to his mouth as if to prevent some outburst of emotion. With each additional step, the image came into focus. At first, he could only make out feet, then legs. With the waist, the twist in his stomach contracted. His slow creep increased with speed as he verified his finding. By the time her blonde hair was visible, John was in a panicked sprint. His remaining optimism evaporated as he knelt down and saw her battered face resting against the asphalt.

John burst into tears as he rolled April onto her back. The pool of blood surrounding her had congealed against the partially frozen street. Her closed eyes were shrouded in a dried maroon, as was her face.

"Oh, my God!" John's entire body trembled with a terrifying combination of horror and revulsion. Her heart was still beating, barely. On his knees, surrounded by blinding fog, John clutched April tightly against his body. A tear rolled down his cheek, fell off his chin, and landed on April's face. The sensation triggered a response in the young woman.

"John..."

The young man ached with regret as two government officials approached. Help had arrived.

*

An hour later, John was sitting on a metal chair leaning forward with his elbows resting on his knees, head in hands.

His mother rushed into the waiting room, arms outstretched to embrace him. "My baby, are you okay?" She pulled away and gently placed her hands on either side of her son's weary face. "You look like hell."

John's inward smile was the first bit of joy he had felt in hours.

Theodore took a seat next to his son.

"How long have they been in there?" Charlotte asked, sitting next to John. The small, windowless room was all white with very little decoration. A few other people sat scattered throughout its confines, though none appeared quite as distraught as John.

"Two hours," John replied. "I don't know what they're doing."

"Where are her parents?" Theodore found it odd they weren't present.

"On their way. They were out of town."

"Your sisters will be here soon," his mother added, tenderly rubbing her son's leg.

"Police are looking into it," John replied. "I'm not confident."

A tall man in a white lab coat appeared. "Mr. Nolan?"

The family abruptly stood up. The handsome, middle-eastern doctor approached with an uneasy aura.

"She is stable," he reported.

John's rigidity eased slightly. *Thank God!*

"We've induced a coma," the doctor said, his delivery callous, yet somehow comforting. "The crash took a lot out of her. There's some head trauma. Although, considering she wasn't wearing a seatbelt, it could be much worse."

"That doesn't make sense," John thought out loud. "No seatbelt?"

"The bruises on her body are fairly minor. There may be some scarring, especially on her face. As for brain damage, time will tell."

"Now what?" John asked, his voice quivering.

"We wait." The doctor's hands were folded at his waist. "Remain optimistic."

The weight of the moment forced John's head to collapse into the rigid embrace of his cupped hands. "Can I see her?"

The doctor nodded. "This way." He left the room in the same remorseful fashion with which he entered. The Nolans reluctantly followed.

April's room was small with just a few feet of walking space on either side of the bed. Dull white, windowless walls, and one giant florescent tube light on the ceiling providing a dim, but adequate amount of light.

When John entered the doorway and saw April's bandaged and reposed body he nearly fainted. The sight of her connected to tubes and wires further crushed his depressed spirit. April was lying on her back, the white sheet covering her body stopping just short of her blackened chin. Battling every emotion and instinct, John stepped into the room.

Theodore and Charlotte remained at the doorway. John's sisters had just arrived and were rushing down the hall. Lizzy's and Rose's eyes revealed grief to a far greater extent than words could express.

Standing at the foot of the bed, John prepared himself with a slow breath, and an equally slow exhale. The hospital was deathly still. The ominous silence was only interrupted by the occasional chirp of the monitor that signaled April's heartbeat. Despite all his efforts to remain strong, a tear formed in his right eye. It managed to break free of his lower lid and streak down his cheek resting at the bottom of his jawline. He reached under the blanket and delicately caressed April's hand. Her lack of a reaction further twisted the crippling knot that enveloped his stomach. In his soul, John believed his very presence and gentle touch would defy the coma and elicit some sort of response. Amidst his grave disappointment, another tear broke free.

*

"What the *hell* was that!?" screamed an indignant Warren Wickham. He threw his drink against the wall. The mug exploded, sending fragments of clay and coffee to the far reaches of the boardroom. A dozen high ranking FreeGB officers sat reticent, not eager to challenge his anger.

"Well?!" he screamed wildly, throwing his hands up in the air. "What happened?" Feeling a migraine coming on, he placed a hand on his forehead.

"Sir," the man stumbled over his words, "we didn't know she was going to be—"

"This was not the plan." Wickham interrupted. "She drives out of the way to meet Manning. He convinces her to work with us in exchange for funding the disabled. And if she doesn't agree, we take her when no one's around to witness it. How hard is that?" He paused to ease his mind. "Now we have a dead cop, she's near death, and we still don't have Nolan."

"The cop's body and vehicle have been taken care of." The woman who spoke was far more calm and collected than the two men. "It will be weeks before any investigation is complete." Wickham listened with arms rigidly folded across his chest. "All we have to do is modify our plan. Instead of kidnapping the woman, we just have to pin the accident on the Crown. His hatred towards them will send him to us."

Wickham grabbed a chair, placing it at the head of the table. "Where do we start?"

*

John sat on a cramped wooden chair next to April's bed, a book resting on his crossed legs. The hospital remained quiet except for that now familiar chirp that instilled in him some hope. It was nearing the end of visiting hours—10:00 at night. Though his family and friends had left for the evening, the remnants of their visit—flowers, cards, and candy, along with numerous books and magazines—remained. It had now been about 11 hours since April's accident.

Like testaments to April's love, gifts spanned the room like trophies—which included one peculiar card that lacked a signature and obvious donor, but contained familiar handwriting no one could quite place.

"Sir," a nurse said politely, sticking her head into the room. "Five minutes."

John flashed an appreciative smile. He stood up and packed his things. One-by-one he placed in his teaching bag what he wanted to take home: a few boxes of chocolate, a couple of books, and April's bloody clothes which were folded neatly in a plastic bag.

He zipped his bag, placed it on his chair, and turned to face the bed. He shuffled forward until his leg pressed against the metal side bars. With his right hand he gently caressed April's blonde hair. His tears had all dried up. He had no more left to shed. John leaned in, giving April a kiss on the forehead.

"I will be here every day," he whispered, pulling back to admire her serene beauty. "Even when classes start in a couple weeks, I'll be here.

We are going to make it through this." John gave her one more kiss on the check. He pressed his nose to her skin, drawing in her scent. He closed his eyes in remembrance of the great times they shared, and the acknowledgment of the difficult times ahead.

John briskly walked out of the room as if to somehow prove he was in control. Never looking back, he marched straight to the elevator. A ding signaled its arrival.

As he walked through the damp parking garage towards his car, two men approached from the rear.

"Mr. Nolan," one called out. "A moment please."

The drained professor turned around to find two towering men dressed in black suits standing before him.

"Can I help you?" he asked, somewhat confused.

"We work for the major general," the one man explained. "He sends his condolences."

John wasn't quite sure how to react.

"The major general wanted you to know our protection for you and your family will be increased."

John nodded. "Do you know what happened?"

"We are investigating. We have one police officer missing; we think that might be connected. He would have known of April's security status."

"Missing?"

"Yes, sir," the other man replied.

"What about the damage to April's car?" John pressed.

"We are investigating."

"Listen," John said, his patience thin, "you guys were supposed to protect her! You were supposed to protect me! I depended on you, and you failed me."

All the anger he had suppressed throughout the day was being released.

"Mr. Nolan, this was not our fault."

"That's the damn problem!" John shouted, his voice echoing throughout the garage. "It's never *anyone's fault!* People promise all this stuff. But when it falls apart, it's never anyone's fault! I'm sick of it!"

In a powerful motion, he let out a bellowing scream and punched the side of his car. Both the sound of the impact and his piercing cry recoiled off the bare concrete walls and parked cars. As he shook the pain from his hand, his breathing slowed. It appeared the only thing he had to show for his outburst was bruised knuckles and a dented door panel.

In an instant, John's anger subsided. In a more mellow and defeated voice, he uttered, "Can I go home, now?"

The man's voice contained little understanding. "We'll be in touch."

John could not have seemed more disinterested as he stepped into his car.

*

The next morning, John awoke alone. As he slowly emerged from his slumber, he groggily rolled over to drape his arm across his girlfriend. His abrupt union with the cold side of the bed served as an abrupt reminder of the day before. Today surely would be another challenge.

KNOCK. KNOCK.

John moaned. The deep thump of someone striking the front door hurt his head. He sat up and dropped his feet to the floor, catching a glimpse of himself in the full-length mirror. The young man barely recognized the disheveled soul that matched his bloodshot stare. He ran his hand over his days-old beard.

KNOCK. KNOCK.

"Hold on!" he called out, shuffling across the bedroom. He threw on the clothes he'd had on the day before, still splattered with April's blood.

He arrived at the door, realizing he'd forgotten to lock it the night before. *Get it together, man.* With a sharp intake of air, he turned the knob and pulled the door open.

"Mr. Wickham?" John was surprised. Wichkam's body was fully covered. Dark glasses and a hat concealed his face.

"I know you have been through a lot, Mr. Nolan. This won't take long."

John stepped aside, allowing his visitor to enter.

Wickham lowered himself onto the sofa. John followed, settling two cushions away.

"I'm not one to deliver bad news, but I think you need to know this." Wickham pulled a dozen or so photos out of his jacket and handed them to John.

"Someone who saw April's accident took these."

The first picture appeared to show a police officer standing next to April's car. The dense fog slightly hid the images, but the blanket of snow on the road and the time stamped on the photos convinced John they were authentic.

"Take a look."

John squinted his eyes, studying the hazy figures, one after another, until he got to the last of the small stack. "Oh, my God!" he whispered, pulling it closer.

Wickham sat by, letting the visuals do the persuading.

This picture was unlike the previous. In the others, the officer merely stood by April's car. In this one he appeared to be on the attack. Much of his upper body was hanging in the vehicle via a shattered window, his long arms grabbing at April's body. Despite the blurry image, John could make out the look on April's face—sheer terror.

The anger John experienced the previous night returned with a vengeance. The culpability he mostly placed on himself for not accompanying her that morning was now entirely directed at those who had assured her safety.

"Can I keep these?" John's glare couldn't break from that final image.

Wickham played it sincere. "They're yours."

"Who took these?" John again paged through the photos, looking for anything he may have missed.

Wickham shook his head. "They don't want to get involved. You understand. I know it's hard, John, but you needed to see these."

In a brief fit of rage, John slammed the pictures down on the coffee table and stood. Wickham instinctively leaned away from John's threatening gestures.

"Goddamnit!" John hollered, stomping to the back of the couch, his hands on his head. He whipped himself around, leering at the photos strewn across the table.

Wickham played it down, silently encouraging the young man to come unglued. He figured a little prodding wouldn't hurt.

"Though we tried to locate the officer, we can't find him." He paused for a few seconds. "The government could be protecting him."

These pictures raised more questions than they answered, and John wasn't sure if he should feel anger or sadness. He didn't know if he ought to scream or cry. Should he feel sorry for himself? For April? Or would it be best if he simply began to plot his revenge?

From the outside, John appeared to be experiencing a meltdown. From the inside, the meltdown had begun the day before. And it all played right into Wickham's plan.

"I'll go, now." Wickham dolefully made his way to the door, applying his hat and glasses. "If you need *anything* let me know."

John was leaning up against the far wall, his elbows propped against the drywall, his head resting in between. The young man acted like he didn't even hear his guest announce his departure. All his thoughts and the memories of the past eight months swirled around his head. He thought back to what the chancellor told him about when you know what is right. He recalled April's comments about standing for a cause while understanding the circumstances. He savored the rage he once had for the Cambridge History Department, and lamented the anguish he experienced while watching tears stream down his mother's face. He considered that enigmatic pamphlet and the government's weak defense of its contents. He felt the pain of millions of his countrymen who desperately needed some hope. He vividly remembered the intense rush he felt when a sea of people wildly cheered his name.

John's conscience was not prepared to deal with this indecision. He had been taught as a child to honor Great Britain, to respect Her; to cherish Her. Yet, he was also taught to act in Her best interest. He contemplated the perils of joining FreeGB while understanding the outcome would determine his place in history. Victors are heroes; losers are villains. His limited role in affecting the outcome—and therefor his own legacy—restrained his full engagement. His name was being used, but his soul had remained neutral.

I know I am a patriot!

I will do what is right.

What is right?

John knew his physical commitment must also be accompanied by a spiritual one. He also knew the two would be difficult to fuse into one. The man he needed to be was obvious, however, that man's principle resolve was not.

I will make a difference!

I will matter!

To this point, John had succeeded in suppressing his own passion and growth. Now, he could no longer be unengaged. His fear of risk had faded with April's chances of a full recovery. His devotion must be absolute. And at that moment, for the first time, it was.

Wickham waited at the door. As he turned the knob to leave, his host called out.

"Wait!" John turned away from the wall to face his guest. His eyes were puffy, his sleeves damp with the remnants of his emotions. "Are you having a rally tonight?"

Wickham stood in the entranceway holding the door open. "Seven o'clock."

"Put me on the list of speakers," John stated, his cheeks flushed. "I have an announcement to make."

*

"Ladies and gentlemen, thank you for coming to this most historical event," began the announcer as he spoke to a capacity crowd. The old barn had never been this full. So many people had attended on this cold December night that televisions and speakers were placed outside the venue to allow the overflow of spectators to join in. "I would like to welcome all of our fellow patriots from around the nation."

The man cheered with raised arms and pumping fists. The congregation joined in. Throughout the country and its provinces, packed assemblies watched on giant screens. This was to be a momentous night and word spread quickly.

"It is my privilege this evening to introduce a great man. A man who conceived of our movement long before any of this was deemed possible." The crowd began to ramp up. "A man who has stood by this cause with great vision and unyielding determination. And look at us now!" he cried, flinging his arm out in recognition of their immense following.

The followers erupted.

"My friends, my countrymen, I give to you the man whose dream is to return this nation back to its rightful owners."

The barn pulsated at a deafening volume.

"Ladies and gentlemen, Warren Wickham!"

Wickham jumped onto the stage amid the zealous cheers and fanatical screams. The dozens of satellite rallies reacted in full. The proud father of the movement approached the announcer with a magical smile. The mic exchanged hands following a celebratory hug. Wickham soon found himself alone on the largest stage of his life. And he was in no hurry to begin.

"Thank you. Thank you," he said repeatedly as the acclaim continued. "Please," he said, motioning for the masses to calm. His humbleness was only accompanied by the famous wave to no one. "I appreciate it, so much. Thank you." The old barn floor produced a level of noise that drowned out his words. "My friends, we have a lot to get to tonight." His admonishment only served to ignite the crowd.

"My fellow patriots," Wickham continued when the merriment finally tapered off. "We've come a long way, haven't we? I remember the first rally we held just a few months ago. I think it took more people to set up than showed up." The crowed offered him a polite chuckle, though the statement was far from true.

"Now we are nearing the level of support that is necessary for us to greatly advance our cause. However, our work is not nearly finished. We will continue knocking on doors, talking to people on the streets, handing out fliers and distributing information. What we are doing is working well. It's vital we continue with the same level of intensity and integrity. The satellite rallies looked on with eager eyes.

"In reality, I realize you are not here to listen to me. You've listened to me enough." His mouth curled up in a humble smile. Again, the crowd appeased him with a muttering laugh. "You came here to witness history. You will not be disappointed." Wickham made his way to the far side of the stage.

"The person that I am about to introduce to you will be a great addition to our movement. Ladies and gentlemen, it is my honor, my privilege, to introduce to you the newest member of our cause and the man who will help lead us to certain victory. The man behind the book, *Constitutional Correctness*. I give you," Wickham shouted into the microphone, "Professor John Nolan!"

The eruption was the most deafening, yet. The people waved their arms wildly. The scene was the same outside the barn, and at every rally around the nation.

John emerged from the shadows of the stage. He had never imagined such a moment in his life. The old barn was so loud it hurt his ears. As he approached the top step, the sheer magnitude of the crowd began to reveal itself. His first rally had been impressive. This one inspired awe. The tingling sensation and sense of worth he experienced before materialized once again. Powerful chills scattered throughout his core. Goose bumps rose on his skin, and he had yet to even reach center stage.

To John, the events seemed in slow motion, like his mind was not able to process it quickly enough. After all, it was only one year ago this young man set out to write the document that would lead to this national moment.

When he finally reached the stage deck, the magnificent vision stopped him. The sea of people cheered wildly, waving flags and holding up signs expressing their devotion to the cause, and to John.

If only April could be here, he thought. *It would be perfect.*

Warren Wickham was in no hurry to present John the microphone. He wanted the professor to take it all in.

"What do you think?" Wickham finally asked, as he approached John and extended his hand. The question required no response, and John didn't bother to give one. They both simply scanned the crazed mob, in admiration of its beauty.

On the opposite side of the stage, the crew rushed to set up the podium from which John would deliver his speech. In the meantime, the two men walked to the front of the stage where Wickham symbolically offered John to the crowd. Wickham stepped aside, extending his arms toward the featured guest.

There was no mistaking the importance of this moment for Wickham and his followers. John's ideas were the basis for their entire movement. Now, they had been legitimized by the very person who had written the Constitution they not only endorsed, but were determined to live by. This was the catalyst they needed to take the resistance to a new level. As the year came to a close, the political momentum heading into the spring and summer would be theirs. And the government, via the Internet, watched it all unfold with troubled eyes.

The goose bumps still had not subsided as John approached the podium. Wickham had since walked off stage, turning over his entire operation to its newest recruit. The masses had not yet begun to yield in their enthusiasm as John prepared to give the speech he had penned earlier that day. He nervously placed it on the podium and glanced over the first few lines. His respiration was frantic and shallow, his brow beaded with sweat. The thought of how many people were watching only increased his desire to throw up. Whether he was ready or not, John was about to give the speech of his lifetime, and what he hoped would become one of the most consequential political sermons in history.

"Good evening," he nervously proclaimed, "I'm John Nolan." The crowd erupted at the mere sound of him officially announcing his arrival. While the mob was loud, large, and intimidating, their acceptance of him served to calm his near-crippling anxiety. Despite previous words of encouragement from party leaders, it wasn't until now that John realized these members were there for him, as much as he was now there for them. These people believed in him and his ideas.

Suddenly, John didn't feel so isolated on that lonely stage. Maybe it was the signs that bore his name, or the shirts stamped with his likeliness. Maybe it was just clearing that frightening barrier that separates us all from similar acts of greatness. Either way, it didn't matter. Whatever *it* was, it supplied John with an immense boost of confidence and bravado. He no longer felt shy or quiet. He no longer felt intimidated by groups of unfamiliar people. He stood tall and proud.

He was ready.

"For thousands of years, all across the globe, humans have sought to master our own governance. Our evolving ideals have led us to follow leaders great and villainous; constitutions strong and weak. Obscure nations have risen to global dominance only to collapse, while some never emerge from despair. Despite our greatest efforts in this endeavor, we have failed. But out of that failure, we have learned." He paused to scan the attentive room.

"A civilization's success lies in but one aspect."

As the masses listened, John honed in on his new voice, which sounded from deep within his chest. He never realized how much his profession had developed his oratory. He spoke with an infectious vigor rarely found on the political scene. The party leaders were ecstatic at his robust delivery. Government leaders were horrified over the influence his powerful speech was sure to garner.

"Our pursuit of societal perfection has undoubtedly been one of sacrifice, with untold millions lost in its venture—a venture pursued at the behest *of* leaders, but not *for* leaders."

"No!" a few in the audience yelled. The mood was such that the satellite rallies also followed.

"A countryman only dies," John lowered his voice, forcing the assembly to closely fixate on his words, "so *his* countrymen can *live*."

His distinct emphasis lay on that final word. The response was thunderous.

"Therefore, it is upon us to define a life worth living, one that assigns a more appropriate relationship between leadership and citizen. Within us lies a human spirit that rejects the limits of unreasonable restraint. However, the natural yearning of those who govern is to govern more, a divide that shapes the principle struggle of our existence.

"Throughout most of civilization, humans have lived at the command of others. We trade our sovereignty—sometimes voluntarily, sometimes not—for the guarantee of a certain quality of life. Often, this deal is made passively through soaring rhetoric and grand promises that the people, not the governor, will most benefit. This relationship, many have simply accepted.

"But we have witnessed over millennia that those in power tend not to serve the many, but to service the few. And their power is often expanded as that of others constricts. Whether this concentration of authority is achieved through brutality or the stealthy guise of less violent means, is irrelevant. Once it is obtained, it is rarely shared, even at the expense of societal collapse. Few nations have implemented a government that empowers the people instead of a person; a government guided by a strong constitution that confines desirous leaders. Yet, those are always the most successful."

John's pragmatic approach at persuasion was alluring.

The colossal release of energy following John's declaration was the grandest yet. John took a second to glance over his notes. The crowd held silent in a pent up restlessness.

"No nation is genetically exceptional. No people hold special talents. None are mentally or physically superior. Only if we are honest with ourselves will we realize that the true measure of a civilization's success lies solely in its ability to adapt.

"Adaptability encourages innovation and the ambition to endure. It is the reason some nations overcome challenges while others succumb to them. But a people cannot adapt if the necessary means of adaptation are restricted by a governmental structure that values more its own authority."

John now spoke in a soft, yet authoritative and passionate tone. "A perpetual union most requires the energy generated by the most powerful tool for lasting prosperity," John pointed to the crowd, "the impartial initiative of its citizenry."

A round of applause accompanied his reserved pitch.

"Government shall only exist to create a basic framework in which to live!" John cried. "And that government must be specifically limited not to allow the systematic weakening of the populace. For when the people are too weakened, the nation will certainly follow. This virtue must not become threatened by those who fear the power it possesses."

"I've never seen a crowd this energized," Wickham commented to Manning as they stood off-stage. His words were barely audible as they battled the exuberance of the mob.

Caught in the allure of the moment, Tony didn't have words. He simply nodded.

John stood tall on the stage, his impassioned voice resonating throughout the land. The dozens of satellite rallies and tens of thousands who filled their ranks cheered wildly for the young man. Millions more watched at home online. At that very instant, he was the most powerful man in Great Britain.

"It is that of inept, self-serving, and dishonest governments that provide the impetus for revolution and societal collapse. But a government cannot be seen as inept or self-serving, and will not be dishonest, if operated by the very *people* who benefit most from its limitations. And those strict and proven Constitutional limitations that come at the expense of the governing are rooted in the belief that the laws of economics and natural rights don't stop at any nation's borders. The balance of influence must always tilt in the citizen's direction, no matter how enticing the political language of the day."

The crowd roared.

With his head still down, he continued in a more somber voice. "For thousands of years, all across the globe, humans have struggled to master the complexities of civilization. But the answer has always been so simple. As long as we believe in *ourselves*, we will be able to adapt to any challenge and survive.

"It is now that we must take the next evolutionary step in human society. It is now that we must hold firm to the values and principles that we know work. It is now that we must lead for ourselves a re-birth of civilization based in the understanding that there is no human authority greater than our own!" John screamed.

He glanced down at his notes. He had written no more, yet he had one last thing to say.

"In the coming days and weeks, we will all have very difficult decisions to make. We will all experience the same uncertainty. We will question what is right. We will question what is patriotic. Our way of life is fragile. It's never more than a generation away from extinction. Within every era there are those who will die to preserve it and those who will die to change it. What will our era do with *its* opportunity? Life is not something you simply inherit. It is something you earn and preserve. Because once it's gone, we may never know it again." He took some time to let his words set in then continued calmly. "I have made my decision. Join me."

John raised an open hand in appreciation of the people's support. They returned the favor in full with their own form of gratitude—fervent applause accompanied by raving cheers.

John walked away from the podium and waved to the crowd as the stage flooded with highly-energized party leaders.

Everyone in the barn and all those watching on the satellites embraced their newly found momentum. The quiet few who remained in a control room in Westminster were not so elated.

CHAPTER TWELVE
SOWING THE SEEDS

Warren Wickham entered a newly decorated boardroom full of his highest ranking officials, which now included John. The room was no longer drab and unkempt, following a surge in donations after John's joining days prior. Large maps of the nation's most populous cities were replaced with framed landscapes of the countryside. New paint adorned the walls and the ceiling tiles no longer hung in disarray. Despite its revised appearance, however, those in attendance still preferred their casual wear.

"I am happy to announce our polling has revealed a little less than half the population of Great Britain is now either fully devoted to our cause, or leans our way," he announced.

The good news generated a temperate applause.

"It's good news, but we cannot be complacent," the leader admonished. "We are not finished." He paused for a few seconds but could no longer fight the triumphant urge. A large smile grew on his enraptured face. "But this feels pretty good, doesn't it?"

The room broke out in laughter, triggering another round of applause.

Wickham waited for the clapping to taper off. "The question is, how do we now gain more momentum?"

He reached inside his briefcase and pulled out a few dozen manila folders. "Pass these out." Splitting the stack into two, he handed one off to each side of the table. "This is our new strategy."

Wickham patiently waited for everyone to receive a copy. Like a grade school boy receiving his first valentine, John opened his.

"Please focus your attention on the first page," Wickham said once everyone had a copy. "This summarizes our short-term plan. By tomorrow, I'd like your opinions and ideas. With the support we now have, we need to mobilize. Before the week is out, we'll begin rebuilding this nation, one worker at time. But first, we must work to stop the violence. If we can help stop the violence—something the government can't do—we'll gain respect."

As the room voiced its conformity, John took it all in.

"If you continue through the pages, you'll see where I believe we should concentrate most of our resources." Wickham continued to the supplemental pages of the report. "Of course, all this is open to change via your input."

*

Beep! Beep! Beep! Beep!

The sound of April's heartbeat being monitored through the electrocardiogram had become a soothing sound for John. After a week of her being in a coma, he still visited his girlfriend every day. The bandages on her face were gradually being removed as her injuries healed.

Like trophies signifying his devotion, the literature John used to keep himself occupied had begun to stack up. Since April's arrival, the bare room had come alive with colorful balloons, flowers, and cards of support. John sat next to her feet, leaning up against the white bed sheets, book in hand.

Outside, the press accumulated on the sidewalk. John had yet to give any media interviews. Every reporter in the world was eager to get the first.

"You're back."

John looked up to see April's doctor standing in the doorway. He smiled, reaching for his bookmark.

"There are many theories about comas," the tall, silver-haired man said, stepping into the room. His hands rested in the pockets of his white lab coat. "I believe she knows you're here."

John looked at April, hoping the doctor was right. "Any news?"

The doctor shook his head regrettably. "When the swelling is down, we can wake her. We'll know more then." He took her medical records out of the plastic container on the wall and scanned them. "The good news is, aesthetically, she is healing well. Let's hope that's true throughout."

John extended his hand to the doctor. "I appreciate what you've done for her. I can't thank you enough."

The doctor placed April's chart back on the wall, nodded at John, and left.

John sat back down and reopened his book. Shifting his body sideways, he leaned against the bed and lifted his feet rest upon the chair rail on the wall. He planned on being there a while.

Except for the occasional nurse shuffling past, the hospital was terribly quiet. The last few months had taken a great toll on every Brit's health, both mentally and physically, which overwhelmed many hospitals. To survive, some only treated patients with active health insurance or those who could pay with cash.

April was fortunate enough to carry insurance through her employer, which still offered it to its remaining employees, but there was no telling how long it would last. But with strong book sales, John took comfort in knowing April would always receive the best care.

"John." Charlotte Nolan gently shook her son's leg. His head rested upon the wall, his book lying open on his chest. "John."

He slowly emerged from his deep sleep. He fumbled around, until his eyes fell upon his mother's loving smile. As she came into focus, he realized he was far more fatigued than he had wanted to admit.

Moments later, John found himself in the waiting room down the hall, surrounded by his family. "How are you, son?" Theodore asked with concern.

John shrugged. "I could be worse."

Charlotte's heart melted at her son's mature perspective. "Oh, honey." She gently rubbed the sides of John's face in a way only a mother could. "I'm so proud of you." Her eyes glossed over with a thin layer of pride and sorrow.

"We *are* proud of you, John," Theodore stated. "Your entire family is."

"Really?" he grinned. "No one has said anything to me, except you and Uncle Tony."

John's parents shared an uncertain glance.

"He's been calling and writing often since April's accident." John continued. "He's genuinely worried. It means a lot."

"We are also very worried," Theodore replied. "We saw your speech. We understand you had to make a commitment and we support you. But we are your parents and—"

"I know," John cut him off. "I know."

While John's parents expressed their apprehensions, his sisters looked on with intrigue. They found John's newfound influence and celebrity enchanting.

"You are on your own now, John," his father continued. "We want to protect you, but we no longer can. As parents, it's hard."

The helplessness Charlotte felt under the gravitas of the situation was terribly difficult for her to handle. Her motherly instincts were to safeguard her children, even when her ability was limited.

"No matter what decisions you make," added Theodore, "you will always have our support and a place to call home."

John and his father looked at Charlotte. If someone had just walked into the room, it would appear she was the one needing comforted.

"Your mother can't help it," Theodore said, gently rubbing her back. "She always wants everything to be perfect with you kids."

John's heart ached for his weeping mother. "I know."

*

262

Warren Wickham's office was dark with the exception of one dim lamp that barely managed to illuminate its own shade. Everyone had gone home hours ago. The vast expanse of the complex visible through the windows displayed few lights and less life. The new day had just begun with the stroke of midnight. Wickham sat alone at this desk, with the phone pressed tightly against his ear.

"Mr. President, we appreciate your willingness to assist us. And I assure you, your hospitality will be returned in full." He paused to hear his reply. "Yes, sir. Goodnight to you."

Wickham placed the phone on his desk and grabbed a pen from a jar. A tablet already sat in front of him. The tablet appeared unremarkable; solid brown with an odd insignia that resembled Inanna's Star, a powerful symbol of the heavens in Sumerian culture. Near the bottom, he found a free line and wrote the following: *France: 10,000,000.*

His addition supplemented a page already laden with the contribution of dozens of nations.

"Is it what we anticipated?"

The lamp cast a dim light on the man who entered. It didn't have to. Only one other person would be around this hour of the evening.

"Yes, sir," Wickham replied. "With this, we surpassed our goal."

The man walked up to Wickham's desk and sat down. The dreary light illuminated the man's face just enough that his demented eyes reflected a clear white.

"Can you believe it was only last year we campaigned for the Centre Party?" reminisced Paul Harris. "While I knew they'd screw up the country, I had no idea it would go this badly."

"Everything is going too well," Wickham agreed. He ran nervous fingers through his matted hair. "Something has to eventually go wrong, Paulie. Our luck can't last forever."

*

"It doesn't matter how we lost him." Despite the dire consequences of his revelation, Major General Bernard Harris remained emotionless. "He chose his allegiance. Now we move on."

"You were assigned to protect him," the prime minister replied sharply. "We deserve an explanation."

Harris' intense lack of respect for the PM blinded him to the fact that the assemblage clearly agreed with his political opponent. "We must move on." His voice appeared to mildly tremble with a rare anger. "Our sources tell us FreeGB is planning sit-ins and marching protests around the country. We must counter."

"How?" one woman in a pinstripe suit—who wore it well—asked. "We can't fight all these little battles."

"She's right," said a thin man with a rugged jaw. "We need a big picture solution."

Any optimism Harris had for a peaceful and swift solution had vanished.

"At the current rate, this economy will take years to turn around." With her trusty calculator in hand, a nerdy woman spoke. "That option is gone."

"Could we work to increase trade?" added the attractive woman in the suit. "We could use the economic headline."

"There is no one to trade with," the prime minister said with a calm certainty. "The world is hurting. Some nations like the Congo have cheap resources, but their memories are long."

For the first time since early in his term the PM felt accepted. The looks he received from his peers appeared to be rooted in respect, instead of disappointment.

"The message FreeGB has is resonating," stated a man dressed in fatigues. He sat at the far end, away from the major players. "Maybe we should work with them."

Harris was curious. "Continue."

"Offer Wickham a cabinet post." He looked at the prime minister. "We can placate his followers while maintaining our authority. There is a chance he may want the *easy* power."

The prime minister seemed intrigued.

The major general was not. "No. He wants revolution. That is what Germany did with Hitler and Italy with Mussolini. The government gave them some power in an effort to control them. It didn't work."

"I think he's got the right idea," the PM said, in defense of the man dressed in fatigues. "Right now our battle is not with the economy or trade agreements. It's with Wickham. We need to get him under control."

For the first time since early in his term, the prime minister also appeared to assume his elected role with confidence. "We need to out-strategize him. Let's track their movements and cut them off. If they plan a protest in the shipping district, we announce an ease of regulations on imports the day before. If they stage a sit-in at power plants, we announce a reduction of utility prices. We can control the headlines and take their momentum. We'll strip away their base."

Harris' recognition of the prime minister's idea rendered everyone speechless.

"We can slowly give concessions and target different constituency groups. This way, we only give as much as needed. Well done, Mr. Prime Minister."

The heads before him nodded.

Harris concluded as he gathered his belongings, "We can't give more than is necessary. We move cautiously."

No one in the room was particularly eager to relinquish authority. But with aching hearts, most accepted the harsh reality. However, not everyone had the altruistic intention of giving in to the demands of the populace, even if they initially volunteered the idea to do so.

*

With his laser pointer in hand, Warren Wickham circled Westminster. "This, my friends, despite all that has happened, is still the pulse of Great Britain." The leader of FreeGB stood in front of a sizable black and white sketch of London. The lights in the room were dimmed, except for the rich glow of an orange fluorescent bulb above the map. With windowless walls of solid concrete, the darkness hid the attendees in a sea of black. Fleeting glimpses of Wickham appeared and disappeared as he paced in and out of the light. On occasion, his words seemed to arise out of the black. Even when he was visible, the ghostly shadows cast upon his face failed to match the pleasant tonality of his voice.

"Ladies and gentlemen, we will concentrate our efforts here." Wickham spoke with great assurance, pointing at the area around Westminster. "We will move swiftly, but delicately, and the media will have to cover it. The world will watch as we start with the streets around our capitol. Gradually, we will branch out to the rest of the city and then the countryside. FreeGB will be seen as the ultimate force for good."

Wickham stepped fully into the orange glow. The contrasts of intense light and pitch darkness threw a glimmering radiance upon his body.

"The government will try to stop us," he admonished. "Our sources tell us they will relinquish control to keep the peace."

A click of a switch illuminated the crowded room.

"My friends," Wickham said inspiration, "our focus has now shifted. Up to this point we were about gaining followers, raising money, and spreading our message. We'll now use our momentum to remake this nation. We'll help people get back on their feet. We'll fight crime, poverty, and hunger. Nail by nail we'll rebuild structures, repave roads. We'll repair our global image. We'll make this nation thrive once again."

Wickham approached the boardroom table, placing his hands on the newly refurbished cherry wood surface. "As far as we are concerned, the national crisis is over, and we'll get the credit for ending it. The next parliamentarian elections are rumored to be this spring." He theatrically peered down at his watch. "That gives us just enough time."

John sat towards the back watching his peers marvel at the ingenious plan. However, he was unable to join them in their rejoicing. April was soon to be awakened from her coma and the uncertainty of her condition consumed his thoughts.

*

BEEEEEP!

It was a call the prime minister was expecting.

He leaned forward to press the button on his phone. "Yes, Delores?"

"The major general is here, sir."

"Send him in." The prime minister took a deep breath to calm his nerves. The afternoon's meeting still festered within him. Sure, the major general had gone along with his plan, though it was now time for the nation's highest elected official to garner some respect.

The prime minister stood as the major general entered the room. He graciously extended his hand towards the antique chairs opposite his desk. "Mr. Harris. Please, sit down."

Harris proceeded silently, appearing miserable and uninspired. But that was not unusual.

The room was barely lit by the evening sun, which struggled to shine through the large windows that overlooked the crumbling city. Despite the desperate state of his nation, the prime minister managed to keep a brilliantly furnished and decorated office. Nothing would keep him from the surroundings he deserved.

"Thank you for coming," the prime minister's said. "I want to make something very clear." He leaned forward onto his desk, locking eyes with his political opponent. "As long as I am prime minister, I still run this nation. You want to make a decision, you consult with me first."

Harris was not impressed by the prime minister's newly found fortitude. He remained reserved and stone-faced.

"How dare you approve *my* plan for implementation? When I presented it, I wasn't asking for your approval. I was announcing our new strategy."

Harris' gut began to churn, yet his disposition remained calm to the point of condescension.

The PM proceeded with a trembling passion in his calm voice. "I was elected to run this country. If you deny that mandate, you will start a war within this government."

The major general had built a career around his ability to remain numb in the wake of unspeakable acts. Yet now, this simple man before him was able to bring out emotions he thought were long dead. It was now obvious Harris loved his country. But he loved his role more.

"If you defy me," warned the PM, "I will do everything in my political and legal power to have you removed from your post."

Harris' brow bent inward and his voice bled with contempt. "Go ahead. I love a challenge."

CHAPTER THIRTEEN
WIN THE FUTURE NOW

At night, London and the Westminster area appeared peaceful and serene. There were no cries for help in the empty streets, and the wails of ambulances shrieking through crowded intersections had all but disappeared. So too did the terrifying echo of gunfire that had replaced the more soothing sounds of city life. The few operating streetlights created a comfortable glow that succeeded in masking the struggles that had befallen the once great metropolis. As dawn approached, the rising orb cast light on a ruinous facade. The depressing sight was difficult for Brits to accept. Most couldn't help but wish for eternal darkness.

This particular December 31st morning called for a beautiful day. The heavens would radiate a bright blue. The cloudless sky allowed the free flow of sunlight to illuminate everything.

When the sun first appeared over the eastern horizon, it sent a powerful ray of warmth over the region. The winter season thus far had been harsh, adding to the already frigid mood of the British people. But a few days of tepid relief was upon them.

As the ball of fire rose into the stratosphere, it gradually erased the dark shadows that hid the bleak expanse of the city. As with every dawn, this one offered the hope that this new day would be better than the last. For most, however, all the sun succeeded in doing was to spotlight a city in disrepair. If nothing changed, by the end of winter the streets would have more potholes than asphalt.

A few shop owners still managed to hold onto their dreams of keeping alive what little commerce remained. The sounds of these hapless entrepreneurs opening the metal doors that shielded their livelihoods from the ravages of poverty could be heard echoing throughout the city with hardly any vehicle or human traffic to muffle the sound.

Due to the weather, most of the homeless had moved indoors. They now occupied the abandoned buildings that littered the city blocks. These men and women wouldn't wake for a few more hours. Like the rest of the nation, they would greet the day with a renewed optimism. The type of enthusiasm where the impossible seemed possible, and life was only limited by one's own imagination.

It was amazing what one beautiful day in the dead of winter could do to the human spirit; especially, a spirit that had been trampled.

A few days of early spring had arrived. And the next 24 hours would be immortalized in the history books. But not because of the weather.

*

"Let's move it!" yelled Warren Wickham to his legions of workers as they packed their cars and trucks. "I want to be there by 8!" He tilted his clipboard to check his watch.

A low-level manager approached. "I think we have most everything, sir. We have a few trucks to fill with food and supplies, and then we're ready."

The energy levels at FreeGB's headquarters were high and rising. The massive fields surrounding the complex were lined with workers preparing to revitalize their struggling nation.

Every slamming door and trunk signaled another envoy ready for departure. Wickham and his followers were not only invigorated by the virtue of their mission, but also by the magnificence of the burgeoning day.

"Tony!" Wickham yelled over to where his friend was assisting some workers with a heavy box.

"One, two, three, lift!" Among grunts and moans, the mammoth box rose from the ground. With it secured in the listing bed of the truck, Tony wiped himself off and made his way towards Wickham.

"Warren, how are you?"

"Wonderful." The fruits of his labor were about to be picked.

"Can you believe this?" Tony gazed out at the thousands of men and women working in their devotion.

"I know, my friend." Wickham sounded equally amazed. "Today will be the first of many good days."

"What do you think they will do?" Tony asked, *they* meaning the *enemy*.

Wickham smiled. "It doesn't matter." Wickham put his arm around his good friend, and they took their first steps towards the convoy that would escort them to their destiny. "Let's go make history."

*

It had now been about an hour since the sun first rose over the horizon, and the homeless were finally beginning to wake. The cities' most downtrodden stumbled from their hollowed-out shelters onto the streets. Mother Nature had indeed brought them a beautiful day. But even at that, many were far too deranged to enjoy it.

Off in the distance, a familiar low roar gradually increased in volume. As it grew louder, a visual accompanied the deep resonance. Lined along the sidewalks, the transients watched in wonderment at what seemed like an endless parade of vehicles entering the city. The few shop managers that remained ventured out to witness it for themselves. For the first time, the resilient entrepreneurs stood with the people they blamed for their misfortunes.

One-by-one, the vehicles broke from formation and rolled to a stop next to the curb. Some of the awestruck city dwellers gravitated towards their guests. Others looked on with intrigue. The workers exited the cars with tote bags filled with fruits, vegetables, and non-perishables. They opened the trunks to reveal bags of clean clothes.

"Good morning," proclaimed a woman whose arms were stacked full of apparel. She approached a group of disheveled men and presented them the gifts. At first, they didn't know what to make of this good will. It seemed too surreal.

"Please," she pleaded with caring eyes, "take it."

Once the first man hesitantly reached out to accept the offer, the others soon followed. As fast as the clothes went, the food went even quicker. London's hungry ripped it from the hands of the volunteers and viciously began to eat it right away. This scene wasn't unique to this specific area. Most every street near downtown was enjoying the same altruistic charity.

"We are with FreeGB," stated one of the volunteers as he passed out the provisions. "We believe this country needs a new direction. If you need shelter, work, a fresh start, please, let us help you."

The homeless, with no other option and plenty of reason to believe, signed up by the truckloads.

"Please, one at a time," politely stated a young woman who directed their newest members into buses.

"I'll be able to get a shower?" a man asked hopefully as the young woman helped him into the bus. His scraggly hair hadn't been washed or cut in some time. The dirt on his face appeared permanent, as did the dark circles under his eyes.

"Yes, sir!" she replied enthusiastically. "You can shower, shave, get a haircut if you wish."

A thankful smile enveloped his face. His eyes sparkled as a rush of optimism lifted his soul. With both hands, he grabbed his shaggy brown beard.

With the first of many buses full, the drivers shut the doors. "Here we go!"

The roar of the engine signaled the end of a long nightmare for those inside. This bus would make this uplifting journey dozens of times, and it was just one of many blazing a similar route. This piece of the puzzle only encompassed a small portion of that day's activities.

*

"Hi, sir." John Nolan stood at the doorstep of one of Center City's last remaining businesses a few blocks from Westminster. The old white haired man who reluctantly answered the door worked alone. His rickety wooden door was kept secure by rusted steel bars, as were the blackened windows on either side. Above the door, a red and white sign announced: OPEN DURING DAYLIGHT HOURS.

The building itself was run-down and littered with graffiti and holes. The corners of the brick edifice were as straight as a country road. Rapid deterioration and acts of meaningless aggression had taken its toll. The architecture had the potential for aesthetic beauty. In fact, at one time, it was surely a dazzling structure.

"My name is John. This is Isabella and Amina." John turned to present his colleagues. "We are from FreeGB."

"Yes. I have heard of you." The old man's brown eyes appeared tired. His dark skin perfectly accented the blotchy white hair that caressed his face and head. His deep, melodic voice complemented his intriguing character.

"May we come in, sir?" John asked.

His bushy white eyebrows bent inward signaling his skepticism.

John saw he needed some convincing. "We are no longer taking part in this depression. We refuse to be victims."

John's words raced through the elderly man's mind. Long ago, he lost his ability to trust strangers. Yet, despite his apprehensions, he stepped aside, allowing his visitors to enter.

*

BEEP, BEEP!

One block away from John, a construction worker in a bright yellow vest guided the dump truck backwards.

"Just a little more!" he hollered, the truck approached the wide expanse of the sunken pothole.

"Hold!"

The man waved the driver out. Grabbing a metal shovel from behind the door, the driver jumped into the hole. In one swift movement, his partner threw the steel latch, raising the tailgate. Gallons of thick, steaming gravel and rock fell into the small crater.

The calm winds of that morning carried the smell of roadwork down the streets and into the allies. The city was once again alive. Even the beeping of the truck, which was once considered an annoyance, had become the sound of progress.

In powerful motions, the man in the pothole spread the asphalt. He executed his job with the vehemence of a man who hadn't worked in months.

"Good!"

His colleague threw the latch, raising the tailgate. Grabbing a rake, he began to smooth the new blacktop that in just minutes would be ready to support its first round of traffic.

*

The original oak floor creaked under John's weight as he stepped into the old man's store. Much to his surprise, opposite the tattered threshold lay a world of enchanting antiquity and delicate charm. As if walking through a portal, the throes of London seemed to give way to a secret treasure. Old wooden Victrolas dating back to the early 1900s lined the wall along the door. On top of old cherry tables near the foyer sat dated postcards and dresser clocks. Framed pictures of historical scenes were mixed with black and white autographed stills of celebrated world leaders. Individual glass containers protected dozens of faded baseball cards. Barbies and Cabbage Patch Kids in their original boxes hid in glass cases, along with original Coca-Cola bottles and Hollywood memorabilia. Toward the rear of the store, multiple bookshelves contained first edition prints of classic novels, along with American election memorabilia, including a tire gauge that read, "Obama's Energy Plan." Every square inch of the small store was utilized to display the old man's passion.

"I can see why he hasn't moved," whispered one of the women. All three looked in amazement at what they had just discovered.

"It would take forever to pack all this," the other woman replied, leaning in towards an aerial picture that caught her eye. The top third of the photograph showed a raging river, and the bottom third appeared to be an empty body of water. Filling the middle third was a breach that resulted from the massive flooding of the lake. Two houses that sat on the edge of the breach's banks were broken in half. The missing halves were not in the picture. The woman used her fingers to trace the path the water must have taken as it rushed from the lake to the river. At the bottom right corner of the picture, she spotted a handwritten title and date: *Lake Delton, WI. June 9, 2008.*

"This is awesome," John muttered, walking further into the store.

An exquisite bronze bust of Winston Churchill, John's historical idol, stopped him. The sculpture was large, more than a foot high. The brilliant finish aided in perfectly depicting the stern resolve of the man who many credited with saving the world. With valor and pride, the prime minister glared off into the distance. The bust sat on a square foundation of granite etched with a quotation. John recited the familiar passage:

We shall go on to the end, we shall fight in France, we shall fight on the seas and oceans, we shall fight with growing confidence and growing strength in the air, we shall defend our Island, whatever the cost may be, we shall fight on the beaches, we shall fight on the landing grounds, we shall fight in the fields and in the streets we shall fight in the hills. We shall never surrender.

"Sends chills up your spine, does it not?" The old gentleman had sneaked up behind his adoring guest.

John nodded.

"Considering what was happening then, he becomes more impressive. He was outnumbered, outgunned, out-treasured. Yet he told the enemy if they wanted this island, they'd have to kill every Brit first, including himself."

By this time, John's female colleagues had joined him in admiration. "We don't have leaders like this anymore," the old man lamented. He then breathed a long sigh. "In time, some tyrant will realize that."

With a creak of the floor, the feeble old gentleman made his way behind the counter. "So, what can I do for you?"

*

"Bring in the roller!" the yellow-jacketed worker called.

With a turn of the key, the mighty engine roared. Plumes of black smoke raced out of its exhaust as the colossal steel cylinder began to turn, gaining speed with each rotation. The two men who filled the hole hopped into their truck to move on. Just forty yards away, another gaping depression demanded attention. Miles of decaying roads would be addressed in the coming weeks.

"I wish those damn trucks weren't so loud!"

Milt Sirrah's laborer could barely hear him over the rumble. They took a break from mixing the mortar to observe the new road. However, their curiosity soon waned. The novelty of working was a powerful lure.

They hoisted their shovels, manually churning the mud in the wheelbarrow. The warm weather was perfect for laying brick. Granted, it was a slight change from the tile work Milt was accustomed to. His contract was simple; repair the exteriors of a given set of buildings.

"Hell! I need more water." The sweat dripped as Milt struggled to work his shovel amongst the thick material. His choice of profession took an ever-increasing toll on his aging physique. Despite the pain, however, his mind wouldn't allow his body to slow down.

His assistant fetched a bucket out of their van and began pouring water.

"Good. Now, grab a shovel and give me a hand."

The roller's engine reduced to a dull idle.

Milt's laborer, a thin boy in his late teens, grabbed a shovel off the sidewalk and shoved it into the mix, scraping the grit against the metal bottom.

"Power that shovel into the mortar and turn." Milt demonstrated. "You learn this trade, Derek, and you'll be thankful. You may get dirty and sore, but you'll always be able to feed your family."

The boy continued to work the mud.

"This looks pretty damn good," Milt stated. "Grab that blue bucket."

As they hauled the mortar and tools to the bricks near the building, Milt commented, "Derek, you should listen to me."

The young man looked at his mentor as if to say, *Why?*

A proud smile grew on Milt's face. "The last laborer I had, is now *our* boss."

*

"We don't want anything from *you*, sir." From his back pocket John brandished a flyer and offered it to the old gentleman. "As I said, FreeGB will no longer participate in this depression."

Placing his glasses on the tip of his wide nose, the old man peered down at the literature.

"Right now, we have people repairing buildings, potholes, and assisting the homeless."

The old gentleman placed the flyer on the glass display case and smiled. "Son, I'm just an old man struggling to keep this little shop open. Why are you here?"

"Sir?" John politely replied.

The old man grabbed one of his canes to assist in his standing. "I have been here a long time," he said humbly. "I appreciate your efforts. But I have made it this long. Making it to the end will not be hard."

"If you don't mind, sir," began one of John's colleagues, "why *are* you still here?" She scanned the room wondering why he wasn't somewhere better.

The corners of the old man's mouth rose, his eyes widened with a gentle glow. "Well, young lady, we opened this shop decades ago after immigrating from America. My wife and I said this would be our last stop. A few years ago, she kept her promise. I intend to keep mine."

"But your business could do better outside the city," she replied, looking through the glass at his collection of old revolvers.

"This is home." He lifting his cane and let it fall freely to the wooden floor, generating a deep, hollow thud.

"Are you doing alright?" John asked. "Do you need anything?"

John could sense his host was growing tired of their visit. He wasn't used to company. "My life has been built here. I saw it rise from nothing and fall back to nothing." His nostalgic words struck an emotion in everyone but himself. "This is where I will remain."

Behind the old gentleman, hanging on the wall, a faded picture of a middle-aged couple standing in front of a large rotunda caught John's eye. The clean-cut professional wore a brown three-piece suit and a wide smile. The ravishing mocha-skinned woman beside him beamed in her colorful spring dress. The grass was a spotty green. The tree branches bore millions of buds just about to explode in color. It was obvious the couple was in love.

The old gentleman couldn't help but notice John's wondering eye. "That is my wife and me outside the U.S. Capitol Building. Now it's just another museum." He reached up to lift the frame off its supports. "What a shame," he sighed.

"You lived there?" John inquired.

He placed the frame on the glass counter facing his guests. "We were born there. We left a few years before the breakup. The greatest regret of my life."

"She was stunning." John's co-worker was truly amazed by the woman's simple beauty.

"You should have seen her in her younger years," he chuckled. His lips pulled back towards the corners of his mouth.

As John and the two ladies conversed with the old gentleman, their FreeGB comrades rigorously carried out another part of the plan—one few knew about.

*

"Stay out of sight," demanded Warren Wickham. The leader stood at the foot of an unmarked van filled with armed men in full protective gear. "When this hatch opens, rush into the buildings and find a position that overlooks as many streets as possible. Stay there as long as time demands. Any questions?"

"Should we expect encounters?"

The van, which was parked in a desolate side alley, contained a few dozen mercenaries. Wickham heard the question, but was uncertain who'd asked it. The warriors' faces were concealed with dark masks and optical shields.

"The buildings should be empty. If you come across anyone, we cannot sacrifice the mission."

Wickham leaned backwards beyond the van doors to check the alley. He climbed in the van and shut the door behind him.

"The government *will* try to stop us. Don't let them! You guys are van five. Six more are on their way, right?"

"Yes, sir." Like the question before it, the voice had no origin.

"Gentlemen," Wickham concluded, "FreeGB expects your full cooperation. Each of you has one of these." Wickham held up a small communication device. "I am linked with your captain." The business card-sized trinket disappeared into his pocket. "Do not act until the command is given. None of us on the ground have guns. The government may take advantage of that."

Wickham placed his left hand on the door latch. "All right, men. Be safe!" In one swift motion he unlatched the door and threw it open. The men darted out of the truck, filtering into the surrounding buildings.

Not all the marked locations connected to this alley. Some of the mercenaries were forced to travel in clear view as they dashed to their destination.

"Don't film that!" admonished Tony Manning. He grabbed the camera from the hand of his assistant. From the relative safety of a few blocks, they watched as darkly dressed, armed men sprinted across the street and entered a building through a cracked window. Manning looked at his photographer. "You didn't see that!"

The confused woman simply nodded.

Manning abruptly started walking in the direction from which they came. The woman followed. Behind them, more dark figures quietly raced across the street.

"How many videographers do we have?" Tony asked the woman. She was weighed down with a still camera, video camera, tripod, and audio equipment.

"About a half-dozen from my company," she responded. "But there are more."

"How long until we can post video and pictures?"

"The *before* pictures, should be up in an hour. The *after* will go up as needed."

They turned the corner onto a busier street and he patted her on the back. "Make us look good."

*

"So if I could, I'd like to get back to my shop," the old gentleman said politely. He appeared to be growing tired.

John turned towards the ladies and nodded. "Head to the next business. I'll be out in a minute."

"There are others?" The old gentleman chuckled.

"The list is short," John acknowledged.

Seconds later the door quietly closed, leaving the two men alone amongst the antiquity.

"It took me a while," John said, "but I figured it out."

"What took a while?"

"You're Bryan Butler."

A smile grew on his old wrinkled face. He adjusted a gold pocket watch on a second tier shelf. "I'm impressed, Mr. Nolan."

John was slightly taken aback, recalling the instant he first introduced himself. *Did I say my last name?*

With his back still turned Butler uttered, "You are not alone in knowing a face."

John was humbled.

The old man stumbled out from behind the counter. The two, at opposite ends of their lives, sat down on an old walnut loveseat. Despite the age of the fabric it still radiated a brilliant purple.

"I have read a lot about you." John barely knew the man, but was highly respectful of his name.

"Have you? All good, I hope."

The man was a controversial figure, one who drew the loyalty of many, and the hatred of few.

"You do not have to answer," Mr. Butler said, and John breathed a silent sigh of relief. "I know what is written about me."

"Congressman, I have—"

"Please, son!" Butler put up his hand. "That is not a title one retains their entire life."

"Sir, I know you've seen this before."

Butler's eyes glazed over in a solemn haze. "I promised myself I would not get involved."

"How similar is it?" John pleaded. "You fought against the American collapse. Tell me, what really happened?"

Butler's aging heart bled with a compassion grown from rare experiences few could understand. His words defied his better judgment. "What we speak of in this room does not leave it."

With a simple nod, John earned his trust.

"I spent a large part of my life in American politics before the breakup, which I saw coming." He snickered. "Many of us did."

The young professor hung on Butler's every word. He was living history.

"Most politicians knew our system was not sustainable, but it didn't matter. Growing party membership was more important. Oftentimes, party politics were designed to create the misfortunes of potential constituents, which allows for political opportunity. But when perception dictates reality, misdirection becomes essential if proving truth. Then again, what do you expect when lawyers run the government?" The two shared a dubious glance. "When I was young, I wanted to believe *in* politics. I quickly learned it's just a *game*. Politicians are the players, the country is the board, and the people are disposable pieces. The players move the pieces with disregard. Some are sacrificed, some are favored, some are used for bluffing. And all too often, the pieces just let themselves be played.

"For years, I tried to warn America of what was really happening. But other politicians called me a fear monger and a demagogue. *That can't happen in the United States*, they would say. Arrogantly, I thought I could win with logic and facts, while they played the populist. And the people bought it. Permanent solutions don't favor politicians, they need problems to solve. Americans were so comfortable in their lives, they were unwilling to face reality and sacrifice that comfort." He paused. "We got what we deserved."

His eyes widened. "Thankfully, my constituents trusted me. Though I never lost reelection, I was shunned politically. I was so frustrated, I left the country. Soon enough, everything I predicted came true. I sat in this store and watched it happen. Despite being right, I could not help but feel guilty. I should have kept fighting. Now, I have to live with that regret every time I look at a map of North America."

"Populist?"

"It's a political strategy rooted in effectiveness, not reality. A populist simply says what the people want to hear. Politics trump consequences. People vote for politicians to run the country because they are busy running their own lives. Most don't pay attention, which politicians exploit. Usually by the time people realize something is wrong, it's too late.

"After we left America, my wife and I built a great life here. As this nation thrived it reminded us of America when it was strong." He lowered his head in disgust. "Now I'm starting to think it doesn't matter where you live. People are people; we can ruin anything."

The old man looked deeply into John's eyes. "We are a self-destructive species, son. Always will be."

John desperately searched for a worthy comment, suggestion, inquiry—anything.

"You want advice?" Butler added with a sincere conviction. "Politics are a stale game with fresh words and new players who work to manipulate the uneducated and corral the influential." He spoke with unconditional certainty. "In today's world, those who win bend the most minds with the slyest rhetoric." The old man's back arched. "You have the right message, son. And you have what I did not—an uncommitted populace."

He leaned in so close John could feel the warmth of his stale breath. "Understand—people seek power to *use* it." He pumped his fists. "Many ideas that seem so brilliant have been tested and failed at great human cost, only to be tried again because the idea itself is appealing. You are close to achieving what I could not. Governance lay in a pendulum.

Educate the people about how nations can avoid disastrous ends. We know what works. In time, trust in the government will run its course and the world will again rise up. But we shall not have to suffer through those years. We can win the future now."

CHAPTER FOURTEEN
ARROGANCE D'ÉTAT

"Suggestions?" Major General Bernard Harris stood at the head of a tired board room.

He had grown highly irritated with the defensive posture he was consistently forced into. "We had no idea this operation would start this soon. They beat us... again."

"Is the media in on this?" With her hair pulled back in a ponytail, the normally striking brunette was not as well-kempt. "Could we defuse their interest?"

Harris shook his head. "They are not covering it, yet. But they will. We must not allow that to happen. The media is still skeptical of FreeGB. If that changes, we'll lose the whole damn country."

While Harris hid it well, he was on the verge of a meltdown. Throughout his decades-long career, he had commanded some of Great Britain's most successful foreign and domestic campaigns: revolutions in South America; nation-building in Northern Africa; and, counterterrorism at home. Now he was being outflanked by a bunch of rogue amateurs. This was beyond humbling. It had crossed the line of embarrassing, teetering on devastating.

"My friends, FreeGB has just given us the break we needed." The prime minister charged into the room and immediately advanced to the head of the table. "Their organization is not ready for an offensive this large. They've overextended. Right now, and only right now, they are vulnerable. We can break the movement. But our window is small."

Harris was instantly indignant at his political adversary's pompous actions, yet the seasoned arbiter managed to reign in his anger. Standing his ground at center table, he spoke with a deep rooted disdain. "What do *you* suggest?"

"Send in troops. They don't have to cause a great disruption, only enough to create a little havoc."

"So you want to fight?" Harris tried to play off his strategy as absurd.

The placid Prime Minister espoused confidence in his delivery. "Just a small disorder. Downtown is known for being unstable and dangerous. We just have to prove it still is. Their workers will panic and leave. We can crush their spirits."

The PM could tell his words had impact on the room.

"FreeGB put all their resources, money, and manpower into this effort. This is it. If we stop them here, they may collapse." He paused for affect. "Then, we're in control."

Harris' aggression towards the Prime Minister began to emerge, "What if FreeGB somehow proves this was our doing?" Harris said aggressively.

"These men are trained by you, Major General. They are the best."

"You don't get it, do you?"

The prime minister was not about to back down from Harris' advance. This was his last chance to prove he could lead. Judging by the favorable reaction of those in the room, his idea was gaining traction. And he didn't have to use his domineering voice or robust stature to rekindle the flame of his leadership.

Harris could see he was losing the argument, and his authority. "We must measure the consequences of our actions against the potential reward," the major general said, addressing the room as if to garner their vote. He stood tall in an effort to intimidate his way to victory. "The creation of instability is impossible to contain. This war can only be won in the arena of ideas."

"How do you think FreeGB grew so powerful?" the prime minister asked, and the focus of the room shifted back to him. "They went into cities and towns and neighborhoods and incited violence. They burned buildings, robbed, and killed. They created fear. We can't play by different rules and expect to win."

"Stand down, Mr. Prime Minister!" Harris' escalating temper finally got the best of him. He was losing power, and didn't know how to cope.

Undaunted, the prime minister continued, his voice at a controlled level. "They did everything they could to destroy us. And we allowed it to happen." He jabbed at his chest with stiffened fingers. "Now we have a chance to *crush* them when they are most vulnerable."

"That's enough!" Harris lunged towards the prime minister, stopping just short of his face. The two stood inches apart, eyes locked in contempt. "That's an order!"

"Need I remind you, Major General," the PM's voice shuddered, "I outrank you!"

Harris took a deep breath, puffing out his chest. The prime minister could feel the flow of the major general's breath as it entered his body.

"You have failed, Major General." The declaration triggered a gasp from the captivated onlookers. The PM shook his head. "It's time for a new direction."

"Sit down," Harris huffed, pointing to a corner chair.

"Admit it, Bernard." The Prime Minister's tone softened even more. Their blood-shot eyes were still locked in scorn. "You've lost."

The room was dead silent.

Harris stepped back and adjusted his suit coat. "*My* hand has shaped this country, and world, for decades. And you, a simpleton from nowhere Great Britain think you can do better?" He snickered. "You propose we create instability?" He addressed the Prime Minister as if he were a child.

The rhetorical question required no reply.

"Let's suppose the resistance does catch us, Mr. Prime Minister. What then?"

"Do what we always do. Blame it on the LAF," the prime minister shot back. "Their hands are not clean."

Harris's bellow filled every corner of the room with a mocking incivility.

"Would you like to tell us what's so funny?" With each exchange, the prime minister secured more confidence.

"You really don't get it, do you?"

The prime minister stood boldly.

"I asked you a question!" Harris screamed, his raspy voice cracking under the strain.   The Prime Minister would not cooperate.

"The LAF doesn't exist!"

Harris appeared unwilling to divulge the information. On the inside, however, he was not so contrite. He had to make the prime minister look weak and sophomoric. "We made it up!"

The prime minister reeled back in shock. He scanned the reaction of the room and felt his edge slipping away.

"Occasionally, we needed cover," Harris explained mockingly. "The LAF provided that cover."

"So the LAF was actually *you*?" The prime minister didn't want to believe it. The Loyalist Ali Front had been involved in horrific acts.

"Sometimes," Harris remarked rudely. "The tactic is common and effective, Mr. Prime Minister. It has allowed the people of this nation, the people of the world, to live their little lives in peace and harmony. You should thank me." He looked about the room. "You should thank all of us."

"You don't even tell anyone of this?" the PM gasped. His heart felt like it had fallen into his stomach.

"We have," Harris smirked. "We just didn't tell *you*."

It would have been less of an insult to spit in his face.

The prime minister had to think fast and find a way to spin the situation to his advantage. "*This* is why we are losing the country." He turned towards those who sat in judgment of his naivety. "The people don't trust us. Don't you see? The Bushtel pamphlet, the reason people believed it, the reason they are rejecting us, is because of this type of corruption." He peered at Harris. "It's because of you and all the people like you. We devote our lives to this republic, only to be betrayed by those we should most trust." He paused to separate his demand from its justification. "Major General, I expect your resignation."

An arrogant Harris sneered at the feeble threat.

At that moment, with dozens to bear witness, their national struggle shifted from one of mere survival, to one of political expedience.

*

The contentious meeting between Britain's governmental elites concluded soon after the political lines had been drawn. Disdain was high and little could be accomplished. Standing in the hallway next to the door, the prime minister waited for his opportunity. "Colonel Levanetz," he called out when the man dressed in military fatigues exited the boardroom.

"Yes, sir?" The warrior saluted his commander.

The prime minister pulled the statuesque man to the side. "What I discussed in the meeting, I want *you* to carry it out." He spoke quietly to limit others from hearing. "We cannot wait for Harris. By then, it could be too late."

The prime minister knew he could trust the colonel. Men of his training were loyal to the end.

Like any good soldier, the colonel nodded. "How would you like it done?"

"Make them wish they never challenged us."

The colonel raised an eyebrow. "Are casualties a concern, sir?" He required authorization.

"No." It was an answer the PM didn't want to give, but had to. "Do what is necessary. We may not get another chance."

"Yes, sir." The colonel saluted once more and marched down the hallway.

"Colonel! No one can find out."

A simple nod confirmed the order.

As the soldier disappeared down the hollow corridor, the prime minister remained to contemplate his command. The ambivalence of the situation made any decision daunting. With the weight of this particular order, he didn't know whether to smile that it would be carried out, or cry because it had to be. For the first time in his life, he'd sanctioned the taking of human lives, many of whom may have voted for him.

*

Harris and a half-dozen members of his inner circle remained in the boardroom after the others had departed. "We must stop the prime minister," he said. "He can't gain a following." Stiff fingers rubbed his aching head. "I don't know where this newfound zeal of his came from, but we have to end it."

"He could have... an accident," said one man, his meaning clear.

Harris smiled. Though interested, he considered the uncertain consequences. "The nation is far too skittish for that. We must strip him of his power. Render him insignificant once again."

"Why not just remove him from office?" declared a sharply dressed woman. "Take care of FreeGB ourselves?"

"She's right," agreed a colleague. "People are concerned with themselves and their families. Plus FreeGB has given us one hell of a distraction. If we do it right, no one will even notice. By the time they do, new leadership will be in place."

"You want to stage a military coup?" Harris was disbelieving what he heard, yet a hint of intrigue crept through him.

The woman huffed, "Maybe we should have considered this a long time ago."

CHAPTER FIFTEEN
WHAT'S SO CIVIL ABOUT WAR?

"Outstanding work, son," Warren Wickham playfully rubbed the red hair of a young boy who was helping his father repaint a fence.

"Thank you, Mr. Wickham," the boy's father replied, carefully pouring more paint into the tray. "We appreciate all you're doing for us." The man's eyes displayed far more gratitude than his words ever could.

"Thank yourself." Wickham smiled with humility. "People like you will rebuild our country, not me."

As the leader of FreeGB continued his walk down the street, one of his assistants approached.

Ashleigh Blair's wrinkled eyes beamed with excitement. A few weeks back, she had left the British News Network's mail room to join the movement. "Sir?"

"Yes, Ashleigh?"

"All the homeless are back at headquarters cleaning up."

"Wonderful."

The two casually walked down the busy street. All around them roads were being repaired, buildings restored, and hope rejuvenated. Oddly enough, the smell of fresh paint mixed wonderfully with the steaming asphalt.

"We have plenty of work for them," added Blair.

"What about the others?"

"Well...." She rifled through her reports. "A few have addiction or health issues. We're getting them help."

"Make sure we get video. Anything is a possible promo."

"Yes, sir." She jotted down his words.

"What about the roads?" asked Wickham, his proud eyes scanning the bustling scene.

"We should have 20 blocks finished by week's end. We have also contacted many of the previous tenants, and most said they'd consider moving back."

Wickham signed off on the clipboard. "Any word from the government?"

"Not yet." Ashleigh smiled and walked away.

Wickham watched Ashleigh disappear amongst the workers. Despite his immense joy, a sickening skepticism managed to dampen Wickham's mood. He knew the government wouldn't simply allow their power to be usurped.

What he didn't realize was how close they really were.

*

Directly under the street where Wickham pondered, with assault rifle in hand, Colonel Levanetz crept along the concrete walls of London's sewer system. A few dozen of his men followed closely behind, each with his helmet light illuminating the way. They were dressed in black, only the whites of their eyes exposed.

"A little farther." His words, along with the slightest of sounds, continuously echoed through the winding maze of concrete passageways.

The old shaft was absolutely dark. The vertically curved walls were moist, and the air possessed a musty, damp quality. The soldiers shuffled to their destination, a few inches of water swirling beneath their feet.

Abruptly, the commander stopped, throwing his fist in the air. On his other arm, a watch indicated their position.

"This is it." The light on his helmet followed the rungs of a rusty ladder up the wall. A few stories above their heads, a storm drain marked their exit. Levanetz threw his rifle around his back. "Get to your position and wait for the command." He looked into the stoic eyes of his men. "Limited contact; we are in and out. Remember, gentlemen, you don't exist."

He turned to the man who would be first out of the hole. "You're our lookout."

The commander checked his watch. "We have thirty seconds. The other squads should be in position soon."

The most difficult part of any military operation is the time one has to ponder the implications. For the next 25 seconds, the men stood by with only their thoughts to keep them company. When these men signed up for the military, they swore allegiance to the Crown and its citizens. Was this a treasonous act which violated the oath that bound them in brotherhood? Or was this their purest act of patriotism? Thankfully for them, twenty-five seconds was not enough time to reach an answer.

"Go!"

The first soldier grabbed the rusted steel rung and scurried up the ladder. His comrades followed, leaving no space between one man's boots and another's protective gloves. The commander anchored the line.

The lead commando stopped just short of the heavy metal cover that lay flush with the street above. Warm gusts of fresh air and streams of light poured in through the drainage holes. A clip anchored his body to the ladder. The permeating sun no longer required the use of his flashlight.

From one of his many coat pockets he removed a small square device. Connected to its base hung a black wire. Bending the length of the wire into the shape of an *L*, he eased it through one of the holes, rotating it with one hand. The other held the base device which displayed a clear picture of the desolate world above.

293

The specialist swiftly disconnected the cord from the phone and stowed the device back in his pocket. Seconds later, the manhole cover began to rotate. In secret, the soldiers rushed out of the sewer and disappeared into what they assumed were empty buildings.

*

"Where have you been?" Tony Manning asked his nephew when they ran into each other on the street.

"Helping a small business owner."

An unknown, middle-aged, woman appeared holding a copy of *Constitutional Correctness*. "Mr. Nolan," she said, brandishing a pen, "would you mind? I really love your ideas. It's an honor to meet you."

John smiled, signed his name, and added a short message: *"Let's keep them honest."*

"Have you signed many today?" she asked, in awe of his presence.

John chuckled. "Only a few dozen." He handed her the book. She carefully shut it as she turned away.

"Great! Follow me." Tony led John towards one of the many control centers set up throughout the city. The white party tents could be assembled in a matter of minutes. Party leaders expected quick turnover, and agility was essential.

Tony draped his arm around his nephew. "We have a lot of people to place."

John looked confused.

"Throughout the day we've been filming our work and posting it online. Thousands have watched our videos and want to sign up."

"Really?" John was truly impressed with not only the scope of the plan, but with the overwhelming support of his countrymen.

Tony pulled out a chair in front of a monitor. John sat next to him. The rest of the tent was empty except for a couple of tables, chairs, and some leftover fruit from breakfast.

"John, I'm really sorry for what happened to April," Tony said gently.

The young man nodded, having already accepted his uncle's sympathies numerous times.

"I never intended for this to happen," Tony said. "She looks so peaceful."

John's stare locked tight onto his uncle's words. John had never seen anyone outside his immediate family at the hospital. Before he had a chance to challenge his uncle's comments, the topic changed.

"We have a few more warm days ahead. We need to use them well." Tony pulled up a file displaying every FreeGB worker and where they were stationed. Another file illustrated population density, economic hardship, and productivity. Tony pointed to the map. "We need to branch out in this direction." The area north of the city was outlined in blue. "These neighborhoods are in better shape. If we can connect with them, we can branch out to the suburbs faster."

Tony reached across John's chest, grabbing a small bundle of papers off the printer. "This is a list of the recruits that signed up today, along with their trade or profession."

John peered at just the top page, which must have contained a hundred names.

"We have to get these people organized so they can be deployed, here." He motioned towards the highlighted area on the monitor.

The MP looked at his nephew whom he'd sworn to his sister he would protect. "What do you think?"

The young professor barely had the words. "It's hard to believe."

"It's working, John," Tony explained with a hint of his own disbelief. "It's working better than we imagined."

*

It took less than 30 seconds from the time the manhole cover was slid open to the moment it was slid back into place and locked. The surrounding buildings were now occupied by some of the Crown's most apt commandos. As planned, FreeGB surveyors had not yet arrived; they would come later in the day.

With striking agility, the commandos rushed up the stairs. Skipping steps and turning the corner, they sprinted upward. A few headed to the roof, which would serve as a lookout. Others would stay a few floors from the top, perched by a window waiting for their orders.

When the men reached their designated posts, they hurled themselves onto the floor, backs supported by the walls. With their rifles clenched tightly in their hands, one near the trigger and the other close to where the barrel met the stock, they'd scan the streets and the surrounding edifices, never realizing the *real* target would be one of their own.

One particular soldier did everything his comrades did. He sprinted up the stairs skipping every other step. He swiftly spun on the landing, propelling himself to the next level. After reaching his designated position a few floors short of the roof, his hasty advance turned covert. Stealthily, the special agent crept down the partially constructed hallway, carefully checking for unlocked doors.

His search led him to an inconspicuous wooden door situated in the middle of the building. Reaching forward, he placed his hand on the knob and applied a delicate clockwise pressure. When the bolt silently cleared the shaft, a gentle push eased it open. The bright room appeared vacant. Unlike the other offices that contained the remnants of past residents, this one was under construction when deserted. A few slabs of drywall leaned up against partially painted support beams, and a couple of five-gallon buckets collected dust in the far corner. Electrical wires and duct work adorned the ceiling. The tracking panels themselves sat in sealed boxes near the fall wall.

Large windows lining the outside wall provided unobstructed views of the street below. A few were even cracked open, allowing the warm breezes of the day to caress what little skin he had exposed.

Comfortable in his appraisal of the location, the soldier stood flat-footed in the doorway, his rifle foolishly aimed at the floor. As the door swung open, the commando's widened eyes fell upon that of a mercenary's. The black figure sat on the ground, knees bent, with his back against the wall in the far corner. Unlike the commando, this man's rifle was not pointing at the floor; it was aimed directly at his unexpected guest.

Neither man was prepared or willing to deal with the situation. The commando knew if he reacted or made any sudden moves, he'd be dead. The mercenary knew if he unloaded a round their clandestine mission would be in jeopardy. As the seconds painfully ticked by, the two highly trained warriors studied each other with panicked eyes. At that moment, with tensions running high, a gust of balmy air blew into the room, kissing the beads of nervous sweat that had developed on the men's skin. Though it was winter, the tepid breeze smelled of spring.

In a desperate attempt at fortune, the commando suddenly jerked his weapon up, depressing the trigger. Reacting instantly, the mercenary fired three successive rounds. Each armor-piercing bullet sliced through the commando's vest, lodging near his heart. His gamble had failed.

A few government-issued bullets ricocheted off the linoleum floor, shattering the windowpanes. As the glass fell towards the streets below, the shots raced around the city. Despite the heavy construction of the surrounding blocks, the roar of gunfire was unmistakable.

The sounds of productivity and hope were replaced with frantic cries of fear and confusion. The blasts were an all too familiar sound, and frightening reminder of London's recent past. Everything good came to an abrupt standstill. In desperation, people rushed for cover. Some ran into buildings, others jumped into cars. A few stood their ground, bravely scanning the surrounding buildings. One of the fearless onlookers was Warren Wickham.

He reached into his pocket for his radio. "What the hell was that?" he hollered into the receiver. People hysterically raced past him in search of shelter.

The leader of the mercenaries immediately replied. "We are looking into it, sir."

For Wickham, the next few minutes would be hell.

*

With blood saturating his uniform, the commando stumbled into the hallway, desperately grabbing at the wall in a vain attempt to remain on his feet. With each pump of his weakening heart, more blood gushed out of the holes in his chest. The bright light that shone through the door and into the hallway began to fade. He collapsed to the floor.

The pain racing throughout his body subsided, replaced with an overwhelming feeling of euphoria. In the last moments of his life, his training and sense of duty took over.

With shaking hands, he pawed at his radio. "Man down in the Weston." His words gurgled as his breath mixed with the blood that filled his throat. He swallowed hard. "They were waiting for us, Colonel." The radio dropped from his hand. His head fell to the floor.

"Man down! Man down!!" his commanding officer, Colonel Levanetz, hollered. His voice cracked in a panic unbecoming of a professional killer. "All hands to the Weston Building! Now!"

Another voice from the radio cried out.

"Ryan!" he pleaded. "Speak to me, man!"

The heart-wrenching calls went unanswered. There would be no goodbyes.

"Sergeant!" The radio inside the room where the gunshot originated sprang to life. The petrified mercenary had not budged since pulling the trigger. His rifle was still pointed at the door. Blankly looking off into space, he lowered his weapon to the floor and reached for the transponder.

"Yes, sir?" His voice was quiet and reserved.

"Soldier, what happened?" The captain of the mercenaries was far more urgent in his delivery.

"He was dressed just like me, sir." The mercenary remained calm, shaking his head. "I had to do it."

"Soldier, get out of there!" There was no mistaking who he had just killed. "They will come for their dead. Get out *now!*"

"They are coming, Captain. I heard the radio." His calm disposition was replaced by an extreme fear, coupled with regret. In his mind, he kept replaying the scene: the sight of the rounds impacting the man's chest; the awful suction sound of the bullet piercing his flesh; the look in his opponent's eyes when he realized what had happened; the pungent smell of sulfur accompanied by his final words; the desperate cries of his comrades.

"Son-of-a-bitch!" cried the captain. "We have to get him!"

In a dead sprint across the rooftop, he screamed into his radio. "All hands to the Weston!" He flung the door open and charged down the stairs. "I repeat. All hands to the Weston! Proceed with great caution!" Leaping five and six stairs at a time, he left his men with a grave warning. "Be prepared for battle!"

On the ground, just a few blocks away, Warren Wickham stood in horror of what he'd just heard. His worst fears had come true, and it threatened to tear apart his growing empire.

*

"Tully!" screamed the captain. He sprinted out of his building and raced across the vacant street.

His contrite sergeant was now standing in the hallway staring down at the life he had taken. The pool of blood surrounding the commando's body advanced closer to his boots.

"I am here, sir."

The captain whipped around the corner of Central Hall and dashed down Matthew Parker Street. The Weston Building, a 25-story square edifice draped in dark reflective glass, stood tall, centered at the end of the street.

"I'm just about at the Weston and—"

BANG!!!

"Ahhhh!" The captain ripped off his headset as the powerful charge reverberated through his ear.

What the hell?

Moments later, the remnants of a rogue gunshot ricocheted off the building walls.

The captain dove behind the corner of a crumbling brick wall. The shot could have come from anywhere. Frantically, he shoved his radio back into his ear.

"What's going on? Somebody talk to me!"

"Man down!" a voice screamed. "Man down in the Weston! Tully's hit! He's not moving!" More gunshots rang out over the airwaves. "Here they come!" The mercenary unleashed a fierce battle cry as he raised his weapon and opened fire on the dark figures at the far end of the hallway. The two bodies that lay motionless in the middle of the melee would be avenged.

Fearing for the safety of his men and the mission, the captain made a rash decision.

"This is Captain Tim Hadduk. We need backup immediately. Send all available forces to the Weston Building. Now!"

Hadduk raced out from his sanctuary and resumed his charge down Matthew Parker Street. The sun glistened off the Weston's brilliant black exterior.

"Get our people off the streets!" Wickham commanded to whoever was close enough to hear. Hundreds of his screaming followers aimlessly raced past him. No one knew from where the gunfire was coming and they didn't care to find out.

Wickham grabbed a young lady who was racing past him in. "Darla, call everyone. Tell them to get away from the Weston. Find shelter." She nodded with certain terror gripping her eyes. "Try to get out of the city, if possible."

In the middle of the chaos, Wickham spotted Tony Manning directing traffic into one of the nearby buildings on Old Queens Street—a few blocks away from the Weston, but still in plain sight.

"Tony!"

They ran towards one another.

"It's coming from the Weston!" Wickham fought to catch his breath.

"Between who?"

"Not sure."

Off to the left, Wickham spotted a few teenagers who had yet to heed his warnings. "Go!" he screamed, pointing to the doors Manning had previously been filing people through. "Now!"

His passion proved more convincing than the barrage of gunfire that loudly reverberated between the buildings. They promptly joined the long line of panicked citizens eager to get inside.

Wickham turned back towards Manning, his eyes scanning the street for more stragglers. "It's between our guys and someone else."

"Government?" Manning inquired.

"Don't know. Where's Nolan?"

Manning pulled out his phone. "I'll find him."

CRACK!!

A stray bullet shattered the fifth story glass of a nearby building. Out of instinct, Wickham and Manning ducked, throwing their bare arms above their heads. The window particles cascaded.

"We'll be in the Harry Building!" yelled Wickham to Manning as they separated. "Find Nolan!"

"What's the status?" Levanetz rushed up to a few of his men staked out in an alley opposite the Weston. The commander was broad but short. What he lacked in height he made up for with his desire to fight.

"There are a few guys with pretty heavy weaponry across the street behind the plumbing store," replied one of his soldiers. "With them there, we can't get inside."

"This ain't no weekend warrior, either," the other soldier added. He leaned beyond the building's corner, eyes fixed on the target. "These guys are trained."

"Mercenaries!" The colonel's brow bent inward. "They hired damned mercenaries."

CRACK! ZOOM!

Three rounds in rapid succession forced the men back against the wall. The bullets shattered the brick, flinging pieces in all directions.

The front man whipped his rifle around the corner and indiscriminately fired four shots.

Levanetz brushed debris off his shoulder. "How many are there?"

"I'd say a few dozen. Maybe more. They have the exits."

"How many do *we* have inside?"

"Counting Ryan, three. Peters and Gregg were stationed on this street. They arrived soon after the call."

"They killed the bastard who shot Ryan." The front man turned around for the first time. "We can't leave them stranded in there, sir. We have to get them out."

"Are they still alive?"

"They're alive." The man had already returned his focus around the corner. "They're too good to die."

The commander fell against the frayed brick wall and looked up to the clear blue sky pondering his next move.

"Sir?" the near soldier asked in anticipation of a strategy.

The commander raised his radio. "This is Colonel Levanetz. Send all available city forces to the Weston Building, immediately."

Before the colonel released the button on his radio he uttered, "Kill 'em all."

*

Bent down low, slowly advancing, Captain Hadduk entered the Weston Building from the rear, below the first level. He carefully lowered each foot, avoiding the slew of particle board, copper wires, and old tools that covered the cracks in the concrete floor. Few windows and no electricity made for a damp, dark dungeon of unfinished construction.

Nerves on alert, he cautiously approached every doorway. Leading with his rifle, he peeked into the room.

For the moment, the intense volley of gunshots had ceased. Radio communication had also been temporarily suspended as each side gauged the opponents and sought a tactic.

SNAP!

Hadduk's head whipped around. He was not alone. And his company was not as careful as he.

The captain carefully approached the noise, leaning his back against the wall. Following a deep breath and controlled exhale, he positioned himself next to the door and leaned towards the opening. His eyes cleared the wooden frame to see an armed man dressed not of his squad. He stood by the far wall, peering through a foggy window.

"Don't move." Hadduk stood in the center of the doorway with his rifle fixed on the commando.

The man dropped his weapon on the concrete and discreetly placed his hands on his head.

Hadduk stepped across the threshold. "No sudden moves."

The brief stretches of ominous silence were separated by the steady drip of a nearby water pipe.

"Turn around."

The commando followed orders. The man who surfaced before the captain was tall and thick. His black uniform complemented his imposing figure. His hazel eyes showed no concern.

"Who are you with?"

Silence.

"This is not the time!" Hadduk violently thrust his rifle in the man's direction.

CRACK!

The sudden resumption of gunfire from the street blew out the window behind the commando. Hadduk dove to the left, sliding behind a thick steel beam. The commando grabbed his weapon and sprinted towards the door, indiscriminately firing in Hadduk's direction.

From his back, the captain raised his weapon and shot. The commando fell hard.

With the gunfire raging outside, the captain crawled to his victim, pushing through the clutter. He checked for a pulse. None. He then checked the body. In the commando's back pocket were two government-issued ID cards, one for Sergeant Ray Peters, the other for Special Agent Edward Gregg.

"Government," he uttered in contempt.

He switched on his headset.

"This is Captain Hadduk." With the echo of gunfire ricocheting off the concrete walls he could barely hear himself. "The enemy has been identified."

Wickham, who had secured his followers in a nearby building, had a direct view of the Weston. Behind him, hundreds of scared men and women embraced in solidarity, their words drowned out by the loud chatter of small arms.

Wickham stood alone by a window with his radio tightly pressed to his ear. The glass of the basement garage barely rose about street level.

Tony Manning and John Nolan emerged from around a corner. "What do we know?" Manning said.

"Government." Wickham's voice bled with disdain.

"Everyone's safe," Manning said, knowing his words were untrue.

John and Tony stood by Wickham, watching their aspirations fade. Their disappointment was only overshadowed by what was happening on the 200 block of Matthew Parker Street.

*

The roar of engines rolling through the city signaled the arrival of additional government soldiers. The heavily armored convoy rolled to a stop one block south of the Weston, and hundreds of camouflaged soldiers exited. The young man driving the final truck was stumpy, and half as wide as he was tall. If not for his intense demeanor, two cavernous dimples would have quartered his full cheeks. His sparkling clear blue eyes matched the color of his civilian name tag which read: C. Blaire.

"Colonel Levanetz." The lead officer immediately reported to his superior, who was hunched over a makeshift table studying the architectural design of the Weston. The echo of gunfire had calmed.

Levanetz greeted his first influx of support with wide eyes. "Share this with the envoys when they arrive. We expect four more."

The lieutenant nodded.

"Mercenaries have taken the Weston. We have one confirmed dead, two trapped. They're entering from the north. We have the south and west secured. They have the north and east."

The sudden succession of random gunfire jolted the lieutenant.

Undeterred, the colonel continued. "In our first attempts to take the building we sustained seven causalities, five fatalities. We took out just as many. But they are well supplied."

"Lieutenant!" Levanetz called as the second envoy arrived. "This is it."

*

Two blocks northeast of where Colonel Levanetz plotted his attack, Captain Hadduk greeted his own assemblage of support troops. The former veteran army officer already had fifty men stationed throughout the Weston and on surrounding rooftops. He stood on a rickety medical table. The vaulted ceilings and windowless plaster walls created a powerful atmosphere. The mercenaries jammed into the room completed the vision.

"Men!" Hadduk cried out, hoisting his rifle above his head. The mercenaries erupted in cheers and raised their own weapons. The exchange of nearby gunfire added to their excitement.

"Who'd have thought this many hate the Crown?" Hadduk proclaimed in jest as a familiar South American accent formed his words.

The men howled at their leader's rhetorical scoff.

"They've sent their best. They want us dead." The warriors felt the rage fester. "But this is *our* battle now!"

The captain reached into his pocket and pulled out the government issued cards of Gregg and Peters. "And, we're off to a good start." He threw the cards onto the ground and spat in their direction.

A firefight erupted on Matthew Parker Street.

"We will hold this building at all costs!" Hadduk screamed over the gunfire. "*This* is where we claim victory!"

*

It was a wonderful day in which to end a terrible year. The kind of day people dream about during the unrelenting surge of winter. Still high in the sky, the sun cast warm rays onto the London metropolis. To the west, ominous dark clouds crept ever closer.

"All the reinforcements are here, sir." The announcement by one of his corporals soothed the colonel's nerves. "The next wave will arrive early tomorrow."

"What are our numbers?"

The young infantryman handed him the report. "Five hundred."

"Five hundred?"

"We can't get more without the prime minister's approval."

The colonel nodded. "Those are my men who are dead. *I* will finish this." Hell bent on revenge, the officer grabbed a bulletproof vest off a supply table. "This treason must not be allowed." He secured the Velcro around his chest plate. "Make sure communication with the prime minister remains blocked."

*

Commander Hadduk now stood in front of hundreds of wildly exited mercenaries. With the cathedral ceiling as his witness, he imparted on them the rationalization for what they were about to do.

"We weren't good enough. We didn't meet their standards." Hadduk was no longer able to suppress his rage. "We were good enough to work *with* them? But not *for* them. They will pay for their disobedience. Their blood will flow through the streets of this city. Make your country proud!" Hadduk proclaimed.

He jumped to the floor and sprinted to the archway that would lead him to Matthew Parker Street. "Make Bolivia proud!"

When Hadduk charged out of the room, his guards began to unload their weapons en masse at the government commando's full-fledged assault. The dark windows of the Weston served to hide the mercenaries' positions, and there was no way to enter the building from below.

With few available openings, the stubborn glass of the Weston limited the number of mercenaries who could stop the advance. Hadduk and his men were forced to charge into the street and face their enemy.

Through the transmitter he shared with Hadduk, Wickham, Manning and Nolan listened to the roar of the captain's loyal devotees before it went dead.

Wickham's exhausted voice bled with guilt. "This was not supposed to happen." He shook his head in disgrace. "They turned this into some vendetta."

John's eyes asked what his mental will could not.

"When we colonized South America, our government bribed the local militias," Wickham explained. "We needed peace for our economic interests to grow. Many Bolivians settled here thinking they'd get government work. When it didn't happen, they turned on the Crown. I didn't think they'd do this."

John's disappointment in the man he once respected was only trumped by the result of his actions.

*

On the opposite side of the city, April Lynn lay motionless and unresponsive in her hospital bed. The faint sound of distant gunshots barely broke the silence between her heartbeats. The halls of the hospital were empty and quiet, the balloons in her room were deflating and listing, and cards were spread out proudly over every flat surface. Yet none of her supporters were around to witness her greatest achievement in weeks, the twitching of an eyelid.

*

"Here is your briefing, sir." The somber young woman handed the prime minister the chronology of the day's events.

He reluctantly reached out to accept the documents. "That will be all, Kelly."

"Yes, sir."

After she left the room, the prime minister placed the briefing right-side-up on his desk and allowed himself a second to mentally prepare. He sat alone. The room was dark with the window shades pulled low, sheltering him from the chaos that had engulfed the city. A single lamp on the corner of the desk provided all the light he desired. Much like the hospital bed where April lay, the faint sound of gunshots barely succeeded in breaking the silence.

The prime minister opened the report, grimacing as he studied the information. He placed his elbows on the desk and dropped his head into his hands.

"What have I done?"

*

Major General Bernard Harris' reaction was not so passive.

"What is this!?" he yelled, throwing the report onto his desk. His officers had yet to find comfort in his newfound emotion. "Who authorized these soldiers to the city!?" he demanded. " W e believe the prime minister, sir."

Harris' eyes bulged and he slammed his fists upon the desk, sending items scattering to the floor.

With his heart pounding and breath pumping, the major general approached a large window that overlooked the city From his position, the upper floors of the Weston were in sight. It appeared peaceful, the black glass and silver lining basking in the midday sun. Much like the hospital bed where April lay and the office where the prime minister sulked, the gunshots were faint and far away.

"This ends, now." Harris' arms were taut behind his back; his chin held high. "Get me the prime minister."

*

While the view from the major general's office appeared innocuous, Chris Nash's perspective was anything but. With the situation rapidly deteriorating, he refused to put one of his reporters at risk, so he went himself. Whether out of guilt or principle, he remained as far from the scene as possible, while still in sight. He stood still; expressionless. One hand hung by his side holding a pen, the other a tablet. Neither were being used. The concussion of the gunfire thumped in his chest and his struggled to separate the shots. Meanwhile, his stomach churned over his involvement. And above all, his mind battled to separate his devotion of country from that to his profession.

*

Such a mental struggle was lost on Warren Wickham, Tony Manning, and John Nolan. They continued to watch in horror. The mounting dead lay in darkening red pools. Dozens of bodies were now strewn across Matthew Parker Street, and more fell by the minute.

The FreeGB members that sat behind them managed to hold themselves together. However, as light began to fade, so did everyone's resolve.

Though many of the other sanctuaries were able to evacuate the city, this building was too close to the Weston. The piercing shriek of stray bullets served as a frequent reminder to stay put. Yet in-between the gunfire, little was said. Most knew what was happening.

"It's begun," averred Tony Manning as the sun set over the city and the last trace of natural light dissolved to black.

Confused, John turn to his uncle, then to Wickham. Neither responded. Both men had succumbed to the realization of what they had done. Until now, neither was willing to recognize that civilization, no matter how strong, is fragile. During its endless formative stages, various factions will spar to protect their own interests, secure their own legacies, and preserve their own images over the nation's future. Few consider the consequences. Yet, they all face the uncertainty of who history will praise or blame for the result.

EPILOGUE

January 1:

I'm writing you from a parking garage off Queen Anne's Street. I have been stuck here for hours. It's now one in the morning. It's been two weeks now since your accident, and a lot has changed.

I joined the movement. Yesterday morning we launched a campaign to help rebuild Great Britain. We started with London. By midday, a gunfight broke out between a group we hired to protect us (The Civilian Army Defense Corps) and government soldiers. Many others arrived with their own guns to fight either for or against the government. There's no telling how many people are already dead. Hundreds, maybe. And the fighting is getting worse as the night goes on. Our original goal was simply to win the next election. I fear that may have changed. I'm supposed to go back to the classroom in two weeks. Tonight may have changed that, too. Tonight may have changed a lot.

I am fairly safe in a garage with a bunch of FreeGB members. Many are calling tonight the start of a Civil War. No one is arguing.

My guess is the nation will split in two. It's been shaping up this way for the past year or so. They want to keep the current government, and we want something better. We can do better. We have to do better. I believe history is on our side. But the human condition might not be.

Our leader is a man named Warren Wickham. I thought we were lucky to have him. He's been a strong leader, but tonight really affected him. I hear the government is in worse shape. I hope it keeps up. It just further proves why our vision is the right one.

Mom and Dad are doing well. Of course, they support my decision to join FreeGB. They didn't join at first, but now they have. So have my sisters. There's a spot for you, if you would like it. Eventually the entire nation will pick a side.

I met a very interesting man, Bryan Butler. He was an elected representative in America before its collapse. I would love for you to meet him. He is a wealth of knowledge.

Book sales have remained strong. As long as care is available, you will always have the best.

I have been thinking a lot about my book and what our nation is going through. I remember Old Sores telling us in class that every civilization will wax and wane, and there can never be a lasting civilization any more than there can be a lasting spring or lasting happiness. He said it's in the nature of man that all he constructs will collapse. I don't want to believe that. I want to believe enough of us are good. In my heart, I truly believe the Constitution I wrote can work—if it's only given a chance.

I thought we did everything right. Now we're on the verge of having nothing. How cruel. How terrible. How predictable.

We were so arrogant to think this time the result would be different. How arrogant to think it wouldn't happen to us. How arrogant to think we could do it better.

It's hard for me to admit this, April, but I am scared, especially since you're in that hospital bed and I can't do anything about it. It tears me up inside.

The power on my phone is getting low. I should go. But as I sit here, I realize how truly important you are to me. I love you, and I can't wait to tell you for the first time.

- John Nolan

ABOUT THE AUTHOR

Chris Papst is a multiple Emmy-award winning investigative reporter and author of the Amazon #1 Best Seller, *Capital Murder*.